The Scientific Romances of
J.-H. Rosny Aîné

THE NAVIGATORS OF SPACE
And Other Alien Encounters

The Scientific Romances of
J.-H. Rosny Aîné

THE NAVIGATORS OF SPACE
And Other Alien Encounters

translated, annotated and introduced by
Brian Stableford

A Black Coat Press Book

Acknowledgements: I should like to thank John J. Pierce for providing valuable research materials and offering advice and support. Many of the copies of Rosny's works and critical articles related to his work were borrowed from the London Library. Also thanks to Paul Wessels for his generous and extensive help in the final preparation of this text.

Visit our website at www.blackcoatpress.com

Table of Contents

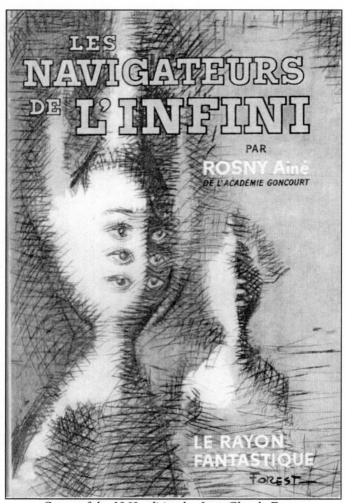

Cover of the 1960 edition by Jean-Claude Forest

Introduction

This is the first volume of a six-volume collection of stories by J.-H. Rosny *Aîné* ("the Elder"), which includes all of his scientific romances, plus a number of other stories that have some relevance to his work in that genre. Although the series includes a volume of prehistoric romances, it omits the prehistoric romance *La Guerre du feu* (tr. as *The Quest for Fire*) that is readily accessible in English translation.[1] I have, however, made new translations of several scientific romances that have been previously translated, including "Les Xipéhuz" (tr. as "The Shapes" and "The Xipehuz"), "L'Autre monde" (tr. as "The Sixth Sense" and "Another World"), "Nymphée" (tr. as "The Warriors of the Waters"), "La Mort de la Terre" (tr. as "The Death of the Earth"), "La Grande énigme" (tr. as "The Great Enigma" and *L'Etonnant voyage de Hareton Ironcastle* (tr. as *Ironcastle*). I have done so in the interests of completeness rather than because the previous translations are unsatisfactory (although one or two of them are).

The contents of the six volumes are:

Volume 1. THE NAVIGATORS OF SPACE AND OTHER ALIEN ENCOUNTERS: The Xipehuz, The Skeptical Legend, Another World, The Death of the Earth, The Navigators of Space, The Astronauts.

Volume 2. THE WORLD OF THE VARIANTS AND OTHER STRANGE LANDS: Nymphaeum, The Depths of Kyamo, The Wonderful Cave Country, The Voyage, The Great Enigma, The Treasure in the Snow, The Boar Men, In the World of the Variants.

---

[1] *Le Félin géant* (*The Giant Cat* a.k.a. *Quest of the Dawn Man*) and *Helgvor du fleuve bleu* (*Helgvor of the Blue River*) will be reprinted in their original English translations in a seventh volume.

J.-H. Rosny *Aîné* is now generally reckoned to be one of the most important pioneers of French scientific romance, not necessarily second in rank to his much more popular and far more widely-known predecessor Jules Verne. Pierre Versins, in his definitive *Encyclopédie de l'Utopie et de la Science-Fiction* does not hesitate to describe him as France's greatest "conjectural author" (Rosny was Belgian by birth but Parisian by calculated cultural affiliation), not excluding Verne. Jacques van Herp, in his introduction to an omnibus collection of Rosny's scientific romances and related tales edited by Jean-Baptiste Baronian, states flatly that "Before Rosny, science fiction did not exist; all that existed was a related literature: anticipation" and, after characterizing that earlier (Vernian) literature as an assembly of tentative extrapolations of the contents of our own world, adds that: "With Rosny, fortunately, everything changed."

Actually, van Herp's judgment is wildly overestimated; any change wrought by Rosny's early ventures into scientific romance certainly did not happen overnight, and was always weighed down by crippling difficulties. In his own day, Rosny's scientific romances went virtually unnoticed at first, and it was not until they were belatedly identified as having a significant kinship with those of H. G. Wells that anyone thought them significant; because Rosny had written several of his key works before Wells made his debut, some French critics became keen to establish the priority of his work, just as they were keen to represent Wells as a follower in the footsteps of Jules Verne. Rosny, however—like Verne, and with equal justice—was quick to deny that the apparent kinship between his work and Wells's was as close as these observers claimed. His protests went unheeded, and he was frequently labeled "the French H. G. Wells" thereafter, but that did not make it any easier for him to publish more work of a similar sort. In respect of the broad evolution of scientific romance as a genre he was a unique pioneer, whose imaginative reach was unprecedented, and has rarely been matched even by the relatively few writers who have undertaken to imitate or extrapolate aspects of his work, but he has never been popular, even among connoisseurs of speculative fiction. That is mainly because his best work was so very unusual, and usually lacking in certain traits guaranteed to encourage the affection of readers—but there is no doubt at all about his originality, or the imaginative quality of the contribution that he made to speculative fiction.

Seen in the context of his long life and prolific literary career, Rosny's contribution to scientific romance was sketchy, problematic and puzzling—but in such a context, it is not necessarily a bad thing to be problematic or puzzling, and the sketchiness of his production was not his fault, being reflective of the intense hostility to speculative fiction that has always been obvious in the literary marketplace, and even more obvious in the chatter of conventional critical opinion. The translation of his work into English, although not entirely neglected, has—until now—been very patchy and rather fugitive, and this has made it very difficult for historians and critics of speculative fiction working in the English language (as the vast majority of them do) to assess his contribution accurately. Hopefully, this collection, and the accompanying commentary, will help to make that much easier.

J.-H. Rosny *Aîné* was the principal pseudonym used by Joseph-Henri-Honoré Boëx, who was born in Brussels in

9

1856. In the beginning, the pseudonym was simply J.-H. Rosny, but he decided after some years of near-fame to share that pseudonym with his younger brother, Séraphin-Justin-François (who preferred the name Justin), and it remained a joint enterprise for a decade and a half, until the two fell out and decided to separate; because both of them wanted to maintain the limited but significant prestige attached to the pseudonym, they divided it into two, becoming J.-H. Rosny *Aîné* (the elder) and J.-H. Rosny *Jeune* (the younger). (The two brothers had five other siblings, but none of the others are of any relevance to their writing career.)

"J.-H. Rosny" was neither the first nor the only pseudonym that Joseph Boëx used. During the most prolific period of his work for periodicals he is known to have sometimes signed himself "Henri de Noville," and he signed some of his early books "Enacryos" before reprinting one of them under the Rosny name, but some of the other names he used have never been identified, so the whole scope of his work remains unknown. There is, however, no doubt that the vast majority of his most interesting work appeared, or was reprinted, under the J.-H. Rosny by-line. He never used his own name in the form that he had received it, although he did sign one nonfictional essay J.-H. Boëx-Borel, the second component of the surname being the maiden name of his second wife.

This set of circumstances has inevitably caused problems for critics, who have never been quite sure how best to refer to Joseph Boëx while discussing his life and work. Most critical and biographical articles settle for "Rosny," in spite of the difficulties thus caused in specifying his young brother's contribution to the name's achievements, but Jean-Baptiste Baronian's supplementary material in the Robert Laffont omnibus of Rosny's *romans préhistoriques* dutifully refers to him as R.A., while designating his brother as R.J. Although that strategy is tempting, "R.A." has too many alternative referents to be free of potential confusion, so I shall stick to "Rosny"—or, occasionally, "Joseph"—in spite of the inevitable contortions this will cause whenever the younger brother comes into the discussion. Fortunately, there is good reason to believe that the younger brother never made any contribution to any of the small number of prehistoric romances or scientific romances that appeared while the two brothers were working in association.

Pierre Versins begins his article on the elder Rosny (his encyclopedia also includes a brief article on Rosny *Jeune*) with an anecdote about the young Joseph Boëx writing a Utopian essay at the age of 11 about a land of free children escaping the persecution of their parents, which allegedly annoyed the father after whom he had been named—but Rosny's similarly-named father had, in fact, died when he was seven, so any annoyance must have been felt by his widowed mother, for whom bringing up seven children cannot have been easy. Young Joseph could hardly have known his father at all, but it may be worth noting that Joseph Boëx senior probably did not like his surname much, having inherited it from a mother who disowned him at birth—after refusing to name his father—leaving him to be brought up as a ward of the Belgian state.

Although Versins' article and the chronology of Rosny's life included in the Laffont omnibus both stress that Joseph junior began writing at an early age—Baronian's chronology credits him with a collection of verse completed at the age of thirteen—and always looked upon it as something of a vocation, he took a long time to get his literary career off the ground, or even to attempt its launch. Indeed, he seems to have formed the opinion, even in his teens, that he needed a long period of education before he could move on to stage two of his life-plan—and also that he needed to plan his own curriculum rather than rely on the one provided by any existing institutional system. He left school at 15 to work in a bank, studying English in the evenings; Baronian records that he published a few articles in Belgian newspapers in 1872, but he did not attempt to build a career on those publications.

In 1875, Joseph took advantage of his English lessons to get a job in London, where he worked for a telegraph company, on the night shift, and continued his program of self-education by day. Baronian says that he published some work in English periodicals, but gives no details, and the pattern of the references contained in J.-H. Rosny's subsequent publications strongly suggests that the bulk of his reading and writing was in French. His self-designed educational curriculum was very heavily biased toward sciences, ranging from physics and astronomy all the way through to newly-emergent social sciences like paleoanthropology.

Although he was not a man to say a great deal about himself, and might even be thought to have been deliberately secretive, Rosny did include some useful reflections on this period of his life in one of his two volumes of literary memoirs, *Torches et lumignons* [roughly, Bright Lights and Guttering Candles] (1921) and some further inferences can be gleaned from the most personal of his three early semi-autobiographical novels, *Marc Fane* (1888), which is a detailed account of the ambitious self-education program designed by the eponymous clerk in a telegraphy office, and the tribulations he experiences in carrying it through. In *Torches et lumignons*, Rosny explains that his passion for science was not only derived from his conviction that such knowledge was more valuable than that provided by a "traditional scientific education;" he states that: "I also remain incomprehensible if one forgets my extreme taste for metaphysics and science. For me, science is a poetic passion; it opens myriads of channels or openings into the universe; it never appears dead to me."

Given this "poetic passion" and the other item of potential incomprehensibility to which the "also" in the above quotation refers back—Rosny describes himself as a complex and essentially contradictory personality, in which "realism is intimately and constantly mingled with the most chimerical idealism"—his self-education cannot have been quite as relentless and methodical as Marc Fane's, but it was certainly patient and elaborate. His life-plan must, however, have been thrown slightly off track in 1880, when he married an Englishwoman, Gertrude Holmes. The family lived in London

for a further five years—probably longer than he had originally intended to stay there—but Joseph paid increasingly frequent visits to Paris, where he intended to go once his embryonic literary career was ready for hatching out. Justin had
already been there for some time, apparently waiting for him,
when the older brother eventually relocated his still-growing
family late in 1884.

Rosny begins *Torches et lumignons* with a description of
his submission by hand, in the autumn of 1885, of what was to
become his first-published novel, *Nell Horn de l'Armée du
Salut* [Nell Horn of the Salvation Army] (1886), a revelatory
study of the world of the London poor, written from occasio-
nally-bitter experience. Although it is based on first hand observation, the central character is only loosely based on Gertrude Holmes, and the fates of the two women are contradictory; while Rosny married Gertrude, Nell's French lover call-
ously abandons her, leaving her with no alternative but to become a prostitute in order to support her illegitimate child.
Gertrude presumably got a better bargain than Nell, but Rosny
apparently came to feel that he had not done nearly as well as
his hero; although it produced four children of whom Rosny
claimed to have been fond, the marriage was direly unhappy,
and eventually ended in divorce.

Although *Nell Horn* must have been recently finished
when Rosny handed it over to Monsieur Giraud in the offices
of the Nouvelle Librairie Parisienne, he had been working on
it for years, alongside numerous other works. Like many aspiring writers, Rosny was far better at beginning projects than
bringing them to conclusion, and had accumulated a vast store
of fragmentary manuscripts and notes while living in London.
In *Torches et Lumignons* he notes that in 1885, after arriving
in Paris: "I retouched *Les Xipéhuz*, I finished my *Livre étoilé*,
which did not see and will not see the daylight of publication;
I assembled the multitudes of *Le Bilateral*, I jotted down *Marc
Fane* and the lineaments of *Daniel* [Valgraive]; I lost myself
in endless dreams of *La Légende sceptique*, I revised
L'Immolation, I sketched out a romance of *Cavernes*."

Assuming that this account can be taken seriously—and there is no reason to doubt the list of titles—it appears that at least four of Rosny's first six published novels already existed in some form before he completed *Nell Horn*, together with drafts of four more works, two of which were never published. Significantly, in the context of the present project, the second group of four includes two of this key works of scientific romance—"Les Xipéhuz" (1887; tr. herein as "The Xipehuz") and "La Légende sceptique" (1889; tr. herein as "The Skeptical legend"). Equally significantly, from the same viewpoint, the two that never reached publication also seem likely, to judge by their titles, to have been in that same genre. If, as seems probable, *Cavernes* was the source of the fragmentary story eventually published as "La contrée prodigieuse des cavernes" (1896; tr. in vol. 2 as "The Wonderful Cave Country"), that would suggest that some of Rosny's later publications in the genre might have been written, or at least imagined, much earlier than their dates of publication.

Rosny was very keen to win friends and influence people once he had launched his literary career, and was ardently desirous of being accepted into Parisian literary society—partly, no doubt, because he understood the importance of networking in building a career, but mainly because he had such a great admiration for that society that he could imagine no greater reward than to be gladly welcomed into it. He sent a copy of *Nell Horn* to Emile Zola, hoping to win some praise for the novel's extrapolation of the Naturalist credo that Zola had made famous, but the famously curmudgeonly Zola was dismissive. Rosny's fortunes took a sudden and momentous turn for the better, however, when he sent another copy of the book to Zola's great rival, Edmond de Goncourt, who was considered by many (not least himself) as the true founder and greater exponent of Naturalism.

Goncourt not only sent Rosny a letter expressing the praise that the younger writer craved, but also invited Rosny to visit him at his home. That meeting changed Rosny's life; it is probably no exaggeration to say that if it had not been for Goncourt's patronage, Rosny might have disappeared into oblivion after the publication of *Nell Horn*—which sold little more than a couple of hundred copies—and never published another book. Instead, Goncourt took the fledgling writer under his wing as a protégé, and introduced him to his weekly literary salon, generally known as the *Grenier* [loft], as a writer of great promise—a judgment that other people, including Albert Savine, the owner of the Nouvelle Librairie Parisienne, and the editors of several notable periodicals, took seriously.

Rosny was by no means the first young writer to have been favored in this way by Edmond de Goncourt—who seemed to some observers to have been desperately seeking a replacement for his younger brother, Jules, ever since the latter had died in 1870—but he was the last, retaining his position until Goncourt died in 1896. He seems to have replaced Goncourt's former favorite, Jean Lorrain, virtually overnight, and he quickly became the central figure of an entourage of young writers who were standard fixtures at the *Grenier* and were regarded there as the up-and-coming generation of Naturalist writers. Although the others had all published material before Rosny published *Nell Horn*, his late start meant that he was a few years older than they were, and his accumulated store of manuscripts meant that he was able to make more rapid progress; those circumstances, combined with his assertive personality, quickly made him the brightest star in the constellation.

The other writers in Goncourt's neo-Naturalist cadre of *protégés* included Paul Bonnetain, Lucien Descaves, Paul Margueritte and Gustave Guiches, with whom Rosny joined in a conspiracy directed against Zola, seemingly prompted by another member of the entourage, Gustave Geffroy. (Goncourt remained ostentatiously uninvolved and was never formally convicted of having masterminded the coup, although his loathing for Zola was well-known and it was widely suspected that he was the ultimate puppet-master of the plot.) The result of the conspiracy was the publication in the August 8 issue of the newspaper *Le Figaro* of an open letter to Zola which came to be known as *Manifeste des Cinq*: a new Naturalist manifesto that put the boot into Zola in no uncertain terms, accusing him of having vulgarized, devalued and debased that literary mode—holding up the recently-published *La Terre* (tr. as *Earth*) as a horrible example—and declaring the independence of their own Naturalist work.

All five of the *Cinq* subsequently regretted having issued the *Manifeste* and repudiated the views sternly and extravagantly expressed therein, but at the time it succeeded in its purpose, which was to cause something of a sensation in the literary community. Although the document had five signatories, Bonnetain was subsequently to reveal that it had actually been written by Rosny, and to allege that Rosny had flatly refused to accept any amendments suggested by his co-signatories. The document was welcomed by the leading French literary critic of the day, Anatole France—a diehard antagonist of the supposed vulgarity of Zolaesque Naturalism—who referred to it in his memoirs of *La Vie littéraire* (1913) as a Revolutionary Terror, in which Rosny represented "a strict literary Dantonism" while his four companons were mere "Jacobins." It was also welcomed by Max Nordau, author of the scathing *Entartung* (1893; tr. as *Degeneration*), who considered Zola's Naturalism to be one more symptom of the degeneracy of modern culture—but cited Rosny's *Vamireh* (1892; tr. in vol. 4) as evidence that Zola's former disciples were only deserting the fold in order to descend further into the cultural mire.

The contemporary impact of the *Manifeste* can be judged by scanning a series of interviews conducted by Jules Huret between three and four years after its publication, initially published in the *Echo de Paris* and swiftly reprinted in book form by Charpentier as *Enquête sur L'Evolution littéraire* [An Inquiry Concerning Literary Evolution] (1891), in which Huret attempted to consult all the luminaries of contemporary French literature as to the direction that French literature was currently taking, initially focused on the explicit question "Is

Naturalism dying?" and the corollary question of whether, if so, the *Naturaliste* school was to be reformed, or replaced by a new school derived from authors recently hailed as *Psychologues* or *Symbolistes*, or victimized by some other convenient label. Although some of the people to whom Huret wrote asking for an interview sent letters instead of actually seeing him, his subjects were, on the whole, extraordinarily co-operative (with the exception of Guy de Maupassant—described by Huret as "the most unapproachable man in Paris"—who did agree to see him at his home, but then flatly refused to talk about literature).

Given that the *Echo de Paris* routinely featured work by numerous members of the *Grenier*'s inner circle—including Rosny and other members of the *Cinq*—it is not entirely surprising that even the minor writers in that circle were all featured in the book, but it is obvious that Huret's basic interrogative agenda was set by the *Manifeste*, and that many of the opinions expressed by the younger writers featured were orientated in relation to it, either for or against. The results were extremely varied—in respect of Naturalism they ranged from Henri Céard's languid "How can Naturalism die, since it has never existed?" to Paul Alexis's urgently-dispatched telegram "Naturalism not dead. Letter follows."—and many of Huret's respondents were brutally dismissive of the conventional critical assortment of writers into *Naturalistes, Psychologues, Symbolistes*, etc., as well as being completely at odds when it came to identifying the writers who belonged in each category, but the terms of the argument are sufficiently consistent to determine that all but a tiny minority of the Parisian *literati* of 1891 knew perfectly how the battlefield was marked out, and judged that the *Cinq* had established a significant strategic position.

One of the things Huret asked his respondents to do was to name the new writers who would play a significant part in the future evolution of French literature, and Rosny's name was one of those most often cited. He was not only named by the other four members of the *Cinq*, Gustave Geffroy and

17

Goncourt himself, but by other "senior" members of the *Grenier's* inner circle, including Joris-Karl Huysmans and Paul Hervieu. Cracks in the solidarity of the *Cinq* were already manifest, however; Bonnetain observed dismissively that "Rosny liked to spoil his enormous talent by an abuse of pharmaceutical neologisms," while Descaves accused him of having "an incommensurable, mad pride, of which he has no conception" and observed that he was "always preaching" at the *Grenier*. The latter judgment was not unchallenged, however; Anatole France presumably had it in mind when he wrote a review-essay on Rosny's work in the same year, focused on *Le Termite* (1890), in which he declared that: "Whatever anyone may say, M. Rosny is not vain. Neither is he proud. He knows nothing of arrogance... He does not admire himself, but he has an infinite respect for that portion of the divine wisdom which nature has placed in him, and if he is full of himself it is due to stoic virtue. He is a man of great integrity, but difficult to improve."

Anyone reading the *Echo de Paris* or the *Enquête* in 1891, therefore, and keeping up with the opinions of the leading critic of the day would have been bound to come to the conclusion that Rosny was an important writer, not only for what he had already accomplished as a *"Neo-Naturaliste"* but for what he might go on to do in future. When Huret reacted to criticism of his ready-made system of classifying writers as *Naturalistes, Psychologues, Décadents et Symbolistes, Parnassiens, etc.* by producing a tongue-in-cheek alternative system, he placed Rosny among the *"Boxeurs et Savatiers"* [Boxers and Kick-Boxers]. The simple fact is, however, that Rosny owed the spectacular reputation he had developed between 1886 and 1890 far more to *salon* gossip and critical back-scratching than to the actual sales of his books, which were—and remained—rather poor.

Rosny had not only become a regular at Goncourt's *Grenier* but had been introduced by Goncourt to other influential writers, most notably Alphonse Daudet, and to other influential salons. Rosny obviously loved that aspect of literary life; the second part of his second volume of literary memoirs is taken up with his nostalgic description of the various salons he attended regularly and the writers he met there; it gives pride of place to Madame Arman de Caillavet's salon, where he met and cultivated the acquaintance of Anatole France, her long-time lover and some-time collaborator. Some of Rosny's descriptions take great care to compliment the food served at those salons which took the form of dinners, for which he may well have been exceedingly grateful in the early days— although the reader might occasionally be inspired to wonder how it compared to the fare that Madame Boëx and her four children were eating at home, where they obviously spent a great deal of time in his absence.

What had first inspired M. Giraud to make an offer of 250 francs for a 1000-copy first printing of *Nell Horn* was an enthusiastic reader's report, whose author is unidentified in *Torches et lumignons*, save for the fact that she was female and was said to have been "touched" by it. Rosny affords scant importance to this, save for his gratitude for the part it played in getting his career moving, but it is worth noting that, although almost all the literary critics of the day were male, publishers were keenly aware of the importance of female readers and, in particular, of the fact that it was female readers who found books "touching" who were responsible for the success of a seemingly-new school of fiction centered on the works of Paul Bourget. Bourget, who was identified by Huret and others as the archetypal *Psychologue*, was a practitioner of a kind of naturalistic fiction that preferred exploring the psychological motivations of characters rather than their morality—whether religiously-defined or not—or their supposed hereditary defects. (Zola's school of Naturalism was "physiological" rather than "psychological" because it sought to explain its characters' moral defects or excesses in terms of hereditary factors modified by the social environment.)

It seems probable that Giraud and his employer, Albert Savine—who was then making a determined effort to expand his business—both hoped that Rosny might have the potential to emulate Bourget. Savine must have been delighted when he saw that one of "his" authors was making such rapid progress in Parisian literary society, meeting all the right people. Rosny's subsequent works turned out to be far less "touching," even when he tried to bring female characters into the foreground and focus intently on the romantic relationships of his characters, but he did manage to maintain himself in a prominent position in the Parisian literary community, suggesting that he might become a great success anyway. Savine seems to have maintained his high hopes of Rosny into 1887, following the critical success of Rosny's second novel, *Le Bilateral* (1886), but he felt forced to modify his publishing plans considerably in the course of that year.

The short story collection *L'Immolation* [The Sacrifice] (1887) in which Rosny included "Les Xipéhuz" as the last of five items, following four naturalistic *contes cruels*, offered a list of volumes "*à paraître prochainement*," not one of which actually appeared; they were *Nouvelles Londoniennes* [Londonian Short Stories], *Le Livre étoilé* [The Starry Book], *La Légende sceptique* and *Grisailles* [Studies in Grey], the last identified as a volume of poetry. Also mentioned as "*sous presse*" was *Les Corneilles* [The Crows], which had already appeared as a serial in the *Revue Indépendante*, one of several periodicals in which Rosny had found a warm welcome thanks to his star status in the *Grenier*. Its editor, Edouard Dujardin, was a regular at the *Grenier*, and it was he who published Rosny's second item of speculative fiction, then called "Tornadres" but later retitled "Le Cataclysme" (1887; tr. in vol. 2 as "The Cataclysm").

Fane: roman de moeurs parisiennes, which was actually the next Rosny book Savine published, as *Marc Fane*, in 1888, was only mentioned as "*en preparation*" in the preliminary material to *L'Immolation*. Savine evidently decided to postpone *Les Corneilles*—a relatively conventional and somewhat anodyne account of resistance to an arranged marriage—and not to publish the other items at all, presumably in response to the relatively poor continuing sales of the three books he had already published. Although *L'Immolation* contained advertisements for a second edition of *Le Bilateral*, accompanied by a sampler of glowing reviews of the first edition, that second edition presumably did not sell very well, and Savine must have deduced from the continuing poor sales of *Nell Horn* that it would be best to avoid any more works set in London. The other cancellations testify to Savine's decision to market Rosny purely and simply as a naturalist novelist—probably somewhat to Rosny's chagrin.

Rosny subsequently arranged the publication of "La Légende sceptique" as a serial in the *Revue Indépendante*, shortly after Albert Savine had bought that periodical from Dujardin and appointed Rosny on its staff as literary editor. Rosny observes in *Torches et lumignons* that he spent long hours mulling over the philosophical notions contained in the piece with the new editor Savine had appointed, François Dere, Comte de Nion—presumably as a means of ensuring its welcome, despite its awesome esotericism and peculiarity, and Savine's reluctance to publish it in volume form. Rosny frankly admits in *Torches et lumignons* that these were the only possible circumstances in which "La Légende sceptique" could ever have got into print, and he must have been equally well aware that the publication of "Les Xipéhuz" and "Tornadres" had also been the result of exceptional circumstances. He obviously accepted Savine's reasoning, however reluctantly, with respect to the mysterious *Le Livre étoilé*, and never bothered to finish *Cavernes*; as his career achieved lift-off, Rosny obviously made a decision to concentrate more exclusively on the aspect of his literary personality that had won him his valuable friends and influenced some influential people. The decision was undoubtedly wise, in terms of his reputation—but by 1890, when Rosny was at the height of his critical fame, the writing was already on the wall with regard to his marketability in any genre, and he must have been keenly aware of the fact.

Although Rosny obviously had other material in hand from the work he had done in the earlier months of 1885 and from his days in London, Savine had every reason to follow up the publication of *Nell Horn* with that of *Le Bilateral*, a novel which must have been entirely written after his relocation to Paris, being based on Rosny's excursions through the suburbs of that city. In *Torches et lumignons* the author observed, while talking about his early years in Paris, that "I was a great roamer. Every day I wandered for three or four hours... [I was] almost always on foot, in spite of an innate indolence. But walking did not seem laborious to me; I was drawn on by a daydream force that no longer allowed me to feel tired. I also loved to chat with unknown people— especially revolutionaries."

Rosny undoubtedly considered the observations he made and the reveries in which he indulged while walking to be an essential component of his creative endeavor, and his conversations with people he met by chance to be the kind of research required of a writer dedicated to quasi-scientific observation. He was, however, evidently interested in what many of his interlocutors had to say—especially the various socialists, anarchists and nihilists, many of them exiles, who had found a refuge in Paris (with whom he could, if necessary, converse in English instead of French). His work in this vein was of interest not merely to Parisians but anyone interested in the awesome complexities of the schism afflicting contemporary socialist thought. A newspaper article Rosny wrote on his findings was translated for publication in America in *Harper's New Monthly Magazine* in 1891, and the discussion it generated was probably influential in recommending some of his short fiction for translation, including two of his scientific romances: "L'Autre Monde" was translated in *The Chautauquan* in 1896 as "The Sixth Sense; or, Another World" and "Nymphée" in *The Eclectic* in 1908 as "The Warriors of the Waters."

Rosny was not himself a socialist, and presumably thought that the neo-Naturalist component of his creative personality required a scrupulous philosophical neutrality, so it is not unduly surprising that his judgment of the political activists to whom he talked was that they were unduly single-minded, quite unable to entertain any viewpoint other than their own. *Le Bilateral* presents a carefully-organized compendium of such "unilateral" characters, subjected to harsh judgment by the character bearing the eponymous nickname, who is allegedly highly unusual in being a complex and essentially contradictory individual, able to see matters from multiple viewpoints.

Although Rosny's commitment to a revisionist form of Naturalism in several of his early works controlled the way that contemporary critics evaluated him, and still colors critical evaluations offered today, his work was always highly idiosyncratic. In the interview he gave to Jules Huret, Paul Hervieu declared that Rosny was not a Naturalist at all, but that even such supposedly realistic works as *Daniel Valgraive* were "hatched in supernaturalist regions of hallucination or dream." Paul Margueritte also denied in his interview that Rosny should be characterized as a Naturalist, arguing that he "merits a separate epithet, specifying all that he brings of the new and the human." Rosny always took care to stress the bilateralism of his personality and the importance of its "poetic" or "chimerical" elements. In *Torches et lumignons* he wrote, stridently:

"I have always considered realism as a fragmentary aspect of literature; from my earliest works on, one will find more fantastic essays than realistic essays: *Les Xipéhuz, Tornadres* and *La Légende sceptique* are as far away as possible from realism. In consequence, the label of naturalist, applied to me, seemed to me to be an insult, and almost a calumny. I have never applied it to myself. If it had not been for that baroque manifesto, even ignorant Parisian critics would not have classified in so narrow a category a writer who interested himself in the entire universe, in all times, and in all dreams."

Even if one leaves aside the other components of Rosny's personality and work, there is no doubt that his brand of

Naturalism was far from Zolaesque—or, for that matter, Goncourtian. As M. Giraud's reader had obviously observed, in addition to its Mayhewesque detailing of the wretchedness of life in London's "underworld," *Nell Horn* contains a strong dose of sentimentality, especially in its treatment of the heroine. In the same way, in addition to its wealth of detail about the myriad schools of revolutionary thought lurking in the back streets of Paris, *Le Bilateral* contains a much stronger dose of philosophical analysis and judgment than was strictly in accordance with scrupulous observation, even of the theoretically-loaded variety licensed by Zola. By far the most idiosyncratic aspect of Rosny's Naturalism was, however, the influence of his equally-idiosyncratic fascination with science—which was, of course, also the progenitor of his adventures in scientific romance.

Rosny makes no attempt in *Torches et lumignons* to explain exactly what he was trying to accomplish in his early days as a writer, but the replies he gave to Huret's questions when he was interviewed for the *Enquête* do offer an account of the sort of revision of which, in his opinion, Naturalism stood in need. After having judged that Zola had spoiled his work with an "excess of triumphant materialism," while setting Goncourt aside as a vital pioneer and Daudet as a unique artist whose supposed association with the school was largely accidental, Rosny claims that what is necessary to carry the tradition forward is "a more complex, broader literature...a progress toward the enlargement of the human mind, a more profound, more analytical and more accurate comprehension of the *entire* universe and the humblest individuals, acquired by the science and philosophy of modern times." In his view, the *Psychologues* were too narrow in their approach, as Zola's hereditary theories had been, while nothing had yet come out of the Symbolist school but "a new stock of metaphors."

For Rosny, a scientific account of human nature had to include the insights of other sciences too, and must not be overly introspective, being obliged to consider people in the broadest possible context, both in time and space. For him, physical anthropology was a vital science, because it placed contemporary human nature and behavior in a context that extended back beyond history into prehistory, and thus to the entire evolutionary process that had produced humankind. As a Frenchman, his version of evolutionary theory owed at least as much to the Chevalier de Lamarck as to Charles Darwin, and it had a marked "ecological" component that was arguably ahead of his time, which gave him a distinctive view of humankind's place in Earthly nature. He was equally insistent on the importance of a human being's relationship with the findings of astronomy; unlike Camille Flammarion, the great popularizer of astronomy, who had become convinced that the stars were important to humans because humans would one day have the chance to live elsewhere in the universe, thanks to serial reincarnation, the thoroughly materialistic Rosny thought that they were of vital importance anyway, simply by providing a measuring-device by virtue of which humans could appreciate the true magnitude of creation—a magnitude that inspired him to a kind of metaphysical extrapolation very different from Flammarion's, and allowed him to develop an even more distinctive view of humankind's place in Cosmic nature.

These interests, and the viewpoints they generated not only led Rosny to repeated early experiments in scientific romance—although he neglected such endeavors for a long time once he had realized that his work in that vein was commercially unviable—but they also affected the manner in which he framed the descriptions included in his neo-naturalistic works, and the kinds of explanations he gave for the behavior of his characters. He was well aware of the fact that he was highly original in this regard, and was right to take some pride in the fact, although he soon learned that readers were often unsympathetic to it—especially the kind of readers that Albert Savine had hoped that he might attract, on the basis of the somewhat misleading example of *Nell Horn*.

Marc Fane, which Savine chose to release after *Le Bilateral* and *L'Immolation*, is the most frankly autobiographical

25

of Rosny's works and must have been in progress for many years. Savine followed it up in the same year with *Les Corneilles* but then seems to have become thoroughly disillusioned; after publishing *Le Termite* [The Termite] (1890) he gave up, cutting Rosny loose, for reasons which Rosny had made painfully clear within the text of *Le Termite*, and which Anatole France highlighted in his review-essay on the text and its writer.

Although *Le Termite* is not, strictly speaking, a *roman à clef*, it contains easily-recognizable portraits of several significant figures in the Parisian literary community, including Edmond de Goncourt (Fombreux), Zola (Rolla) and Alphonse Daudet (Guadet). The central character, Noel Servaise, is a purely hypothetical straw man—an unsuccessful and embittered neo-Naturalist who probably would not even have been invited to sign the *Manifeste des Cinq* had he actually existed—who is there mainly to be insulted for his lack of imagination, but the text is less interested in what the leading lights of literary Paris think of Servaise than what they think of a more promising writer named Myron, who is very obviously based on Rosny himself. Fombreux/Goncourt—painted, somewhat riskily, with less obvious sympathy than Guadet/Daudet, though far more than Rolla/Zola—likes Myron's work but disapproves of his incessant use of scientific language and thinks his style "tortuous;" Rolla/Zola likes it far less, but is keen to make exactly the same criticisms in somewhat stronger terms. Even the narrative voice makes no bones about the relevant tendencies in describing Myron:

"A bitter disputant, full of confidence before the old masters, he appeared a presumptuous as well as a tiresome and emphatic repeater of arguments; he was at the same time tolerant and pig-headed. He repelled Servaise, by reason of his involved style and prophetic poses, at every point at which an exuberant nature may clash with a sober and depreciative one."

Given this self-judgment, it is hardly surprising that Anatole France, while obviously wishing to praise Rosny's good points, also feels obliged to admit that he cannot abide his "terrible defects," which he sums up, brutally, in a single clause: "he lacks taste, proportion and clarity." Later, having summed up all the arguments that Myron/Rosny repeats against himself, France concludes that: "M. Rosny is no man to listen to these timid counsels. He will never give up." France was wrong about that—Rosny had already given up on the more exotic produce of his poetic passion and was about to start soft-pedaling the other tendencies to which his friends objected—but he was right to observe a certain resentful stubbornness in Rosny's character, which would persist in rearing its head in later life. Albert Savine—who might well have thought that there was a little of his own staid philosophy in the "anti-metaphysical mind" of Noel Servaise—had been even quicker to give up on what he had come to consider a lost cause.

By 1890, therefore, Rosny's career had reached a crossroads, and the prospect of a long struggle lay ahead of him. It was not only his association with *La Revue Indépendante* that had suddenly become problematic, but his ready welcome at many of the other periodicals that had taken him up while he was fashionable, and he was condemned from then on to a relentless search for new outlets.

There is little doubt that the optimistic period that began in 1886 was the happiest of Rosny's life, save for the stresses of his unhappy marriage, and there is an exceedingly powerful nostalgia in his reportage of it in *Torches et lumignons*, but it did not last long. The situation was further confused by the fact that, from 1891 onwards, Rosny began to advertise the fact that he was no longer one writer but two. *Daniel Valgraive*, which Rosny had been working on since the mid-1880s but did not publish until 1891, was the first J.-H. Rosny novel in which the younger brother's contribution was acknowledged by the elder, and most of the work published thereafter was completed without any such contribution, but that did not inhibit Joseph from making much of the name's now-dual ownership.

The reasons for the publicization of a collaboration that might have been more apparent than real remain stubbornly unclear, although Rosny reported in his own published comments that it was a possibility that the two brothers had discussed long before it became any sort of actuality. Lucien Descaves mentions the move in his interview in Huret's *Enquête* in terms suggesting that he thought it a mere publicity stunt, and clearly believed Rosny had entered into the allegedly-close collaboration partly in order to imitate his mentor, who had worked so closely with his own younger brother, and partly because such a collaboration was so "rare and difficult" that his supposedly overweening vanity simply could not resist the challenge.

The memoirs that Rosny *Aîné* wrote, long after the sharing of the pseudonym had been formally ended in 1907, make almost no mention of the younger brother beyond the essential, perhaps reflecting the fact that their falling out had by then become a kind of cold enmity. There is, however, a brief memoir by Jules Renard, recorded in the printed version of his *Journal*, reprinted in the Laffont omnibus of Rosny's prehistoric romances, in which Renard recalls snatches of various conversations he had with Rosny prior to March 1908 (when the record was first made), in which Renard alleges that: "He does not collaborate with his brother; they juxtapose themselves. His brother finishes a book commenced by his elder, and reciprocally." He quotes Rosny as having said "My brother has fewer words than me at his disposal, but we think the same thing."

This is an extremely flimsy, and perhaps unreliable, basis for evaluating the terms of the Boëx brothers' literary association, but if it is combined with the appearance of the works themselves, it seems highly likely that the vast majority of the works published under the Rosny name while it was being shared were produced by Joseph alone, with a minority—mostly consisting of short stories—that were produced by Justin alone, and a relatively small number of novels that were the result of one brother finishing off a fragmentary work that the other brother felt incapable of completing. The most compelling reason for considering this likely is the pattern and volume of their subsequent publications once they had split the pseudonym in two. It must be admitted, however, that the components of Joseph's own personality seem always to have been working "in juxtaposition" rather than collaborating, and the patchiness of his solo work is so extreme that it is difficult to identify instances in which another hand might have been involved.

Although he claimed in *Torches and lumignons* to have "revised" some of his works, Rosny's texts give absolutely no indication of being anything other than first drafts, often cobbled together, or at least strung together, as patchworks that the author never made the slightest attempt to amalgamate into coherent wholes. The principal reason that reading his works remains so frustrating is that so many of them seem to be continually changing course, stubbornly refusing to seek any kind of overall unity of direction, theme or ambition. This tendency is particularly obvious in scientific romances, the composition of which was unable to take advantage of the natural dynamic that comes from setting carefully-designed characters to work in familiar social contexts, where both they and their imagined situations have an intrinsic narrative momentum. When dealing with extraordinary characters and/or extraordinary circumstances, that natural dynamic and its corollary narrative momentum are lost, and authors who are used to making their stories up as they go along very often find themselves floundering when producing "heterocosmic" texts; Rosny was not only no exception to this rule, but might well be reckoned its most obvious exemplar. Given the inherent difficulty of picking up such texts, it is hardly surprising that Justin—who had no poetic passion for science—seems only to have taken over texts of a much more conventional character.

If Lucien Descaves was right to think that the original basis for the advertisement of the fact that "J.-H. Rosny" was two people working in uncanny sympathy was a desire to emulate Edmond and Jules de Goncourt, at least in Edmond's eyes, it is not difficult to see why Rosny might have wanted to do that. Rosny must have been aware of the value of his status as Goncourt's favorite, and also of the precariousness of that status. Although it would be unjust to be unduly cynical about it, that value went beyond mere matters of influence; it actually had a promise of hard cash attached to it, which must have been doubly attractive to Rosny, in that the commercial failure of his novels ran parallel to an increasing desire to divorce his wife—a move that was bound to prove expensive, given that he would have to make formal financial provision for their four children.

The reason that Edmond de Goncourt's favor had a cash value is that the ageing author had no direct heirs, and made no secret of his intention to pass on his fortune to a select society of writers, who would constitute a kind of "alternative Academy" fostering and sponsoring writers excluded by the notoriously conservative Académie Française—to which Goncourt had never been elected. The society would also have the duty of obtaining publication for the journals that the Goncourt brothers had maintained for many long years, but which were still considered far too scandalous for publication by contemporary publishers. To say that Goncourt "made no secret" of this intention is, in fact, a drastic understatement, for it was a carrot he continually dangled over the heads of his entourage, perpetually teasing them with the possibility that they might or might not be included.

Rosny was obviously desperate to be named as one of the members of this select company; indeed, he testified to the pride he took in his membership by altering his by-line as soon as his appointment was confirmed. His signature then became "J.-H. Rosny de l'Académie Goncourt," and Joseph's literary signature remained "J.-H. Rosny *Aîné* de l'Académie Goncourt" after the split with his brother until the day of his death—after which his publishers promptly dropped the latter part as an unnecessary embellishment (and, strictly speaking, an inaccurate one, since the organization's official designation was as a *Societé* rather than an *Académie*, although the latter appellation became almost universal). Joseph Boëx clearly considered that it was J.-H. Rosny's appointment to the Académie Goncourt that confirmed and symbolized the status he had so eagerly sought, and it became a key component of his identity, as he conceived it. It presumably seemed all the more valuable to him because he had to live so long in expectation of it, not merely while Edmond de Goncourt was still alive, but for seven long years after the latter's death in 1896.

Rosny's own version of the story of the problematic foundation of "L'Académie Goncourt" is told in the long essay that begins his second volume of *Mémoires de la vie littéraire* [Memoirs of Literary Life] (1927), and is usually reckoned to provide its title because it appeared in larger type on the cover and title page than the overall title. The essay explains how Goncourt's will was challenged by a group of distant relatives, who took the challenge through the available courts, all the way to the Conseil d'Etat (which, as the notional regulator of the real Académie, was rumored to be implicitly hostile to the founding of a rival). Thanks to their lawyer, Raymond Poincaré, however, the surviving writers named by Goncourt to occupy the seats of the new Societé (Alphonse Daudet had died in the interim) won the day, and the Goncourt Academy was finally founded in 1903. Unfortunately, Goncourt's investments had only been worth half what he had expected when he drafted the provisions of the will, with the result that the salaries attached to the seats were only 3000 francs per annum, instead of the anticipated 6000. Even so, that salary was far from trivial, in terms of contemporary literary incomes—especially the incomes of writers who sold as poorly as Rosny.

Although the Academy had ten seats, at its inception, it only had nine names, because the appointment of "J.-H. Rosny" required two of them. The problem of Daudet's death was solved by allowing his son Léon to inherit his seat. Rosny dutifully notes in his memoir that Goncourt's former favorite,

Jean Lorrain, was devastated to find that he had not been named, although Rosny did not repeat the observation he had earlier made while describing Lorrain in *Torches et lumignons*, when he mentioned that the Academicians "dared not" repair Goncourt's omission by electing him to one of the seats that subsequently fell vacant. Lorrain had, alas, tainted his literary reputation by tackling too many subjects deemed dubious on moral grounds, and had failed to escape the censorious cut that had let in Joris-Karl Huysmans (who had reverted to piety as well as Naturalism after penning the controversial Bible of Decadence *À rebours*) and Octave Mirbeau (who had not yet written the equally Decadent *Le Jardin des supplices*), along with Elemir Bourges, Léon Hennique, Paul Margueritte, Gustave Geffroy and Lucien Descaves.

Although Rosny's great expectations had been somewhat delayed, and were eventually reduced by half, he nevertheless went through with his divorce in 1896, having already become reconciled to the fact that he would have to cut his literary cloth more to market expectations if he was to make a living from his pen. He was married again, to Marie Borel, in 1900, and that presumably put a further burden on his finances, requiring him to concentrate even more intently on the commercial viability of his published work. Although he did not give up entirely on eccentric productions—*Les Femmes de Setnê* [The Women of Setne] (1903), which he signed Enacryos, is set in ancient Egypt and briefly features an exotically-populated lost land—the work published under the J.-H. Rosny name after 1896 remained carefully conventional, occasionally descending to such blatant popularity-courting endeavors as *La Tentatrice* [The Temptress] (1897), *Les Amours d'un cycliste* [A Cyclist's Love-Affairs] (1899), *Le Crime du docteur* [The Doctor's Crime] (1903) and *Le Millionnaire* [The Millionnaire] (1905). Whether or not this seems regrettable in retrospect, the collaboration did maintain the two brothers' production at a reasonably prolific level; they averaged about three novels a year from 1894-1906, and rarely reached that level thereafter, even when the production of the divided pseudonym is added together.

Although "J.-H. Rosny" did publish a handful of scientific romances after Joseph had announced his collaboration with his brother, most were brief or conscientiously moderate, and it is probable that the more adventurous examples were based on material written many years previously. Jean Morel, who wrote two articles on Rosny's prehistoric romances and scientific romance for the *Mercure de France* in 1923 and 1926 (the former in collaboration with Pierre Massé) said in both that he had "good reason to believe" that the younger brother had not made any contribution to the relevant work; if he did not get that information directly from Rosny he presumably obtained it at only one remove, *via* Alfred Vallette; the *Mercure*'s editor. The situation was slightly confused by Pierre Versins, whose article on J.-H. Rosny *Jeune* dutifully included a list of relevant titles produced during the period of collaboration, but Versins was equally careful to state that any contribution Justin might have made must have been "minimal," and all the other available evidence suggests that it was nonexistent. Although he produced two items of lost land fiction after the pseudonym was split, neither of which involves any kind of alternative evolution, Versins observes that J.-H. Rosny *Jeune*'s only work based in scientific speculation was *Le Destin de Marie Lafaille* (1945), produced some years after his brother's death and perhaps intended as a belated homage to him. For the duration of the collaboration, however, even Joseph wrote little or nothing new in a speculative vein, and the naturalistic novels he wrote on his own—whichever ones they might have been—also became conspicuously less idiosyncratic. The change of direction and modification of ambition the brothers quickly routinized after 1893 did not, alas, prevent something of a backlash against the brief hyping of Rosny's work as the promise of a brighter literary future. The spearhead of that backlash was Anatole France's review-essay, but the relatively sympathetic tone of that piece was decisively set aside by a cruelly sarcastic demolition of Rosny's work and reputation in an 1895 issue of the prestigious *Revue de Deux Mondes* penned by René Doumic—a critic renowned for carrying out hatchet-jobs, on behalf of a steadfastly conservative literary philosophy that eventually won him election to the Académie Française in 1909.

Doumic's article on *"Les Romans de M. J.-H. Rosny"* begins by inviting the reader to transport himself forward a few years, into an era in which "the tendencies that have begun to manifest themselves in education have conclusively triumphed. Letters have finally been exiled to information... The University has realized its desire to be modern... For everything concerning art and literature, the younger generation have entered a world where their gaze is no longer saddened by the vestiges of ancient things; everything is recent. It is not that the times have attained ignorance; quite the reverse; men have never been so wise. They know everything, once they have been to school... They have been taught all the sciences, for there is no useless science. Every year brings its new quota of discoveries. The brain of every French citizen is like an encyclopedia; it is a repository of formulas, a storehouse of scientific ideas. Humankind has crossed an important threshold. It has entered, under full sail, a positivist and utilitarian era, frankly democratic and resolutely scientific."

Doumic goes on to ask: "In a society thus constituted on its true foundations, will people continue to read books? It is to be feared so, for perfection is an ideal toward which poor men may well extend all their efforts, but they will never attain it. Literary vanity still has a fine future ahead of it. What sort of books will be written in that time following ours? Let us assume writers endowed with fine faculties, capable of observation and provided with imagination, laborious and respectful of their pens, haunted by generous dreams. Let us assume that they will write novels. What will these novels be like? The question is not idle, and to resolve it we are not constrained to content ourselves with hypotheses; we have an easy means to answer it with some precision, and that is to consult the novels of Monsieur J.-H. Rosny."

Doumic notes that less than ten years have passed since *Nell Horn* was published, and asks his reader to recall the movements of ideas, currents of sensibility and influences that has provided the literary atmosphere of those ten years, when Naturalism was in decline, perishing "by the excess of its own narrowness and vulgarity." By virtue of its complexity, he claims, the modern soul "attracted and troubled the most subtle analysts," especially with respect to the "eternal problem of love," which has become even more problematic because "from all points of the worlds of reality and dream a wind of sadness had desiccated hearts." In Doumic's eyes, this problem has been solved by authors who have "reinvested" in tenderness, charity and pity, if not formal evangelical religion, but Rosny, he claims, has remained defiantly immune from such influences, remaining "as far from the psychologists as the dilettantes, and from the neo-Christians as from the aesthetes." Reading Rosny, according to Doumic, "one has the impression of traveling in a strange land, in which characters, questions, ways of thought and language are disconcertingly different."

The essay continues: "M. Rosny, although he has already written a great deal, is little known, and his books, full as they are of talent, have few readers. A few enthusiasts for his work reckon that the semi-indifference of the public is one of the great injustices of the modern epoch, and a confirmation of our frivolity. It is only just to acknowledge that M. Rosny has not made any concession to easy success; he has not lowered himself to employing any of the assured means that certain authors of the era have used to sell their books." Doumic also notes that Rosny "offers no indiscretions" regarding his person. "All that is known," he adds, "is that person is double; J.-H. Rosny is one author in two individuals: his books are the collaboration of two brothers arrived at such a degree of intellectual penetration that on any given subject, their ideas being communal, they can set to work, each writing the same page on his own account. Compared with this fraternity, that of the Goncourts was, as is evident, a fraternity of enemy brothers."

"What first leaps to the eyes," Doumic says, when he moves on to a consideration of Rosny's actual texts, "is that the author of these books has, I certainly do not want to say a scientific turn of mind, but a taste for science. Almost all the characters he puts on stage are, if not scientists, half- or quarter-scientists. This one is a physician, that one a medical student, others chemists of some sort. They are writing a considerable work, whether it is on *The Elimination of the Nordic type from the Aryan Family* or a *History of Modern Migrations*; if they are not dreaming of some *Metaphysics of Animals* it is because they are absorbed in a project on *Tranformist Legislation*. Each one following his aptitudes and his tastes, they are trying to pick up some crumbs of universal knowledge. There is the young telegraphist Marc Fane. He has, as yet, only received a professional education when he conceives a project of working for the benefit of humankind. Persuaded that everything is contained in the history of ideas, and that to accomplish the most meager progress for humankind it is necessary to know all the needs of modern society, he sets out to complete his studies. He outlines a program for himself compared with which Pico della Mirandola's was child's play. All the sciences will be represented therein, and each will have its ration of time. 'The ration of some branches would only be five minutes a week—design, astronomy, music. Gradually, that would increase to ten hours of politics and twenty hours of sociology.' Naturally, the sciences that attract Marc Fane preferentially are the least advanced, the least complete, those which have the least scientific certainty and the most apparatus thereof. Marc Fane thus acquires all the elements of knowledge, with no guidance, no criticism and no order, pell-mell...

"I am wary of confusing M. Rosny with his characters and assuming that he is fabricating their biographies with fragments of his own. I merely remark that all the sciences inscribed in Marc Fane's program have left some memory of themselves in M. Rosny's novels. Astronomy holds an important place there. Constellations, planets and stars are noted there by their names... Geology, paleontology, anthropology, ethnology, zoology and a few related sciences are for M. Rosny the ordinary repertoire of his comparisons...

"M. Rosny effortlessly makes himself the contemporary of cave-men. While our gaze timidly ventures into a corner of society or the soul, for him moves easily into a period of time more than twenty thousand years in the past, and which has no limit in the future. Little interested in individuals, he attaches himself passionately to questions of species and race... It is from the same viewpoint that M. Rosny envisages social questions; natural rights, the division of labor, the division of wealth, heritage, family, Malthusianism, population, depopulation and repopulation. Science presents the question of adultery to him in an aspect which, in order not to be the sentimental and passionate aspect to which novelists usually confine it, has no more probability of being its true aspect 'the indomitable instinct that desires a renewal of selection'...

"This worship of science is, in M. Rosny, essential and fundamental. It is that to which all his theories are attached or subordinate; it is the reason that he has devoted himself to literature, and it is the source of his aesthetics... To extract from the scientific work of the century the elements of literature that it contains—such is the task that he has assigned himself and to which he attempts to adapt the form of the novel."

I have quoted this at such length because, setting Doumic's obvious disapproval aside, it is an accurate and perceptive account of the basic outlook of Rosny's early work, establishing the ideative context from which his early scientific romances emerge. After more detailed consideration of *Nell Horn* and *Le Bilateral*, Doumic brings his textual analysis to the conclusion that: "All these novels are those of a good pupil of the naturalist school. One could say the same of *Immolation*, a peasant study reminiscent of the most brutal short stories of Maupassant [and] *Le Termite*, a study of literary mores, the most frankly detestable I think, of the author's books, simultaneously pretentious and dull." Having ignored Rosny's other scientific romances, perhaps on the grounds that they were too short to qualify as *romans*, he tries to accommodate *Vamireh*, Rosny's first *roman prehistorique*, to his argument by claiming (inaccurately) that "in spite of its title and subtitle, [it] is nothing but a novel composed according to the formula and by the ordinary methods of the documentary school..."

Doumic does concede that Rosny's more recent works are of a different kind, being more accessible in form and containing more human interest—he adds that they are less "hair-raising"—but is keen to progress to an account of Rosny's literary faults, and thus pays no detailed attention to anything published after *Vamireh*. His primary complaint is the lack of continuity in the novels. "The episodes succeed one another at random, devoid of connection rationale or appreciable utility, developed in inverse proportion to their importance: no order, no proportion, no choice, no taste." He also complains bitterly about Rosny's neologisms and odd forms of expression, which "do not enrich the language," claiming that he violates the rules of grammar because he does not know them and suggesting that his improprieties of expression are based in murkiness of thought, although he "hastens to remark" that such faults are less common in the more recent works.

All of these criticisms have some justification, although the oddness of Rosny's modes of expression is not so obvious in translation, where a necessary adaptation to English grammatical and syntactical conventions inevitably obliterates some of their eccentricity in respect of French conventions. It is, however, worth noting that Doumic does not seem to realize that the lack of continuity in Rosny's works is a by-product of their patchwork method of composition rather than a deliberate artifact, and that he completely ignores the most important factor mitigating all these supposed facts: that Rosny's imaginative reach, if not his grasp, was unprecedented.

The simple fact is that Rosny would not have been able, let alone willing, to grope so far into the unknown for new ways to look at human nature and the cosmic environment of humankind had he been the kind of writer who planned his works more meticulously in advance and adapted his works more carefully to patterns of reader demand, in terms of their structure as well as their content. In brief, his work could not have been so worthwhile in some respects had he not been so seemingly faulty in others; Doumic, who had very rigid ideas about what writers ought to be doing and how, could not even see the merit in Rosny's imaginative endeavors, and thus thought it appropriate to condemn him—but lovers of speculative fiction inevitably take the opposite view: that his achievements in the realm of speculation justify and excuse the essential awkwardness of compositional method.

Inevitably, Doumic rounds out his essay—after a few mildly hypocritical paragraphs complimenting Rosny for certain merits he retains despite his faults, though not the one just identified—by returning to the futuristic thrust of his opening paragraphs, venturing into prediction: "But even though it is of today, his *oeuvre* has its right to significance. It will be yet another ornament of an epoch in which that which was once high intellectual culture will founder... That is what we have followed with sympathetic curiosity in M. Rosny's novels: it is the future of the novel in an enlightened barbarism, in which art and literature have beaten a retreat before triumphant sociology."

In this respect, of course, Doumic was utterly and absolutely mistaken; not only was Rosny's early work not a symptom of things to come in the broader literary world, but it was not an indication of the way in which his own career would be forced—and, indeed, had already begun—to develop. The scientific outlook that he tried to cultivate did not triumph, either in education or literature, but fell instead into a peculiar and perverse ignominy, treated almost universally with the kind of blind and stupid hostility of which Doumic was so proud. That might easily have prevented Rosny from ever venturing back into the realms of speculative fiction, but in fact it did not, and once Joseph Boëx was free of the shackles of his "juxtaposition" with his relentlessly unspeculative younger brother, he soon found several reasons for doing so.

After the serial publication of "La Légende sceptique" in 1889, there was an evident hiatus in the publication of Rosny's scientific romances, although *Vamireh* certainly warrants consideration as a literary extrapolation of late-19th century discoveries and (mostly mistaken) theories in paleoanthropology. The novel was serialized in 1892 in the early issues of a new periodical, the *Revue Hebdomadaire*, whose editor was probably pleased to acquire a contribution by such an up-and-coming writer, who had already published in many of the prestigious periodicals of the day. The same periodical went on to publish Rosny's naturalistic novel *L'Impérieuse Bonté* in 1893-94.

The editor of another new periodical, *Le Bambou*, was also sufficiently interested in Rosny to be willing to serialize work of this sort in 1893, beginning with the *roman préhistorique Eyrimah* (reprinted in book form 1896; tr. in vol. 4) and continuing with an account of unknown human races surviving in a remote part of Asia, "Nymphée" (tr. in vol. 2 as "Nymphaeum"). Both stories are conspicuously patchy, and the second is finished off in a brutal fashion, after having already undergone some awkward changes in direction, so it seems highly likely that both were cobbled together from pre-existent materials dating back to the mid-1880s.

During the remainder of the two brothers' partnership, only four short scientific romances and one further prehistoric romance appeared under the J.-H. Rosny name. The brief sardonic prehistoric romance, "Nomaï" (tr. in vol.4) appeared in the *Revue Parisienne* in 1895. "Un Autre Monde" (*Revue de Paris* 1895; tr. herein as "Another World"), which extrapolates—rather uneasily—an idea sketched out in "La Légende sceptique," was almost as ground-breaking as "Les Xipéhuz," but the other items are noticeably more conservative. As previously noted, "La contrée prodigieuse des cavernes" probably derives from the mid-80s manuscript identified by Rosny as

Cavernes, and "Les Profondeurs de Kyamo" (1896; tr. in vol. 2 as "The Depths of Kyamo"), which features a further adventure of the same protagonist, may well come from the same source. Both are in the same vein as "Nymphée," featuring the discovery of variant "dominant species" in remote "lost land" enclaves. Although there is no detailed bibliography of Rosny, and the full extent of his periodical publications has not been mapped, it is possible that these two stories were not published in periodicals, but appeared for the first time as the first two items in a collection issued by Plon under the title *Les Profondeurs de Kyamo*, whose other contents, carefully separated in the table of contents, are all mundane.

"Le Voyage" (1900; tr. in vol. 2 as "The Voyage") is also a lost land story, which could easily have featured the same protagonist as "La contrée prodigieuse des cavernes" and "Les Profondeurs de Kyamo" but refrained, perhaps because it begins in a very different style, with an extrapolation of one of the prose poems patched into "La Légende sceptique." It too seems to have been dropped into a collection of mostly-naturalistic stories rather arbitrarily, without any previous periodical appearance having been noted by modern bibliographers, and probably antedated that publication by some—perhaps many—years. No more prehistoric or scientific romances appeared in print while the two brothers' partnership lasted—or, indeed, for two years thereafter, in spite of the fact that H. G. Wells had demonstrated in the interim that scientific romance could be popular, as well as interesting in its extrapolations.

References to Rosny as a "French Wells" began to be made as early as 1896, when the press associated with the *Mercure de France*—whose literary editor, Henry Davray, was H. G. Wells's French translator—issued a small volume entitled *Le Cataclysme*, containing the title story and "Les Xipéhuz," presumably in order to cement the claim to his priority. Such references did not, however inspire Rosny to any immediate further attempt to justify the label, or to emphasize the distinctness of his own speculative fiction. In spite of his "poetic passion" for science and speculative thought, Joseph Boëx seems to have resolutely refused to embark on any further ventures of that kind between the publication of "L'Autre monde" and the formal termination of his literary partnership with his brother.

We can only speculate as to the role Justin Boëx might have played in dissuading his elder brother from experiments in scientific romance while they were sharing their pseudonym, but it seems highly probable that their collective change of status to "J.-H. Rosny de l'Académie Goncourt" also had much to do with it. In spite of the fact that the Goncourt Academy had been conceived as a protest against the conservatism of the official Académie, its members were nevertheless defensive of their own aesthetic credentials.

Oddly enough, the first Prix Goncourt, awarded in 1903, did go to a work that some might consider to be a scientific—or, at least, metaphysical—romance, *Force ennemie* [Hostile Force] by John-Antoine Nau (Eugène Torquet), but it was the work of an already-respectable writer who never did anything else of a similar ilk, and the Prix Goncourt was never subsequently awarded to anything of that sort, or to anything else that might be considered a "genre" novel rather than a "literary" novel. Three of the first 20 winners (Claude Farrère, Henri Barbusse and Ernest Pérochon) did do some work in the genres of scientific or prehistoric romance, but they won the prize for works that were very different in character. Rosny seems to have felt, once he was appointed to the Académie Goncourt, that he was somehow obliged to shun such work as unbefitting a writer of his status. He did, however, eventually borrow the speculative premise of *Force ennemie* for adaptation to his own speculative context in one of his more interesting exercises in hackwork, *La Jeune vampire* (1920; tr. in vol. 6 as "the Young Vampire").

Rosny left no precise record of the reason why he changed his mind about the propriety of writing genre fiction, but he made no bones about the fact that, as a man who had to make a part of his living from his pen, he was obliged to do a certain amount of hackwork. In all probability, there were two significant factors involved in his decision to include some speculative fiction within that aspect of his production; one was the foundation in Paris of a number of new "middlebrow" periodicals in imitation of such English periodicals as *The Strand*, which had been briefly hospitable to scientific romance, and the other was the fact that he began attending a weekly *salon* run by Maurice Renard.

I have already produced a five-volume set of Maurice Renard's scientific romances similar to this one,[2] whose supplementary materials map out that author's association with the genre in great detail, but it is sufficient to say here that Renard was Wells's most fervent admirer in France, and a diehard enthusiast for what he called the "scientific marvelous" and the potentialities of "scientific marvel fiction." Because he came from a wealthy mercantile family, Renard had a private income when he first settled in Paris in 1908, and was able to indulge in a relatively lavish lifestyle. Salon culture had been in steep decline for some time by then, but Renard was as eager to join it as Rosny had been 20 years before, and set out to do so from the opposite direction, by starting one of his own. Although many notable writers and editors became regulars, the writer he was most eager to attract was Rosny, not because of his membership of the Goncourt Academy or his now-deflated reputation as an important neo-Naturalist, but simply because he was an anticipator of H. G. Wells. When Renard penned his "manifesto" for scientific romance, "Du Roman merveilleux scientifique et de son action sur l'intelligence du progress" (*Le Spectateur* octobre 1909; tr. as "On Scientific Marvel Fiction and its Influence on the Awareness of Progress"), he gave almost equal attention to Wells and Rosny as the pioneers and supposed masters of the fled-

---

[2] *Doctor Lerne, A Man Among the Microbes, The Blue Peril, The Doctored Man* and *The Master of Light*, Black Coat Press, 2010.

gling genre—an opinion he had already made known to Rosny in no uncertain terms.

Perhaps Renard actually succeeded in persuading Rosny that scientific marvel fiction really would acquire the prestige in future that it had been so contemptuously denied in the past, but it seems more likely that he only managed to persuade him that such fiction now had a potential marketability that it had not had when Rosny had first tried it out. That potential proved short-lived, as did Renard's optimism, but while Renard's *salon* was still going, Rosny was persuaded to try his hand at "scientific marvel fiction" again, in a vein clearly influenced by Renard's manifesto—and, in one instance, by one of Renard's own novels. The two of them never collaborated, but they definitely "juxtaposed," each of them taking sufficient influence from the other to enliven his own work considerably, if only for a while. Oddly enough, they were very different writers; Renard was by far the better craftsman, planning his work carefully and revising it assiduously in order to build coherent and intricate plots, but he never had Rosny's imaginative reach, and the reach he did have owed more than a little to his interest in refining and further extrapolating ideas he had found in Rosny's work.

Significantly, Rosny never suggested that any of Maurice Renard's novels might be worthy of consideration for the Prix Goncourt, and never proposed him for election to the Academy itself (to which his namesake in Jules Renard had earlier been elected). The elder Rosny was prepared to allow Maurice Renard to influence his hackwork, to a degree, but he remained very conscious of the fact that the latter was only a genre writer, and hence a cut below him in terms of apparent status—even though Renard, having been pauperized by the Great War, never sank so low while making his living from his pen as to write pure pulp fiction, while Rosny did so without an atom of conscience.

Rosny's first contributions to the principal French imitator of *The Strand*, *Je Sais Tout*—which had been founded in

1905—were conventional varieties of popular fiction. "Le Lion" [The Lion], a novella serialized in 1908, was a straightforward African adventure story, and "La Flèche au curare" [The Curare-tipped Arrow] (1909) was in a similar vein; either might equally well have appeared in the more downmarket *Journal des Voyages*, which was one of the last surviving refuges of Vernian fiction, mostly featuring mundane adventures set in far-flung corners of the ever-shrinking globe. His third sale to the magazine was, however, the serial novel *La Guerre du feu* (1909; tr. as *The Quest for Fire*), a new prehistoric romance that revamped the essential substance of *Vamireh* in the context of a more coherent adventure story, with a more urgent narrative thread. The novel became Rosny's most successful work, eventually giving rise to the notable 1981 film adaptation by Jean-Jacques Annaud.

It is possible that Rosny initially intended the first of his "Renardian" scientific romances, "La Mort de la Terre" (tr. herein as "The Death of the Earth"), as a serial for *Je Sais Tout*, but it did not appear there, being serialized instead in *Les Annales Politiques et Littéraire* in May-July 1910 before being reprinted as the title-story of a Plon collection in 1912. The story clearly owes some inspiration to Wells's *The Time Machine*, but both Rosny and Renard were well aware that Wells's novel had had a French predecessor in Camille Flammarion's *La Fin du monde* (1893; tr. as *Omega: The Last Days of the World*) and Rosny was, in effect, knowingly carrying forward a French tradition parallel to the English one. Indeed, Rosny took the trouble to equip the book version with a preface, in which he dissented from the opinion that he was a Wellsian writer:

"It has sometimes been said that I was a precursor of Wells. A few critics have gone so far as to say that Wells had drawn part of his inspiration from such of my writings as *Les Xipéhuz*, *La Légende sceptique*, *Le Cataclysme* and a few others that appeared before the English writer's fine novels. I do not think that this is true, and I am even inclined to think that Wells has not read any of my works. He certainly does not share the monstrous ignorance of his compatriots in matters of continental literature, but the notoriety of *Les Xipéhuz, La Légende sceptique, Le Cataclysme,* etc. etc. was negligible in the era in which he started to write—and if he had read my modest books, I would deny all the same that he had been subject to any influence by them. *The War of the Worlds* and *The Island of Doctor Moreau* are *original* works, which it is necessary to admire without reserve. Besides, there is a fundamental difference between Wells and me in the manner of construction of *unknown* entities. Wells prefers living beings that still offer a considerable analogy with those that we know, while I willingly imagine creatures on a mineral sort, as in *Les Xipéhuz*, or made of a matter other than ours, or even existing in a world regulated by other forces than ours; the Ferromagnetals that appear episodically in *La Mort de la Terre* belong to one of these categories.

"In sum, save for a few points in which all writers occupied with the marvelous are similar, there is only an apparent resemblance between Wells and me, although it was probably not unnecessary to point this out."

Rosny's second Renardian romance—which obviously took its inspiration, and its basic narrative framework, from Renard's *Le Péril bleu* (1911; tr. as *The Blue Peril*)—was *La Force mystérieuse* (tr. in vol. 3 as "The Mysterious Force"), which was serialized in *Je Sais Tout* in 1913. This novel went to some lengths to emphasize the point made in the preface to *La Mort de la Terre*, by introducing phenomena and life-forms even stranger than the ferromagnetals of the earlier novella or the Xipehuz, and much stranger than any featured by Wells or Renard. Curiously enough, however, this story too became accidentally entangled with the history of British scientific romances when readers began to notice coincidental parallels between its opening sequence and a novel that began serialization a couple of months later in *Je Sais Tout*'s model, *The Strand*. Again, Rosny was prompted to add a preface to the book version issued by Plon in 1914:

"On March 11, 1913 an American friend sent the following note to me: 'Have you given an English writer—one of the most famous—the right to rewrite your novel that is currently appearing in *Je Sais Tout*; have you given him the right to take the central thesis and such details as the disturbance of the lines of the spectrum, the agitation of populations, the discussions of a possible anomaly of the ether and the poisoning of humanity, in their entirety? The famous English writer is publishing this at the present moment without naming you, without any reference to Rosny *Aîné*, placing the setting in England.'

"In consequence of that letter, I read the issue of the *Strand Magazine* in which my British colleague, Monsieur Conan Doyle, had begun publication of a novel entitled *The Poison Belt*. There are indeed annoying coincidences between the theme of his story and the theme of mine, including the disturbance of light, the phases of human panic and depression, and so on—coincidences that will be obvious to any reader of the two works. I confess that I cannot, in view of the extreme particularity of the thesis, restrain certain suspicions—all the more so because, in England, it quite often happens that writers *buy* an idea, which they then exploit as they please: someone might have proposed my idea to Monsieur Conan Doyle.

"Certainly, a coincidence is always possible, and for myself, I am inclined to be trusting. Thus, I have always been convinced that Wells had not read my *Xipéhuz*, my *Légende sceptique* or my *Cataclysme*, which appeared well before his fine stories. That is because there is in Wells a certain individual stamp that Monsieur Conan Doyle lacks. In any case, my objective is not to make any claim. I admit the possibility of a transmission of ideas between Monsieur Conan Doyle and myself, but as I know, from fairly long experience, that one is often accused of following those who follow you, I think it useful to establish a time-scale and to point out that *Je Sais Tout* had already published the first two parts of *La Force*

Mystérieuse when *The Poison Belt* began to appear in the *Strand Magazine*."

In fact, the time-scale proves beyond all reasonable doubt that the coincidences between the two novels were, indeed, purely coincidental; the fact that Rosny draws no such conclusion is presumably due to the fact that there was a long tradition in France of *feuilletonistes* writing daily newspaper serials, who delivered their copy on the day before the issue went to press. British magazines worked on a much more leisurely schedule, so the overwhelming probability is that Doyle had delivered the entire text of *The Poison Belt* to the editor of the *Strand* before anyone could possibly have told him about the theme of Rosny's serial in *Je Sais Tout*. In any case, the divergence of the two stories after their opening sequences is very marked indeed, so any question of imitation rapidly disappears, and could never have seemed likely to anyone but readers who had only read the first episode of each serial.

Maurice Renard was so delighted with *La Force mystérieuse* as an example of "scientific marvel fiction" that he wrote an extravagant essay in praise of it: "Le Merveilleux scientifique et la *Force mystérieuse* de J.-H. Rosny Aîné," published in the June 15, 1914 isssue of *La Vie*. When he wrote the essay, Renard was still hopeful that such examples might pave the way for a glorious future for the nascent genre with which he was infatuated, and there seems to be every reason to believe that he and Rosny would have continued to juxtapose such works for at least a little while longer had not circumstances intervened. Unfortunately, they did intervene, in the crushing form of the Great War, into which Renard—who had experience as a cavalry officer—was immediately drafted. By the time he returned to civilian and literary life, impoverished but not yet in despair, the world had changed drastically, and Rosny was all too well aware of the implications of that change.

In fact, Rosny probably did begin work on a third item of scientific marvel fiction in 1914, but did not manage to get it ready for publication for some time thereafter. Although it is no less of a patchwork than many of Rosny's other works, the interpolation two-thirds of the way through the finished text of an entirely irrelevant episode in which the hero sinks a German submarine suggests that he felt obliged to modify it in order to fit in with the pattern of wartime propaganda fiction, and that some such insertion was the price of obtaining publication for it in 1917 as *L'énigme de Givreuse* (tr. in vol. 5 as "The Givreuse Enigma"). He had not published any books at all in 1915 or 1916, and his other 1917 publication, *Perdus?* [Doomed?] (likewise issued by Flammarion) was a straightforward exercise in propaganda fiction, as was his 1918 collection *Confidences sur l'amitié des tranchées* [Secrets of Friendship in the Trenches].

When popular fiction got under way again after the trauma of the war—as Maurice Renard found to his cost—the public mood had turned against science, because of the contribution new technologies had made to the slaughter, and scientific romance was completely out of fashion. The same did not apply, however, to prehistoric romance or more conventional forms of adventure fiction, and that was the kind of hackwork to which Rosny reverted in earnest. Even before the war had ended, he had attempted to repeat the triumph of *La Guerre du feu* with *Le Félin géant*, which was serialized in *Lectures Pour Tous* in May-July 1918 before being reprinted in book form by Plon in 1920. Although it did not do as well as its predecessor, it was translated into English for publication in America. Although the book—*The Giant Cat*—did not appear until 1924, Rosny might have been aware of the rights sale well in advance of that date, because the lost land adventure *L'Etonnant voyage de Hareton Ironcastle* (1922; tr. in vol. 3 as "Hareton Ironcastle's Amazing Journey") has the appearance of having been constructed with the idea of a similar sale in mind, featuring an American hero and seemingly mimicking the formulae of the pulp magazines.

Rosny also published a very brief lost land story in *Lectures Pour Tous*, "La Grande énigme" (1920; tr. in vol. 2 as "The Great Enigma"), in which he offered a brief glimpse of a conventional lost land preserving relics of the Palaeolithic era rather than featuring a variant evolution—a theme swiftly expanded in another adventure story, *Le Trésor dans la neige* (1920; tr. in vol. 2 as "The Treasure in the Snow"), in which he brought back the protagonist of "La Contrée prodigieuse des cavernes" and "Les Profondeurs de Kyamo" for one last fling.

The extent to which Rosny was in communication with Maurice Renard once the war was over is difficult to estimate, since Renard could no longer afford to host a weekly salon, but the two undoubtedly met on occasion, and presumably shared Renard's despair with regard to the fortunes of the new genre he had tried to nurture and had virtually been forced to abandon after publishing a truncated version of "L'Homme truqué" (tr. as "The Doctored Man") in *Je Sais Tout* in 1921. There was certainly nothing in either man's experience to encourage them to write more scientific marvel fiction thereafter—but Renard kept trying to get his existing work in that vein into print, and Rosny did manage to place one more novella of that sort in the periodical *Oeuvres Libres*, which had published Renard's mock-Wellsian "L'Homme qui voulait être invisible" in 1923 and was also publishing a whole series of "mad scientist" comedies by André Couvreur, who was better known as a Zolaesque Naturalist.

The scientific romance that Rosny contributed to *Oeuvres Libres* was *Les Navigateurs de l'infini* (tr. herein as "The Navigators of Space"), which appeared there in 1925. It is an account of the first voyage to Mars, and the life-forms discovered there. The text makes Rosny's intention to write a sequel clear, but none materialized at the time, and Rosny abandoned scientific marvel fiction for good, apparently agreeing with Renard that the genre had no future in France. Twenty years after his death, a story called "Les Astronautes" [The Astronauts] was published in a paperback edition of *Les Navigateurs de l'infini* as if it were the second part of a composite novel. Although I have translated "Les Astronauts" for this collection, in the interests of completeness, the close acquaintance I developed with the idiosyncrasies of Rosny's style while carrying out this series of translations convinces me that only the first 5000 or 6000 words are actually his, the remaining 20,000 having been juxtaposed by another hand. The new text added nothing significant to Rosny's scenario.

Les Navigateurs de l'infini might have been inspired by an interest in the actual possibilities of space travel, although it was the cause rather than an effect of Rosny's subsequent adoption as an honored member of Robert Esnault-Pelterie's Nouvelle Societé Scientifique de Recherches pour l'élaboration de fusées destinées aux futures voyages interplanétaires [Scientific Society for Research into the Development of Rockets Designed for Future Interplanetary Journeys] in 1928.

Not unnaturally, after the failure of his final venture into scientific marvel fiction, Rosny reverted to more familiar ground. Although *L'Etonnant voyage de Hareton Ironcastle* had failed to sell in America, as he might have hoped, his next prehistoric adventure story, *Helgvor du fleuve bleu* (1930) had better luck, translation rights being sold to the pulp magazine *Argosy*—probably for a far greater sum than was paid for French rights. It was serialized there in 1932, a date attached in some bibliographical lists to Rosny's next adventure story, *La Sauvage aventure* (tr. in vol. 5 as "Adventure in the Wild") although I can find no evidence of its appearance in a periodical before the Albin Michel book edition of 1935. *La Sauvage aventure* is an even more unashamed venture in pulp fiction than *L'Etonnant voyage de Hareton Ironcastle*, although it is a calculated expansion of a novelette in a very different style (and with a very different ending), which had appeared in a collection of items by different authors in 1929: "Les Hommes-Sangliers" (tr. in vol. 2 as "The Boar Men"). Like its predecessor, *La Sauvage aventure* failed to sell to its intended ultimate market, and Rosny did no more work in that vein— although the fact that he was now in his seventies was probably the decisive factor in that respect.

La Sauvage aventure contrasts very markedly with a near-contemporary novel that was initially published as a serial in the *Mercure de France*, and was then reprinted as a book under that periodical's imprint: *Les Compagnons de l'univers* (1934 tr. in vol. 6 as "Companions of the Universe"). If the former was Rosny's ultimate experiment in pulp fiction, then the latter was his ultimate experiment in Naturalism, tending towards Existentialist fiction in its relentless focus on inner experience and a very peculiar form of *angst*. Some commentators have likened it to "La Légende sceptique," some sections of which also have quasi-existentialist leanings, but while the earlier text focused on the *angst* of social isolation and illness, the later one focuses on sex, with an extraordinary cynicism that belies Rosny's earlier (mostly highly idealized) treatments of the subject, although it has certain affinities with "Les Hommes-Sangliers" and the last-published of Rosny's scientific romances, "Dans le monde des Variants" (1939; tr. in vol. 2 as "In the World of the Variants"). The novel does, however, have a minor component of scientific romance, which connects with certain other passages in "La Légende sceptique," via a chain of reasoning and endeavor that needs special attention if Rosny's work is to be fully understood.

"La Légende sceptique" is the most diverse of all Rosny's patchwork texts, and demonstrates in no uncertain terms that his early writings were much more various in style and affiliation than his published novels suggested. It includes a sequence of eleven prose poems, clearly reflective of his admiration for Baudelaire—the author most frequently quoted by his characters—although their subject-matter is derived from his reading of scientific texts. It also includes a brief advice-manual for anyone desirous of founding a new religion, and a remarkable account of the progression of a disease, among other eccentrically introspective materials, but the heart of the enterprise is a collection of earnest philosophical essays derived from the author's omnivorous reading of scientific works, which discuss the nature of the universe and the possibilities of human evolution.

To the contemporary eye, the ideas contained in this set of philosophical speculations must have appeared utterly bizarre, and some of them still seem bizarre to the modern eye, although others have either become manifestly obsolete or much more familiar. There is, however, no doubting the awesome scope of their ambition, nor that there is a component of brilliance contained within them. The manner in which the collective patchwork gropes for suitable literary formats in which to express such ideas, and fails to find any that is satisfactory, is sufficient explanation of the fact that Rosny largely abandoned that quest thereafter, and remained conspicuously tentative in the attempts he did make—but he did not abandon the further development of the ideas he had sketched out in the philosophical essays, and he continually returned to that development in print, in a series of non-fictional endeavors that were ignored at the time and have attracted no attention since.

The most substantial of these further essays, published as a book by Alcan was *Le Pluralisme, essai sur la discontinuité et l'hétérogéneité des phénomènes* [Pluralism: An Essay on the Discontinuity and Hetreogeneity of Phenomena] (1909), which appeared with the signature J. H. Boëx-Borel. It was successful enough for Alcan to issue a companion volume updating its argument in 1922, under the signature J.-H. Rosny Aîné, entitled *Les Sciences et pluralisme* [The Sciences and Pluralism], which sold well enough to be reprinted twice, in 1930 and 1932.

The most conspicuous of the author's other essays in this vein appeared in the seemingly-unlikely venue of the *Mercure de France*, which had begun life as the semi-official organ of the Symbolist Movement and maintained a certain defiant originality long into the 20th century, as that movement faded away. It was in the pages of the *Mercure* that the notion of Rosny as a significant pioneer of the *roman scientifique* was most thoroughly developed, primarily by Jean Morel, and where his self-representation as an offbeat natural philosopher

53

was also given space for display and maturation. The periodical's editor, Alfred Vallette, had been another regular at Maurice Renard's salon in 1908-1914, and had apparently taken some inspiration therefrom; although he only published one story by Renard he published a number of significant items of speculative fiction by other writers, including Gabriel de Lautrec, Henri Falk and Marcel Rouff.

In the July 1, 1921 issue of the *Mercure* Rosny published "Le Temps et l'espace" [Time and Space] a 10,000-word article that elaborated the thesis of the pamphlet in a three-part study, the first discussing the concept of "plural space" in the context of contemporary discussions of "geometric space" and "non-Euclidean space," the second examining the debate initiated by Henri Bergson as to whether the scientific concept of time and the experience of time can be reconciled, and the notion of time as a "fourth dimension," and the third discussing relativity theory, with particular reference to the implications of the Michelson-Morley experiment, Albert Einstein's denial of the ether, and the ideas of Lorentz and Fitzgerald.

In the August 15, 1925 issue, Rosny supplemented his discussion of the relationship between space and time in "Le Puralisme intégral" [Integral Pluralism], which recruits various items of evidence and argument to oppose the assumption by scientists that the seeming complexity of the observable world is reducible to some kind of underlying simplicity, in which the world of the infinitely small involves the transactions of a few particles making up all kinds of atoms, and the entire universe is imagined as a repetitive sequence of stereotyped stars arranged into sidereal systems. In the February 15, 1931 issue Rosny further elaborated the consequences of his pluralistic thesis in the purely speculative "Vers le Quatrième Univers" [Toward the Fourth Universe] in which he proposes that "pluralism" exists on every conceivable scale—that complexity is, in fact, irreducible to simplicity, that everything is different from everything else—and that what we think of as the "whole" of existence is nothing of the sort, but only one aspect of an infinite number of existences.

In a sense, this argument is a straightforward extrapolation of the old theological argument about "the plurality of worlds," which argued that it was an insult to God's creative power to think that he had only created one world, and had been used in support of the Copernican hypothesis, to justify the assertion that the planets were also worlds, and that other stars must have planets of their own after the fashion of the sun. The plurality of worlds had frequently been coupled with "the principle of plenitude," which argued that God could not have created all those other worlds only to leave them empty, and that each of them must therefore have its own life, including its own equivalent of the human race—a principle that inevitably had an exceedingly powerful influence on the development of scientific romances dealing with journeys to and the population of other worlds.

Rosny, however, took this argument a step further in "Vers le quatrième univers" and *Compagnons de l'univers*, in which he elaborated brief statements made in several of his earlier scientific romances with regard to "innumerable coexistence." Briefly stated, his fundamental proposition is that the apparent emptiness of the space within atoms and between stars has to be an artifact of our senses rather than an objective reality—like Aristotle, he found the notion of "void" essentially abhorrent—and that, in accordance with the principle of plenitude, space must actually be full. In Rosny's view, it has to be full not merely of matter that is inapprehensible by our senses but of an infinite series of cosmic aggregations of such matter, each one inapprehensible by all the rest—each one, in fact, in accordance with the principle of pluralism, quite different from all the rest, none of them being a simple variant of any of the others.

Since Rosny wrote his essays on pluralism, of course, physicists and scientific romances alike have become familiar with the notion of an infinite series of "alternative universes" and with the notions of "dark matter" and "dark energy" that hold the observable universe together while not being directly perceptible. The notion of a "multiverse" containing all possible alternative universes is now commonplace in science as well as science fiction, if not yet entirely respectable. It must be noted, however, that the imaginative reach of Rosny's thesis remains substantially greater than these subsequent developments.

The conventional view of alternative universes displaces them in a hypothetical fourth spatial dimension, and allows each of them to retain its component of void as well as its fundamental subatomic simplicity; the extent to which they differ from our own is very often seen in terms of cosmically-trivial variations in Earthly history, and even the bolder versions that imagine alternative universes with different laws of physics are nevertheless still based on the notion of tweaking a fundamental simplicity. Rosny's version of "the fourth universe" (his version of the multiverse) is much more ambitious, both in its packaging and its range—so much more ambitious, in fact, that it becomes very difficult indeed to package in conventional narrative, or any other literary form.

The history of Rosny's dabblings in scientific romance, from the first three examples that reached publication in 1887-1889 all the way through to "Les Compagnons de l'univers" and "Dans le mondes des Variants" half a century later, is that of a series of attempts to incarnate some fraction of his vision of the universe in literary form, thus to prompt or inspire readers to move beyond their conventional way of thinking. The vision underlying his speculations, although it was not to be fully and explicitly developed for a long time, was already so far ahead of the visions underlying scientific romances and science fiction stories by other hands that no one working in the latter genre has yet got as far. Rosny was quite right to deny that he was some sort of equivalent of H. G. Wells, who only moved beyond theological assumptions about the essential humanity of the inhabitants of other worlds to suggest that the inhabitants of other worlds might be the products of alternative processes of evolution essentially similar to our own.

From the very beginning, Rosny was only interested in alternative evolutions as trivial variants, although he was certainly prepared to attempt to imagine such variants and find them fascinating; what he was really interested in was imagining beings and forces that defied our conventional classifications system: life forms that were not only not human but not animal or vegetable, being genuinely *alien*. Nor was he much interested in conventional cataclysms, such as earthquakes or ordinary cosmic collisions; what really interested him was the possibility of cataclysms of a different sort, resulting from the brief and peripheral interaction of alien universes, coexisting in the same unempty space as our universe but normally imperceptible and unknown to one another. In that, he was alone, not only in 1887 but also in 1939—and, for that matter, today. It was an originality that did him no favors, in terms of finding an admiring audience, but it was an originality that was surely worthy of pride, and perhaps even of a pride that seemed to some people, to borrow Lucien Descaves' epithets, "mad" and "incommensurable." It was not merely in his relation to Naturalism that Rosny really deserved a category of his own, but also in relation to scientific romance; there was not, and never has been, anyone else like him.

Nowadays, with the aid of hindsight, we can take the conceptual framework offered in *Le Pluralisme* and "Vers le quatrième univers," apply it to much earlier works like "Les Xipéhuz" and "Le Cataclysme," and see in those stories a kind of sense that was quite inapprehensible to their contemporary readers, and to many readers since. That is the way that they ought to be read—or, at least, that is the way that they can be slotted into the whole fabric of his speculative fiction in such a way as to allow the essential coherency of that work to be seen—a coherency that is sufficient to have prompted the ever-perceptive Pierre Versins to assert that Rosny had "only written one novel, of which 'La Légende sceptique' is the preface and *Les Compagnons de l'univers* the conclusion." This collection of his works is, in effect, a translation of that sprawling patchwork "novel."

I shall not proceed in this general introduction to more detailed analyses of particular stories, leaving that to introductions and afterwords to the individual volumes, but it is within the context of this general introduction that the contents of the whole six-volume project need to be seen and evaluated.

In planning the contents of this introductory volume it seemed sensible to begin at the beginning, placing "Les Xipéhuz" ahead of "La Légende sceptique," even though the latter is, as Versins points out, a sort of preface to the whole of Rosny's work in the genre of scientific romance. "La Légende sceptique" is, I fear, by no means a reader-friendly work, being filled to the brim with all the "defects" of which Anatole France and René Doumic complained, and it might well make considerable demands on the patience and understanding of readers of this volume, but an understanding of its concerns and concepts really is vital to an understanding of what Rosny was trying to do in his scientific romances, and why. Given that he made so little effort to include explanations of the events and entities featured in his imaginative works within the works themselves, some knowledge of the world-view displayed in the piece is invaluable to their comprehension; hopefully, it will compensate readers for their necessary effort with its originality, imaginative audacity and sheer bizarrerie.

I then thought it appropriate to supplement "Les Xipéhuz" with three further accounts of exotic alien life, for the purposes of comparison. Other accounts can be found in other Rosny works—most notably in *La Force mystérieuse* and "Dans le monde des Variants"—but these three are the stories in which alien life comes most clearly into focus as a key theme. As a group, "Les Xipéhuz," "Un Autre Monde," "La Mort de la Terre" and "Les Navigateurs de l'infini" offer a reasonably comprehensive sketch of Rosny's ideas in relation to the distribution, evolution and ultimate destiny of life within the "fourth universe."

The version of "Les Xipéhuz" translated here is the one contained in the Mercure de France volume of 1896, which appended it to *Le Cataclysme*. The text of "La Légende Sceptique" that I used for translation is the one reprinted in the Marabout collection *Récits de Science-Fiction* (1975). The version of "Un Autre Monde" that I translated was taken from the collection bearing the same title, published by Plon in 1898. The version of "La Mort de la Terre" was taken from the eponymous Plon collection first issued in 1912 (although the copy I used was the sixth edition, dated 1914). The version of *Les Navigateurs de l'infini* that I used was the one issued in volume form in 1927 by *La Nouvelle Revue Critique*. The version of "Les Astronautes" I used was the one in the 1996 Grama edition of *Les Navigateurs de l'infini.* (There is no discussion of the last-named text in the afterword because I consider it to be inauthentic.) I have no reason to think that any of these versions differs substantially from the versions reproduced in other collections, although the version of "La Mort de la Terre" contained in the Marabout *Récits* has a brief prefatory passage that is not in the Plon version.

Brian Stableford

REFERENCES

Doumic, René. "Les Romans de M. J.-H. Rosny" *Revue des Deux Mondes* 129 (June 15, 1895). pp. 935-946.

France, Anatole. "J.-H. Rosny" in *On Life and Letters: Third Series*, tr. by D. B. Stewart. London: John Lane, 1922. pp. 267-276 and pp. 352-353. [The essays cited were first published in French in 1891.]

Huret, Jules. *Enquête sur L'Evolution littéraire.* Paris: Charpentier, 1891.

Morel, Jean, with Pierre Massé. "J.-H. Rosny et préhistoire." *Mercure de France*, November 15, 1923. pp. 5-25.

Morel, Jean. "J.-H. Rosny aîné et le merveilleux scientifique" *Mercure de France*, April 1, 1926. pp. 82-94.

Renard, Jules. Extracts from *Journal inédit* reprinted in *J.-H. Rosny Aîné: Romans préhistoriques*. Paris: Robert Laffont, 1985. pp. 687-688. [The *Journal inédit* was originally published by Bernouard in 1927; the relevant entries were originally made in 1908.]

Renard, Maurice. "Le merveilleux scientifique et la *Force mystérieuse* de J.-H. Rosny *Aîné*." *Maurice Renard: Romans et contes fantastiques*. Paris: Robert Laffont, 1990. pp. 1220-1226. [Originally published in *La Vie* in 1914.]

Rosny, J.-H. *Aîné. Mémoires de a vie littéraire: L'Académie Goncourt; Les Salons; Quelques éditeurs*. Paris: Cres, 1927.

-------. *Torches et lumignons: Souvenirs de la vie littéraire*. Paris: Editions "La Force Française," 1921.

Van Herp, Jacques. "Introduction: Et la science-fiction naquit...." In *Récits de science-fiction* by J.-H. Rosny aîné, edited by Jean-Baptiste Baronian. Verviers, Belgium: Marabout, 1975.

Vernier, J. P. "The SF of J. H. Rosny the Elder." *Science-Fiction Studies* 2:2 (July 1975). pp. 156-163.

Versins, Pierre. "Rosny aîné, J.-H." and "Rosny jeune, J.-H." in *Encyclopédie de l'utopie et de la science fiction*. Lausanne: L'Age d'Homme, 1972. pp. 775-778 & 778-779.

THE XIPEHUZ

To Léon Hennique,[3]
His friend and admirer
J.-H. Rosny Aîné

Part One

I. The Forms

It was a thousand years before the aggregation of civilization from which Nineveh, Babylon and Ecbatana emerged. As evening approached, the nomadic Pjehou tribe was making its way through the wild Forest of Kzour in a sea of oblique sunlight. The setting Sun swelled up, hung in the air and sank into its harmonious bed.[4]

---

[3] Léon Hennique (1850-1935) was the co-executor—with Alphonse Daudet—of Edmond de Goncourt's will, and a founder member of the Goncourt Academy, whose president he became from 1907-12. He had once been a friend of Zola's, but split with him over the Dreyfus Affair; he was best known as a playwright.

[4] There is a series of *doubles entendres* here, whose key item is untranslatable; *chant*, which can mean "placed edgewise" with reference to a coin and is used in that sense here to refer to the disk of the Sun, usually means "song;" the supplementary references retain both the mundane implication and the musical metaphor.

Because everyone was tired, they were silent, in quest of a beautiful clearing in which the tribe could light the sacred fire, make the evening meal and go to sleep, protected from wild animals by a double row of red fires.

The clouds became opaline, polychromatic countries wandering above the four horizons, nocturnal gods breathing a cradle song, and the tribe moved on. A scout returned at a gallop, with news of a clearing and a stream of pure spring water.

The tribe raised three long cheers; everyone pushed on more rapidly, childish laughter rippling. Even the horses and the donkeys, accustomed to the realization that a halt was imminent when the scouts returned and the nomads cried out, raised their heads proudly. The clearing appeared. The charming spring hollowed out its course between mosses and bushes; and a phantasmagoria was revealed to the nomads.

To begin with, there was a great circle of bluish translucent cones, points uppermost, each one about half the size of a man. A few bright streaks and dark circles were distributed over their surfaces; near the base, each one had a star, as dazzling as the mid-say sun. Further away, and equally eccentric, planes reminiscent of birch-bark, spotted with multicolored ellipses, were posed vertically. There were also quasi-cylindrical Forms here and there, similarly multicolored; some were thin and tall, others short and stout; all were bronze in color, dotted with green. Like the planes, all of them possessed the same characteristic points of light.

The tribe stared in amazement. A superstitious dread chilled the bravest, increasing further when the Forms began to undulate in the grey shadows of the clearing.

All of a sudden, their stars trembling and flickering, the cones became elongated, while the cylinders and the planes made a noise like the hiss of water thrown on a fire, and they all came toward the nomads, their velocity accelerating.

The entire tribe, bewitched by this prodigy, was rooted to the spot, continuing to stare. The Forms reached them. The impact was frightful. Groups of warriors, women and children collapsed on to the forest floor, mysteriously struck down as if by a bolt of lightning. Then dark terror lent strength, and the wings of agile flight, to the survivors—but the Forms, at first massed and organized in ranks, scattered with the tribe, clinging pitilessly to those in flight. The frightful attack was not infallible, however, killing some and stunning others but inflicting no wounds. A few red droplets sprang from the nostrils, eyes and ears of the dying, but the others, intact, soon got up again, resuming their fantastic flight through the wan twilight.

Whatever the nature of the Forms was, they acted like living beings, not like weather phenomena, having the inconsistency and diversity of movement of living beings, evidently choosing their victims, and not confusing the nomads with plants, or even with animals.

Soon, the fleetest runners perceived that they were no longer being pursued. Exhausted and anguished, they finally plucked up courage to go back toward the site of the prodigy. In the distance, between the tree-trunks bathed in shadow, the resplendent pursuit was continuing—and the Forms were preferentially running down and slaughtering the warriors, often disdaining the weak, women and children.

Seen thus, at a distance, now that darkness had fallen completely, the scene seemed even more supernatural and more overwhelming to their barbarian brains. The warriors were about to resume their flight when an important observation made them pause: it was that, whether they were chasing warriors, women or children, *the Forms abandoned the pursuit beyond a fixed boundary*. However tired or impotent the victim was, even if they fainted, as soon as that invisible frontier was crossed, all peril ceased.

This very reassuring observation, soon confirmed by 50 instances, calmed the frantic nerves of the runaways. They dared to wait for their wives and their poor children, escapees from the slaughter. One of them—their hero—initially stunned and scared by the superhuman nature of the incident, eventually recovered the spirit of his great soul, lit a fire and sounded a buffalo-horn to signal the fugitives.

Then, one by one, the wretches arrived. Many of them were lame, dragging themselves along with their hands. Mothers, with indomitable maternal instinct, were protecting, herding and carrying the fruit of their loins through the panic-stricken crowd. Many donkeys, horses and cows came back, less frightened than the humans.

They spent a dismal, sleepless night in silence, during which the warriors continually felt shivers down their spines—but first light came, palely insinuating itself through the dense foliage, and then the dawn fanfare of colors and singing birds: an exhortation to live and cast off the terrors of Darkness.

The Hero, the natural chief, assembled the crowd in groups and began a head-count of the tribe. Half the warriors, some 200, were missing, having probably been killed. The losses were much less among the women, and almost none among the children.

When the count was finished and the livestock had been assembled—few animals were missing, thanks to the superiority of instinct over reason during crises—the Hero disposed the tribe according to the customary arrangement; then, ordering them to wait, he headed for the clearing, pale and alone. No one dared follow him, even at a distance.

He went to a spot where the trees were widely spaced, a short distance within the limit identified the day before, and studied the scene. In the distance, in the cool transparency of the morning, the delightful spring was flowing. On the banks, reunited, the fantastic troop of Forms was resplendent. Their color had changed; the cones were more compact and their turquoise tint had become greener, the cylinders were tinted with violet, and the planes resembled virgin copper. Inside each of them, however, the star shed its radiance—which was dazzling, even in the daylight.

The metamorphosis extended to the shapes of the phantasmagorical Entities, the cones tending to broaden out into cylinders and the cylinders to spread out, while the planes had become slightly curved. As on the day before, though, the Forms suddenly began to undulate, their Stars flickering.

The Hero slowly went back across the frontier of safety.

II. A Hieratic Expedition

The tribe of Pjehou stopped outside the door of the great nomad Tabernacle, into which only chiefs entered. In the star-filled depths, three high priests stood beneath the male image of the Sun. Lower down, on the gilded steps, were 12 sacrificers of inferior rank.

The Hero went forward and gave a detailed account of the incident in the Forest of Kzour, to which the astonished priests listened very seriously, sensing a diminution of their power in confrontation with this extra-human adventure.

The supreme high priest demanded that the tribe offer a dozen bulls, seven onagers and three stallions to the Sun. He recognized the divine attributes of the Forms and decided to mount a hieratic expedition after the sacrifices. All the priests and all the chiefs of the Zahelal nation would take part in it.

Messengers were sent into the mountains and plains 100 leagues around the place where the Ecbatana of the mages would eventually be built.[5] The sinister tale made people's hair stand on end everywhere, and all the chiefs made haste to respond to the sacerdotal summons.

One autumn morning, the Male pierced the clouds and inundated the Tabernacle, reaching the altar where the bloody heart of a bull was smoking. The high priests, the immolators and fifty tribal chiefs uttered a triumphant cry. Outside, 100,000 nomads assembled in the fresh dew, echoed the cla-

---

[5] Ecbatana, at the foot of Mount Alvand, was the capital of the Astyages before being integrated into the Persian Empire by Cyrus the Great. Rosny might have chosen it as a location because the name meant "place of gathering."

mor, turning their tanned heads toward the prodigious Forest of Kzour and shivering slightly. The omen was favorable.

Then, with the priests at their head, an entire people marched through the woods. About three hours into the afternoon, the Hero of the Pjehou called the multitude to a halt. The large clearing had been turned russet by the autumn; a flood of dead leaves extended majestically, covering its moss. On the banks of the stream, the priests perceived that which they had come to adore and appease: the Forms. They were gentle on the eyes in the shade of the trees, with their tremulous hues, the pure fire of their stars, and their tranquil circulation on the edge of the spring.

"It is necessary," said the supreme high priest, "to offer the sacrifice here, so that they will know that we are submissive to their power!"

All the old men bowed. One voice was raised, however; it was that of Yushik, of the Nim tribe—a young counter of stars; a pale prophetic watcher of nascent renown—who audaciously requested permission to approach the Forms more closely. The old men, whose hair had turned white in the exercise of wise words, prevailed, however; the altar was constructed and the victim led forth: a superb stallion, a fine servant of humankind. Then, in the silence, while the people prostrated themselves, the bronze knife found the animal's noble heart.

A great moan rose up, and the high priest said: "Are you appeased, O Gods!"

In the distance, among the silent tree-trunks, the Forms were still circulating, polishing themselves, preferring the locations where the sunlight streamed more densely.

"Yes! Yes!" the enthusiast cried. "They are appeased!" Seizing the warm heart of the stallion before the curious high priest could utter another word, Yushik launched himself into the clearing. Howling fanatics followed him. Slowly, the undulating Forms drew together, skimming the ground. Then they suddenly precipitated themselves upon the temeritous invaders, and a lamentable massacre terrified the 50 tribes.

Six or seven fugitives, hotly pursued, were able to reach the boundary by a great effort. The rest, including Yushik, were dead.

"They are merciless gods!" said the supreme high priest, solemnly.

They decided to erect a circle of stakes outside the line of safety. In order to determine the extent of that ring, they decided to force slaves to expose themselves successively to the attack of the Forms, around the entire perimeter. This was done. Under threat of death, slaves went into the circle. Very few, however, perished there, thanks to the excellence of the precautions. The frontier was firmly established, rendered visible to everyone by its perimeter of stakes.

Thus, the hieratic expedition was successfully concluded, and the Zahelals believed themselves to be protected against the subtle enemy.

III. Darkness

The preventive measures taken by the council were, however, soon shown to be impotent. The following spring, the Hertoth and Nazzum tribes, passing close to the circle of stakes without any suspicion of danger, in slight disarray, were cruelly assaulted by the Forms and decimated. The chiefs who escaped the massacre told the great Council of Zahelal that the Forms were now much more numerous than they had been the previous autumn. As before, they were limiting their pursuit, but the boundary had been extended.

This news disturbed the people; there was much mourning and many sacrifices. Then the Council decided to destroy the Forest of Kzour by fire. In spite of their best efforts, they only succeeded in setting fire to its fringes. Then the priests, in despair, declared the forest sacred, forbidding anyone to go into it.

Two summers went by.

One October night, the encampment of the Zulf tribe, two bowshots from the fatal forest, was invaded by the Forms while the tribesmen were asleep. Another 300 warriors lost their lives.

After that day, a sinister and mysterious story, corrosive of belief, went from tribe to tribe, whispered in the evenings of the vast starry nights of Mesopotamia. *Humankind was going to die.* The *others*, still broadening out with every passing day, in the forests and over the plains, indestructibly, would devour the doomed race—and that black and dreadful conviction haunted their poor minds, sapping all the fighting strength and superb optimism typical of young races. The human wanderer, thinking about that, no longer dared to love the sumptuous native pastures, and sought on high with his weary eye for the constellations to halt their progress. It was the Millennium of the infant populations, the knell of the end of the world—or, perhaps the resignation of the red man of the Indian savannah.

And in that anguish, primitive meditators developed a bitter religion: a cult of death preached by pale prophets, a cult of Darkness, more powerful than the Stars; a Darkness that would engulf and devour the holy Light, the resplendent fire.[6] Everywhere, in the fringes of the wilderness, one encountered the immobile, emaciated figures of the inspired, silent men who periodically spread out through the tribes, relating their frightful dreams of the approaching Dusk of the great Night, and the death-throes of the Sun.

---

[6] Rosny's earlier reference to "Ecbatana of the mages" suggests that he is associating the region where his story is set with the origins of the religion renewed and reformed about 600 years B.C. by the *Zend-Avestra*, a sacred text credited to Zarathustra. The religion in question was fundamentally dualistic, setting human existence in the context of the essential power of good, Ahura-Mazda or Ormazd, against the ultimate power of evil, Anra Mainyu or Ahriman. This passage sets up Rosny's story as an "explanation" of sorts for the origins of the religion in question.

IV. Bakhoun

Now, at that time, there lived an extraordinary man
named Bakhoun, a member of the Ptuh tribe and a brother of
the foremost high priest of the Zahelals. In his youth he had
abandoned the nomadic life, choosing to settle in a beautiful
wilderness in a narrow and lush valley between four hills,
through which ran the musical clarity of a spring. He had fa-
shioned a fixed tent from slabs of rock, forming a cyclopean
dwelling. Patience, regular harvests and the careful husbandry
of cattle and horses had made him wealthy. With his four
wives and 30 children, he lived an Edenic life there.

Bakhoun professed singular beliefs, which might have
got him stoned to death without the respect in which his elder
brother, the supreme high priest, was held by the Zahelals.
Firstly, he believed that the sedentary life, in a fixed abode,
was preferable to nomadic life, conserving a man's strength to
the advantage of his mind. Secondly, he believed that the Sun,
the Moon and the Stars were not gods, but luminous objects.
Thirdly, he said that men should only believe firmly in things
proven by Measurement. The Zahelals credited him with magic powers, and the boldest among them sometimes took the
risk of consulting him. They were never sorry that they had
done so. It was claimed that he had often aided unfortunate
tribes by distributing food to them.

Now, in the dark hour when the melancholy alternatives
presented themselves of abandoning the fecund regions or
being destroyed by the inexorable divinities, the tribes thought
of Bakhoun, and the priests themselves, after struggling with
their pride, sent three of the most important members of their
order to him as a deputation.

Bakhoun gave the most anxious attention to their story,
making them repeat it, and asking numerous and precise questions. He asked for two days to meditate. When that time had
elapsed, he simply announced that he was going to devote
himself to the study of the Forms. The tribes were a little dis-

69

appointed, for it had been hoped that Bakhoun would be able to save the land by magic. Nevertheless, the chiefs expressed their satisfaction with his decision, hoping for great things.

Then Bakhoun established himself in the borders of the Forest of Kzour, withdrawing when it was time to sleep, and made observations all day long, mounted on the swiftest stallion in Chaldea. Soon, convinced of the superiority of the splendid animal to the most agile of the Forms, he was able to begin his bold and scrupulous investigation of the enemies of Humankind—the study to which we owe a great cuneiform book consisting of 60 large tablets, the most beautiful lapidary book that the nomadic ages have left to the modern races.

It is in this book, admirable for its patient observation and sobriety, that evidence is found of a system of life absolutely dissimilar to our animal and vegetable kingdoms: a system that Bakhoun humbly confesses to being unable to analyze, save for its grossest and most external appearance. It is impossible for Humankind not to shiver on reading this monograph on the beings that Bakhoun calls the *Xipehuz*, and the objective details—never extended to marvelous systematization—that the ancient scribe reveals in relation to their actions, their modes of locomotion, combat and reproduction, which demonstrate that the human race has been on the edge of extinction, and that the Earth almost became the inheritance of a Sovereignty of which we have lost even the concept.

It is necessary to read the marvelous translation by Monsieur Dessault, the fruit of his unexpected discoveries in pre-Assyrian linguistics—discoveries unfortunately more admired abroad, in England and Germany than in his own fatherland. The illustrious savant has deigned to put at our disposition the salient passages of the precious work, and these passages, which we offer hereafter to the public, will perhaps inspire a desire to read the Master's superb translations.[7]

---

[7] Rosny inserts a footnote here: "*The Precursors of Nineveh* by B. Dessault, octavo edition, published by Calmann-Lévy. For the benefit of the reader I have converted the following

V. Extract from Bakhoun's Book

The Xipehuz are evidently Living Beings. All their movements reveal the free will, capriciousness, co-operation and partial independence that serve to distinguish animals from plants or inert objects. Although their mode of locomotion cannot be defined by comparison—they simply glide over the ground—it is easy to see that they control it as they desire. They can be seen to stop abruptly, turn around, launch themselves in pursuit of one another, move around in twos and threes, and manifest preferences that cause them to quit one companion in order to draw away and join another. They do not have the ability to climb trees, but they succeed in killing birds *by attracting them*, by undiscoverable means. They can often be seen to surround forest animals or to lie in wait for them behind bushes; they never fail to kill them and then consume them. One may posit as a rule that *they kill all animals*, without distinction, if they can reach them, and without any apparent motive—for they do not eat them, but simply reduce them to ashes.

Their manner of consumption does not require fire; the incandescent point that each one has at its base is sufficient for that operation. Ten or 12 of them gather in a circle around large animals they have killed and converge their radiance upon the carcass. For small animals—birds, for example—the radiance of a single Xipehuz suffices for the incineration. It should be noted that the heat that they are able to produce is not instantaneously violent; I have often intercepted the radiation of a Xipehuz with my hand, and the skin only begins to get hot after some time.

I do not know whether it can be said that the Xipehuz have different species, for they can transform themselves successively into cones, cylinders and planes, and can do so with-

extracts from Bakhoun's book into modern scientific language."

71

in a single day. Their color varies continually, which I think it necessary to attribute, in general, to the metamorphoses of light from morning to evening and from evening to morning. Some variations of shade, however, seem to be due to individual whims, especially to their *passions*, if I might use that term, and thus constitute veritable expressions of physiognomy—even the most simple of which I am quite unable, in spite of ardent study, to determine other than hypothetically. Thus, for instance, I have been unable to distinguish an angry hue from a tender one, which would surely have been the most elementary discovery of that sort.

I have used the word *passions*. Previously, I had already mentioned their preferences, which I shall call their *friendships*. They also have their *hatreds*. One Xipehuz constantly keeps its distance from another, and vice versa. Their fits of anger seem violent. I have seen them colliding, with movements identical to those observed when they attack large animals or human beings, and it was those same combats that taught me that they are not immortal, as I was initially disposed to believe, for on two or three occasions I have seen Xipehuz die in these encounters—which is to say, to *fall, condense and solidify*. I have carefully preserved some of these bizarre cadavers,[8] and perhaps they will be able, at a later date, to assist in the revelation of the nature of the Xipehuz. They are yellowish crystals, irregularly shaped, streaked with blue lines.

From the fact that the Xipehuz are not immortal, I have deduced that it must be possible to fight them and defeat them,

---

[8] Rosny inserts a footnote: "Kensington Museum in London and Monsieur Dessault himself possess several items of mineral debris similar in all respects to those described by Bakhoun, which chemical analysis has been powerless to decompose or to combine with other substances, and which cannot, in consequence, be entered in any classification of known substances."

and since then I have begun a series of experiments in warfare, of which more will be said in due course.

As the Xipehuz are always sufficiently radiant to be seen through thickets, and even behind thick tree-trunks—a broad aura emanates from them in every direction, giving warning of their approach—I have often been able to venture into the forest itself, confiding myself to the speed of my stallion at the slightest alert. There I have attempted to discover whether they have constructed shelters, but I admit to being frustrated in that research. They do not move objects or plants, and appear to be strangers to any kind of *tangible and visible* industry—the only industry appreciable to human observation. Consequently, they have no weapons, in the sense in which we use the term. It is certain that they cannot kill at a distance; every animal that has been able to run away without being subjected to the *immediate* contact of a Xipehuz has escaped, without exception—I have witnessed that on many occasions.

As the members of the unfortunate Pjehou tribe have already noticed, they cannot cross certain invisible barriers in pursuit of their victims, but these limits have always increased from year to year and month to month. I was obliged to attempt to discover the cause of this.

Now, this cause seems to be nothing but a phenomenon of *collective increase*, and, like the majority of Xipehuz phenomena, it is inaccessible to human intelligence. In brief, this is the general principle: the limits of Xipehuz action are enlarged in proportion to the number of individuals—which is to say that, as soon as there is a procreation of new creatures, there is also an extension of the frontiers; but while the number remains invariable, every individual is utterly incapable of escaping the habitat attributed (by the nature of things?) to the whole race. That rule was suggestive of a more intimate correlation between the group and the individual than the similar correlations observed in humans and animals. The reciprocity of that law has been subsequently observed, for as soon as the Xipehuz began to diminish in number, their frontiers were proportionately restricted.

In relation to the phenomenon of procreation itself, I have little to say, but the modicum is significant. Firstly, procreation occurs four times a year, shortly before the equinoxes and solstices. The Xipehuz gather together in groups of three, and these groups gradually end up forming a single close-knit amalgam, disposed in a very long ellipse. They remain in this state all night, and throughout the morning, until the Sun reaches its zenith. When they separate, vague forms are seen to rise up in the air, enormous and vaporous. The Forms slowly condense and contract, transforming themselves at the end of ten days into amber-tinted cones, still considerably larger than adult Xipehuz. It requires two months and several days for them to attain their maximum development—which is to say, their maximum contraction. At the end of this time, they become similar to other beings of their kind, their colors and forms variable according to the time, the weather and individual caprice. A few days after their development, or contraction, is complete, the frontiers of action are extended. That was, naturally, shortly before the redoubtable moment when I pressed the flanks of my worthy Kouath in order to establish my camp further away.

Whether or not the Xipehuz have senses like ours it is impossible to determine. They certainly have apparatus that serve the same purpose. The ease with which they perceive the presence of animals—especially humans—over long distances evidently shows that their organs of investigation are at least as good as our eyes. I have never seen them confuse a vegetable and an animal, even in circumstances where I might very well have made such an error, deceived by the sub-branchial light, the color of the object and its position. The fact that it takes twenty to consume a large animal, when one alone can attend to the incineration of a bird, proves that they have an accurate understanding of proportions, and that understanding seems even more accurate when one observes that they sometimes employ ten, twelve or fifteen, always according to the relative size of the carcass. A better argument still in favor of both the existence of organs analogous to our senses and their intelligence is the manner in which they behave in attacking our tribes, for they rarely attach themselves to women or children, while they hunt down warriors pitilessly.

Now, the most important question: do they have a language? I can answer that without the slightest hesitation: Yes, they do have a language—and that language is composed of signs, some few of which I have been able to decipher.

Let us suppose, for example, that one Xipehuz wants to talk to another. To do that, it is sufficient to direct the radiance of its star toward its companion, which is always perceived immediately. The summoned individual stops, if it is moving, and waits. The speaker then rapidly traces a series of small luminous characters on the actual surface of its interlocutor— it does not matter where—by means of a modification of the radiation emanating from its base. These characters remain fixed for a moment, then fade away. After a short pause, the interlocutor replies.

Prior to any kind of combat or ambush, I have always seen the Xipehuz employ the following characters:

)—(—

When they were talking about me—and they often were, for they were determined to exterminate my brave Kouath and myself, the signs:

□—v⟩

were invariably exchanged—among others, like the word or phrase:

)—(—

given above. The ordinary sign of appeal is:

_∏_

and it causes the individual receiving it to approach. When all the Xipehux are invited to a general meeting I have never failed to observe a signal in this form:

□ΛΙ

representing the triple appearance of these beings.

The Xipehuz also have more complicated signs, not corresponding to actions similar to ours but to an utterly extra-human order of things, none of which I have been able to decipher. There is not the slightest doubt about their ability to exchange ideas of an abstract nature, probably equivalent to human ideas, for they can remain motionless for long periods doing nothing but conversing, which testifies to veritable accumulations of thought.

My long sojourn in their company ended up, in spite of their metamorphoses—whose sequences differ for each one, no doubt slightly, but with characteristics sufficient for a stubborn observer—allowing me to get to know several Xipehuz in a rather intimate fashion, by revealing particulars of their individual differences...dare I say personalities? I identified taciturn ones that almost never said a word; expansive ones that inscribed veritable speeches; attentive ones; and chatterboxes that spoke at the same time, interrupting one another. There were some who liked to withdraw and live alone and some that evidently sought society; there were ferocious ones that were perpetually hunting wild beasts and, by contrast, merciful ones that often spared animals, letting them live in peace. Does all that not open an enormous highway to the imagination? Does it not lead to the supposition of variations in aptitude, intelligence and strength analogous to those of the human race?

They practice education. How many times have I observed an old Xipehuz sitting in the midst of three young ones, radiating signs to them, which they then repeated one after another, and which they began again when the repetition was imperfect! These lessons were quite marvelous to my eyes, and nothing, out of all that concerns the Xipehuz, has preoccupied my sleepless evenings more. It seems to me that it was there, in that primary education of the species, that the veil of mystery might be partly lifted, that some simple and primitive idea might perhaps emerge to clarify a sector of that profound darkness for me. No, nothing put me off; I watched that educative process for years, attempting innumerable interpretations. How many times have I thought I grasped therein, like a fugitive gleam, the essential nature of the Xipehuz: an extrasensory light, a pure abstraction—which, alas my poor flesh-embedded faculties never succeeded in following!

I have said previously that I thought for a long time that the Xipehuz were immortal. That belief having been destroyed by the sight of the violent deaths occurring in consequence of collisions between the Xipehuz, I was naturally led to seek their vulnerable point and to apply myself every day thereafter to find means of destroying them—for the Xipehuz were increasing in number to such an extent that, having overflowed the Forest of Kzour to the south, the north and the west, they were beginning to intrude on the plains on the eastern side. Within a few years, they would have dispossessed humans of their earthly abode.

To begin with, therefore, I armed myself with a sling, and as soon as a Xipehuz emerged from the forest within range, I aimed at it and launched my stone. I did not obtain any result by this means, although I hit the individuals I aimed at on every part of their surface, even the luminous points. They appeared to be quite oblivious to my attempts and none of them ever move sideways to avoid one of my projectiles. After a month of trying, it was necessary to admit that sling-shots could do nothing against them, and I abandoned that weapon.

I took up the bow. As soon as I shot my first arrows I discovered a keen sense of dread among the Xipehuz, for they turned away, keeping out of range, avoiding me as much as possible. For a week, I tried in vain to hit one. On the eighth day, a party of Xipehuz—carried away, I suspect, by its zeal for the hunt—passed close to me while chasing a beautiful gazelle. I launched a few hasty arrows, without any apparent effect, and the party dispersed, with me in pursuit, using up my ammunition. I had no sooner fired the last arrow when they all came back at great speed from different directions, blocking me in on three sides—and I would have lost my life there and then had it not been for the prodigious speed of the valiant Kouath.

That adventure left me full of uncertainty and hope; I spent an entire week inert, lost in the vague depths of my mediation, in an excessively exciting and subtle question, worthy to dispel sleep, and which filled me with pain and pleasure at the same time. Why were the Xipehuz afraid of my arrows? Why, on the other hand, out of the large number of projectiles with which I had hit those in the hunt, had none had any effect? What I knew of the intelligence of my enemies did not permit the hypothesis of a terror without cause. On the contrary, everything led me to suppose that an arrow, fired in particular conditions, must be a redoubtable weapon for use against them. But what were those conditions? What was the vulnerable point of the Xipehuz?

Suddenly, the thought occurred to me that it was the *star* that it was necessary to hit. Momentarily, I was certain of it—blindly and passionately certain. Then I was seized by doubt. Had I not aimed at that target several times with the slingshot, and hit the target? Why should an arrow be more fortunate than a stone?

Night had fallen: the incommensurable abyss with its marvelous lamps, spread over the Earth. With my head in my hands, I was dreaming, my heart darker than the night.

A lion started roaring; jackals passed by on the plain—and the little light of hope ignited again. It occurred to me that a stone and a sling are relatively large, while the Xipehuz star was so small! Perhaps, in order to have an effect, it was necessary to pierce it with a sharp point and plunge to a profound depth within it. That way, their terror of arrows could be explained!

Vega was turning slowly round the pole though, dawn was approaching, and weariness had been putting the world of thought within my skull to sleep for some time.

In the following days, armed with the bow, I was constantly in pursuit of Xipehuz, going as far into their circle as wisdom permitted. They all avoided my attacks, though, keeping their distance, out of range. There was no question of lying in ambush; their mode of perception permitted them to observe my presence through obstacles.

Toward the end of the fifth day, an event occurred that, on its own, proved that the Xipehuz were creatures both as fallible and as perfectible as humans. That evening, at dusk, a Xipehuz deliberately approached me, with the constantly accelerating speed that they adopt for attacking purposes. Surprised, with my heart racing, I flexed my bow. Still advancing, like a turquoise column in the gathering gloom, it came almost within range. Then, to my amazement, as I got ready to fire my arrow, I saw it turn around and hide its star, without ceasing to move toward me. I only just had time to urge Kouath to a gallop and get out of the reach of that redoubtable adversary.

Now, that simple maneuver, of which no Xipehuz had thought before, in addition to demonstrating once again the individuality and personal inventiveness of the enemy, suggested two things: firstly, that I had chanced to reason correctly in relation to the vulnerability of the Xipehuz star; and secondly, less encouragingly, that the same tactic, if it were adopted by all of them, would render my task extremely difficult, and perhaps impossible. However, after having done so much to arrive at the truth, I felt my courage growing in confrontation with the obstacle, and dared to hope that my mind had the subtlety necessary to turn the tables.[9]

VI. Second Extract from Bakhoun's Book

I returned to my solitude. Anakhre, the third son of my wife Tepai, was a skilled maker of weapons. I commissioned

---

[9] Rosny inserts a footnote: "In the following chapters, which are mostly in the narrative mode, I shall stick close to Monsieur Dessault's translation, but without feeling obliged to reproduce the tiresome division into verses or unnecessary repetitions."

him to construct a bow of extraordinary range. He took a branch from a Waham tree, as hard as iron, and the bow he made from it was four times as powerful as the one used by the shepherd Zankann, the best archer in the thousand tribes. No living man could have drawn it, but I had thought of a trick and once Anakhre had put my plan into action, he found that the immense bow could be flexed and released by a sickly woman.

Now, I had always been expert in launching darts and arrows, and within a few days I had learned to use the weapon my son Anakhre had built so perfectly that I never missed any target, be it as small as a fly or as swift as a falcon.

Having done all that, I went back to Kzour, mounted on Kouath with the eyes of flame, and resumed prowling around the domain of the enemies of humankind. To inspire confidence in them, I fired numerous arrows with my usual bow every time one of their parties approached the frontier, and the arrows fell harmlessly short. In this way, they learned the exact range of the weapon, and consequently thought themselves utterly out of danger beyond a certain distance. A suspicion remained, however, which made them skittish and capricious when they were not in the cover of the forest, and led them to hide their stars from my view.

By virtue of patience, I wore down their anxiety, and on the sixth morning, a troop came to take up position in front of me, beneath a large chestnut tree, at three times the range of ordinary bows. As soon as I saw them there I released a host of futile arrows. Their vigilance relaxed progressively then, and their movements became as free as in the early days of my sojourn.

It was the decisive moment. My heart was beating so strongly that I felt impotent at first, and I paused, for the redoubtable future depended on one single arrow. If that one failed to strike the intended target, the Xipehuz might never again lend themselves to my experimentation—and how would I know, then, whether they were accessible to human aggression?

By degrees, however, will-power triumphed, quieted my heart, made my limbs supple and strong and my eye calm. Then, slowly, I raised Anakhre's bow. Out there in the distance a tall emerald cone was standing motionless in the shade of the tree; its bright star was turned toward me. The enormous bow flexed; the speedy arrow leapt into the air, whistling...and the Xipehuz, struck, *fell, contracted and solidified.*

A loud cry of triumph sprang from my breast. Extending my arms in ecstasy, I thanked the Unique.

The frightful Xipehuz were, therefore, vulnerable to human weapons! There was, therefore, hope that they might be destroyed!

Now, without fear, I allowed my heart to hammer away; I let it beat out the music of delight—me, who had feared so desperately for the future of my race, who beneath the course of the constellations and the crystal blue of the abyss, had calculated somberly that within two centuries, the vast world would have seen all its limits burst by the Xipehuz invasion.

And yet, when the superb, beloved, pensive Night came again, a shadow fell over my bliss: grief for the fact that humankind and the Xipehuz could not co-exist, that the life of the one would depend on the brutal condition of the annihilation of the other.

Part Two

I. Third Extract from Bakhoun's Book

The priests, the elders and the chiefs listened to my story, awestruck; their couriers went to report the good news to the remotest parts of the wilderness. The Great Council ordered the warriors to gather at the sixth moon of the year 22,649, on the plain of Mehour-Asar, and the prophets preached the holy war. More than 100,000 Zahelal warriors arrived, and a large number of combatants from foreign races—Dzoums, Sahrs and Khaldes, attracted by rumor—came to offer their services to the great nation.

Kzour was surrounded by a ten-deep ring of archers, but all the arrows failed by virtue of the Xipehuz tactic, and imprudent warriors perished in great numbers. Then, for several weeks, a great terror prevailed among humans...

On the third day of the eighth moon, armed with a sharp-pointed dagger, I announced to a vast crowd that I would go to fight the Xipehuz on my own, in the hope of overcoming the mistrust that had begun to arise concerning the truth of my story.

My sons Loum, Demja and Anakhre were violently opposed to my project, and wanted to take my place. "You cannot go," said Loum, "for if you die, everyone will believe that the Xipehuz are invulnerable, and the human race will perish." Demja, Anakhre and many chiefs having said the same thing, I found the reasoning compelling, and withdrew my offer. Then Loum, having taken possession of my horn-hilted knife, crossed the mortal frontier, and the Xipehuz came hurrying toward him. One of them, much swifter than the rest, was about to reach him, but Loum, subtler than a leopard, sidestepped, went around the Xipehuz, and then, with a mighty leap, pounced on it and thrust with the sharp point.

The motionless multitude saw the adversary collapse, contract and solidify. A hundred thousand voices rose up in the blue morning, and Loum was already returning, having crossed the frontier. His glorious name circulated through the armies.

II. The First Battle

At dawn on the seventh day of the eighth moon of the year 22,649, the horns sounded and heavy hammers struck the brazen bells for the great battle. A hundred black buffaloes and 200 stallions were immolated by the priests, and my 50 sons prayed with me to the One and Only.

As the solar globe was engulfed in the red dawn, the chiefs galloped to the front of their armies, and the clamor of the attack swelled with the impetuous rush of 100,000 combatants.

The Nazzum tribe was the first to engage the enemy, and the combat was formidable. Impotent at first, scythed down by mysterious blows, the warriors soon mastered the skill of striking the Xipehuz and killing them. Then all the nations—Zahelals, Dzoums, Sahrs, Khaldes, Xisoastres and Pjarvanns—roaring like the oceans, invaded the plain and the forest, surrounding the silent adversaries everywhere.

For a long time, the battle was total chaos; messengers continually came to tell the priests that men were dying in hundreds, but that their deaths were being avenged.

At the hottest hour of the day, my son Sourdar with the agile feet, dispatched by Loum, came to tell me that for every Xipehuz annihilated, a dozen of our men perished. My soul was dark and my heart beat feebly, but my lips murmured: "Let it be as the Only Father wishes!" And I remembered the head-count of the warriors, which had given the number of 140,000. Knowing that the Xipehuz numbered about 4000, I thought that more than a third of the vast army would perish,

83

but that the Earth would belong to humankind. Now, the army might have been insufficient.

"It is a victory, then," I murmured, sadly.

But as I thought of these things, the clamor of the battle made the forest tremble more violently; then, the warriors reappeared from every direction, with cries of distress, fleeing toward the frontier of Safety.

Then I saw the Xipehuz emerge from the edge of the forest, no longer separate from one another but united in 20-strong circles, their fires turned inwardly. In that formation, invulnerable, they advanced upon our helpless warriors and massacred them frightfully.

It was a defeat, and a terrible one. Even the boldest combatants thought only of flight. In spite of the grief that grew in my heart, though, I patiently observed the fatal incidents, in the hope of finding some remedy in the very depths of misfortune—for a venom and its antidote often exist side by side.

For that confidence in the power of thought, fate gifted me with two discoveries.

Firstly, I noticed that in places where our tribes were multitudinous and the Xipehuz few in number, the killing, initially incalculable, gradually slowed down, and that the enemy's blows were having less and less impact, many of the victims getting up after being briefly stunned. The strongest ended up being completely resistant to the shocks, continuing to flee after numerous strikes. The same phenomenon being reproduced at various points on the battlefield, I boldly concluded that the Xipehuz were becoming weary, and that their power of destruction did not exceed a certain limit.

The second observation, which complemented the first marvelously, was furnished by a group of Khaldes. These poor men, surrounded on all sides by the enemy and losing confidence in their short daggers, ripped up bushes and used them as clubs, with the aid of which they tried to clear a passage. To my great surprise, their attempt succeeded. I saw Xipehuz losing equilibrium by the dozen, and about half the Khaldes escaped through the gap thus made. Singularly enough, though, those who made use of bronze weapons instead of shrubs—as a few chiefs did—killed themselves in striking at the enemy. It must also be noted that the blows of the clubs did no appreciable damage to the Xipehuz, for the ones that had fallen righted themselves promptly and resumed the pursuit. Nevertheless, I considered my double discovery to be extremely important with respect to future battles.

Meanwhile, the rout continued. The ground reverberated as the vanquished fled; before nightfall, no one remained within the Xipehuz limits but our dead and a few 100 combatants who had climbed trees. The fate of the latter was terrible, for the Xipehuz burned them alive by bringing a thousand fires to bear on the branches that sheltered them. Their frightful cries resounded for hours beneath the vast firmament.

III. Bakhoun the Chosen

The next day, the tribes made a count of the survivors. It transpired that the battle had cost about 9000 men; a modest estimate put the Xipehuz losses at 600—with the result that the death of each enemy had cost 15 human lives.

Despair entered into many hearts, crying out against the chiefs and talking about abandoning the frightful enterprise. Then, amid the murmurs, I advanced into the middle of the camp and began loudly reproaching all of them for the pusillanimity of their hearts. I ask them if it were preferable to let all men perish or to sacrifice a fraction; I demonstrated to them that, within ten years, the entire Zahelal country would be invaded by the Forms, and the lands of the Khaldes, the Sahrs, the Pjarvanns and the Xisoastres within 20 years. Then, having thus awakened their consciousness, I made them recognize that a sixth of the endangered territory had reverted to humans, and that the enemy had retreated into the forest on three sides. Finally, I told them about my observations; I made them understand that the Xipehuz were not indefatigable, and that wooden clubs could knock them down and force them to expose their vulnerable points.

A great silence reigned over the plain; hope returned to the hearts of the innumerable warriors who were listening to me. Then, to increase confidence, I described a wooden apparatus that I had conceived, appropriate for both attack and defense. Enthusiasm was reborn; the tribes applauded my speech and the chiefs laid their emblems of command at my feet.

IV. Metamorphoses of the Armaments

In the days that followed, I had a great many trees felled, and I provided a model of light, portable barriers of which this is a summary description: a frame six cubits long and two wide, connected by bars to an internal frame one cubit wide by five long. Six men—two porters, two warriors armed with stout wooden lances and two others similarly armed with wooden lances but with exceedingly sharp metal tips, and also provided with bows and arrows—were able to position themselves inside it comfortably and circulate within the forest, protected from immediate contact with the Xipehuz.

On arrival within range of the enemy, the warriors provided with blunt lances would strike, tipping the enemy over and forcing them to expose themselves; then the archers would take aim at the stars, either with their bows or their lances, according to circumstances.

As the average height of the Xipehuz was little more than a cubit and a half, I designed the barriers in such a manner that, when on the move, the external frame did not exceed a height above the ground of a cubit and a quarter. For that it was sufficient to incline the supports linking the internal frame by about a hand's width. As the Xipehuz were unable to pass over steep obstacles, nor make progress other than in an upright position, the barrier, thus constructed, was sufficient to shelter its occupants from their immediate attack. They would certainly make an effort to burn these new weapons, and might well succeed in more than one instance, but as their fires were scarcely effective beyond the reach of an arrow, they would be forced to expose themselves in order to attempt that incineration—which, not being instantaneous, would also permit the employment of displacement maneuvers, which would, in many cases, take them out of harm's way.

V. The Second Battle

On the 11th day of the eighth month of the year 22,649, the second battle against the Xipehuz took place, and the chiefs made me commander-in-chief. I divided the tribes into three armies. Shortly before dawn, I launched 14,000 warriors against Kzour, armed in accordance with the barrier apparatus. The attack was less confused than the one on the seventh day. The tribes moved slowly into the forest, in small troops arranged in an orderly manner, and the engagement began.

The advantage lay entirely with the humans for the first hour, the Xipehuz having been completely disconcerted by the new tactic; more than 100 of the Forms perished, scarcely avenged by the death of a dozen warriors. Once the surprise had been overcome, though, the Xipehuz began to attempt to burn the barriers. In certain circumstances, they were able to succeed. A more dangerous maneuver was the one they adopted toward the fourth hour of daylight. Taking advantage of their speed, groups of Xipehuz, tightly massed together, began rushing the barriers, and succeeded in turning them over. A very large number of men perished in that fashion, to the extent that a part of our army lost heart as the enemy gained the upper hand again.

Toward the fifth hour, the Zhelal, Khemar and Djoh tribes, and parties of Xisoastres and Sahrs, began to retreat. Wanting to avoid a catastrophe, I dispatched couriers protected by strong barriers to say that reinforcements were coming. At the same time, I prepared the second contingent to attack. First, though, I issued new instructions: the barriers had to be maintained in groups as tight as movement within the forest would permit, and be arranged in compact squares as soon as they approached a substantial troop of Xipehuz, without abandoning the offensive in so doing. Having said that, I gave the signal.

In a short time, I had the joy of seeing that the victory was reverting to the tribal coalition. Eventually, toward midday, an approximate count—which estimated our army's losses at 2000 men, and those of the Xipehuz at 300—revealed in a decisive fashion the progress we had made, and filled all our hearts with confidence in a conclusive triumph.

Even so, the proportion varied slightly to our disadvantage toward the 14th hour, the human losses then amounting to 4000 individuals and the Xipehuz 5000. It was then that I launched the third corps, and the battle attained its greatest intensity, the enthusiasm of the warriors increasing by the minute until the hour when the Sun was about to set in the west.

As that moment approached, the Xipehuz went on the offensive again to the north of Kzour. A retreat by the Dzoums and Pjarvanns made me anxious. Judging, in addition, that darkness would be more favorable to the enemy than our own troops, I ordered the sounding of the general retreat.

The troops' return was accomplished calmly and victoriously; a large part of the night was spent celebrating our success. It had been considerable; 800 Xipehuz had been killed and their sphere of action reduced to two thirds of Kzour. It is true that we had lost 7000 of our men in the forest, but those losses were far inferior, in proportion to the result, to those of the first battle.

So, filled with hope, I began to formulate a plan for a more decisive attack on the 2600 Xipehuz that still survived.

VI. The Extermination

On the 15th day of the eighth moon of the year 22,649, when the red star rose over the oriental hills, the humans were in battle formation before Kzour. My heart swelling with hope, I finished talking to the chiefs, the horns sounded, the heavy hammers resounded on the bronze, and the first army marched into the forest.

The barriers had been strengthened and slightly increased in size, enclosing 12 men instead of six, save for about a third, which were constructed on the old model. Thus, they became more difficult to burn, or to turn over.

The first maneuvers of the battle were favorable; after the third hour, 400 Xipehuz had been exterminated, and we had only lost 2000 men. Encouraged by this good news, I launched the second corps. The fury on either side became terrible then, our combatants becoming accustomed to triumph, and the antagonists manifesting the obstinacy of a noble Kingdom. From the fourth to the eighth hour, we sacrificed no fewer than 10,000 lives, but the Xipehuz paid 1000 of theirs, with the result that only 1000 remained in the depths of Kzour.[10]

From that moment on, I was certain that Humankind would have possession on the world; my last doubts disappeared.

At the ninth hour, however, a great shadow was cast over our victory. By that time, the Xipehuz were only showing themselves in enormous masses in clearings, hiding their stars, and it had become almost impossible to knock them over. Excited by the battle, many of our men would charge these masses. Then, with a rapid movement, a company of Xipehuz

---

[10] The arithmetic of this calculation does not correspond to the number of surviving Xipehuz calculated at the end of the previous chapter, but the figures may be approximate.

would separate from the mass, knock down the reckless attackers and massacre them.

A thousand perished in this manner without the enemy sustaining any perceptible losses. On seeing that, the Pjarvanns cried that all was lost; a panic set in that put more than 10,000 men to flight, a great number even being sufficiently imprudent to abandon the barriers in order to run more rapidly. It cost them dear. A hundred Xipehuz set off in pursuit, and slew more than 2000 Pjarvanns and Zahelals—and terror began to spread through all our ranks.

When the couriers brought me this awful news, I realized that the day would be lost if I did not succeed in regaining the lost positions by means of some swift maneuver. Immediately, I sent orders to the leaders of the third army to attack, and announced that I would take command of it. Then I took these reserves rapidly in the direction from which the fleeing men were coming. We soon found ourselves face to face with the pursuing Xipehuz. Drawn on by the ardor of their slaughter, they did not re-form very quickly, and in a few moments I had them surrounded. Very few escaped. The immense acclamation of our victory restored the courage of our troops.

From then on, I scarcely had to reorganize the attack; our maneuvers were limited to continually separating segments of enemy groups, then surrounding these segments and annihilating them.

Soon, understanding how unfavorable to them this tactic was, the Xipehuz resumed attacking us in small groups, and the massacre of two realms, one of which could only survive by annihilating the other, increased terribly. All doubt as to the final outcome had, however, disappeared even from the most pusillanimous souls. Toward the 14th hour, scarcely 500 Xipehuz remained, fighting against more than 100,000 men, and that small number of antagonists was enclosed within increasingly narrow boundaries—about a sixth of the forest of Kzour—which greatly facilitated our maneuvers.

The dusk was sending streams of red light through the trees, however and fearing ambushes in the gloom, I called a halt to the combat.

The immensity of the victory swelled all our hearts; the chiefs talked about offering me the sovereignty of the tribes. I advised them never to confide the destiny of so many people to one poor fallible creature, but to worship the Unique, and to adopt *Wisdom* as their earthly ruler.

VIII. The Last Chapter of Bakhoun's Book

The Earth belongs to Humankind. Two further days of combat annihilated the Xipehuz; the entire domain occupied by the last 200 was razed; every tree, every plant and every blade of grass was destroyed. And for the benefit of future tribes, aided by my sons Loum, Azah and Simho, I finished inscribing this history on stone tablets.

Now here I am, alone, on the edge of Kzour, in the wan night. A copper half-moon is suspended in the west. Lions are roaring at the stars. The river wanders slowly through the willows; its eternal voice speaks of times past and the melancholy of perishable things. And I have buried my forehead in my hands, and a lament is rising from my heart—for, now that the Xipehuz are extinct, my soul regrets their loss, and I ask the Unique what Fatality dictated that the splendor of Life should be spoiled by the darkness of Murder!

THE SKEPTICAL LEGEND
A Fictionalized Essay

I. Luc

Luc lived in a dream of the 20th century. A creature of mysticism, essentially responsive to the beauty of things, a spiritual brother of Mesopotamian contemplators in the abysm of science, he drank to excess of a mystery more profound than the vanished religions and visions refined by the sentiment of forms and forces conceived by the people of Europe. The natural quality of his sensitivity, his vibrant nerves, and the youth of a brain whose amplitude stored thought without effort, ensured that he would not be rigidified by the study of things that would be the life of art, poetry and ecstasy of future humankinds. For him, the artistic and religious terror of his contemporaries in confrontation with the splendors of discovery was merely the incomprehension of an infidel confronted by the Parthenon. To have enlarged the sense of nature, and revealed the charming transformations of matter in elements tinier that those contained in ponderous ancestral thought, did not seem to him to be the decadence of the Ideal but a widening of frontiers, the blossoming of more complex and more polished dreams.

The ancient and infantile conceptions of being—the universe populated by gross hieratism, the Ptolemaic firmament rotating in its cycles and epicycles, the waters of the abyss separated by the hand of Jehovah, the gods of Aeschylus and Phidias, Krishna and Christ broadcasting vague parables, the symbols of Ahriman and Agni, the enigmatic metempsychoses, the voyages of the Egyptian soul, the Occidentals hunched in the gloom of cathedrals and the dreamy Semites of the holy city—retained a retrospective charm, but the mainspring of his being, the breath of the unknown, the bliss and the frisson of all the Beyonds, he only found in the gnosis of the modern era. Is the grace of a beech-tree standing on a hill any less proud and svelte to the dreamer who plunges into the invisible work of vesicles, osmosis and the capillary ascendancy of fluids, into the leaf weaving the light, into the labor of love in the minuscule tabernacle of the sexes? Will the dawn be less divine to the mind and the senses for knowing about the spectrum of radiation, for being aware of the potentials varying with light and heat, the fabrication of electricity linked to the formation and disappearance of clouds, for sensing oneself living in a current of indefinitely nuanced forces and abandoning oneself to the dream of knowing more? Would not the mystery that is blended therein, the religious sensibility that emanates from it, the vertigoes and the adorations of being have been unapproachable quintessences for the ancients?

Ill-adapted to social life, a stranger to the gross movements of human beings, gone astray in the disputes of the struggle for existence, and not understanding their ponderous logic, built of frail timidities and excessive tactilities, Luc lived in dread of contacts, even fearful of love, having a particular horror of conversations into which hatred, brutal joys and base vanities were poured. His soul, however, went out to people with the desire for their happiness and offerings of timid affection. To individuals as delicate as himself, in amities that were few and far between, he eventually confided his thoughts and his mysticism. An ideal of life in a muted voice, whispers alternating with long silences, was combined with a slight intolerance of his solitary life and its meager quality.

His days were passed in patient study, with an extreme preference for the nooks and crannies of science, in which exceedingly delicate phenomena were revealed: the polarization of light, electromagnetic induction, electrolysis, diffusion, spheroid bodies, the physiology of nerves, hypnotism. It was more than study, however, captivating him in long ecstasies of

futurition,[11] prostrations before the unknown, his entire substance being perpetually drawn to unscientific, nebulous creations, the hope for prodigious futures, hypotheses regarding
the utmost depths of things. There, he was no longer in the
realm of knowledge, nor invention, but in a state of mysticism
that suited his nature, in the intimacy of his ascetic brain. And
he dreamed in two ways: one still investigative, deductive and
logical, the other in invocations, prayers and great harmonious
hymns, running between his meninges. He named the former
lucid dreams, the latter *obscure dreams*.

II. Anthem

His thinking about things wandered within an appeal to
atoms, an unfurling of branches and tiny creatures drying their
downy feathers, Unease still trembling on the fringes of the
cloud. The metaphysics of the Ephemeral emerged from the
quivering of moist earth, the semi-desuetude of leaves, in all
the relativities and pauses of Dream and the Psyche, the Babel
of colors, the reflection of light from grass, the attitudes of
hills, the softness of clay and the firmness of stones—and the
suggestion of the Absolute became transparent as merely a
profound gap hollowed out within nimbus clouds.

---

[11] I have preserved this neologism rather than attempt a substitution that would not quite do justice to the notion. The piece
contains several other innovative variations of more-or-less
familiar terms, most of which I have reproduced straightfor-
wardly and without further comment, considering their intended meaning to be transparent. In some passages of this
work Rosny gives free rein to the spontaneous excesses of his
"poetic passion for science," thus exaggerating his occasional
tendency—noted by his friends and critics alike—to lose contact with normal expression and ordinary meaning.

Standing on the old inexhaustible Earth, Luc dreamed that the moment had been improvised for him, that it was for him that the Mother would devour tomorrow without scruple, but in him that she had determined, after countless attempts, that the vicissitudes of Force should be inscribed, corresponding to the stages of the amorous matter of Being.

He was tired of studying. Print, the black and white of pages, still floated before his eyes, providing slight distraction from an inclination to solitary, random speech: a reaction to silence and congestion—the restitution, reconstruction and combination of ideas accumulated under too much tension in his skull.

"I am one of those, Mother, for whom you are always present, of those who reassimilate you perpetually in the palingenesis of the Ideal...of those who believe that no originality can increase without your contemplation."

As skiffs of slate bore away earthenware clouds, opening an embrasure to the huge setting sun: "The Trinity left ajar in the margins of Dogma is you, Sun, Earth and Moon, who—after billions of changes of course, every movement lost in an infinity of orbits like a note in a symphony, after phases in which the twenty-five thousand years of the Precession are a bubble in a marsh—have created my humble ecstasy!"

As happens after too much reading, Luc was possessed by a tender electricity, a mystical bliss. Kneeling down, he intoned something analogous to the ancestral psalms, but orientated in a different direction: "Thank you, vibrations of the sunlight, geometry of organisms, cryptogams struggling through vicissitudes, inferior animals, prehistoric ancestors, all of you who have labored for life, all of you who have run through the eternal hour-glass!"

The words emerged, borne by a melancholy voice, clad in crepuscular charm, while Luc's eyes grew languid and his breast seemed full of extraterrestrial charm.

A soft repetition continued within him, accompanied by emotion drawn from the finest nervous cords, the mysticism of the old European animal returning to the great Mother after centuries of Idolatry.

He was leaning forward, nourished by the transformation of clouds, a mirror of the ambiance, a microcosmic human in which an entire nocturne of the vast musician was duplicated. He seemed to be drinking in the evening electricity, the nervous and drowsy atmosphere, a thousand inductions inverted by the departure of the Star, a thousand new polarities over the vegetable and the mineral.[12]

Small creatures were emerging: crane-flies, crepuscular moths and, already, the silent, fleecy silhouette of bats, imbued with a charming mystery. Luc adored their furtive flight, their life restricted to an hour of penumbral nourishment, their equivocal nature, mammalian tending to avian, rough-hewn by nature with a mysterious objective, a delicate sketch that horrifies us only by virtue of its abortion.

"I love to think about your wings, little disinherited bats, so delicate and tactile, so electric that they have become eyes, perceiving objects at a distance. I love to dream about you, sleeping through the winter in your dark retreats, your lethargy saving up your meager lives during the glacial days...the days devoid of insects!"

Long-eared bats went back and forth, more jerkily than swallows, but more harmoniously than the common run of perching birds. Luc was daydreaming lethargically.

"Old Demoiselle Duhennin...her jaundiced cadaverous face...who made us tremble as she offered us marzipan...one day they put her in her coffin...Knock knock! Old Brother Duhennin mimed the scene admirably...well, it was doubtless an atavistic return...a bat or a marmot reincarnated in Made-

---

[12] Rosny remarks in *Torches et lumignons* that he once had a habit of watching the sky for hours on end, and suggested that, in all probability, no one else had ever spent as much time in such rapt contemplation—although it might be worth noting that the Chevalier de Lamarck would have provided stiff competition.

moiselle Duhennin...and deep down? An isolation...an electrical state separating a life from the environment and conserving its vital charge?"

From the distant slopes on the horizon, blurred animals, cattle or horses, made an impression on Luc's retina. His sensitivity took possession of them in order to complicate his dream.

"*Bos in Aegypto etiam numinis colitur*...dear Pliny![13] How gentle was your gravity, your belief in animal religions...your elephants descending from the forests of Mauretania to the banks of the Amilius to adore the rising moon. What did you think about lethargy and electricity? 'When friction has dispensed life and heat to it, it attracts wisps of straw....' The humble infancy of the terrible force! There was already, it's true, the mystery of lightning, but so distant...in the depths of the Roman firmament, where the augur's eye roamed..."

The hymn became complicated in the depths of the Tabernacle. On the trees, tormented by autumnal necrosis, there were tremors of iridescence and light crystals everywhere. From polished sulfurs, half-way to the firmament, gem-like salts and basins of Tyrian purple, Luc constructed creatures as light and ephemeral as the dusk, Forms living for an hour among the Alleghenies, the Carthages and Lake Arals that the wind and the light composed and decomposed, while he murmured, with a smile that "they are the children of the sines of the angles of incidence and the angles of refraction!"

He saw them, light, undulous and feminine, in the faces of eider-down clouds, in the sashes of pale green silk trailing in the distance over a gulf, in the translucent tresses of the ashen spiral floating over the incarnadine river of the occidental base.

---

[13] The quotation is from Book VIII of Pliny's *Natural History*; the English equivalent is "In Egypt, an ox is worshipped as a god."

"Day by day, the fluid monster was entangled by the humble chains of experience. Rude and barbarous at a remove of three generations, brutal in the Leyden jar, it was disciplined and stolen by the delicate work of the Voltaic pile, the disintegrator with countless fingers and prodigious reconstructor. Finally, it suppressed space, crossed the ocean...and then developed speech...its magnetic ear opened to language and to harmony..."

Luc's attention was caught by a half-completed building. Set against its walls of brick and quarried stone, there was a platform full of tools, a simple technology: a windlass, pulley-blocks, lifting-gear, a wheelbarrow, slender masts fixed at intervals. Before the half-dead sky, the last sighs of purple—the lattices, the darkly-looming scaffolding, and the pulleys seen as projections—caused Luc to dream of a future architecture, as fine as that of mystics, as harmonious as the human form, or, alternatively, an enigmatic page, a charming hieroglyph inscribed on the coppery page of the sky, an ebony handwriting, encrusted on a scarlet papyrus or the resplendent lining of the wing of a Sudanese flamingo.

Then, the deepening of the shadows, the enigma of the constellations, the sensation of being bathed in the ether in which stellar salutations were multiplying—and Luc thought about the timid pioneers, the patient researchers who were weaving an intimacy with the Infinite. An infinitely gentle hymn sang to him upon his lips.

"In modern Analysis, very humble Research striking at all the posterns of Matter, concentrates the ancient impulses of mysticism and the distressed cries of men frightened by the multitudinousness and power of phenomena. Modest and gentle, plowmen of the furrows of the Unknown, enemies of Negation, kneeling before the mystery of forces, the analyst-priests patiently supply the terms of revelation and order the Chaos. They suppress neither human pain nor human doubt; they do not reject the possibility of a principle; they do not flee from conjecture or hypothesis; but in the honesty of their nature and the resignation of their work they find the sensuality of living in spite of suffering. Without stupefying themselves by the affirmation of an absolute, they make use of theories, albeit as a method subordinate to research rather than tyrannical entelechies. To that laborious humility the sanctuaries of the molecule have opened up, the atoms have revealed their waves, and the cathedrals of the Universe resound with the canticles of submissive force...forever adding to the transparency of the infinitely scattered Beauty of art or science, the sovereign utility of any exploration of things and their harmony with one another and with us. The ephemeral disdains collapse in the face of the accumulation of bodies of work and narrow skepticisms surrendering to the dictates of nervous complication. The useful, enlarged from its logical definition, embraces the joy of creating beauty and truth; the conquest of immediate practical problems does not raise any obstacle to the more elevated fabrication of the future, the genesis of ever-superior humankinds...

"Are not the algebra and geometry of light, weavers of organisms and the consciousness of things, the generator of the cerebral? How can one talk about the delicacy of the environment, the fever and the serenity of landscapes, the troubled hours of the firmament and the poems of the setting sun and the convolutions of insect flight without amplifying the intimate domain? Oh, how tolerant that localization is, infinitely respectful of corollary manifestations, merely imagining that the impenetrability of nature does not have fixed boundaries! Modern research, adorable modesty that combs the great darkness, discoverer that has condescended, after the abstract impertinences of scholasticism, to toil, you who have sanctified your levities in the limpidities of investigation, you who have made the abstract an instrument and not a limit, O incommensurable spiral circling the profundities of space into which the human mind rises in brushes with the immanent!"

III. Lucid Dreams

1. Metamorphoses

The singularity of a certain substance, chemically identical to another but differentiated by the analysis of polarity, had led researches to propose the hypothesis that "molecules that have lived retain their original attitude over time." [14] Would it be reckless to complicate this hypothesis with the belief that even more subtle heterogeneities exist, elevations of power in the complexities of vitalized atoms? In infinitesimal experiments, scalar differentiations will doubtless be established between molecules that have been incorporated into innumerable living organisms through the ages and others that have only emerged from the inorganic for centuries or hours, so that a restricted number of substances selected from those most extensively reheated in the furnaces of existence will be identified in the annals of the synthetic biology, history and prehistory of the animate that are being written today in the lumpen capital letters of contemporary and fossil flora and fauna.

Leaning over the gulf of these hypotheses, in which all electrometers, thermoscopes, polarizers and microphones are combined in inexhaustible series, Luc inevitably slid into visions of the destiny of a planet and its humble role in the life of the Cosmos. What repercussions do the palingenesis of its labor, the continual mutation of its surface, and the kneading of corpuscles into ever-more-complex individualities, have in

---

[14] Most organic molecules can exist in two different three-dimensional forms, which are mirror-images of one another. Earthly life is "laevo-rotatory" in its polarization, and Earthly organisms could not metabolize "dextro-rotatory" molecules produced in a laboratory—a situation dramatized in several 20th century science fiction stories, most notably David Lake's *The Right Hand of Dextra* (1977).

the work of the Universe? Might it be itself, within the universal crucible, *a dextro-rotatory or laevo-rotatory molecule?*

In continually recommencing its work, spitting out shreds of its plutonian entrails through its volcanoes, which will live in their turn, is it simply serving some humble function in an immeasurable chemistry of suns and nebulas? And is all the passion of a sidereal bee, metamorphosing solar honey in ontological palpitations, expended in view of the time when it will die—the time when, as a glacial voyager around a black sun, it will implicate enough vital combinations, enough memories of forms and movements, enough attempts at mysterious perfection to be an integral part of *a whole built from expired worlds*, of worlds in which, light and heat having been banished, the forces will be higher, the gloomy glacial abysses being populated with new life?

Why not collapse the present conjectures of our science regarding the death of the planet, why not imagine resurrection *only* by a fall into some sun or some fiery nebula? Why should our assimilation of life to heat and light not be a belief as naïve as the hypotheses of Heraclitus? What logic prevents us from conceiving the immensities and subtleties of organic forces in an Infinite Darkness and an Infinite Cold?

2. Ontological Pathways

In its cold generality, the destiny of a planet scarcely interrupted Luc's train of thought. It was a desert of thought, immeasurable and beautiful, inhabited by an excessively unique absolute, bounded by crystalline metaphysics, the primordial joy of which soon vanished into sadness and vertigo, into avid and monotonous abysses, vegetations and abstract mortuaries floating on the immutable. He preferred to go back to the particular aspects of the thesis, to analyses relevant to the perpetual metamorphoses of souls, such as conjectures regarding the transmutations of fauna and the terrestrial surface. For a long time his dreams dwelt on a simple transformism, a perpetual generation of humankinds appropriate to environments and continuing for an infinite time.[15] Then his ideas swerved; the thesis of an indirect descendance seemed more probable to his instinct and he constructed a romance of the entire animal and vegetable kingdoms preparing the Earth for a further, quasi-virtual reign, the "transport of a pollen of forces and forms by humankind for the advent of a superior being."

If one examines the phenomena recently integrated by analysis, one is surprised by their extremely "organic" appearance. Electrolysis, electromagnetic induction, radiophony and microtelephony, accumulation in the Planté[16] manner and electrical effluvia make one dream of an era in which mechanisms, properly speaking, will disappear from our apparatus, giving way to appropriations of lines of force.

With the wheel and the lever abolished, one may imagine labor by molecular penetration, the transportation of people and things confided to passages of magnetic currents and ac-

---

[15] "Transformism" is a kind of evolution in which species are engaged in an eternal process of transformation into new species—a cornerstone of Lamarck's theory of evolution. The idea of a future evolution of humankind according to this pattern is extrapolated in numerous scientific romances, most spectacularly Olaf Stapledon's *Last and First Men*, but Rosny used the notion primarily in association with his prehistoric romances and lost land stories, imagining dozens of alternative humankinds produced alongside our own in the past but eliminated—save, perhaps, for fugitive remnants—by natural selection. His futuristic fantasies, as this passage suggests, follow the course of the deflection identified and sketched out here, in which humankinds and their equivalent species are seen as exemplary of a transitory phase in the development of planetary life, fated to be superseded by life forms entirely alien to the spectrum of the animal and vegetable kingdoms.
[16] Gaston Planté (1834-1889) was the French physicist and pioneer of electrical technology credited with the construction of the first accumulator.

cumulations of fluids. The Earth, stripped of mechanical devices, having disciplined all conductivities and resistances, will become the passive and unconscious reservoir of what humankind has acquired over the millennia. Furthermore, why should our race, at the ultimate of its power and already prepared to descend from the summit of the curve, not equip its dynamic condensers with infinitesimal procedures of nutrition and generation that will ensure its duration through infinite periods of time, and "saturate the inanimate with the gnostic heritage of the animate?" In the present embryonic state of knowledge, in which dynamos already excite one another mutually, do not magnetic reversibility and the accumulation of current in a Faure apparatus[17] leave the field free for vaster hypotheses of *auto-organic reconstitution*?

As a side-effect of vital development, metamorphoses inscribed in every atom by the phases of life, a scientific retention in the unconscious would also increase, after a fashion: a fixation of central memory on the surface of the habitat, doubling the power of the action of the heavenly body, for future struggles.

Now, Luc imagined the beings that would live on this improved Earth, which exists in a rudimentary state all around us, from our epoch onwards. One effect—and sometimes, undoubtedly, a cause—of our scientific discoveries and organic duplications, in confused correspondence with our sensitivities, is that every one of our acquisitions has its echo in their increase. In truth, it might not only have been corpuscles analogous to cells that floated for billions of centuries on the primitive waters before becoming complex; there might also have been simple poles of movement; it is not impossible that they became an integral part of our flesh and our blood. Why should one not imagine these parasites as an integral whole

---

[17] Emile Alphonse Faure (1840-1898) improved Planté's accumulator in 1881 by coating the lead plates to increase their efficiency, making the large-scale commercial production of batteries feasible.

and one of the reasons for our progress, a principle of future death and of contemporary vital acceleration, with the result that, supposing them to be indestructible, we would be more severely damaged by their extermination than by submitting ourselves to their development, and could not even slow down their progress except by immobilizing ourselves in our present sciences and arts or descending towards animality? Or, to sum up in a sentence: Although they are factors of our final annihilation, are they not—at present—the surest guarantee of our duration?

Let us, however, imagine the era in which they will transform themselves into more complex organisms. Will they be tangible or not, susceptible to being seen and embryonically defined by humans? What will be their mode of nutrition? Will they enter into conflict with us? Will they attempt to annihilate us, as the various branches of the animal kingdom have done?

Luc thought that their mode of nutrition, like their mode of reproduction, would be totally different from ours. The mere notion that they would employ, as humus, the aggregations of magnetic force, induced the conclusion that they would renew their being by the direct absorption of force. Vegetable nutrition seems to be a partial realization of that concept, but as plants only make use of light and chemical decomposition, it is necessary for us to imagine a superior organic phase. The form of future physical agents integrated into the planet will be exceedingly complex, in no way analogous to any simple radiation; all the directions that we can realize by means of receivers orientate themselves in the ether according to the trajectories of origin. Proceeding from simple force to complex force, one therefore imagines contrasts analogous to the difference between a piece of crystal and a morsel of flesh.

As for reproduction, they will accomplish it in an indirect fashion, by "induction" of the female principle by the male principle. In these conditions of existence, Luc deemed the struggle between the two kingdoms futile. The new life would pass through the old, like light through a window, by means of penetrations and superimpositions, and modifications of polarity, not—save for certain accidental cases—by antagonism. That is how the apparatus of human beings would produce the nutritive elements of superior beings without the elements being fatally "deducted" by the effort. If we imagine, roughly, some absorption of power in the field of a dynamo, might that absorption not be independent of "useful work?" Complicating the hypothesis, nothing prevents our imagining the successors of our "reign" nourishing themselves in a manner liable to favorize our labor rather than opposing it, and that concept embodies the notion of a superior harmony adequate to a progressive circulation of the Universe. Thus might recur, in the distant future, the possibility already expressed by the present: Although factors of our final annihilation, will not the new reign be the surest guarantee of our duration?

As for the probability of humankind acquiring some knowledge, superficial or profound, of the nature of its successors, that was one of Luc's gentle chimerical torments. Undoubtedly, if one thinks about the inevitable reversibility of things, it is legitimate to induce that our scientific acquisitions contain, at the least, fragmentary information about the vertiginous future—but the difficulty lies in disentangling it from so many complex phenomena, obtaining an irreducible remainder or an ensemble of notions worthy of synthesis. On the other hand, if, in the matter of tangibility and visibility, the problem seems reasonably facile, how such conditions multiply if one admits that a future being might be composed of lines of force, rendered stable for the duration of a life—save for the inevitable balance of increase and decrease—which move through matter while preserving their individuality, form, intensity and velocity.

At any rate, in order to build at least a humble scientific hypothesis regarding a fourth kingdom, Luc imagined the realization of a series of organo-scientific hypotheses, such as: *planetary physiology, double life, a new sense and cerebral penetration...*

3. Planetary Physiology

If Luc granted some generative priority to planetary phy-siology over bipolar life,[18] a new sense and cerebral penetra-tion, it was not because he intended a strict ordering of these phenomena. Imbued with principles of reversibility and corre-lation, they appeared to him as a cluster, with enigmas and lacunas that rendered uncertain the original demarcation of the Animal and the Vegetable, which often encroached upon one another in the sciences in which he specialized. Contemplated from that angle, planetary physiology lent elements to double life and cerebral penetration, whose circulation nourished it further even though the analytical sum weakened the preferred classification.

A pleasant reverie, for Luc, was the thesis of a "physio-logical tissue of heavenly bodies," of stellar anastomoses[19] concomitant with gravitational modalities, but much frailer and finer. Is there a circulation through the astral Being as different from orbits and emissions of light as protoplasm

---

[18] Rosny's substitution of "bipolar" for "double" is bound to seem slightly confusing to modern readers familiar with the conventional usage that has redefined "manic depression" as "bipolar disorder," so it may be as well to specify that the two "poles" he has in mind are consciousness and sleep—but the notion becomes more complicated as it is extrapolated.

[19] An anastomosis is a link between two different organs or other biological systems; what Rosny is hypothesizing is that the physical linkage of gravity is supplemented by some fur-ther link, which binds heavenly bodies into some kind of greater organism. It is not entirely clear from what he says, but he appears to have a vitalistic theory of life, which imagines life as a kind of force binding molecules and cells together; he appears to consider the laevo-rotatory preference of Earthly organic chemistry to be a manifestation of this force.

from quartz? Is there, in virtuality, a physiological auscultation of the infinitely large?[20]

Firstly, Luc recapitulated gross examples, ancient and modern: the Sun as the father of life, the losses and gains of heat and pressure at aphelia and perihelia, the planetary conjunctions taking our globe further away from or nearer to its hearth, tidal disturbances, the magnetic distortions linked to the course of a solar flare of sunspot. Then, dominated by the ideas of the decadence of Floras and Faunas attributable to large-scale phenomena, and migrations of population in accordance with magnetic currents, in a direction opposite to the Earth's rotation,[21] he soon plunged fully into the Chimerical.

---

[20] Auscultation is what a doctor does with a stethoscope, listening to the beating of the heart and the sounds made in the pleural cavity by the action of the lungs. Rosny's concept of "virtuality" is not the same as the modern notion of "virtual reality," but it stems from the same source: the distinction made in optics between a "real" image, which can be brought into clear focus by being cast on a screen, and a "virtual" one, which remains essentially vague and thus, seemingly, somehow external to, although interwoven with, reality. His notion of a "fourth kingdom" additional to the animal, vegetable and mineral "kingdoms" obviously partakes of a certain "virtuality," which he identifies as something already present in the mysteries of the electromagnetic spectrum, and already active in the evolution of Earthly life. The notion of a future evolution of life to embrace the inorganic was not original to this essay, but the version set out here is much more subtle and sophisticated than the cruder ones satirically explored in such contemporary texts as Samuel Butler's *Erewhon* and Didier de Chousy's *Ignis*.

[21] Rosny made much in his prehistoric romances of the effect of westward migrations of early humans, based on fanciful accounts he found in contemporary paleoanthropology, but he refrained from citing this hypothesis that such migrations were guided by the Earth's magnetic field.

In the same way that an electric current produces an acid taste in the mouth, should not the arrival or departure of large inductive bodies like our companions in celestial migration in some sense acidify or alkalinize the Earth, affecting the accelerations and decelerations of plants and acting on animal nervous systems, *independently* of any gravitational influence?

In order not to have the character of "power," do these phenomena not act in the depths of being, as do so many ideas apparently supplementary but actually determinative? Besides, by virtue of their more psychic character, are they not delayed, emitted in nuances, only becoming massive long after their passage and, by virtue of that fact, confused with immediate characteristics?

If the approach of a planet, a cometary presence, or a traversal of the hyperaeolithic medium developed some floret in the depths of the woods, if the stages of Jupiter's progression aborted some insect generations and multiplied others, affecting diseases, the coloration of plumage or petals, that would be an influence of planetary physiology. The marvelous charm that operates on the melancholy of oxen, the fever of ewes or donkeys, the recrudescence of bees and the depression of spiders will doubtless one day be attributed to cosmic pulsations as precise and as sustained as a mathematical series.

The soul is doubtless gently stirred by the thought that sidereal causalities are echoed in the annelid worm, and that, to the effects of the frightful influence of certain microbes in the human Fatum, will be added the demonstration of the Martian and Saturnian influence of the life of those same microbes and on the arrival of new species. A profound delight accompanies the hypothesis that ancient astrology, its confused prescience of the perturbations of the whole upon the part, will be reborn by analysis, clarified and rationalized; that the obscure notions of hesitant brains, the lies of the Mage and the Fortune-Teller, and the principal features of the necromantic grimoire, will appear as the symbols of profound verities, as the disturbed prophetic instinct of that which will gather the sons of man into the entrails of the Infinite.

Nevertheless, the disentangling of these threads linking human flesh to astral contingencies, to some slight degree, was not for Luc a science conceived, but merely its prolegomena. In the utmost depths of his dream, he calculated the probability of vital reactions organizing the Milky Way via threads of nervous conductivity, rules determining that the beings living on their surfaces had a direct effect on one another, that being one of the causes of transformations, and that if these calorific vibrations and pressures had an ontological geometry, the influences in question were the differential and integral calculus. By their continuity, by the exquisite receptivity of all their components, by the infinite variety of their form, these directive forces employ ponderous dynamics, as a mechanism puts immeasurable power in the hand of a frail human animal. Thus, the universe actually reflected itself in every individual world, and although the flora and fauna of space must have the infinite variety dictated by their environments, a harmonic repercussion unified them, the evolution of each one summarizing the evolution of the whole.

Let it be clearly said that Luc dismissed any idea of *lucid* communication of mechanisms constructed by more-or-less similar creatures, similarized by the general laws of intellect eventually creating an intercosmic intermediary, an interstellar telegraphy.

Anyone imagining a sidereal telegraphy, in fact, from the contemporary era on, can hope for the good fortune of an identity between our abstractions and those of a planetary fauna. Far from there being any unknown force or any substantial novelty involved, one may deem it infinitely probable that success is dependent on a fairly broad convergence, that the signals will be imprinted on elements less complex than our knowledge. In sum, the problem has some analogy with the relationship between explorers and islanders, in which all the ingenuity on both sides is concentrated on the most obvious and most commonplace notions common to human beings. As regards planetary physiology, it must, by necessity, arise independently of any individual communication and any dialogue, its role being to integrate the "animal vibrations" or "organic lines of force" of Space: vibrations varying in intensity but included in a unique phenomenon, as the rays of the spectrum are in the formal identity of lumino-calorific undulation.

To put it briefly, astral telegraphy will probably never furnish any information regarding planetary physiology, and vice versa. The former rests on a notion within our immediate reach, soluble by our most rudimentary sciences, the latter on a hypothesis transporting the imagination toward infinity and unknown forces; one is almost scientific, the other suggestive of the most profound mysticism.

So Luc, his soul in torment, in a singular and vertiginous delight, enclosed himself perpetually in "directions" of experience, with the confused intoxication of indefinables that seemed to be perpetually coming into contact with definables. They were edifications of electrometer-nerves, receptors traced in animal tissues, but reinforced by automatic scales; it might well take hundreds of thousands of years to extract, from the bosom of perturbations of a merely electrical, luminous or gravitational order, any clearly cosmo-organic perturbation isolated from terrestrial influences.

"Oh, sometime in the mystery of the ages, such an apparatus will be constructed, whether it be an anesthetized animal or a network of fibers still endowed with life, while luminous balances, balances of induction, pressure and gravitation will have neutralized every effect of known phenomena, every torsion and every polarity determined by infinitesimal measures.

"Constructed and reconstructed, willed by successive generations, each of its microscopic elements, simultaneously due to prodigious probes and extraordinary intuitions, the moment will finally come when the apparatus, in the darkness, during a determined phase of the moon, will have captured the physiological force of the cosmos, the first feeble tremor that will whisper the great secret of things. Oh well! Even then, might it not be necessary to wait thousands of years before the manifestation is duplicated, before the slightest complementary evidence is added to the initial experiment? How long, alas, was the magnet known to peoples who integrated its magic into some legend or Oriental tale; how long did the compass guide Chinese, and then European, ships; how many prehistoric children had vague electroscopes, before the era arrived in which the exterior notion sprang forth from profound science!"

And Luc, saturated by silent hypothesis, standing beneath the nocturnal mantle, turned toward the nearest planetary body, the beautiful satellite plowing its course among the asterisms, and from which the initial stammers of cosmic physiology undoubtedly emanated.

"Moon, once almost equal to the Sun for the peoples of the world's infancy, as for those of the adult period of Hellenic times and those of the Medieval fever! Then, having established your actual smallness, your role as a celestial mirror, at the same time as science attributed Life and its complications to the solar hearth, to thermal and luminous play and the infinity of their variations, you fell into scientific discredit as a 'creator of beings.' Even so, satellite, compensating by nearness for your smallness, to the point of becoming the conductress of oceans, will you not, in the planetary psyche of tomorrow, be the counterbalancing agent of the sun? Infinitely variable in gravitational phenomena all our blood and every one of our nerves is subject to your phases, and the millions of ancestral human generations that have been subject to them have incorporated them in order to protect themselves against them and make use of them. Evident electrical inductrice, varying our potential every day, colossal Electromagnet whose syzygies and quadratures express the coefficients of forces, whose rapid course through the firmament symbolizes the ruptures and closures of currents, nurturer of nocturnal animals and plants, of which the former are our ancestors and the latter our fodder, your light varies the polarization of the terrestrial surface infinitely, transmuting minerals and flowers. Oh, raiser of tides, if all littoral zones feel the power of your metamorphoses, all subject to the mechanical variations that your force imposes on ours, if you administer the plethoras, is it not infinitely probable that you engrave harmonies in the foundations of the nerves and that your fauna—for it exists—whispers confidences to ours?"

Then, descending to the simple poetry of the Earth:

"Oh, with what charm one reposes in some vale where meadow and forest grow together, where there are springs and fecund streams, when a great lunar segment is rising or setting... The leaves have resumed a little of their diurnal activity, languishing, like spinners dreaming of love...sharp-eyed animals prowl in the grass or beneath the arborescent plush... The Star pours forth its electro-luminous life...its inappreciable chemical currents, while over there, beyond the horizon, the cliff roars, sending a thrill of emotion into the entrails of the rocks, bringing forth phosphorus colossi armed with a hundred thousand hammers, combating the mobile stones impelled by the waves against the inert frontiers of the bank. Oh, Lunar creator, floating over the Imponderable, it seems that one can perceive you toiling in the Abyss as you progress, and that your rays are merely the forerunners of your force, as the spark flies faster than the shell!"

4. Bipolar Life

Will the inertia of sleep always be the mode of repose adopted by nature? Luc, being frail and nervous, fervently desirous that *every* minute of his brief terrestrial sojourn should be conscious, had a horror of the moment when normal life has palpitated in the brain for too long and the vanishment of consciousness abruptly interrupts the currents of the muscles and the nerves. Thus, he found great consolation in building the hypothesis that nature is working to replace the present oscillation with a system in which repose will simply consist of dynamic antitheses, of distortions of life rather than its mysterious suspension.

On the blessed evenings when the firmament is disseminated over the earth, while the portals of the sunset hollow out a moving carillon of light, Luc pursued his chimera into the Infinity of Ontology. For a long time, he preferred recourse to Intuition, to the bliss of reflections of thoughts and shadows of sensation. They were the unstable impulses of being, the hope of a hope, figurations of life in two dimensions, or in one dimension. On the taciturn meadows, an exceedingly slow, diminishing fanfare, a confidential voice of insect flight, the curling up of petals, all the tender luxuries of last light, whispering discreetly, like the arts of a very ancient civilization, accompanied in Luc a course and discourse of Eternities and Postulates of final causes...

In that gentle voyage beyond the tangible, in which the Abstract bordered on Instinct, Luc wondered whether there might be an indication therein of the other Repose. One evening, when his conceptions were becoming ever more uncertain, he attained a state of mind similar to that of a Fakir and perceived that he was collapsing into an ecstatic brutalization, in an immobilization of sensitivity and, finally, into "true sleep."

Awakening beneath a network of branches, clouds and constellations, a desire for the Concrete took hold of him.

"If Sleep is due to disappear someday—although that duplication must be a consequence of Planetary Physiology, I nevertheless see the problem as more typical of, and restricted to, contemporary animality—by means that the eternal Mother has been preparing since the dawn of time, some definite trace of those means must already exist. To the curious gaze of the analyst, data might well up from the organic mystery and reveal its outline, as a thermal balance measures the approach of a human body.

A barn-owl brushed the silvery ash of an aspen saturated with starlight. Luc's soul pursued it into the shadows; the night was magnetized by the mystery of Raptors; charming arguments rose above the level of the meadows. Then, in the gap between a rose-mallow and a laburnum, the admirable tale of nocturnal and diurnal animals appeared to inscribe itself. In the languid waves of Time and Space, the utopian reads the effort of matter haunted by the dream of life, the groping attempts to coexist under all the appearances of day and night.

"Those creatures which wake up in the shadow of a marine rock, the inferior creatures that make their own light and drift in the depths like the stars in the sky...those which wake up in the borders of deserts on moonless nights and go forth with eyes gleaming like glow-worms...those which burrow in subterranean melancholy, blind and velvet-furred, patient laborers and destroyers of larvae...have they, in the formation of their sensitivities, some molecular orientation that, subsequently acquired by the human animal, can contrive the doubling of life by suppressing sleep?"

And Luc wandered through the patient zoological research of our century, through penetrating dissections and profound explorations of the primitive cell, into the caverns of physiology, where the plant-animal prowls, where the primordial menstrual flow hesitates to divide the realm of life.

"Ah! Humus of poetry, obscure metaphysics of origins, so similar in uncertainty to the birth of a Thought...are you not, then, a Sign, a diffuse delineation that is favorable to my Dream...from which it is necessary to rise again to superior life, free to return to you, in the final analysis?"

There was a frisson, like the tremor of a cashmere scarf, and Luc saw the barn-owl—or another—pass by again, the first link in the chain of his current fantasy:

"Beautiful bird of prey, subtle incarnation of so dark a Dream, of such sad and moving annals born in the nocturnities of the skull...and young quadruped brothers, the lynx, the jaguar, the Lord with the huge head of Atlas...aristocrats of Darkness...aristocrats with luminous eyes...with pupils dilating in the play of light and shadow as a river broadens in the plain and shrinks between hillsides..."

On the plain, amid the diffuse islands of foliage, phosphorescent eyes seemed to be scattered like fireflies, lying in ambush in every covert. Luc glimpsed the yellow eyes of tigers, the vertical slits of their pupils, contrasting with the horizontal slits of herbivores—one doubtless adapted for flight, for

115

the circular exploration of plains, for the vague perceptions searching for an infinite number of perils in every direction, the other for ambushes, for the sudden, direct bound, in which it is necessary to set aside all sideways vision to concentrate entirely on the perpendicular direction of the target. Then, recalling the gaze of a cat—the gaze of a superior creature, so foreign to our own gaze, whereas the gaze of a dog understands and absorbs ours—he was able to wonder whether the elements of the double life might not lay there, as the secret idiosyncrasy of a powerful animal lies dormant in a few spermatic vesicles, and whether the differentiation of a feline pupil and a herbivore pupil might embody the secret of abolishing sleep.

With a powerful wing-beat, Luc's mind made a rapid survey of animal sight: the stemmata of insects, the appendices of crustaceans, pigmentary stains, the frigid pupils of fish, the pink eyes of albinos, the troubled gaze of oxen, the enormous pupils of owls, the swift and sinister lucidity of falcons—a resplendent world, gentle and terrible, formidable in the subtlety of its tints, the genius of the flesh in creating receptacles for the most rapid of phenomena, weaving micronervous tissue to measure the reports of etheric vibrations!

Does not the almost universal closure of the eyelids during sleep, while the other senses remain open in a quasinormal fashion, provide an indication of the enormous importance of the organ for the imagined thesis? If the objection is raised of its delicacy and extreme sensitivity, can one not say that the sensitivity in question is a secondary effect, of the same sort as pleasure in love—that it is an excitation maintaining the rule of the closure of the organ during unconsciousness? The same argument applies to the preponderance of vision in cases of fascination, or Braidism, those terrible instances that precipitate birds into the mouths of serpents, or put hysterics to sleep by means of a bright light.[22] There is

---

[22] Rosny inserts a brief footnote to this paragraph: "The preponderance of sight seems proven in cases of fascination, but

evidently no doubt that the other senses are subject to the same regulation, but with less intensity. Now, Luc had no intention of denying that all the senses must contain some information relating to the double life, but he directed his research into the easiest path, toward the part of the organism most specifically impregnated with the conditions of the problem.

Thus, the pre-eminence of the visual apparatus suggested hazardous experiments: saturating eyes with polarized light; grafting the eye of a panther into a human orbit to obtain a duplication of the optic nerve; trying out combinations of forms before the pupil with an objective opposite to hypnotism, awakening instead of putting to sleep; passing light through powerful magnetic fields before directing it at the retina, and so on.

One morning, remembering a madman's pupil—the oval, feline pupil of a lunatic submissive to the phases of the moon, who slept rarely and lightly, and whose thoughts were subtle, immaterial and argumentative—he thought of something curious the man had said about "the eternal wakefulness of the soul." Mingled with metaphysical conceptions, that was the age-old utopia of the nocturnal voyage, in which the soul roams through time and space. Exceptionally, when carried away by excessively distant adventures in the divine world, the soul forgot or was slow to recover its body, death or catalepsy ensued. Among these beliefs, antithetical to Luc's, one of the madman's affirmations remained singularly troubling:

---

not for other instances of hypnotism." "Braidism" (after James Braid, who attempted to liberate hypnotic techniques from the theoretical residue of "animal magnetism") was normally used as a straightforward synonym for hypnotism, but Rosny appears to be using it in a narrower sense, implying entrancement by means of visual stimuli rather than aural ones. The mythology of the hypnotic power of spinning or swinging pendants was as firmly entrenched in the late 19th century imagination as the equally-suspect myth that snakes are capable of hypnotizing birds.

the latter claimed, in fact, in the times when he was fully conscious, that his monomania was an active sleep, as restful as normal sleep, and cited as proof, in addition to the fact that he almost never slept, the periodicity of his fits, thirty hours apart, each one lasting eight and a half hours, which he could predict perfectly, and which were preceded by a period of uncertainty and fatigue, like quotidian repose in other men. Active sleep! And Luc compared the hypnotic sleep provoked by the eye's obsession with an object with the madness provoked by the *direct obsession* of the brain—and sometimes another organ—with an object or a thought. By subtle conversion, perhaps instruments might one day be constructed to act on the eye so as to provoke temporary insanity, just as sleep is provoked today—and how many experiences might be created at that time!

A fascinating chimera, that madness might be the means adopted by nature to realize the problem of double existence, and that perhaps, in times precursory to that realization, humans might come to understand that progress in seeing madness generalized, channeled and, above all, "rationalized" among them. Unexpected, sudden, cataclysmic fits of madness, if one might put it that way, would become increasingly rare. Their periods would be mathematically anticipated by the alienated themselves. The latter would withdraw voluntarily, in good time, to appropriate habitations: comfortable, even luxurious, refuges. In cases of necessity, fits might be delayed, by the will-power of the monomaniac, as we can delay sleep. From then on, all horror would disappear; subject to general and fixed oscillations, madness would re-enter the regime of organic needs. Slowly extended to all humankind, initially with lacunae of memory and logic, a lack of communication with rational life, it would end up in complete harmony, reconnecting the sparse phenomena of hypnotism, preparing the bipolar life by means of a profound knowledge of all organic deviations, creating new arts, revealing the secret of Fevers, extracting from epidemics the principles that might render it as

118

beneficent and fecund as it presently seems sinister and corrosive!

5. A New Sense and Cerebral Penetration

A new sense, sketched by the polarizations of the Double Life, perhaps nurtured but certainly strongly facilitated by Planetary Physiology, can be imagined either as a sort of synthetic harmony of other senses, or as a new localization. It might perhaps be a simple development of the tactility observed in bats, which, although blind, can fly inside a cavern or a building without bumping into the walls, or the directive faculty of birds, or the lateral lines of fishes and salamanders, etc. Has not the supposition of a "homing instinct" in animals, in fact, some analogy with the repetition (for it is evidently a repetition) of music, of the rhythmic singing voice in the human mammal? Monkeys, dogs and pachyderms—all viviparous animals—have either lost the art of *singing* or not yet acquired it. Birds—descended, like us, from reptiles—had it for millions of years in the midst of unharmonious mammals, in which one can scarcely find a certain coarse and primitive beauty in the roar of the lion or the buffalo. And we, descendants of monkeys, are rediscovering that voice and that harmony, proving that nature can suspend a faculty—emerging from a sense—and subordinate it to ulterior development as well as definitive atrophy. From which follows the quasi-impossibility of classifying organs as superior or inferior *in essence*, not knowing what future conditions might add to embryonic faculties, and the legitimacy of the hypothesis of further complications of the homing instinct in species of inferior order.

Using logic of a similar kind, a new sense might be indicated by the as-yet-rudimentary phenomena of hypnotism, or perhaps by a refinement of taste, sight or—most particularly—hearing. Indeed, if one moves forward 50 or 60 precessions of the equinox,[23] when barometric pressure has fallen to a half or a quarter of what it is at present (between 250 and 350 millimeters) the difficulty of hearing will have increased in proportion. Moreover, according to Luc, the atmosphere would have been subject to slow modifications of its innate structure, by virtue of new cosmic conditions, and its coefficient of elasticity might have risen in spite of its cooling, the velocity of its aura being considerably increased in consequence, and the ear subject to concomitant metamorphoses. In various attempts at accommodation to the new environmental conditions, the organ could have been modified to the point of perceiving a number of *longitudinal vibrations* infinitely larger than seems to be demanded *a priori* by the problem, so that hearing would be replaced by a kind of *phonic sight*, capable of discerning pulsations in the ether comparable in velocity to light, although retaining the fundamental qualities that constitute sound-waves. That would give rise to a series of data relating to the nature of pressure and the infinitesimal actions and reactions of terrestrial, intersidereal and intermolecular fluids. In consequence, the luminous diaphanousness of certain bodies would be supplemented by a phonic transparency, which would complicate Atomic science considerably.[24]

---

[23] The precession of the Earth's equinoxes completes a full rotation of the planet's orbit in 25,765 years, so 50 precessions would be 1,288,250 years.

[24] Rosny adds a footnote to this paragraph: "For want of precise terms, and to avoid tiresome circumlocutions, in this chapter I employ the words light, heat and their derivatives, as well as the words acoustic, phonic, sound and their derivatives, in much broader meanings, the former as characteristic of transversal vibrations, the latter of longitudinal vibrations, an abstraction derived from the impression produced on our present-day senses by these phenomena." The terms in which the fundamental distinction is made are now obsolete, but the general point still holds. The subsequent analogy that Rosny draws between electricity and sound-waves seems rather ridi-

This theme is connected in one sense to the development of a sense electrical in nature or whose nature is "symmetrical" to electricity. Sound waves, in fact, present themselves as a calculation of successive modifications of pressure, and electrical potential—especially the charging and discharging of condensers—offers a close analogy with barometric reactions, which could be represented hydraulically in suitable apparatus. If one adds to this the particular fact that sound is the sole agent that has so far lent itself to intimate metamorphosis and electrical reversibility—which is to say, being transformed into induced electric currents that can be retransformed into sounds identical in form and yield (save for intensity) to the originals—then the secret analogies between sound and electricity seem even more striking.

If we examine the case of a new sense now, the mode of electrical representation is that every molecule of a body is perceived by an increase in potential, variable or fixed, *separate from neutralizations of potential in the interior of the body.* That is to say that every body will be defined by the new sense as some differentiation of its general electrical state in the context of the environment defined by the series of its magneto-atomic atmospheres. This very rudimentary definition is that of all the senses; it is sufficient to substitute the words light, touch, etc., for that of magnetism or electricity. Its value is, moreover, considerably diminished by special difficulties. If, for example, one admits that nervous conductivity is an electrical conductivity, either direct or inductive, it seems necessary to conclude that hearing, sight and touch are homologues of telephony, in which sound is only transmitted by metamorphosis, so that the impact of an exterior phenomenon is not perceived in itself but by the modifications it imports to

---

culous nowadays, when the much closer analogy between electrons and photons is solidly established, but that was far from obvious in 1889, when subatomic physics was still in an embryonic state. The amazing thing is that he ventured into such deep and murky intellectual waters at all.

internal currents, and perhaps by retransformations in apparatus as-yet-undefined.

Given this, one is tempted to conclude that the perception of the environment requires at least two factors, one reacting upon the other, unless one prefers to suggest the introduction of inverted orders of conductivity—for example, a neuro-luminous or neuro-phonic conductive network integrated into our *hypothetical* electrical conductive system, a transformation so important that only seems to be realized in differentiating us as much from ourselves as vertebrates from protozoa. If one rejects the inversion of conductivities, it is necessary either to deny that our internal conductivity is electrical, or to overcome the objection of two factors. In the latter case, the solution would be symbolically analogous to the construction of some inductive balance indicating variations which, *as such*, would be electrical in form, while known balances only vary in the form of the augmentation or diminution of sounds, contacts, withdrawals, approaches, etc., modifying the conductivity of circuits or the flow of motive forces.

Now, this construction, which is beyond our present means of imaginative representation, leads, every time one tries to get past it, to the attribution to the magnetic atmosphere of atoms of a characteristic number of vibrations, and, the perception of *transversal* vibrations already being perceived by one of our senses in a condition of excessive velocity, the mind is more inclined to admit prodigiously rapid *longitudinal* vibrations—with the result that, as previously observed, the problem of the electrical sense appears to have a much greater affinity with the problem of a much improved phonic sense.

This viewpoint receives some further confirmation if one reflects on the "harmonic" proportionality of chemical combinations, the simple rules of volume that so closely resemble musical rules and make one think of a symphony of atoms too infinitesimal in the present time to be perceived by our atmosphere-attuned ears. Now, Faraday has added electrical equivalents to chemical equivalent; does this not prove that, in the phenomenon of electrolysis, the output of electricity is a form of sonorous—musical, even—etheric wave regulated by geometrical laws analogous to those of the dimensions of strings, blades and tubes?

In sum, the hypothesis of a localized electric sense was therefore connected, for Luc, with the progression of static phenomena of etheric barometry and of dynamic modifications of etheric pressure of a sonic form. This solution set aside the objection of two factors, either by separating or fundamentally unifying electricity and sound. In the former case, the longitudinal vibration of atomic atmospheres *accompanies* the potential without being confused with it, but always reveals itself by its vibratory proportionality; in the second case, undulation and electricity are synonymous and nature has thus far resolved the problem in hearing, sound only being differentiated from electricity by effects of atmospheric mass opposed to effects of etheric mass, which one might suppose, in the refinement of the new sense, with less intensity, the relationship air/ether being replaced by the relationship $ether^n/ether^m$.

Luc's preferences, however, did not go so far as denying that the new sense might originate outside phonomorphic phenomena. The researches of Faraday, Maxwell and many others, open up the seductive hypothesis of lumino-magnetic links, a theory of molecular vortices: electrical effects on rotatory polarization seem, in the relevant experiments, confirmative of these ideas, although the influence of a current or a magnet on polarized or normal light is not fundamentally incompatible with a phonoelectric theory (inasmuch as Becquerel's objection, suggesting the deformation of experimental substances, is plausible).[25]

---

[25] This reference is not to Henri Becquerel, who discovered radioactivity some years after Rosny published "La Légende sceptique," but to his father Alexandre-Edmond Becquerel, who was intensely interested in the chemical effects of light and electricity, especially those leading to decomposition.

Luc was also able to forge a hybrid, phono-luminous, theory by proposing that the perpendicularity of the two effects of a current is symptomatic of the fact that electromagnetism is, in the final analysis, a lumino-phonism, flow along linear wires and the pile being assimilated, etherically, to a longitudinal vibration, and the transversal effect being assimilated to sub- and hyper-luminal vibrations of the spectrum, or *vice versa*. Nevertheless, these imaginations seemed less fecund, for the conception of a New Sense, than the first, phono-electric, conception; they demanded a refinement of the eye, or a hybrid oculo-auricular sense.

Now, a refinement of the eye, when that organ already measures such infinitesimal etheric pulsations, lends itself poorly to the dream, and the hybrid sense comes back in the end to the analysis of each of the two combined senses—so Luc preferred to immerse himself in the thesis of an independent, morphologically essential electricity, an abysm full of entities, full of vagueness and mysticism, in which the theorem of the two factors posed itself more rigorously, and where the seductive chimera of something "symmetrical" to electricity could react upon itself. In truth, in respect of that symmetry, Luc's imagination could scarcely get past concepts of functional inversion—for example, that conductivity might be manifest in present day dielectrics, that threads of silk, resin and gutta-percha might transmit currents from piles or new dynamos: ideas as seemingly absurd as admitting to bodies reputed to be limp, an elasticity complementary to that of elastic bodies.

"Is it not analogous tendencies that lead the mystical soul beyond all the nebulas, to alternative Matter, to the pole of Creation opposed to the Infinity, Reason and Equilibrium of ours? There, the Unknowable is not divided into heavenly bodies; there, the Mysteries of Genesis do not lie in the sanctuaries of Suns, Heat and Light, Electricity and Sound, and the Mechanics of Solids, Liquids and Gases are not modes of Existence. The very Essence of Forces, Mass and Density, Difference and Similitude, Space and Duration, still accompany phenomena there, but are strangers to our Geometry, ungraspable by our analysis. Plunged into the reverie of that gulf, where *no* form is conceivable for us, a fundamental passion, an invincible instinct attracts our being, without hope trembling in our soul for a single second in perceiving some infinitesimal notion, without our ceasing to sense that distance is, for us, the offspring of the Other Pole, Unreachable in the Eternity of Time and Space. A dream confused and empty, then, forever futile and awakening neither image nor thought within us? Whoever has plunged into it, however, comes back from that inconceivable vagueness with a subtle and profound fever, a mysterious ability to penetrate deeper into our own universe, the sharp impression of having obtained nothing but anguish and terror from the *Other* Matter, the Pole of Creation opposed to the Infinity, Reason and Equilibrium of Ours, unable to be indifferent to the development of our Being, and especially to our enlarged concept of the possible."

The new sense is connected to the nature of Cerebral Penetration.[26] In all probability, none of the future developments of the organism arouse more mysterious terror and vague hatred. The violation of the self, the devirginalization of nascent thoughts, seems execrable even on the part of adored beings, and the repulsion of the idea of cerebral sharing is so violent that few people can endure the communion—superficial as it is—of reading a book or a newspaper while tortured by the neighborhood of an eye scanning the same words as their own eyes.

That our volitions might be rendered as perceptible as our physical actions, every delicate soul conceives with the most legitimate horror—and does not the supposition that custom might erase the repugnance deprive us of a charming modesty, in direct relation to the progress of being, the inferior

---

[26] The term "telepathy" had not yet become the common currency of discussions of this sort, "psychic research" still being in its infancy in 1889.

man and the beast being infinitely less sensitive to it? Thus, the mind likes to imagine new defensive means, isolations of thought similar to the isolation of an electrical apparatus, interpositions of obscuring forces relying on the investigative forces.

The transcendent man already finds a shield in transcendence itself, his lofty speculations becoming closed to mediocrities in terms of etheric transmission as well as aural transmission. But that is too little, in truth, inasmuch as the power of a creator does not shelter him from assimilatory souls. What does sheltering a few rare ideas matter, if our sensations and quotidian thoughts, the very foundations of our life, become anyone's prey? No impressionable person can resign himself to that; everyone would prefer to keep his inner being hermetically sealed—and how can the conclusion be avoided that the determination in question, perpetually transmitted through human generations, must have created defenses against cerebral penetration and discovered superior laws of organic dissimulation; that, to the finesse of the attack, being must have opposed a finesse of reception warning of the concentration of another thought upon our own, inviting us to closure; and that lies and equivocation by etheric means must present more subtle analogies with oratory lies and equivocation?

According to Luc, cerebral penetration will develop in phenomena distinct from mental suggestion by hypnosis, and even more so from deductive divination. In divination by hypnosis, the factors are due, it is believed, to phenomena of concomitance, to a synchronic preparation of the induced individual and the inducing individual, or even a mere assistant. The surroundings, the succession of contingencies and the involuntary metamorphoses of the physiognomy form as many signs, as many elements of language, and as many cryptographic themes from which the Subject—in an extreme state of concentration and psycho-nervous refinement, endowed with tactilities and visibilities that permit the fluid interpretation of any contraction of nervous fibers—obtains a maximum of interpretation. Now, the transmission of thought, after the ac-

126

quisitions of the double life, planetary physiology and the new sense should not be based on any indirect deduction or reading.

One might object that mental suggestion, outside of spiritualist theories, is not strictly localized to deductive mediations, that it lends itself to a direct transmission of language. It seems sufficient to posit that, all our thoughts being in the form of words, or at least accompanied by words, our vocal apparatus vibrates to a greater or lesser degree in accordance with the nature of our meditations, that our vocal apparatus speaks concomitantly every time an idea presents itself to intimate sensation. Now, this microphonic movement of the vocal apparatus is no more revealed to the ear by the air than an excessively delicate current reveals itself to an insufficiently sensitive galvanometer. If it exists however, it can, become perceptible to a hypersensitized organ, just as the most minute variation of current is perceptible in a telephone, and hypnosis incontestably creates exacerbations that justify this hypothesis. Consequently, somnambulistic mental suggestion, in theory, can be explained by a reading of thought as direct as reading by conversation, and the former will be much finer and more reliable than the second if it is true that we speak *all* our thoughts internally, while we disguise the majority of them when we address ourselves to one another.

To this, Luc replied that cerebral penetration will originate independently of the vocal apparatus and any organ transmitting a "convention" akin to language. Humankind armed with planetary physiology, a double life and the new sense, will create means of communication drawn out in the form of the living fiber, in the functional development of the cell, and no longer in the embryonic hieroglyphs of writing and speech. Thus, he did not believe for a moment that the phenomenon would begin with a human penetration of human beings, but rather with an intimate understanding of inferior organisms.

Studying the mystery of primitive protoplasm, humankind will one day conceive its harmonies not merely scientifically but organically. At will, by magneto-nervous insufflation, man will succeed in decomposing it and recomposing it by means of a sort of intellectual electrolysis. He will be able to transport protozoans over a distance galvanoplastically, molecule by molecule, recombining their molecules around the appropriate poles. Eventually, in his unity, he will be able to see them evolving and living within himself, forming his individuality piece by piece; he will acquire *immediate* consciousness of the fact that he is a colony of multiple animal colonies, a soul compounded of myriads of synthesized souls. He will thus learn to substitute ontological thought for verbal intermediation, after having passed cerebrally, with the same slowness, through all the phases through which it evolved in climbing the scale of living beings.

Before clearly deciphering the thoughts of his neighbor at a distance, man will read the instinct-notions of radial creatures, inferior vertebrates and then, coming closer and closer, the gentle poetry of almost-fraternal animals, his domestic companions. In the depths of mute organisms, their dreams, their logics, their humble desires, their efforts to understand things, he will discover infinite sources of poetry and philosophy; he will acquire the ability to created new mnemonics within them, faculties of retention and abstraction that will lead some of them gradually to participate in our knowledge.

At the divine chimera of animal society, the dream of delicate souls over the centuries, Luc paused, in the bosom of his hypotheses, as if at an aromatic oasis, in the consoling peace of branches, in an exceedingly long and mysterious semi-dusk, beneath the fluid clouds of mercy and love. Future ages there acquire the penumbral poetry that reminds us of ages past, both being saddened by the same idea of Ephemerality, one symbolizing the death of distant ancestors, the other our own death, lost in the forest of millennia!

When that stage is reached the penetration of humans by humans will finally arrive in its plenitude: the conductivity of thought independent of all language and all convention, such that the ultimate ontological evolution will have been instituted, and such that organic conditions would permit its transmission through space. On that day, humankind will attain the summit of his trajectory. On a planet already half-obscure, where water no longer exists as anything but crystals of snow and ice, where the oceans lie in immutable mineral rest, where forces more subtle have become manifest in the thin air and on the harsh surface, humankind will divine a progress toward new Verities and Beauties, and will resign itself to its decrepitude, sounding its century-hours to the tocsin of Eternity. All its mystical aspiration will expand to comprehend the superior Kingdom that will follow the animal Kingdom.

By means of the marvelous acquisitions of scientific generation, by means of planetary physiology, the new sense and cerebral penetration, humankind will undoubtedly discriminate the slightest magneto-nervous modifications, the organic components of the Kingdom furnished by the stellar expanses, the generative inductions vaguely imitated by organo-electrolytic recompositions, the evolutionary relationships of new beings to old, the polarities analogous to that of the double life...

And Luc, in the ultimate minutes of a winter day, standing on a beautiful and funereal promontory in Holland, recapitulated all these shadows, these chimerical phantoms in which his mystical soul loved to bathe and lose itself. The moment was in harmony with his dreams, the hour of supreme frost, immobile in the vastness of smooth seas.

The Occident was in mourning, with purple and ponderous reefs, in the North, the glint of an aurora borealis was scintillating: a frail magnetic light, a sad, imponderable and profound kiss between the electricities of Earth and Sky. Behind him were plains paled by a snow reminiscent of moonlight, the immobility of crystal lagoons, the silence of high latitudes, the tremulousness of cold asterisms in the firmamentary glaciers; everywhere there was a mineralization and etherization of substances, even on the hesitant breast of the ocean, even in the magical glide of navigation-lights and the enveloping rotation of lighthouse beacons.

Luc imagined that every magnetic pole, like that Northern evening, is emitting a subtle auroral conflagration; that every creature is trembling in an ocean of fluids; that all the phenomena of hypnosis—the subtle nervous transmission, even levitation—are the infancy of a prodigious animal dynamism. As the last light expired, the Darkness crouched down upon the Silence and the aurora borealis rose up among the stars in melodious undulations, it seemed to Luc that he no longer had weight, that he was drifting in the web of lines of force, in the infinite intersection of waves that Life, Electricity and Light weave in every corner of Space; he felt that he was floating in the New Realm, around the obscure Earth, condensed in his own being, dreaming of the patient economy of forms that Eternity and Immensity do not allow to accumulate by Individuation for a second.

Like an Apocalypse, all his chimeras clamored simultaneously in his head; he thought that he could touch the utmost depths of the problem and coerce the indefinable forms with which he loved to nourish his soul; he immobilized himself in meditation like the humble monks of the Thebaid or Benares...

But the momentary display vanished, the breast of the oceans gasped toward the promontory, a heavy and rapid breath passed from wave to wave, the night moved on and lived its contemporary life. Luc found himself powerfully and cruelly attached to the earth, in the flagellation of a north wind, his humanity gripping his chest—and he went slowly back toward the lagoons, aware of the inanity of every one of his mystical aspirations, adoring them with a humble heart and a fervent intelligence.

IV. Dream Interlude

Although Luc deemed all mystical aspiration to be quenched by the promises of Knowledge, all poetry and all ascension toward the Enormous and the Vaporous securable in the infinities of Scientific Hypothesis, it was nevertheless necessary to admit—in more troubled souls—a desire for fixed beliefs and formal promises. The troubling and fascinating enigma posed to the ancient Aryan intellectuality, religious Palingenesis, bogged him down on days when a storm threatened without resolving itself, when earthworms writhed in the troubled soil.

In lucid Europe, on our roads bristling with rails, is there still room for a fomenter of mystical Cataclysm, a Buddha, a Christ or a Mohammed? Without pyres and gibbets, are not our notions of the Ephemeral and the Unstable—our beautiful dream of matter, speech transmitted over long distances through metal wires, the transportation of Force, Thermodynamics and transformist philosophy, the pages of the book of prehistory open in the bowels of the Earth—unbreakable foundations on which any Prophet would be bound to fracture his skull?

Luc meditated upon Mormonism, the Salvation Army, the Shakers, the Spiritists, the mad Summer of Nihilism, and above all our Revolutionaries, the most avid types of contemporary religious Instinct, more sincere than the residues of Christianity or the cultivators of Entities or scholastic Kabbalists, for an entire summer month, an August saturated with vapors, when, in the warm darkness, the atmosphere sometimes discharged itself in phosphorus gleams.

His nerves chased him in nocturnal hunts in which he circled stone Symbols, Temples or Pantheons. Downpours of large raindrops, interrupted by lightning, were dried up by the passage of an oppressive hot breath that seemed to be the respiration of the clouds; the points of ogives, squared Hellene frontons, a dome perched on high, the chiaroscuro joy of colonnades and interconnected towers, the pale flesh of pillars, gladioles and the rocks of ancient Christians, the silk and metal of sunlight on windows, the slow recompositions of lightning at the summits of edifices, immersed him in the abysms of Folktale and Miracle, and the Element humanized and symbolized therein by the dreams of vanished multitudes.

The *element!* Four ancient substances, confused and terrible phenomena. If the Bible were to be reborn once more, Anthropomorphism would no longer cling to the breath of the Desert, to the Beyonds of the Cloud, to the Voice of the Thunder, it would no longer admonish Neptune or Behemoth, Mylitta the fecund[27] or Siva the transformer.

As in the obscure origins when prehistoric people formulated the first codes of hope and supernatural terror, no religion can be born outside the mysteries of the Element. Multiplied and divided, however, its gross manifestations reduced and analyzed, the Element is only adorable now in its acquired subtlety, in the specifications of Science, in its most tenebrous elements. Only a Prophet armed with modern discovery, endowed with the lucidity indispensable to select the parts "still unexplorable for a long time," the mysterious fractions of advanced physiology, of vital mechanics, would perhaps be able to build a new Religion, but it would be infinitely more transitory than the religions of the Past.

Luc, his soul smitten with the problem, constructed the Bible involuntarily. His being was possessed by the double frisson of the creator who identifies himself with the game of hypothesis and the poet whose nerves thrill with the joy of communicating intellectually with his fellows. The obscure materials furnished by hypnosis and mental illness, the influences of one being on another, he catalogued in their extreme manifestations, then, amassing them in an introduction to a book, vivifying them with transformist terminology, he gradually arrived at suggestions, dogmatic affirmations, vague laws

---

[27] Mylitta was a Sumerian fertility goddess, the equivalent of Ishtar and Astarte.

and rules. There commenced the hieratism, the recitals, lapidary in appearance, indecisive and troubled in reality, like so many mirages in which luminous magic sculpts granites, gems and bronzes.

It was necessary to posit, without miracles, without incarnation and without direct divine confidence, the Being; it was necessary to dress him with will-power, arm him with judgment, electrify him with scientific and vital metaphors. In order not to lapse into simple deism, it was necessary to find a new revelation, a possible link between the Human prophet and the Infinite, the Immutable, the Omnipotent.

The story having commenced, the slow Ascension of an intelligence, Luc proceeded gradually to build a new and near-miraculous apperception—but he nevertheless displayed hyper-hypnotic notions, polarities that were, if not defined, at least suggested in nuances, in developments of savant poetry.

The Prophet, he supposed in advance, would be immune to cerebral fatigue. In contrast with ancient doctrines, he would not submit him to fakirism, nor to ascetic disciplines, to Christan fasting or Buddhist annihilation; he repudiated all emaciation of being for the sake of local faculties. Proceeding towards entire superiority, he made him increase his sensory power as a direct result of intellectual progress; he rejected Trials as illusory, destructive of a part of Being. The Prophet's harmonious ascension; his vascular and nervous systems followed the evolution of his brain, and it was in complete physical health that he came to live "in the field of action of all the ambient molecular forces" without ceasing to increase his concept of the infinite.

At the stage when—here Luc partially echoed his speculations regarding thought transmission and planetary physiology—the Prophet perceived carnally the intimacies of Substance, when he saw metamorphoses like those of light absorbed by the blackness of smoke, little by little a mental sense, not of the Universe entire but of the greater part of Our

Nebula,[28] increased, analyzed itself and then synthesized itself within him. Eventually, increasingly with every passing day, he felt that he was an atom in complete communication with the whole, succeeding in reflecting and condensing the essential phenomena of the Whole.

Then, transhumanized, he had within him, not a Voice, but the representation we attribute to an assembly of speaking sensations. For, indeed, in the Prophet's inner being, by virtue of an effort toward a new cerebral power, his life in the field of action of molecular forces becoming unified, he was becoming a creature listening to a symphony without paying particular attention to any of the instruments contributing to it, although he continued to hear them all...

Revelation originates in that. Profoundly moved, by virtue of the recital and the transformist prolegomena as well as the crepuscular anxiety in which the nerves command the brain, the mystic reader is ready to receive the Precepts. Vibrant with the spirit of modernity, selected from the highest sources, clad in enigma everywhere that they are not essential, their accord with the principles of the Era will cement the Tendency to Belief developed by the preceding chapters. Much simpler, in total, than at the outset of the revelation, they will not require complex Artistry, but will nevertheless necessitate an absolute tangibility, a faculty of infinitely subtle choice between the various moral conclusions drawn by contemporary philosophers. The maxims of the struggle for existence, spiritualized and socialized, will be recombined there with the charitable entities to which they can be reduced in the final analysis; the methods of the Positivist school, its rules of

---

[28] Rosny's use of the term "nebula" is consistently odd; rather than using it to describe star-clusters or clouds of gas, he uses it to mean the entire observable cosmos—which is, in his view, merely an exceedingly tiny fraction of the vastly greater collectivity that he was ultimately to call "the fourth universe."

research, will adapt themselves marvelously to the new religion's laws of Work and Solidarity.

That will be the termination of the Genesis. The Work of Propaganda will now begin. The Bible, printed and widely distributed, will run through the social strata with marvelous rapidity, the number of mystics transformed by the marvelous news being incalculable. And it is here, in consequence of the faculties of the very advanced comprehension and very advanced originality of the brain that will have conceived the Bible, that a series of complimentary conditions, rigorous but not impossible to unite in a single man of the Aryan race, will come into play.

Firstly, the man who has conceived the regenerative Religion will sacrifice himself, not assuming the role of Prophet, but that of propagator of the Bible. He will take every possible measure to establish the belief that the Revelator is dead. He will be endowed with faculties indispensable to the propaganda: oral authority, physical grace and especially—by nature and by virtue of very long and laborious study—unrivaled as a hypnotist. He will not disguise his hypnotic power, nor even his recourse to stimulant materials; he will not employ hypnotism as a miraculous element but as a physical and metaphysical demonstration. Finally, he will not be a Pauper; he must never soil himself, in word or in action, with any of the works of Edification or Organization undertaken by the Faithful. He will have no friends. He will live alone and will only appear on days of propaganda; he will refuse all debate as prejudicial to the dignity of his priesthood, having in any case posited, as a first principle, absolute Tolerance, and that the regenerative Religion is not a dogma of condemnation...

For a long time, Luc wandered through the labyrinth of this Dream. When the anemia of October arrived, he pursued it through the morning silences, standing in the bare fields at dawn, having taken refuge in some village of olden times. The frail beauty of browns, the exquisite death of enfeebled plants, the exodus of small creatures in the indefatigable navigation of clouds, abundantly nourished the images and Abstract sensa-

135

tions of his Conception. He experienced the life of the Prophet, the frisson of the faithful, the delightful dread of multitudes; he perceived the astonishment of the human race in the
tremulous expectation of a return of Youth, of a new Promise
in harmony with the Revelations of Science.

Then, he tired of it. In accordance with the fury of the
elements, the gallops of cyclones over hillsides, the supplica-
tions of forests, the lacerations of the firmament under the
claws of the Equinox, while the splendors of foliage died as
the twilight dies in collision with Shadow, his soul felt slightly
ashamed and regretful; it returned to the sincere charms of
actuality, to pure visions gathered from the rich humus of disinterest, exempt from the sickly vegetation of priesthood.

After the fevers of the Storm, in the final remnants of the
Sunlight, as November approached, when the cities of Branch
and Twig padded the buds of the future against the frost,
transmuting the last rays of sunlight into resistance, and the
universe of the infinitely small buried itself in warm cavities,
Luc revived the vertiginous hypotheses, the circumnavigations
of the archipelagos of Conjecture, until the return, in spring, of
the softening of grains, the haste of embryos devouring their
starch, projecting their roots into the realm of Darkness and
their stems into the heights, of the joys of the petal harvesting
its beauty in Light, of the creaking of vegetal blood in the tall
trees.

In the obscure and hesitant disturbance of those days, the
lucid Dreams vanished, the joy of young flesh caused seeds to
germinate in Luc as innocent and puerile as those of April,
and, with the flux and reflux of his arteries, his brain fell prey
to *obscure dreams*.

V. Obscure Dreams

1.

It is the crepuscular hour: its softness, its immensity, its formidable defervescence; it crumbles, descends into the abyss of carillons of color, into slow symphonies on the slender faces of prisms.

Soon, in a lower register, the vibrations darken, Orange weighing upon the collapsing depths. Then, for some time, the Red plaint, the suave and monotonous death-throes of the curved glow, the paling and vanishing of occidental streaks, the heavy crêpes of Purple and Ash-grey.

Then, the twinkling of Antares in the moonless opacity.

Then the brain, ceasing to vibrate in lucid labors, in a superabundance of sensuality, abandons the straight line of Consequence, the exhausting tension of directed Effort. In the august magnificence of contemplation, untroubled by logic, it accepts the impressions that surge forth, the Dreams without denouement, the beauty of Disorder, the breakage of the flux of Thought by the reflux of Instinct.

And these are the things that flow in the dark Room, the chromatic events of the Brain contemplated by the Brain!

2.

Sediment of Great Rivers, which the centuries refine, O, go back to your Point of Departure, when the Frost and Chemistry, and the impacts of the Storm and the efforts of the Lichen mortified the old mountain contemporary with the Secondary Ocean, whence emerged the Beasts of Fable: Pterodactyls with scaly wings, Iguanodons standing in the mire of marshes, lifting their jaws to the tops of tall trees.

Sediment, there was an era when the bare mountain, glacial and arid, seemed an offspring of Eternity, immobile for Eternity—but on the day when the primal snows melted, when the waters and glaciers hollow out the veins of the rock, Sedi-

137

ment, you began to descend in heavy blocks. Wedged into fissures, the torrent tormented you, and you had scarcely progressed a hundred cubits in a century when the marvelous Gothic spires of the summits began to sketch themselves, slender Steeples alternating with cavernous Pyramids. Sediment, you descended then in round pebbles, and then became the fine dust of sand, and finally you fertilized the plains and ran as far as the immeasurable depths...

O, rivulets and great rivers, symbols of the red fluid which carries the Sediment in our arteries and will fertilize the valleys of the Flesh and the ravines of the Encephalum, O, go back to your Point of Departure, when the Frost and Chemistry, and the impacts of the Storm and the efforts of the Lichen mortified the old mountain contemporary with the Cretaceous Ocean!

3.

Marsupials, in the Jurassic matrix, when the atmosphere still weighed so heavily and you appeared, timid and exceedingly humble among the dominant beasts...

The Reptiles had warmer arteries then, and those which advanced on to the promontories, and those which soared on their membranous wings, were the icings of a half-deaf and taciturn Creation. Crouched between the plantules,[29] the pressure of oxygen would only have to remain constant, Marsupials, and you would have remained timid and exceedingly humble debris of the animal register. The King of Creation, clad in scales, with the three-chambered heart, would doubt-

---

[29] Strictly speaking, the French word *plantule*, and its English equivalent, refer to a plant embryo, but Rosny subsequently couples the term with "animalcule" in a fashion that makes it clear that he is using it to refer to primitive plants, and I have taken the liberty of importing his improvised second meaning into English.

less have been some Reptile-Human, immensely tall and oviparous.

Ah, if the rocks had not drunk the atmosphere; if, in the lighter fluid, the blood of Saurians had not chilled their vanished wings and the colossi of their class had not died in the stagnating marshes, what would their world have become, and what subtleties, what variations of the pattern, what organic auxiliaries and corollaries, what languages and what labors, what weavings of forms would have been born of the Reptile-Human, with the three-chambered heart? What attitudes would he have imposed on matter, what metamorphoses on the terrestrial surface?

Oh, Marsupials, if you had not known the gentler pressure, your loins would never have elaborated our Ancestors, Dinotherium, Hipparion, Machaerodus, and the day would never have come when the Anthropoid emerged mysteriously from the bosom of the tall trees!

Marsupials, in the Jurassic matrix, when the atmosphere still weighed so heavily and you appeared, timid and exceedingly humble, among the dominant beasts!

4.

Do not imagine, Plum-Weevils, Vine-Beetles and you, Grain-Weevils, that the poem of your battle against Humankind does not move my soul. While your legions rise up in the mysteries of cereals and foliage, opposing the power of numbers and fecundity to the weapons of your ponderous adversary, I think of the subtleties of your series on organic algebra and my soul has never desired your annihilation more.

Grasshoppers, Crickets and Locusts, avid and rapidly-multiplying races, when the stridulations of your love rise up, my heart enters into the tumult and trembles with mercy. Oh, when the Dragonfly and the Mayfly rise up from the banks of ponds, or a cloud of Midges drift in the arborescent summits, or hordes of Gnats couple in their millions on warm evenings, or the armored Ground-Beetles emerge at the corners of paths, fraternity torments me, purifies and enchains me in the gulfs of Life, in the menstrual flow where animal Colonies flourished, Isidae, Gorgonians, Madrepores,[30] in the primitive time when the waves grew cold, where the lace of mother-cells floated in pale clouds and the troubled Energies confused Animalcules and Plantules.

Oh, my nerves soon remember those abysms of Genesis, my flesh whispers mysterious debuts, and everything in my higher self, in my sensitive fibres complicated by millions of years, comes back and narrates their effort to construct me: Hydras, Nostocs and Thallophytes, Colonial Polyps, Tube-worms and Saurians crouching in the terrestrial marshes.

Then, Plum-Weevils, Vine-Beetles and you, Grain-Weevils, and you, Locusts, Grasshoppers, Dragonflies on the banks of ponds, Gnats buzzing on warm evenings, resplendent warrior Ground-Beetles, I see you sketched in my bones and in my veins. Offspring of the same origins, formed by the same harmonious anastomoses, and the poem of your battle moves more intensely and more suavely, while your legions rise up in the mystery of cereals and foliage, opposing the power of numbers and fecundity to the weapons of your ponderous adversary!

5.

Great Dynamo rotating to the chaos of the wave, captivator of Forces whose subtle power runs along nerves of metal...

---

[30] These are all species of coral, although the names contain mythological echoes of which Rosny was doubtless conscious. I have generally followed a policy of using common names for the various creatures named in the prose-poem rather than Latin ones—although there is a much greater overlap between the two systems of nomenclature in French, because it is a Latin-derived language (which makes it much easier to distinguish different kinds of weevil, coral, and so on)—but I had no alternative but to retain Isidae.

Great Dynamo, through space along your frail conductors, here comes Life, and far from torrents, on the edges of Cities, the Wheels of the future are turning in silence and clarity, the Labors of the future whispering without exhausting the Artisan and without rusting his face. The horrible respiration of industrial monsters has vanished into Legend.

Great Dynamo, over Metropolitan pallor, your Hymn is euphonic; a natural Atmosphere strays over the walls, and if it is not yet bliss, here at least is purity; overly harsh famines abolished humankind is elevated in the vital hierarchy, a creature of brain and blood exonerated from muscular weariness.

The fevers of the Ocean and the wrath of the Abyss are your captives, Dynamo, and nourish you as much as the rays of the summer sun. From your rotating heart, slender veins extend through roofs and underground; and your supple force obeys the whim of accumulators, reducible to infinity, the slave of the humblest.

Great Dynamo rotating to the impacts of the wave, captivator of forces, whose subtle power runs along nerves of metal!

6.

Long after the death of the Sun, on the Earth roaming the cosmic darkness, a light greyness quivered, the nebulosity of an infinitesimal gleam. A timid vermilion floated, suspended from a vault, scattered in unreal powder, then became grey-green. Then it extended a beam of light, a thread of stellar Spider-silk, exceedingly long, and on that filament perched some kind of Apparition with wings: wings of primrose-yellow and nemophila-blue, which opened, trembled and closed again over centuries...

But as the wings paled, a metamorphosis occurred, into leaves of living paper, which persisted in opening, vibrating and closing, laying down through Infinity a library of delicate books. And they were the works of Humankind, extinct for billions of years; it was the vibration on the diaphanous Spid-

141

er-Silk of thoughts inscribed in the bowels of the Star by the metamorphoses of the Brains, which vanished into some nebula in genesis, and which began to nourish young Creations...

Then, in further centuries, punctuated by a soft comet appearing in vaults of ink, the greening of Space paled tenderly, in a symphony of lilac sown with snowdrops and beams of light, and the works of humankind faded away. Then, in the death-throes of nuances, a frightful multitude of white worms began to climb slowly up the mountains, the most distant microscopic, twisted by the summits, the nearest vast, like pale boa constrictors: exceedingly soft boas, horribly blind, with neither pupils nor orbits.

Then came the Frost again, eternal, and the eternal darkness, the Firmament on high strewn with the immutability of crystal stars, the fading away of all forms in the Immensity of Chaos, in the Immensity of Silence.

7.

There will be born, in the soul of the human elite, the horror that awakes in rare exquisite brains, the idea *that the chain of Being has been broken*. A prescience, instinctive today, reasoned tomorrow, will reveal how important it is that the ontological symphony conserves all its notes, and the peril stemming from an extermination of Genre, Species and Race. The terror is doubtless prophetic that thrillers in profoundly naturalistic individuals at the thought of an animality reduced to a minimum of types. It is the invasion of sterility: the certainty that the most adorable of our acquaintances, the gropings of the Eternal Artist, the genius of the infinitely delicate and the infinitely complex , the great poem of animal strophes, are threatened with absence.

In order that the elephant or the giraffe might perish before their time, or the great Arabic Lion, or the fascinating Beasts inhabiting the plateau and the forest, the Axis Deer, the Bison or the poor crepuscular long-eared bat, or the colossi of the Ocean and any shade-loving plantule it is necessary, without very long hesitation, that there should be religious attempts at preservation.

So, for the beasts useless as nourishment or in the service of humankind, Edens will be built. Calculated for all the inhabitants of the Earth, furnished with jungles or savannahs, brushwood or high forests, marshes, ponds, streams and heathlands, the poetic Beast and Plant, conserved *solely* for the sake of Art and Science, will live there in relative liberty and not in the horrible cloisters of our Sewers of Acclimatization.[31]

Thus, in spite of the abominable struggle for existence, the beauty of creation and the sentiment of ontological grandeur will never be lost to humankind; and uniquely created, on this principle, out of respect for the venerable Mother, perhaps, over the centuries, the Gardens of Eden, the Arks of the Industrial Deluge, will eventually become saviors from cataclysms, or at least such precious indicators of the very progress of Humankind that our disinterest will be rewarded a hundred times over.

8.

Subtle sensuality of humid weather, beatitudes of the Hydrophile, when the cracked lips of the glebe have drunk the Storm, when the pure wells open in the shredding of the clouds! The blanched tiny creatures strewing the Earth, the sweet flower of renewal opens, and the clothes of the Hydrophile acquire a marine viscosity, an ineffable freshness strays over his pupils, bringing a tremor to the brackish lichen of his

---

[31] The original purpose of modern botanical and zoological gardens—as opposed to mere menageries—was to investigate the practicalities of transplantation of crops and domestic animals for the purposes of colonization; several such projects were labelled *Jardins d'Acclimatation* [Acclimatization Gardens] in France. *Cloaques d'Acclimatation* [Sewers of Acclimatization] is, therefore, Rosny's unsympathetic characterization of zoos.

beard, and dips his soft leather shoes in the mire? Implacable, the blue Ether sets about drinking the moisture of the clay, and the Hydrophile gradually dries out, dries out and dies...

Subtle melancholy of arid weather, terror of the cracked lips awaiting the Storm, when the frightful firmament is denuded of clouds with palpitating edges! Will the moment return when the tiny creatures strewing the Earth, when the Hydrophile dips his soft leather shoes in the mire?

9.

The Spark! She has seized in her feeble grip the frail tip of a blade of grass. She launches forth, animating herself, overtaking the fearful gallop of hinds, surpassing the bounds of panthers in distress, the hectic wing-beats of wood-pigeons. She hummed at first like an insect buzzing above the branches, but her voice has amplified into a tempest, swelling the horizons, drowning out the breathless clamor of lions, elephants and zebras. She has seized everything in her enormous claws, she agitates the ashen purple of its tresses, devours ancient forests, crosses eternal rivers, fleeing with the wind, insatiable and destructive—she, the Creator!

She speaks, in her thunderous voice, in the sonorous bosom of the globe, she flows there, bearing away the fuliginous sulfurs, striking in resounding dust-clouds against the heavy walls, pupil of a hearth of thunderbolts, projecting prodigious lavas into the air, creating a growling fête at the summit of a mountain.

Gentler, a friend of life, she filters subtly through avid pores, penetrates particles, swells roots, incenses flowers. Luring in the pulp of fruits, guiding the pistil toward the stamen, ardent to complete the amorous pollens, dilating the hearts and circulating the red rivers, she is the delicate enchantment inexhaustible and merciful!

10

"Soul of things, whisper of the Expanse, when, on nights like this, the old hieratics constructed their adorable lies, did they glimpse Dynamos, Transmutation, Atoms and Luminous Oscillation? For me, the shadows remain, and god subsists in Force, and the disturbance of this darkness, the tremor of infancy, the aspiration of ecstasy in the dull contact of shadows, the Darkness in the depths of sensitivity!"

"Is the answer written in the margins of the Abyss rather than in a few atoms? If Egypt makes Astronomical Science sacred, if the herdsman becomes a priest, is an understanding of the delicate prescience of Genesis preferable to the hypnotism of Enormity on simple brains? Are not the laws that radiate through Space contained in a corpuscle floating on a tide, O, wailing of the Infant-Human, verse of the young Word inscribed in Bibles?"

"Are the harmonies seeking to weave the Beautiful, as the radiance of stars to weave worlds from the feeble light of empty space? Missal of the Petal, canticle of the amorous Beast, tremor of the Root, is your initial esthetic power surpassed, your feeble beacon flickering on the cliff?"

"Does uncertainty alone exist? Every day, though, adds an affirmation to affirmations acquired. The incalculable horizon of probabilities shrinks before certainty, a wholly charming clarity dissipates the ancient shadows. No, not doubt but science. Whoever seeks may find. *I seek*."

"Is it necessary to marvel at mystery and not distress oneself with analyses: the brutalization of things, the annihilation of social joys, opposing the serenity of a Dream? Is it necessary to animalize oneself to the sensualities that muffle renunciations, mineralize oneself in causeless scorn, and *wait*?"

"Ophiuchus, and you, Corona, and you, Capella, are you not the oil-drop of the Slide?[32] And must I still, in the abysm of Space, demand the fundamental Principle? Simply to continue, without tiring, always condemned to imperfection, always aspiring to perfection, moving forward, erring, losing myself continually...but persevering, no matter how tremulous the beacon is! The road has no end! It is necessary to refuse to sit down, in dark despair, because, for each stage covered, a tremor of joy follows, in spite of the fact that infinity still extends ahead! *I seek*."

11.

Your gropings, Planet, the sickly appearance of your Phenomena, the chaotic Destructions, the Negligences, the Ferocities, the Waste, the Injustice and the Inconsequence, bring forth, in indolent eras, the idea of some pupil of the Infinite, an Individual involved in nebular genesis to whom a parent or educator has given the problem of our corner of Space to resolve. Bent over our Universe, he slowly works upon it, and from the depths of his brain, the Theme has emerged, which he will vary according to inspirational phases. As the Duration and Logic of his actions are proportional to his power and longevity, however, as a Precession of Equinoxes is for him a drop in the timetable of billions of centuries, we promulgate *laws* in accordance with one page of his studies, the page that covers our igneous period (a sort of sketch and vague exordium) and our ontological period (a sort of narration by the sidereal Schoolboy, in which he attempts to move, hesitatingly, toward Order).

In spite of the vertiginous transcendence of such an Individual, however, in spite of the complication of his methods and their exhausting harmonies, we have already discovered

---

[32] The reference is to a microscope slide, on which preparations for examination were often contained within a drop of oil in the late 19th century.

146

the lacunae that make impossible for us the conception of a merciful or omnipotent God, which allow us to glimpse that the incommensurable brain leaning over us is merely *relative*. And by virtue of that, belief in Rules, in the reality of all Ideality as well as all Experience, flows away—and the end of Logic, the vanishment of all our laws will be some caprice of the Individual in posing the problem differently, to the extent that neither Chemistry, nor Physics, nor the courses of the Planets will any longer correspond to our poor formulas!

VI. Dispersal

1.

Luc fell ill. The existence of populations of tiny fibers was painfully disrupted. Less curious, they received life in a dream, forgetting to re-elaborate themselves. The blood went to sleep in such vessels; in their narrow vestibules, the nerves scarcely reacted to the environment. That caused his eyes to grow pale, hammer-blows in the left side of the skull, and his skin and hair to become dull.

That's very distinguished, Luc thought.

Indeed, it was an aristocratic condition of the entire system, the refusal of atomic artisans to work freely. The thousand collisions of Light, Scent and Sound seemed half-colored, like October mornings. Shape, anti-crystalline and flexible, acquired a vegetable slackness. Thought ploughed ahead with unrestricted expressions of tenderness, scarcely making contact, enemies of sensuality and noise.

That was at the outset, in the morning. Luc tottered from one item of furniture to another, sometimes sunk into an armchair, sometimes dragging himself along like a tortoise. His head, a trifle heavy on his neck, seemed to him to be his carapace.

These cerebral and sensory ramblings took firmer hold toward mid-day. Quite involuntarily, effortlessly, as if by a mechanical disposition, the preludes of the morning combined to recreate Luc's old state of ill-health, in a mnemonic process similar to that of a drunkard who can only find a hidden object while in a similar state of drunkenness. The weak joints and problems of articulation he had suffered in his sixth year reappeared, the hardness and excessive softness of a bed during bouts of malarial fever.

Delicate migraines revived, refined states of existence in which the dorsal spine and the chest attained the charm and melancholy of superhuman and plaintive organs. He also reverted to the days of dilated and tired pupils, when shapes and colors are gently monstrous and cruel. Oh, the torment of nature assailing a poor organism, the fluid, ferocious and angelic play of complementary colors and electrical potentials on morbid flesh, and senses slightly deviated to the right or left along planes of unknown polarization!

Above all, the memory reappeared of times when Luc grew too rapidly, when his arms weighed heavily upon his shoulders, or, after a short walk, he felt a weariness between his shoulder-blades. In those days he had lain down on the ground, stepping himself in complete sadness. At the slightest spring breeze he had felt cold.

The Universe seemed very long, very narrow and quite unsteady. He felt the fever in blades of grass, in his clothing, in the feathers in his pillow, and especially in the odor of water, the stirring of aquatic animals. On July evenings, he got up in the night, suffocating, and opened his window, to feel the fresh air on his naked body—but the coolness quickly became icy, and cold fever flowed over his horizon, over the trees in the orchard. If he covered himself up again then, the heat returned more ferociously, and the fever was as heavily warm as the vapor of a Turkish bath.

The night felt sharp, the croaking of the frogs was sharp, the stars were threatening, the perfume of the orchard injurious. He was afraid; he would have liked to hide but could not do it, for in a corner or underneath his bedclothes he was immediately overtaken by the black fear of asphyxia...

Melancholy scenes were intimately connected with these memories of adolescence:

The evening when his father died, the whisperings, the sound of doors, perhaps other things, all alerted him; a breath of horror shoved him out of his room and set him prowling along the stairs. Then, having seen his mother and the nurse come out, he went down on tiptoe, and went into the mysterious room. Someone had begun, and then stopped, dressing him; the cadaver lay half-naked, with a stony smile, the eyelids closed, the funereal arms folded across his broad chest, in the spectral flickering of candlelight. Luc fled outside, toward the corner of the sky in which the red crescent was descending.

Oh, the funereal grandeur of that night, the oscillation of the solitary heart, the information of sobbing, voices whispering in the meadow, and on the pale *shore of the sky, between two mounds, obsession with the* pale *bed, the* pale *candles, the* pale *cadaver. When he was weary and drained of strength, sitting in a corner of the path, for a long time he saw two eyelids lifting over the gleam of two dead eyes, for a long time he saw the dead man rising up on the horizon, the smile on the blue lips wandering amid the stars, the funereal arms folded over the bright breast of the Milky Way...*

Once, even as a human being, Luc had loved a certain corner of the earth, a sickly wrinkle on the face of Pan, so sad, so personal. Bushes tormented by necroses grew there, with anemic trunks, yellowed leaves and worm-eaten branches dying of ulcers. Alburnums with pitted bark and frightful vermin everywhere, cancers and vegetable farcies. Holed and tattered leaves, hordes of parasitic fungi, plaintive chloroses—and yet it was life, a painful effort in the midst of implacable fatality!

"How," Luc murmured, "in examining these memories of morbidity or heartbreak, which are so clear, can I avoid attributing to some enemy—some interval of semi-dyspepsia, some prolonged dazzle during weeks of divine toil—a creation of knowledge and poetry, to every order of malady or state of disequilibrium, a very particular development of the art of

149

metaphysics, a development that neither threatens nor is threatened by other factors if the disease passes a certain level of oscillation? The ecstasy of imagining little cells laboring in the depths of the organism! The condensers and minuscule piles, at every deformation, continually inducing the passing blood and forcing the deposition of certain basic or acidic atoms, according to whether the lesion affects a positive or negative form! Even in the most inorganic corners, the aggregations are minimally affected by the precise idiosyncrasy of the disease. In the nervous and vascular centers, there is not only the aggregation, the synthetic architecture of the edifice, but a torsion of every atom—a modification that will, perhaps, subsist!"

2.

For several days the illness remained composed by slight migraines and Luc's joints still echoed the fragility and cramps of a growing and malnourished adolescent: a slight anguish in the hips, an uncertainty in the vertebrae, the taste of fruit and shellfish. When he had stretched out or curled up for a quarter of an hour in the depths of his rocking-chair, it seemed when he got up that his sensitivity was cured. The atmosphere became charged with delight. Then, pain in the lower back, moistness in the palms, and every hair distilling a bead of sweat at its root. At the same time, a mercurial glow, with a sort of grey-green tint, settled over everything.

Luc felt that his connecting nerves were losing their equilibrium, furnishing contradictory thermal currents with disharmonic extensions and contractions of his muscles. He tottered, he was exceedingly miserable, but delights and etherizations of his flesh consoled him, like summer breezes on an arid plateau.

"What is it that the atoms are creating?"

In that curiosity, he thought he could perceive the arrival of currents of pain in the encephalum: this one a depressor of energies; this one an awakener of old ideas torpid beneath the

150

strata of the grey matter; this one a confuser of logic, this other a provoker of prescience, together producing some sonorous phenomenon and some luminous phenomenon which would otherwise never have been fused; this one discovering confused analogies; this one predisposing the cells to adopt a perception of the external world impossible in any other state of equilibrium.

A mystery equal—and superior, in its delicacy—to that of a monk dreaming of spirits and angels, which transported Luc into the utmost depths of matter and force, where human flesh is, so far as we are concerned, the maximum of complication.

Slumped in his chair again, his heartbeat accelerated, its jolts torturing him, he persevered nonetheless in pursuing his dream of panmetamorphosis—except that, weary of imagining magnetic currents and molecular evolutions, he preferred to observe the passage of impressions:

Violet colored patches float above the floor like raindrops, eventually uniting in a sheet. The sheet quivers like a fluid in the wind, then like a gulf from which an amber vapor is rising. Then the sheet or gulf is clarified, transmuted into pale sulfur-yellows and indecisive off-whites. Winglets appear, in billions, tremulous columns of tiny insects flying above the pale and dark patches.

Luc murmurs: "The violet transforming itself into yellow, and the black into white, is the physical play of complementarities...but I'm evidently deceived, and it's no longer my illness that is evoking these trichoceres, but the simple memory that, in the family of *Tipula*,[33] the columns of some species like to float over white surfaces, and others over black

---

[33] *Tipula* is a *genus* of water-spiders. The term trichocere is normally applied to a kind of cactus with hairy spines, which might seem somewhat reminiscent of a spider to a confused individual, but it is compounded out of Greek terms for "hair" and "wax" and Luc may well be using the term more generally.

surfaces, by virtue of the profound philosophy of *preferences*, against which our abstract logic struggles eternally."

Forms circulate before him, rising up and descending in curved trajectories, without relief, painted on empty space like Assyrian symbols on stone. He ends up discovering their regular movement in the quivering of an agitated weather-vane on a roof facing him, which, set before the Sun, is casting its shadow on the window-sill.

For other phenomena, metallic noises, tapping noises, sudden whiffs of odors not present in his surroundings, insipid tastes on his tongue, he can find no immediate application, but he takes note of them anyway, hoping to discover therein the psychology of his illness.

3.

Luc's suffering grew worse.

Fruits and shellfish became repulsive to him, then even the slight perfume of lime and orange, and the taste of sugar. He wished for tastelessness and odorlessness, a clear atmosphere devoid of sunlight, the immobility of the landscape. The pallor of his face became earthen, his back became weaker, breaking out in sweat at the slightest movement.

Luc felt a part of what he had originally been disappearing—something delicate and refined. His sluggishness, his slow, painful respiration, the feverish taste in his mouth, were remaking his substance, a diseased dynamic as forceful as full health. The electric flux, at first gently disturbing, was transformed into the gross charges and discharges of poles and condensers. Congestions were perpetually warming some part of his body, chills appearing in others, then, abruptly, a boiling sensation, a great equilibrating effort that made his heart and spine shiver.

Through this distress, however, Luc persisted in interrogating his brain, in observing the history of these crises and drawing it out of very distant and infinitesimal phenomena. It was a time of great hope and great despair, the immersion of his soul in more ardent invocations of the mystery of forces. The earliest times of his scientific life reappeared, when he had hoped to reform laws, construct a new theory of the Universe, discover the essential nature of things. He saw once again his immature theoretical book, the vague immensity of formulas, the peremptory tone of demonstrations. As the stages of his fever progressed, the smile that these memories brought forth transformed itself into a return of certainty, a reinflation of the soul. He thought then that, perhaps, with a little more meditation and a little more patience, those large hopes might be resolved, revealing the reformation of universal theories to him. He forgot his delicate work, his work on physiologized physics, on extrasubtle chemistry, the illness beginning to rob him of the supreme qualities of his being.

The stages of the disease continue to progress. From sluggishness and dullness he progressed to intoxication. After long writhings a drastic increase in temperature occurred, his periphery shivering, his skin livid and glacial, the roots of his hair coming out while hot flushes ran beneath the dermis. His eyes bulging, his breath harsh and gasping, his teeth clenching in vain, and chattering, Luc imagined himself prey to an organic phenomenon analogous to the spheroidal state.

Then came all the phenomena provoking chills: radiation, evaporation, chemical mixtures swelling in abscesses where the nerves and human blood capable of dividing temperature into zones, according to the direction of vibration, according to positive and negative undulations, were refined into mere torsions and relaxations.

Soon, the increased chill imposed an impression of Crypts on his poor flagellated body, a glacial and violent intoxication and an insatiable thirst, and delirium displayed him to himself as a symbol of the Earth. In the same way that his health was like a fine season in which the surface is mild and warm, and a slight illness like the anemia of days when vegetation perishes, now he was a wintry symbol, a surface of ice extending through space while the terrestrial bosom heats up and broods, volcanoes rumbling beneath the glacier snows.

This was no longer, for him, some allegory but a sharp truth, almost the certainty that a human being, not only in the brain but throughout the body, is an imitation and reduction of his habitat, reflecting the phases of the planet moving through space.

In consequence of these crises, he was afflicted by a fear and an immense desire for full health, the combination of which brought back all the periods in which he adored movement, especially certain extreme scenes that marked the summits of his corporeal life, like these:

Over the plateaus of his homeland, where the vegetation is hard and slow, in the black declivities through which glacial waters flow, the light body of twenty-year-old Luc bounded untiringly. An entire winter of ancestral shadows awoke within him, making his soul bellicose, eager to brave perils. He went up, therefore, to the crests where the glacial snows are treacherous; he filled his arteries with magnetic blood; he stung his flesh with nocturnal storms and precipitated himself, naked, into icy torrents. His hair grew over his shoulders, the fire of the Sicambri[34] lit up in his pupils; he lived with the spirit of the forests, the rude psyche of meadows, the dialogues of caverns; the alacrity of his muscles made up for their slenderness.

Now, through the pride of age, through the labyrinths of his studious life, he had retained from that epoch a barbarous pride in the following incident. In the middle of a gorge in that Realm there was a ledge jutting out toward the other edge, leaving a gap of about 20 meters. At the thought of jumping across it, Luc experienced a frisson, perhaps an instinctive memory of an ancestral herdsman who had attempted the adventure. One morning when cirrus clouds were chilling the firmament, and an angry wind bounded toward the Sun, with

---

[34] The Sicambri (*Sicambres* in French) were a Germanic tribe; they have a particular relevance in French history because St. Remy, in baptizing Clovis, the first of the Merovingian kings of the Franks, designated him as a member of that tribe.

the intoxication of the cold and the vertigo of the snow at his temples, Luc marched toward the Realm. When he got there, he stepped back to prepare for the jump, bracing his slender calves. He set off in a rush, and reached the ledge. There, standing over the abyss, as his heart thrilled with delight, the cry of victorious nomads, the cry of massive warrior spirits rose to his lips; he would never forget the profound joy of it, the sensation of spending animality...

One day, he wandered for 12 hours among oak trees. The leaves silently filtered the rays of sunlight. Humble, in the moist bosom of the Mother, the cryptogams were borrowing the shade. Luc sat down, and at first his heart beat rapidly, following labor with inertia. Then a gentle weight, in accord with the susurrus of foliage, and a subtle light between his meninges, warm and pale and his bones becoming fluid, his forehead dipped and his flesh took on the unconsciousness of plants...

Meanwhile, through the filtering branches, a kind of speech fell upon him, an insinuating breath lifted up his hair. The Earth had moved on, the forest plunged into its nocturnal cone. A window opened above Luc's head, framed with trembling lace, in the wall of an oak. Through it slid a sidereal traveler, a pink Arcturian arrow, pure and fresh, after such a peregrination through the Expanse! All around, the opaque wood was traversed by a faint vegetable phosphorescence. A psalm wept on the branchiate cords, the twisted boles, the silky cymbals of the leaves.

Luc walked on, sometimes bumping into trees, hatching a thousand little active, palpitating dreams, amorously mingled with the roots of his hair. His blood traveled, vividly red, from his breast to his brain, alimenting his being; the divine tenebrous forest was like an incarnation of his nervous system, a syllabication of Pan, evocative of hamadryads...

The things that inhabit us and wish to live, the atoms that sigh the canticle of Love, rose up one morning all together, growling in Luc's breast. The orchard was displaying its spring Greenery, the petals of the great Sacrifice, the snows of germination and the tips of branches everywhere. Harmonious pollens were flying in the Light, the male birds singing their triumphant battle-songs, the rivers bearing ovules, and the old earth was trembling with the laughter of sunlight. Then, Luc went out beneath the stamens, into sunken paths where the nave of hedgerows concealed adventures, and met *the other*.

Little virgin, he knows the cashmeres of your throat, your confidence like the whispers of rivers, your grace shaped by myriads of human generations, your hair spun on the wheel of the ages, the threats of your sex-appeal; he has no fear of Death, of long months attentive to the folds of your dress, the slave of your gestures.

He submits to you until the end of May, when the manifold arborescence grows heavy, when the beetles are more dazzling on the undersides of corollas, when the light feet of the breeze settle on the edges of storm-clouds, on the crests of precipices, when the litanies of Eros drift, and the growling fluids of the Earth espouse those of the Firmament, generating the rapid rains, fabricators of incense and intoxication!

The fevers eased; an extreme debility of the muscles succeeded them. In Luc's brain, after the gross turbulence of the malady, there was calm, but also a diminution of intellectual vitality. Reduced to thoughts of a secondary order, he descended further into infancy. Soon, impressions of the age of the desert island held exclusive sway in his brain.

He forgot his scientific preoccupations, or, rather, retained only the elements that he had possessed when he had dreamed of Rafts, Voyages and Oases. If, sometimes, fragments of complex problems still haunted him, he was almost immediately wearied by them. Shreds of his memory tore away like the bark from the trunks of plane-trees. The world appeared to him as a simple mystery, the marvels of which were as they should be, and the blessings and sadnesses of which existed without motive and without measure.

It seemed that the elegance and distinction of the early phase of the malady returned then, but thinner in complexity. He resavored the timid awakenings of the charming young dreamer that Luc had been at the age of ten, amorous of shelter amid moist vegetation, kind to the frogs that fled from the edges of fountains, not inclined to "material appropriation," and thus ignorant of the ferocious joys of little owners of insects and fledglings.

On his frail legs, he thought himself as nimble as a kid goat in the jutting edges of ruins, discovering the secrets of jackdaws or, silently and patiently observing the mysteries of widgeons and the rustling of gorse. A religious veneration caused his hair to bristle when, in the woods, the gentle royal herbivore with the antlered forehead passed by with his troop of hinds, and all those tawny bodies, candid eyes and slender feet symbolized for him the angelic quality of forests.

Soon, however, Luc descended even further into childhood. He was the little creature roaming from room to room, the collector of rags and debris in niches similar to those of thieving magpies, the stammerer sitting in the laps of those who like frail children; his brain as half-empty, but infinitely laborious and curious, about a thousand locked rooms, all admirably disposed to receive visitors. Oh, the endless labor in the suppleness of chairs, the arrival of the first ideas, like the invasion of a virgin territory by immigrants! As in the wilderness, as in the forests of a conquered continent, in the child of the Aryan race the fertile humus, the alluvion full of potential, is ready for the labor of populations, little immigrant ideas that the environment attracts in multitudes. In the same way, though, that an evening twilight is symmetrical with a morning twilight, but whose gradations descend into the gulf instead of rising from it, so that infantile re-existence was lived inversely, from the complex to the simple, from speech to mime, from sentences to words, moving towards a period of mutism, toward sensation without terminology, embryonic thought—visual, tactile and odorant—without shape and nameless.

In that singular collapse of his being, however, reactions persisted: recurrences of active thought, virile and complex but as transient as the attempts of certain plants can be to flower again in the autumn. In sum, his being simplified itself chromatically, so that he only experienced fleeting terrors once the full-blown fevers were past, and he was only aware of his decline during his very rare returns of adult memory.

On the day when his memory was stripped of words, however, when his vocabulary sank into the darkness of Un-consciousness, when he was no longer any more than a scarce-ly-thinking individual traversed by vegetative circulations, all sadness was erased from his life.

When he became a newborn infant, however, when his pupils drank the light as mountains drink clouds, when his ears vibrated to sounds as bays to the breeze, was there not still a great soul within him, a superior personality, like an adorable beauty in the depths of the Earth, like some fossil fern dead for hundreds of millions of years?

His individuality, for those who watched over him, seemed, in its mutism, suave, gentle and manageable, his smile exquisite, even when he degenerated further, when he descended further than infancy, when he recapitulated the epoch in which he was growing in his mother's womb, then that in which he was formed by the contact of the generative animalcules, then the infinite periods in which the encounters of individuals slowly united the ovules from which he would be born—and it was in that surge, in the division extended to infinity, in the passage upstream toward geneses, one morning, when the first greyness tinted the west-facing windows, that Luc, without a sigh or a start, dispersed.

ANOTHER WORLD

To Anatole France

I.

I am a native of Gelderland. Our patrimony was reduced to a few acres of heath-land and stagnant water. Pines that made a metallic sound as they quivered were growing on its borders. The farmhouse only had a few habitable rooms, and was falling apart, stone by stone, in isolation. We were an old family of herdsmen, once numerous but now reduced to my parents, my sister and myself.

My destiny, bleak at the outset, has become the finest imaginable; I have met someone who understands me; he will learn that which only I knew before—but I have been suffering for a long time. I was in despair, prey to doubt and loneliness, which ended up eroding everything of which I was once certain.

I came into the world with a unique constitution. From the very beginning, I was an object of astonishment. Not that I seemed deformed; I am told that I was more graceful in body and face than is usual in the newly born—but I had the most extraordinary skin color: a kind of pale violet, very pale but quite distinct. By lamplight, especially that of oil-lamps, that tint paled further, becoming a peculiar off-white, like that of a lily submerged in water. That was, at least, how I appeared to other people—for I saw myself differently, as I saw everything in the world differently. To that first peculiarity others were added, which were revealed in due course.

Although born apparently healthy, my development was difficult. I was thin and cried incessantly; at the age of eight months, I had not yet been seen to smile. My parents despaired of my ever growing up. The doctor in Zwartendam declared that I was suffering from a congenital weakness; he saw no other remedy but rigorous hygiene. I continued nonetheless to grow weaker; I was expected to perish at any moment. My father, I believe had resigned himself to it, somewhat dented in his self-respect—his Dutch pride in order and regularity— by his infant's bizarre appearance. My mother, by contrast, loved me all the more for my strangeness, having ended up finding the color of my skin pleasant.

That was how things stood when a very simple occurrence came to my rescue; as everything concerning me was abnormal, though, the event was a cause of scandal and apprehension.

When one of the servants left, she was replaced by a vigorous Friesian girl, very hard-working and honest but inclined to drink. I was confided to the newcomer. Seeing that I was so weak, she took it into her head to give me, secretly, a little beer and water mixed with *schiedam*—a sovereign remedy, in her opinion, against all ills.

The curious thing is that I was not long delayed in recovering my strength, and showed thereafter an extraordinary predilection for alcohol. The young woman rejoiced secretly, not without taking some pleasure in puzzling my parents and the doctor. Under interrogation, however, she ended up revealing the secret. My father was extremely angry; the doctor railed against superstition and ignorance. Strict orders were given to the servants and I was removed from the Friesian woman's care.

I began to grow thinner and weaker again, until, heedless of everything but her affection, my mother put me back on a diet of beer and *schiedam*. I immediately recovered my vigor and vivacity. The experiment was conclusive; alcohol was revealed to be indispensable to my health. My father felt humiliated; the doctor got himself out it by prescribing tonic wines. Since then, my health has been excellent, although no one hesitated to predict a future of drunkenness and debauchery.

Shortly after this incident, a further anomaly was observed by those around me. My eyes, which had seemed normal to begin with, became strangely opaque, acquiring a horny texture like the wing-cases of certain beetles. The doctor predicted that I would lose my sight, but confessed nevertheless that the ailment seemed absolutely bizarre, and that he had never had an opportunity to study one like it. Soon, the pupil was so confused with the iris that it was impossible to distinguish between them. It was noticed, in addition, that I could look directly at the Sun without any discomfort. In truth, I was not blind at all, and it had to be admitted eventually that I could see perfectly well.

I reached the age of three. According to our neighbors, I was then a little monster. The violet color of my skin had hardly changed; my eyes were completely opaque. I spoke badly, with incredible rapidity. I was clever with my hands and well-adapted for all actions that demanded more agility than strength. No one denied that I would have been graceful and good-looking if I my skin color had been natural and my pupils transparent. I showed intelligence, but with gaps that those around me could not fathom, inasmuch as, save for my mother and the Friesian woman, no one liked me very much. To strangers, I was an object of curiosity, and to my father a constant thorn in his side.

At any rate, if my father had conserved any hope of seeing me revert to normality, time certainly disabused him. I became increasingly strange, in my tastes, my habits and my abilities. At six, I nourished myself almost entirely on alcohol, only rarely eating a few mouthfuls of fruit and vegetables. I grew with prodigious rapidity, but I was incredibly thin and light. I mean "light" in terms of specific gravity, which is the opposite of thinness; thus, I could swim without the slightest difficulty, floating like a plank of poplar-wood. My head was no more inclined to sink than the rest of my body.

I was as nimble as I was light. I could run as fast as a roe deer, easily jumping ditches and obstacles that no other man would even have tried to jump. I could reach the top of a beech-tree in the blink of an eye, or—which was even more surprising—leap on to the roof of our farmhouse. On the other hand, the slightest burden was too much for me.

All these things, in sum, were merely phenomena indicative of a special nature, which, in themselves, would only have served to single me out and make me unwelcome; no one would have classified me as other than human. I was undoubtedly a monster, but certainly not to the extent of people born with horns or animal ears, the head of a calf or a horse, fins, devoid of eyes or with a supplementary eye, four arms, four legs or devoid of arms or legs. My skin, despite its unusual tint, was not so very different from sun-tanned skin; my eyes were not repulsive in spite of their opacity. My extreme agility was a talent. My need for alcohol could pass for a mere vice, a hereditary addiction—the country folk, in any case, like our Friesian housemaid, only saw it as a confirmation of their ideas regarding the "power" of *schiedam*, a slightly exaggerated demonstration of the excellence of their tastes. As for the rapidity and volubility of my speech, which was impossible to follow, that seemed little different from faults of pronunciation—stammering, lisping and stuttering—common to many young children. I did not, therefore, have any marked characteristics of monstrosity, even though the ensemble was extraordinary. The most curious aspect of my nature was invisible to those around me: no one was aware that my vision was strangely different from normal vision.

Although I saw some things less well than other people, I could see a great many that no one else saw. That difference manifested itself most obviously in colors. Everything that other people called red, orange, yellow, green, blue and indigo appeared to me as varying shades of darkness, while I perceived violet, and a series of colors beyond that—colors that were nothing but darkness to normal people. I eventually realized that I am able to distinguish 15 colors as dissimilar as, for instance, yellow and green—with infinite gradations, of course.

Furthermore, transparency does not manifest to my eyes in ordinary conditions. I can only see poorly through a window or through water; glass, for me, is brightly colored; water noticeably so, even when very shallow. Many crystals said to be clear are more or less opaque; by contrast, a large number of substances called opaque do not inhibit my vision. In general, I can see through far more substances than you can, and translucency—modified transparency—is so often present that I can say that, for my eyes, it is the general rule of nature, while complete opacity is the exception. Thus, I can discern objects through wood, foliage, the petals of flowers, magnetized iron, coal and so on. At a variable thickness, however, these substances—such as a stout tree-trunk, water a meter deep, a large lump of coal or quartz—become obstacles.

Gold, platinum and mercury are black and opaque; ice is quite dark. Air and water vapor are transparent, but colored, as are certain kinds of steel and very pure clay. Clouds do not prevent me from seeing the Sun or the stars, although I can clearly distinguish those same clouds suspended in the atmosphere.

This difference between my vision and that of other people, as I have said, went largely unnoticed by those around me; they simply thought that I was color-blind—which is too common an infirmity to attract much attention. It was inconsequential for the meager activities of my everyday life, for I saw the shapes of objects in the same fashion—and perhaps more subtly—as the majority of people. The designation of an object by its color, when it was necessary to distinguish it from another object of the same shape, only caused me difficulty if they were unfamiliar. If someone called the color of one waistcoat *blue*, and that of another *red*, it scarcely mattered what color the waistcoats seemed to me to be; *blue* and *red* became purely mnemonic terms.

163

Given that, you might think that there was some sort of correspondence between my colors and those of others, and that it amounted to the same thing as my being able to see their colors, but as I have already said, red, green, yellow, blue, and so on, when pure—as the colors of the prism are—I perceived as shades of darkness; they were not colors to me. In nature, where no color is simple, it is not the same; one substance called green, for example, is for me a certain composite color,[35] while another substance called green—which is an identical shade so far as you are concerned—is by no means the same color to me. You can see, therefore, that my scale of colors has no correspondence with yours; when I consent to call both brass and gold "yellow," it is rather as if you were consenting to call a cornflower "red" as well as a poppy.

II.

If the difference between my vision and normal vision stopped there, it would be extraordinary enough, to be sure. That is very little, however, compared to what I still have to tell you. The different coloration, transparency and opacity of the world; the ability to see through clouds, to see the stars on the most overcast nights, to see through a wooden partition-wall what is happening in the next room or outside a house—what is all that compared with the perception of a *living world*, a world of animate creatures moving alongside and around human beings, without humans being aware of it, without them being alerted by any kind of immediate contact?

What is all that, compared with the revelation that there exists on this Earth a fauna other than our fauna, and a fauna with no resemblance to ours in its form, its organization, its

---

[35] Rosny's narrator inserts a footnote: "And that composite color, of course, does not include green, since green is darkness to me."

mores, or its manner of growth, birth and death? A fauna that lives alongside and in the midst of ours, influencing and influenced by the elements that surround us, nourished by those elements, without our suspecting its presence. A fauna which—as I have proved—is as ignorant of us as we are of it, as insensible to our movements as we are insensible to its movements. A living world, as varied as ours, as powerful as ours—perhaps more so—in its effects on the planet's surface! A kingdom, in sum, extended over land and sea and in the atmosphere, modifying that land, sea and atmosphere in fashions very different from ours but with a very formidable energy—and, by virtue of that, indirectly influencing us, and our destinies!

This, however, is what I—alone among men and animals—have seen; this is what I have *studied*, ardently, for five years, after having spent my childhood and adolescence merely *observing* it.

III.

Observing it! For as long as I can remember, I have been instinctively subject to the seduction of that creation, foreign to our own. At first, I confused it with other living things. Perceiving that no one was troubled by its presence—that everyone, on the contrary, seemed indifferent to it—I scarcely felt any need to point out its peculiarities. At the age of six, I was perfectly conscious of its distinction from the plants in the field, the animals in the farmyard and the stables, but I still confused it slightly with inert phenomena like fire and light, running water and clouds. That was because these creatures were intangible; when they touched me, I did not experience any effect of their contact. Besides, their forms, although very various, had the singularity of being so thin in one of their three dimensions that they were comparable to moving drawings, surfaces and geometric lines. They passed through all organic matter; on the other hand, they sometimes seemed to be halted or hampered by invisible obstacles...but I shall describe them later. For the present, I only want to call attention to them, to affirm their variety in shape and size, their near-absence of thickness and their impalpability, in combination with the autonomy of their movements.

By the time I was eight years old, I was perfectly able to distinguish them from atmospheric phenomena as well as the animals of our kingdom. In the excitement that this discovery gave me, I tried to communicate it, but I was never able to succeed. Apart from the fact that my speech was almost completely incomprehensible, as I have said, the extraordinary nature of my vision rendered it suspect. No one took the trouble to interpret my words and gestures, nor was anyone ready to admit that I could see through wooden partitions, even though I gave proof of it many times over. Between me and other people there was an almost-insurmountable barrier.

I became discouraged and took to daydreaming; I became a sort of young recluse; I provoked unease in the company of children of my own age, and was aware of it. I was not exactly a ready-made victim, for my agility put me out of range of infantile malice and gave me a means of avenging myself easily. At the slightest threat, I was far away, mocking any pursuit. No matter how many of them there were, mischief-makers never succeeded in surrounding me, much less in taking hold of me. There was no point in even trying to catch me by trickery. Although too weak to carry any load, my agility was irresistible, freeing me immediately. I could return unexpectedly, and crush my adversary—adversaries, even—with rapid and well-aimed blows. I was, therefore, left in peace. I was taken for both an innocent and something of a magician—but a magician of an unintimidating sort, who could be treated with scorn. By degrees I cultivated an outdoor life, wild and meditative, but not devoid of gentleness. The only humanizing influence I had was my mother's affection, although, being busy all day long, she found little time for caresses.

I shall try to describe, briefly, a few scenes from my tenth year in order to make the preceding explanations more concrete.

It is morning. Broad daylight illuminates the kitchen—a pale yellow glow for my parents and the servants, very various for me. Breakfast is being served, bread and tea—but I don't drink tea. I've been given a glass of *schiedam* and a boiled egg. My mother is taking care of me, affectionately; my father is asking me questions. I try to answer him, slowing down my speech; he only understands the occasional syllable, and shrugs his shoulders.

"He'll never be able to talk!"

My mother looks at me compassionately, convinced that I am a little simple-minded. The domestics and farmhands are no longer even curious about the little violet monster; the Friesian woman returned to her homeland some time ago. As for my sister, who is two years old, she is playing beside me, and I have a profound affection for her.

When breakfast is over, my father goes off to the fields with the farmhands, and my mother makes a start on her daily chores. I follow her into the farmyard. The animals come to her. I watch them with interest; I like them. The other Kingdom is, however, moving all around us, and captivates me more; it is a mysterious domain known to me alone.

A few forms are extended over the brown earth; they move, they stop, they vibrate at ground level. There are several sorts, different in shape, in their movement, and especially in the arrangement, design and color of the linear features they display. These features constitute, in fact, the major part of their being; even as a child, I can take account of them very well. While the bulk of their form is dull and dark, the lines are almost always sparkling. They form exceedingly complicated networks, emanating from centers, radiating outwards until they become blurred and fade away. Their hues are innumerable, their cures infinite; those shades vary even in a single line—as, to a lesser extent, does their form.

As a whole, each creature is made up of a somewhat irregular but quite distinct border, by centers of radiation, and by multicolored lines that intersect profusely. When it moves, the lines quiver and oscillate, and the centers contract and dilate, while the outline scarcely varies.

All this I can already see quite well, although I am incapable of defining it; an adorable charm possesses me as I contemplate the Moedigen.[36] One of them, a colossus ten meters long and almost as broad, passes slowly through the farmyard and disappears. That one, with a few stripes as broad as cables and centers as large as an eagle's wing, interests me greatly, and almost frightens me. I consider following it momentarily, but others attract my attention. They are very various in size; some do not exceed the length of our smallest insects, while I have seen others more than 30 meters long. They advance over the surface of the ground, as if solidly attached to it. When a material object—a wall or a house—presents itself, they move over it by molding themselves to its surface, always without any significant modification of their shape—but when the obstacle is living matter, or matter that was once alive, they pass directly through it. Thus, I have seen them a thousand times over emerging from a tree, or beneath the feet of an animal or a man. They can also pass through water, but prefer to remain on its surface.

These terrestrial Moedigen are not the only intangible beings. There is an aerial population of a marvelous splendor, subtlety and variety, incomparably spectacular, compared with which the most beautiful birds are dull, slow and ponderous. Here too, there is an outline and linear features, but the back-

---

[36] Rosny's narrator inserts a footnote: "This is the name that I gave them, spontaneously, during my childhood, and which they have retained, although it does not correspond to any attribute or form of the creatures in question." *Moedigen* is the plural of *moedig*, which signifies "brave" in Dutch.

ground is not dark; it is strangely luminous, sparkling like sunlight, and the lines stand out as vibrant veins, the centers throbbing violently. The Vuren,[37] as I call them, are more ir-regular in form than the terrestrial Moedigen, and generally navigate with the aid of rhythmic dispositions, increases and decreases of which, in my ignorance, I cannot keep track, and which confuse my imagination.

Meanwhile, I am making my way through a recently-mown meadow; a conflict between one Moedig and another attracts my attention. These conflicts are frequent; they inter-est me passionately. Sometimes, there is a battle between equals; more often, a strong individual attacks a weak one—the weaker one is not necessarily the smaller. In the present instance, the weaker, after a brief defense, is put to flight, hot-ly pursued by the aggressor. In spite of the speed at which they are traveling, I follow them and contrive not to lose sight of them before the moment when the fight is resumed. They hurl themselves at one another, solid to one another—hard, even rigid. As they collide, their lines glow, heading toward the point of impact, their centers fade and shrink.

At first, the struggle is fairly equal, the weaker one dep-loying the more intense energy, even succeeding in forcing a truce from its enemy. It takes advantage of that to flee again, but is rapidly overtaken, forcefully attacked and finally gripped—which is to say, maintained in an indentation in the other's outline. That is exactly what it was trying to avoid, in responding to the stronger one's thrusts with less forceful but more rapid thrusts of its own. Now, I can see all its lines shi-vering and its centers throbbing desperately. Gradually, the lines fade and thin out, the centers blurring. After a few mi-nutes, it is set free; it draws away slowly, dull and debilitated. Its antagonist, by contrast, is gleaming more brightly; its lines are more colourful, its centers clearer and more active.

The battle has impressed me profoundly; I think about it, comparing it to the contests I have seen between our animals

---

[37] *Vuren* is the plural of *vuur*, which signifies "fire" in Dutch.

and their smaller kin; I am vaguely aware that the Moedigen, on the whole, do not kill one another—or very rarely—and that victors are content to *absorb strength* at the expense of the vanquished.

The morning wears on; it is nearly 8 a.m.; the school at Zwartendam is about to open. I run back to the farm to get my books—and here I am among my peers, none of whom is aware of the profound mysteries that are happening around them, and none of whom has the vaguest idea of the living creatures through which all human beings pass, and which pass through human beings, without any indication of that mutual penetration.

I am a very poor student. My handwriting is no more than a hasty scrawl, formless and illegible; my speech remains incomprehensible; my distraction is manifest. The master continually shouts: "Karel Ondereet, have you finished watching the airborne flies yet?"

Alas, my dear master, it's true that I watch the airborne flies, but how much more interested I am in the mysterious Vuren passing through the room! And what strange sentiments obsess my childish soul in observing everyone's blindness—especially yours, earnest shepherd of minds!

V.

The most painful phase of my life was between the ages of 12 and 18. Initially, my parents tried to send me to secondary school; I found nothing there but misery and frustration.

At the cost of exhausting labor, I succeeded in expressing the most commonplace things in a vaguely comprehensible fashion. Slowing my speech down considerably, I enunciated the syllables awkwardly and with the intonation of the deaf. As soon as anything complicated came up, though, my speech resumed its fatal speed, and no one could any longer follow what I was saying, so I could not make my progress manifest orally.

On the other hand, my handwriting was atrocious; my letters sprawled over one another and, in my impatience, I omitted syllables and whole words; it was monstrous gibberish. In any case, to me, writing was a torture perhaps even more intolerable than speech, of an asphyxiating ponderousness and slowness. If, sometimes, by dint of effort and much sweat, I succeeded in starting an assignment, I soon ran out of strength and patience and felt faint. Then I preferred my masters' remonstrations and my father's fury, punishments and privations to the horrid labor.

I was, therefore, almost totally deprived of means of expression; already an object of ridicule because of my thinness and bizarre complexion, and my strange eyes, I was also taken for some kind of idiot. It was necessary to take me out of school, and become resigned to making me a farm-laborer.

On the day when my father decided to renounce all hope, he said to me, with an unaccustomed gentleness: "You can see, my poor boy, that I've done my duty—everything I can! Never reproach me for your fate!"

I was profoundly moved; I wept profusely; I had never felt my isolation in the midst of humankind so bitterly. I dared to embrace my father tenderly, and murmured: "It's not true that I'm an imbecile, though!"

In fact, I felt superior to those who had been my fellow pupils. For some time, my intelligence had been developing remarkably. I read, I understood, I deduced, and I had immense subjects of meditation—far more than other human beings—in the universe that was visible to me alone.

My father could not make out what I said, but he was softened by my embrace. "Poor boy!" he said.

I looked at him. I was in frightful distress, knowing only too well that the gulf between us would never be bridged. My mother, thanks to the intuition of love, saw at that time that I was not inferior to other boys of my own age; she looked at me tenderly, and said naïve and sweet things to me from the

171

bottom of her heart, but I was condemned nonetheless to cease my studies.

Because of my weak muscular strength, I was put in charge of the sheep and cattle. I acquitted myself marvelously; I had no need of a dog to look after the flock and the dairy herd, and no colt or stallion was as agile as me.

From 14 to 17, therefore, I lived the solitary life of a herdsman. It suited me better than any other. Free to observe and contemplate, and also to do a certain amount of reading, my brain never ceased to develop. I compared the elements of the double creation I had before my eyes incessantly, extracting therefrom ideas as to the constitution of the universe, vaguely sketching hypotheses and theories. Although it is true that my thoughts were not perfectly ordered at that time, not forming any lucid system—for they were adolescent thoughts, uncoordinated, impatient and enthusiastic—they were nevertheless original and fecund. That their value depended exclusively on my unique constitution I shall certainly not deny, but they did not derive all their force therefrom. Without the slightest vanity, I think I may say that they surpassed considerably, in subtlety as in logic, those of ordinary young people.

They alone brought a certain consolation to my sad life as a semi-pariah, devoid of companions or any real communication with those around me, even my adorable mother.

At 17, life became quite unbearable to me. I was weary of dreaming, weary of vegetating on a mental desert island. I fell into idleness and ennui. I sat motionless for long hours, disinterested in the entire world, inattentive to everything that was happening in my family. What good did it do me to know about things more marvelous than other men knew, since that knowledge was bound to die with me? What was the mystery of living organisms to me, or even the duality of the two vital systems that passed through one another without knowing it? These things might have intoxicated me, filling me with enthusiasm and excitement, if I had some way of communicating them or sharing them—but what could I do? Vain and sterile, absurd and miserable, they contributed instead to my perpetual psychic quarantine.

Several times, I thought of writing down some of my observations, to make a permanent record anyway, even at the cost of continual effort—but since I had left school I had abandoned the pen permanently, and I was already so poor a scrivener that I barely knew how to trace, with difficulty, the 26 letters of the alphabet. If I had still had any hope, perhaps I would have persisted—but who would take my wretched efforts seriously? Where was the reader who would not think me mad? Where was the sage who would not treat me with disdain or irony? What was the point, then, in devoting myself to that vain task, that irritating torture, not so very different from that of an ordinary man obliged to engrave his thoughts on marble tablets with a coarse chisel and a titanic hammer? My writing would have to be a kind of shorthand, so far as I was concerned—and a shorthand even more rapid than usual!

I did not have the courage to write, therefore—and yet, I longed fervently for something to happen, some strange and fortunate eventuality. It seemed to me that there must exist, in some corner of the world, impartial, lucid, inquiring minds capable of studying me, of understanding me, or of extracting my great secret from me and communicating it to others—but where were these men? What hope did I have of ever meeting them?

And I fell back into a vast melancholy, into the desire for immobility and annihilation. For an entire autumn, I despaired of the Universe. I languished in a vegetative state, from which I only emerged to utter long groans, followed by painful protests.

I became even thinner, to the point of becoming fantastic. The people of the village called me, ironically, *Den Heyligen Gheest*—the Holy Ghost. My silhouette was as tremulous as those of young poplars, as slight as a shadow—and I attained, along with that, the stature of a giant.

Slowly, I formulated a plan. Since my life was sacrificed, since none of my days was joyful and everything was darkness and bitterness to me, why stagnate in inaction? Even if no mind did exist that could respond to mine, was it not, at least, worth the effort of making sure? Was it not, at least, worth leaving my bleak homeland to go in search of scientists and philosophers in the big cities? Was I not an object of curiosity in myself? Even before calling attention to my extra-human knowledge, could I not excite a desire to study my person? Were not the physical attributes of my being worthy of analysis in themselves: my sight, and the extreme agility of my movements, and the peculiarity of my nutrition.

The more I thought about it, the more reasonable it seemed to hope, and the firmer my resolve became. When the day arrived that it became unbreakable, I confided in my parents. Neither of them understood it very well, but they both ended up yielding to my repeated insistence; I obtained permission to go to Amsterdam, free to return if things did not work out for me.

I left the next morning.

VI.

The distance from Zwartendam to Amsterdam is about 100 kilometers. I covered that distance easily in two hours, without any other incident than the extreme surprise of passers-by on seeing me run at such a speed, and a few crowds gathering on the edges of little villages and larger towns that I shorted. To ascertain my route I spoke to solitary old men on two or three occasions; my sense of direction, which is excellent, did the rest.

It was about 9 a.m. when I reached Amsterdam. I went into the city resolutely, going along the beautiful canals where merchant fleets are quietly maintained. I did not attract as much attention as I had feared. I walked quickly, in the midst of busy people, enduring the occasional gibes of a few street-urchins. I decided, however, not to pause. I had gone back and forth through the city in every direction before I finally resolved to go into an inn on one of the quays of the Heerengracht.

It was a pleasant spot; the magnificent canal extended, full of life, between shady rows of trees, and among the Moedigen that I saw circulating along its banks, I thought I perceived a new species. After some indecision, I crossed the threshold of the inn and, addressing the proprietor as slowly as I could, I asked him if he would be so kind as to direct me to a hospital.

The landlord looked at me with amazement, suspicion and curiosity, took his stout pipe out of his mouth and put it back again several times, and eventually said: "You're from the colonies, no doubt?"

As there was no point in contradicting him, I replied: "Indeed!"

He seemed delighted with his perspicacity, and asked me another question. "Perhaps you come from that part of Borneo that no one has ever been able to get into?"

"Exactly."

I had spoken too rapidly; is eyes widened.

"Ex-act-ly!" I repeated, more slowly.

"You're having difficulty speaking Dutch, aren't you? So it's a hospital you want? Presumably, you're ill?"

"Yes."

Customers were drawing nearer. The rumor was already going round that I was a cannibal from Borneo; even so, they looked at me with far more curiosity than antipathy. People were coming in from the street. I became nervous and anxious. Nevertheless, I put on a brave face, coughed, and added: "I'm very ill."

"It's the same with monkeys from that region," said a fat man, benevolently. "The Netherlands kill them!"

"What funny skin!" said another.

"And how does he see?" asked a third, pointing to my eyes.

The circle drew closer, enveloping me with 100 curious stares—and newcomers were still coming into the room.

"How tall he is!"

It was true that I was a head taller than the tallest of them.

"And thin!"

"Cannibalism doesn't seem to be very nutritious!"

Not all the voices were malevolent. A few sympathetic individuals defended me: "Don't crowd him like that—he's ill!"

"Come on, friend, be brave!" said the fat man, observing my nervousness. "I'll take you to a hospital myself!"

He took me by the arm; taking it upon himself to clear a way through the crowd, shouting: "Make way for an invalid!"

Dutch crowds are not very aggressive; they let us pass, but went with us. We went along the canal, followed by a compact multitude, and people called out: "It's a cannibal from Borneo!"

Finally, we reached a hospital. It was visiting time. I was taken to an intern, a young man with blue-tinted spectacles, who greeted me sulkily.

"He's a savage from the colonies," my companion told him.

"What do you mean, a savage?" the intern exclaimed. He took off his spectacles to look at me. Surprise immobilized him momentarily. "Can you see?" he asked me, abruptly.

"I can see quite well."

I had spoken too rapidly. "It's his accent!" said the fat man, proudly. "Again, friend!"

I repeated the words, and made myself understood.

"Those aren't human eyes," the student murmured. "And that skin-color! Is that the color of your race?"

Making a terrible effort to speak slowly, I said: "I've come to be examined by a scientist."

"So you aren't ill?"

"No."

"And you're from Borneo?"

"No."

"Where are you from, then?"

"Zwartendam, near Duisburg."

"Then why does your companion claim that you're from Borneo?"

"I didn't want to contradict him."

"And you want to see a scientist?"

"Yes."

"Why?"

"To be studied."

"To earn money?"

"No, for nothing."

"You're not a pauper? A beggar?"

"No!"

"What makes you want to be studied?"

"My constitution…" But I had spoken too rapidly again, in spite of my efforts. I had to repeat myself.

"Are you sure that you can see me?" he asked again, staring at me. "Your eyes are like horn…"

"I can see quite well…" And, going from right to left, I rapidly picked objects up, put them down again, and threw them up in the air in order to catch them.

"That's extraordinary!" said the young man. His softened voice, almost friendly, gave me hope. "Listen," he said, eventually, "I'm sure that Dr. Van den Heuvel will be interested in your case. I'll go and inform him. You can wait in the next room. And by the way…I've forgotten…you're not actually ill?"

"Not at all."

"Good. Wait in here…the doctor won't be long."

I found myself sitting among monsters preserved in alcohol: fetuses, children in bestial form, colossal batrachians, and vaguely anthropomorphic saurians.

It's an apt waiting-room, I thought. *Am I not a candidate for one of these alcoholic sepulchers?*

When Dr. Van den Heuvel appeared, I was overcome by emotion; I felt the thrill of the Promised Land: the joy of reaching it, the fear of being banished therefrom. The doctor, who had a vast bald forehead, a powerful analytical gaze and a soft but obstinate mouth, examined me silently—and, as with everyone else, my excessive thinness, my lofty stature, my ringed eyes and my violet complexion caused him considerable astonishment.

"You say that you want to be studied?" he asked, eventually.

"Yes!" I replied, forcefully—almost violently.

He smiled approvingly, and asked me the usual question: "Can you see well enough with those eyes?"

"Very well. I can even see through wood and clouds..." I had spoken too rapidly though. He looked at me anxiously. I started again, sweating heavily: "I can even see through wood and clouds..."

"Really! That would be extraordinary. Well, what can you see through that door there?" He pointed to a closed door.

"A big glazed bookcase...a carved table..."

"Really!" he repeated, in amazement.

My chest swelled; a profound contentment descended upon my inner being.

The scientist remained silent for a few seconds, then said: "You speak very awkwardly."

"I speak too rapidly otherwise. I can't speak slowly."

"Well, say something in your natural voice."

I then recounted the tale of my entry into Amsterdam. He listened to me with extreme attention, and an intelligent and observant manner that I had never encountered among my peers. He did not understand any of what I said, but he demonstrated the sagacity of his analytical capability:

"If I'm not mistaken, you're pronouncing 15 to 20 syllables a second—which is to say, three or four times as many as the human ear can perceive. Your voice, moreover, is much sharper than any human voice I've ever heard. Your gestures, excessive in their rapidity, correspond perfectly with that speech. Your entire constitution is probably more rapid than ours."

"I can run faster than a greyhound," I said. "I write…"

"Ah!" he interjected. "Let's see your handwriting…"

I scribbled a few words on a writing-pad that he gave me, the first ones fairly readable, the others increasingly scrambled and abbreviated.

"Perfect!" he said, a certain pleasure mingled with his astonishment. "I believe that I shall be very glad to have met you. It would certainly be very interesting to study you…"

"That's my keenest—my only—desire."

"And mine, of course. Science…" He seemed preoccupied, thoughtful. Eventually, he said: "If we could only find an easy means of communication…"

He started pacing back and forth, frowning. Suddenly, he stopped. "How stupid I am! You'll learn stenography, of course! Eh?" A cheerful expression appeared on his face: "And I'm forgetting the phonograph…the perfect confidant. It'll be sufficient to slow down the playback more than the recording. It's settled: you'll stay with me during your sojourn in Amsterdam!"

The joy of a vocation satisfied, the delight of not spending vain and sterile days! In the presence of the intelligent personality of the doctor, in that scientific environment, I felt a delightful sense of well-being; the melancholy of my spiritual solitude, the regret for my wasted abilities, the long misery of the pariah status that had weighed upon me for so many years, all vanished, evaporating in the sentiment of a new life, a real life, a destiny of salvation!

179

VIII.

The doctor made all the necessary arrangements the following day. He wrote to my parents; he provided me with a stenography instructor and obtained phonographs. As he was very wealthy and entirely devoted to science, there was no experiment he did not propose to undertake; my vision, my hearing, my musculature and the color of my skin were subjected to scrupulous investigation, which made him increasingly enthusiastic,

"This is prodigious!" he exclaimed.

"I understood perfectly, after the first few days, how important it was that things be done methodically, proceeding from the simple to the complex, from slight abnormalities to marvelous ones—so I had recourse to a little artifice, which I did not try to hide from the doctor, which was only to reveal my abilities to him gradually.

The rapidity of my perceptions and my movements claimed his attention first. He was able to convince himself that the subtlety of my hearing corresponded to the rapidity of my speech. Graduated experiments with the most fugitive sounds, which I imitated with ease, and the speech of ten or 15 individuals talking at once, which I could distinguish perfectly, demonstrated the matter beyond all question. The velocity of my vision was no less proven, and comparative trials of my ability to resolve the gallop of a horse and the flight of an insect, against those of instantaneous photographic apparatus, were entirely to the advantage of my eyes. As for perceptions of ordinary things, the simultaneous movements of a group of people, children at play, the movement of machinery, stones thrown into the air or little balls tossed into an alley in order to be counted in flight—they stupefied the doctor's family and friends.

My runs through the large garden, my 20-meter jumps, the instantaneity of my seizing objects and putting them back again, were even more admired, not by the doctor but by his entourage; and it was a continual pleasure for my host's wife and children, during a walk in the country, to see me outrun a galloping horseman or follow the flight of a swallow. There is in fact, no thoroughbred to which I could not give a start of two-thirds of the distance to be covered, whatever it might be, nor any bird that I cannot easily overtake.

The doctor, increasingly satisfied with the results of his experiments, defined me thus: "A human being endowed, in all his movements, with a speed incomparably superior, not merely to other human beings, but also to that of all known animals. That speed, found in the slightest elements of his organic make-up as well as the whole, has created an individual so distinct from the remainder of creation that he merits a special category in the hierarchy of animals all to himself. As for the curious constitution of his eyes, and the violet hue of his skin, it is necessary to consider them as mere indications of that special status."

Tests having been carried out on my muscular system, he found nothing remarkable therein, except for an excessive thinness. No more were my ears furnished with any unique attributes; nor, save for its color, was my epidermis. As for my hair, which was dark—a violet-tinted black—it was as fine as spider-silk, and the doctor examined it minutely.

"I'd have to be able to dissect you!" he said several times, laughing.

The time passed pleasantly in this fashion. I had learned stenography very quickly, thanks to the ardor of my desire and the natural aptitude I showed for that manner of transcription—into which I introduced, moreover, a few new abbreviations. I began to take notes, which my stenographer translated. Furthermore, we had phonographs manufactured according to a special design made by the doctor, which were perfectly adapted to reproduce my speech, considerably slowed down.

My host's confidence eventually became perfect. In the first weeks, he had been unable to help being suspicious—which was entirely natural—that the uniqueness of my abilities might have given rise to some madness, some cerebral derangement. Once that fear was set aside, our relationship became entirely cordial—and, I think, as captivating for each of us as for the other. We carried out analytical tests of my perception through a large number of substances reckoned opaque, and of the dark coloration that water, glass and quartz acquired for me at a certain thickness. You will remember that I can see quite well through wood, the foliage of trees, clouds and many other substances, that I had difficulty distinguishing the bottom of a body of water half a meter deep, and that a window, although transparent, is less so for me than for ordinary people, and rather dark in color. A thick piece of glass appears almost black to me. The doctor convinced himself of all these singularities at his leisure, being particularly struck by my ability to make out the stars on cloudy nights.

It was only then that I began to tell him that I also perceived colors differently. Experiments established beyond doubt that red, orange, yellow, green, blue and indigo were as invisible to me as infra-red or ultra-violet to normal eyes. On the other hand, I was able to provide evidence that I perceived violet and, beyond violet, a whole series of shades: a spectrum of colors with at least twice the range of the spectrum that extends from red to violet.[38]

This astonished the doctor more than anything else. The investigation was long, scrupulous and, moreover, conducted with infinite artistry. It became, in the hands of that skillful experimenter, the source of subtle discoveries in the order of sciences classified by human beings, giving him the key to

---

[38] The narrator inserts a footnote: "Quartz gives me a spectrum of about eight colors: extreme violet and the seven colors following in the ultra-violet—but there still remain some eight colors that quartz does not separate, which other substances separate to a greater or lesser degree."

arcane phenomena of magnetism, chemical affinity and the power of induction, and guiding him toward new notions in physiology. You can easily imagine what an ingenious scientist might be able to deduce from such data as knowing that some metal manifests a series of unknown hues, variable with pressure, temperature and electrical state, and that the most transparent gas has distinct colors even at low density; learning about the infinite richness of the tones of objects that seem more or less black, and that they present a more magnificent spectrum in the ultra-violet than all the known colors; and, finally, knowing how the unknown hues of an electric circuit, the bark of a tree, or the skin of a human being vary from day to day, hour to hour and minute to minute.

At any rate, these studies plunged the doctor into the delight of scientific novelty, compared with which the products of the imagination are as cold as cinders compared with fire. He repeatedly said to me: "It's obvious! Your extra-luminary perception is, in sum, merely an effect of the speeding-up of your organic constitution."

We worked patiently for an entire year without my making any mention of the Moedigen; I wanted my host to be absolutely convinced, to give him innumerable proofs of my visual abilities before venturing upon the supreme confidence. Finally, the moment arrived when I thought that I could reveal everything.

IX

It was the morning of a mild Autumn day, overcast with clouds that had been traveling across the vault of the sky for a week without any rain falling. Van den Heuvel and I were strolling in the garden. The doctor was quiet, fully absorbed by speculations of which I was the principal object. Eventually, he began to speak.

"It's pleasant, mind, to imagine being able to see through these clouds…to penetrate as far as the ether, when we're… blind as we are…"

"If only the sky were all I could see!" I replied.

"Oh, yes—the entire world is so different…"

"Much more different than I've told you!"

"What!" he cried, with avid curiosity. "Have you been hiding something from me?"

"The most important thing of all."

He planted himself in front of me, stared at me with a veritable anguish, in which a certain mysticism seemed to be mixed.

"Yes, the most important thing of all!"

We had arrived beside the house; I rushed in to ask for a phonograph. The instrument that was brought was state of the art, much improved by my friend, capable of recording a long speech. The servant deposited it on the stone table at which the doctor and his family took coffee on fine summer evenings. The fine apparatus, miraculously accurate, lent itself admirably to conversation. We could talk almost as easily as in a normal conversation.

"Yes, I've hidden the most important thing from you, wanting to have your entire confidence first. Even now, after all the discoveries that my constitution has permitted you to make, I fear that you might have difficulty believing me, at least to begin with."

I paused in order that my words might be repeated by the instrument. I saw the doctor go pale: the pallor of a great scientist confronted with a new aspect of matter. His hands were trembling.

"I'll believe you!" he said, with a certain solemnity.

"Even if I claim that our creation—I mean our animal and vegetable world—is not the only life on Earth—that there is another, just as vast, as numerous and as complicated…invisible to your eyes?"

He suspected occultism, and could not help saying: "The world of the fourth dimension: souls, phantoms and spirits."

184

"No, no—nothing like that. A world of living beings, condemned, as we are, to a brief existence, organic needs, birth, growth and conflict…a world as frail and ephemeral as ours; a world submissive to laws as fixed as ours, if not identical; a world similarly imprisoned by the Earth, similarly vulnerable to contingencies…but also completely different from ours, without any influence upon us, as we have no influence upon it, save for the modifications it makes to our common foundation, the Earth, or the parallel modifications to which we subject that same Earth."

I don't know whether Van den Heuvel believed me, but he was certainly in the grip of a keen excitement. "In brief, they're fluid?" he queried.

"That's something I can't say, for their properties are too contradictory to the idea we've formed of matter. The Earth is as resistant to them as to us, as are the majority of minerals, although they can penetrate some way into humus. They are also quite impermeable—solid—with respect to one another, but they pass through plants, animals and organic tissues, albeit with a certain difficulty, and we pass through them in the same way. If one of them could see us, we would probably appear fluid in relation to them in its eyes, as they appear fluid in relation to us in mine—but it would probably be no more able to *conclude* that than I am; it would be struck by parallel contradictions.

"Their form has the strange quality of having very little thickness. Their size is infinitely variable. I've known some of them to reach a hundred meters in length, and others as small as our tiniest insects. Some of them derive nutrition at the expense of the Earth and weather phenomena, others at the expense of weather phenomena and the individuals of their kingdom—without, however, that being a cause of murder, as among us, since it is sufficient for the stronger to draw energy, that energy presumably being extractable without exhausting the vital source."

The doctor asked me, abruptly: "Could you see them when you were a child?"

I guessed that he had formulated the hypothesis that this was, in essence, some disorder that had overtaken my organism fairly recently.

"Since infancy!" I replied, forcefully. "I can provide you with the necessary proofs."

"Can you see them now?"

"I see them—the garden contains a considerable number of them."

"Where?"

"On the path, on the lawns, on the walls, in the air...for there are aerial as well as terrestrial ones—and also aquatic ones, although those rarely leave the surface of the water."

"Are they numerous everywhere?"

"Yes, and scarcely less numerous in towns than in the fields, and in houses than in the streets. Those that prefer enclosed spaces are smaller, though, doubtless because of the difficulty of moving around—although wooden doors are no obstacle to them."

"What about iron...glass...brick?"

"Impermeable to them."

"Would you care to describe one of them—preferably a large one?"

"I can see one of them near that tree. Its form is extremely elongated, and rather irregular. It is convex on the right, concave on the left, with bulges and indentations; one might imagine it to be a cross-section of a gigantic, thickset caterpillar—but its structure isn't characteristic of the kingdom, for structure is extremely variable between species, if one may use that term in this context. Its infinitesimal thickness is, on the other hand, a universally general quality; it can scarcely be more than a tenth of a millimeter, although it is five feet long and 40 centimeters broad at its greatest width.

"What defines it most obviously, and its entire kingdom, are the lines that cut across it in every direction, terminating in networks that thin out where two systems of lines meet. Each system of lines is equipped with a center, a sort of swollen patch slightly elevated above the mass of the body—or sometimes, by contrast, hollowed out. These centers have no fixed shape, sometimes being almost circular or elliptical, sometimes twisted or spiral, sometimes divided by several constructions. They are astonishingly mobile, and their magnitude varies on an hourly basis. Their borders vibrate very rapidly, by virtue of a sort of horizontal undulation. Generally, the lines emerging from them are broad, even though there are also some very thin ones; they diverge, finishing up as infinitely delicate traces that gradually vanish.

"A few lines, however, much paler than the others, are not engendered by centers; they remain isolated within the system and grow without changing color. These lines have the ability to move around within the body and to vary their curvature, while the centers and the lines connected to them remain stable in their respective situations.

"As for the colors of my Moedig, I must renounce any attempt to describe them to you, none of them being in the register perceptible to your eye, and none of them having any name for you. They are extremely bright in the networks, less so in the centers, and very faint in the independent lines—which, in compensation, are highly polished, with an ultraviolet metallic quality, if I might express it thus.

"I have assembled a few observations on the mode of life, nutrition and autonomy of the Moedigen, but I don't want to show them to you for the moment."

I fell silent. The doctor had the recorded words repeated twice over by our impeccable intermediary, then remained silent for some time. I had never seen him in such a state; his features were rigid, mineralized; his eyes vitreous, cataleptic; an abundant sweat was running down his temples and moistening his hair. He tried to speak, but could not. He made a tremulous circuit of the garden, and when he came back his expression and mouth expressed a violent, fervent, religious passion. One might have thought him a disciple of a new faith rather than a placid hunter of phenomena.

Finally, he murmured: "You've overwhelmed me! Everything you've just told me seems perfectly lucid—and have I any right to doubt it, after all the marvels you've already shown me?"

"Doubt!" I told him, hotly. "Doubt fervently...your experiments will be all the more fecund for it!"

"Ah! He went on, in a dreamy voice. "It's prodigy itself—and so magnificently superior to the vain prodigies of Fable! My poor human intelligence is so small by comparison to such knowledge! My enthusiasm is infinite. Something within me, however, doubts..."

"Let us work to dispel your uncertainty. Our efforts will be rewarded a hundredfold!"

X.

We worked. A few weeks sufficed to dispel all the doctor's doubts. Ingenious experiments, undeniable concordances between each of my affirmations, and two or three fortunate discoveries regarding the influence of the Moedigen on atmospheric phenomena left no room for equivocation. The assistance of Van den Heuvel's eldest son, a young man with the greatest aptitude for science, further increased the fecundity of our labors and the certainty of our discoveries.

Thanks to the methodical mentality of my companions, and their skill in investigation and classification—faculties that I gradually assimilated—it did not take long for my presently-uncoordinated and confused knowledge of the Moedigen to be transformed. The discoveries multiplied, the rigorous experiments gave firm results, in circumstances that would, at most, have suggested a few seductive diversions in ancient times, or even in the last century.

We have now been conducting our researches for five years; they are far—very far—from reaching completion. An initial account of our findings will not be ready for quite some time. We are, in any case, strictly determined not to do anything in haste; our discoveries are too important in kind not to be revealed in the greatest possible detail, with the most sovereign patience and the most careful precision. We do not have to get in ahead of any other researcher, we have no patent for which to apply, nor any ambition to satisfy. We are at a height at which vanity and pride fade away. How can we reconcile the delightful joys of our work with the wretched lure of human renown? Besides, is not the mere accident of my constitution the sole source of these things? How petty it would be, therefore, to glorify ourselves?

We live passionately, always on the verge of marvelous things, and yet we live in an immutable serenity.

I have had an adventure that has added to the profound interest of my life, and which, during my hours of leisure, completes my infinite joy. You know how ugly I am, and stranger still, liable to frighten young women. I have, however, found a companion who can accept my affection to the point of enjoying it.

She is a poor hysteric, neurotic girl, whom we found one day in a hospice in Amsterdam. She is considered to be wretched in appearance, as pallid as plaster with hollow cheeks and wild eyes. To me, she is pleasant to behold, and her company is charming. My presence, far from astonishing her, like everyone else's, seemed from the outset to please her and comfort her. I was touched, and wanted to see her again.

It did not take long to perceive that I had a beneficial effect on her health and well-being. On further investigation, it seemed that I influenced her magnetically; my proximity, and especially the imposition of my hands, communicated a veritably curative gaiety, serenity and mental equilibrium to her. In return, I found pleasure in being with her. Her face seemed pretty to me; her pallor and thinness were merely delicacy; her eyes, capable of seeing the glow of magnets, like those of sufferers from hyperesthesia, did not seem to me to have the quality of wildness of which others disapprove.

In a word, I found her attractive, and she returned the sentiment passionately. Soon, I decided to marry her, and easily attained my goal, thanks to the good will of my friends. The marriage has been a happy one. With my wife's health restored, although she remained extremely sensitive and frail, I tasted the joy of being, in the most important aspect of life, like other men. My destiny has been especially enviable for six months; a child was born to us, and that child reproduces all the characteristics of my constitution. In terms of color, vision, hearing, extreme rapidity of movement and nutrition, he promises to be an exact replica of my physiology.

The doctor is watching him grow with delight; a delightful hope has been born in us: that the study of Moedig life, of the kingdom parallel to ours, which requires so much time and patience, will not come to a stop when I die. My son will doubtless pursue it in his turn. Why should he not find collaborators of genius, capable to take it to further extremes? Why should there not be born, to him also, seers of the invisible world?

May I, too, not expect more children? May I not hope that my dear wife will one day give birth to other offspring of my flesh similar to their father? And as I think about that, my heart quivers, and I am filled with an infinite bliss, feeling myself blessed among men.

THE DEATH OF THE EARTH

I. Speech at a Distance

The frightful north wind had died down. For a fortnight its malevolent voice had filled the oasis with dread and sadness. It had been necessary to put up the storm-shields and the elastic silica hothouses. Finally, the oasis began to warm up.

Targ, the Great Planetary's[39] watchman, felt one of those sudden joys that illuminated human life in the divine Time of Water. How beautiful the plants still were! They took Targ back through the ages, to a time when oceans covered three-quarters of the world and humans flourished amid springs, streams, rivers, lakes and marshes. What freshness animated the innumerable generations of animals and vegetables! Life was abundant everywhere, including the utmost depths of the

---

[39] This story was written at the very dawn of wireless communication and aviation, so Rosny improvises terms for numerous devices that have since come into being, albeit in somewhat different forms, and have thus acquired their own terminology. I have attempted to conserve the spirit of his improvisations by transcribing some terms—including *planétaire* [planetary]—directly, and translating others, such as *planeur* [glider] "literally," even though the meanings of the words have changed in the interim (*planeur* is used here to refer to powered aircraft). In a few cases, however, I have preferred more informative translations of words to which Rosny has attributed new meanings—thus, for instance, substituting "dish" for *conque* [shell, as of the ear] with respect to the receivers built into the radio-transmitting "planetaries"—and have made similar compromises with respect to some neologisms, notably *ondifère*, which I have rendered as "radiolink."

191

seas. There were meadows and forests of algae, just as there were forests of trees and grasslands. An immense future opened up before all creatures; humans had scarcely any inkling of their distant descendants who would tremble at the approach of the world's end. Did they ever imagine that the death-throes would last for more than a hundred millennia?

Targ raised his eyes to the sky, in which clouds never any longer appeared. The morning was still cool, but by midday the oasis would be torrid. "The harvest is almost ready!" the watchman murmured.

He displayed a swarthy face, eyes and hair as black as anthracite. Like all the Last Men, he had a broad chest and a narrow abdomen. His hands were slender, his jaws small, and his limbs gave more evidence of agility than strength. A garment made of mineral fibers, as supple and warm as ancient wool, was fitted exactly to his body; his whole being was redolent with resigned grace and a fearful charm that emphasized his thin cheeks and the pensive fire in his eyes.

He lingered in order to contemplate a field of tall cereals and rectangular trees, each of which bore as many fruits as leaves, and said: "Prodigious dawns of the Sacred Ages, when plants covered the young planet!"

As the Great Planetary was in the borderlands of the oasis and the desert, Targ could see a sinister landscape of granite, silica and metals: a plain of desolation extending as far as the foothills of bare mountains devoid of glaciers and springs, with not a blade of grass or plaque of lichen. In that desert of death, the oasis, with its rectilinear plantations and its metallic villages, was a miserable patch.

Targ felt the vast wilderness and implacable mountains weighing upon him; sadly, he raised his head toward the dish of the Great Planetary. That dish was a brimstone corolla in a gap in the mountains. Made of arcum and as sensitive as a retina, it only received the wavelengths emanating from the oasis and, according to the setting, suppressed those to which the watchman need not respond. Targ loved it, as an emblem of the rare adventures still possible to human beings; when he felt sad he turned toward it, expecting to draw courage and hope from it.

A voice caused him to shiver. With a weak smile, he saw a young woman with a harmonious figure climbing up to the balcony. She wore her dark hair loose; her upper body undulated, as flexible as the tall stems of the cereals. The watchman looked at her lovingly. His sister Arva was the only creature in whose presence he recovered those sudden, unexpected and charming moments when it seemed that a few forces in mysterious depths might still be working for the salvation of humankind.

Suppressing a laugh, she exclaimed: "The weather's fine, Targ. The plants are happy!" She breathed in the consoling odor that welled up from the green flesh of leaves; the black fire of her eyes flickered. Three birds flew over the trees and swooped down to the edge of the balcony. They were shaped like ancient condors: forms as pure as those of beautiful feminine bodies, with immense silvery wings sprinkled with amethyst, whose tips emitted a violet light. Their heads were large, their beaks very short and flexible, as red as lips, and the expression in their eyes was almost human. One of them, raising its head, voiced articulate sounds.

Targ took Arva's hand anxiously. "Did you understand that?" he said. "The earth is stirring!"

Even though it was a very long time since any oasis had perished in an earthquake, and their amplitude had greatly diminished since the ominous era in which they had broken human power, Arva shared her brother's anxiety—but a capricious idea passed through her mind. "Who knows," she said, "whether, having done so much harm to our kin, earthquakes might not be more favorable to us?"

"How?" asked Targ, indulgently.

"By causing some of the waters to reappear!"

He had often thought of that, without having told anyone—for such a thought would have seemed stupid, and almost blasphemous, to a fallen humankind in whom planetary upheavals evoked all kinds of terrors.

"You think so too, then!" he exclaimed, excitedly. "Don't tell anyone! You'll offend them deeply."

"I haven't told anyone but you."

Groups of white birds were coming from every direction; the ones that had joined Targ and Arva were hopping about impatiently. The young man spoke to them, employing a particular syntax—for, as their intelligence had developed, the birds had been initiated into language: a language that only admitted concrete terms and imagistic phrases. Their notion of the future remained obscure and abbreviated, their foresight instinctive; since humans no longer exploited them as nourishment, they lived happily, incapable of imagining their own deaths, let alone that of their species.

The oasis played host to about 1200 of them, whose presence was exceedingly soothing and very useful. Because humans had not been able to regain the instincts lost during the period of their dominion, the present environmental conditions left them at the mercy of phenomena that even the most delicate apparatus inherited from their ancestors could hardly register, but which the birds could detect. If the birds—the last vestige of animal life—had disappeared, human souls would have been subject to even more bitter desolation.

"The danger isn't immediate!" Targ murmured.

A rumor was running through the oasis; humans were emerging from the edges of villages and cereal-fields.

A thickset individual whose massive skull seemed to be directly posed on his torso appeared at the foot of the Great Planetary. His eyes were wide open and feeble, in a face the color of iodine; his flat rectangular hands were shaking at the ends of his short arms. "We shall see the end of the world!" he groaned. "We shall be the last generation of human beings."

Cavernous laughter was heard behind him. The centenarian Dane appeared, with his great-grandson and a woman with wide eyes and bronze-colored hair, who walked as lightly as a bird. "No," she said, "we shan't see the end of the world. The death of human beings will be slow. The water will dwindle away until there are only a few families around a well—and that will be even more terrible."

"We shall see the end of the world!" insisted the thickset man.

"So much the better!" said Dane's great-grandson. "Let the Earth drink up the last springs this very day!" His exceedingly narrow and sinuous face displayed a boundless sadness; it astonished him that he had not put an end to his own existence.

"Who knows whether there might not be some hope!" muttered the old man.

Targ's heart beat faster; he looked down at the centenarian with eyes sparkling with youth. "Oh, Father!" he cried.

The old man's features had already become frozen again; he fell back into the taciturn reverie that made him resemble a block of basalt. Targ kept his thought to himself.

There was a growing crowd in the borderlands of the desert and the oasis. A few gliders took off, coming from the Center. An era had been reached in which humans had scarcely any work to do; they merely had to await harvest-times, for there were no surviving insects or microbes. Huddled in narrow domains, outside of which all protoplasmic life was impossible, their ancestors had mounted an effective war against parasites. Even microscopic organisms were no longer able to maintain themselves, deprived of the opportunities resulting from dense agglomerations, large open spaces and perpetual displacements and transformations.

Besides, master of the distribution of water, humans disposed an irresistible power against creatures they wished to destroy. The absence of ancient domestic animals and savages, incessant vectors of epidemics, had brought the hour of triumph further forward. Humankind, the birds and the plants were now permanently safe from infectious diseases.

They did not live any longer; many benevolent microbes had disappeared with the others, the inherent infirmities of the human machine had increased, and new maladies had emerged that were thought to be caused by "mineral microbes." In consequence, humans found enemies within analogous to those that had threatened them from without, and, although marriage was a privilege reserved for the fittest, the human organism rarely attained an advanced age.

Soon, several hundred people had gathered around the Great Planetary. There was only a feeble tumult; the tradition of misfortune had been handed down through too many generations not to have drained the reserves of fear and dolor that are the price of powerful joys and vast hope. The Last Men had a restrained sensibility and little imagination.

Even so, the crowd was troubled; a few faces were contorted. It was a relief when a quadragenarian leapt out of an electric car and shouted: "The seismic apparatus isn't showing anything yet. The quake will be weak."

"Of what are we afraid?" shouted the wide-eyed woman. "What can we do and expect? All possible measures were taken centuries ago. We're at the mercy of the unknown; it's terrible stupidity to ask questions about an inevitable peril."

"No, Hélé," the quadragenarian replied. "That's not stupidity; it's life. As long as people have the strength to ask questions, their days will still have some pleasure. Afterwards, they'll be dead as soon as they're born."

"Would that it were so!" jeered Dane's great-grandson. "Our miserable joys and sickly sadnesses are worse than death."

The quadragenarian shook his head. Like Targ and his sister, he was still mindful of the future, and still had strength in his broad chest. His frank gaze encountered Arva's clear eyes, and a delicate emotion quickened his breathing.

Meanwhile, other groups were assembling in various sectors of the periphery. Thanks to radiolinks distributed at 1000-meter intervals, these groups could communicate freely; one could hear at will the rumors of a district or even that of the entire population. That communication condensed the mentality of crowds and acted as a strong stimulant—so there was a kind of excitement when a message from the Redlands oasis vibrated in the Dish of the Great Planetary and echoed from radiolink to radiolink. It announced that it was not only the birds but also the seismographs that were advertising distant subterranean upheavals. This confirmation of the danger drew the groups closer together.

Mano, the quadragenarian, climbed up on to the balcony; Targ and Arva were pale. As the young woman shivered slightly, the newcomer murmured: "The very smallness of the oases, and their restricted number, ought to reassure us. The probability that they'll be located in the danger-zones is tiny."

"Few as they are," said Targ, supportively, "it's their locations that have saved them before."

Dane's great-grandson had heard; his jeering laughter was heard again. "As if the zones didn't vary periodically! Besides, wouldn't a feeble quake be sufficient, if it struck in the right place, to dry up the springs?" He drew away, full of bleak irony.

Targ, Arva and Mano shuddered; they remained momentarily taciturn, and then the quadragenarian spoke again: "The zones vary with an extreme slowness. For two hundred years the strongest shocks have occurred deep in the desert; their repercussions haven't altered the springs. Redlands, Devastation and Occidental are the only ones close to the dangerous regions…"

He studied Arva with a gentle admiration, in which the flower of love was growing. Widowed three years before, he was suffering pangs of loneliness. In spite of the rebellion of his strength and affection; he had resigned himself to it— marriages and births were regulated by rigid laws—but several weeks before, the Council of Fifteen had inscribed Mano's name among those who might remake a family, and the image of Arva had undergone a metamorphosis in Mano's soul, the obscure legend being illuminated once again.

"Let's mingle hope with our anxieties!" he exclaimed. "Even in the marvelous Epochs of Water, wasn't every man's death the end of the world for him? Those who now live on the Earth run fewer risks, individually, than our forefathers of the Radioactive Era!"

He spoke fervently, for he had always rejected the lugubrious resignation that devastated his peers. An excessive atavism had doubtless only permitted him to escape it intermittently; nevertheless, he had known the joy of living in the sparkling present moment more often than most.

Arva listened to him gladly, but Targ could not imagine being neglectful of the future of the species. If, like Mano, he happened to be abruptly gripped by a fugitive sensuality, he always mingled it with that great dream of Time that had guided his ancestors. "I can't be disinterested in our descendants," he replied. Pointing toward the immense wilderness, he added: "How beautiful existence would be if *our* reign extended over these frightful deserts! Don't you ever think that there used to be seas, lakes and rivers there...countless plants and—before the Radioactive Era—virgin forests. Oh, Mano!—virgin forests! And now, an obscure life is devouring our antique fatherland!"

Mano shrugged his shoulders meekly. "It's a terrible thought that, outside the oases, the Earth is so uninhabitable for us—perhaps more so than Jupiter or Saturn."

A rumor interrupted them; heads were being raised attentively; a new flock of birds had just arrived. They announced that some distance away, in the shadow of the mountains, an unconscious young woman had fallen prey to the ferromagnetals.

While two gliders set off over the desert, the crowd thought about the strange magnetic creatures that were multiplying on the planet's surface as humankind declined.

Long minutes went by; the gliders reappeared. One of them was bringing back an inert body, whom everyone recognized as Elma the Nomad. She was a strange orphan girl, not much liked, for she had the instincts of a wanderer, whose savagery disconcerted her peers. Nothing could prevent her occasionally fleeing into the wilderness.

She was deposited on the balcony of the Planetary; her face, half-hidden by the long black hair, seemed to be livid, and strewn with scarlet dots.

"She's dead!" declared Mano. "The *Others* have drunk her life."

"Poor little Elma!" cried Targ. He gazed at her with pity—and, passive as it was, the crowd growled hatefully against the ferromagnetals.

The loud clamor of the resonators, however, deflected their attention.

"The seismographs have detected an abrupt shock in the vicinity of Redlands..."

"Oh! Oh!" cried the plaintive voice of the thickset man. No echo replied to him. Faces turned toward the Great Planetary. The multitude waited, shivering with impatience.

"Nothing!" exclaimed Mano, after two minutes of waiting. "If Redlands had been affected, we'd already have heard..."

A strident voice cut his speech short, and the Dish of the Great Planetary proclaimed: "Immense quake...the entire oasis is shaking...Catas..." Then, confused sounds, a muffled collision...and silence...

Everyone waited for a further minute, as if hypnotized. Then the crowd breathed in hoarsely; even the least emotional were excited.

"It's a great disaster!" announced old Dane.

No one doubted it. Redlands possessed ten broad communication planetaries, which could be orientated in any direction. For all ten to fall silent, either they must all have been uprooted or the consternation of the inhabitants must be extraordinary.

Orientating the transmitter, Targ sent forth a long appeal. No response. A dull horror weighed up their minds. It was not the ardent disturbance of the people of yesteryear, but a slow, idle, all-consuming distress. Narrow ties bound together High Springs and Redlands. For 5000 years, the two oases had maintained a constant relationship, by means of the resonators and frequent visits by glider and electric car. Thirty relay-stations furnished with planetaries marked out the 1700 kilo-

199

meter highway between them, which linked their two populations.

"We have to wait!" Targ shouted, leaning over the balcony. "If panic is preventing our friends from replying, they won't take long to recover their composure."

No one believed, however, that the people of Redlands were capable of such panic; their race was even less emotional than that of High Springs; although capable of sadness, it was scarcely amenable to fear.

Targ, reading incredulity on all the faces, said: "If their apparatus has been destroyed, messengers can reach the first relay-station within a quarter of an hour..."

"Unless the gliders have been damaged," objected Hélé. "As for electric cars, it's improbable that they'd be able to get through ruined outskirts in a short time."

Meanwhile, the entire population was moving toward the southern zone. Within a few minutes, gliders and electric cars were pouring out thousands of people in the vicinity of the Great Planetary. Rumors increased, like long sighs punctuated by silences—and the members of the Council of Fifteen, the interpreters of the laws and determinants of unanimous actions, assembled on a balcony. Everyone recognized old Bamar by her triangular face and long salt-white hair, and the bulging head of her husband, Omal, whose 70 years of life had not been able to pale his tawny beard. They were ugly but venerable, and their authority was great, for their children were unblemished.

Bamar, ensuring that the Planetary was correctly orientated, sent forth a few waves in her turn. Before the receiver's silence, her face darkened further.

"Thus far, Devastation is safe," Omal murmured, "and the seismographs haven't indicated any quakes in the other human zones."

Suddenly, a strident appeal sounded, and while the multitude straightened up, hypnotically, the Great Planetary was heard to growl: "From the first Redlands relay-station. Two powerful quakes have shaken the oasis. The number of dead and wounded is considerable. The crops have been annihilated. The waters seemed to be under threat. Gliders are departing for High Springs."

There was a stampede. People, gliders and electric cars surged forth in torrents. An excitement unknown for centuries elevated resigned minds; pity, dread and anxiety rejuvenated that Last Age multitude.

The Council of Fifteen deliberated, while Targ, trembling from head to toe, replied to the message from Redlands and announced the imminent departure of a delegation. In tragic times, the three sister oases—Redlands, High Springs and Devastation—were obliged to come to one another's rescue. Omal, who had a perfect knowledge of the tradition, declared: "We have provisions for five years. A quarter might perhaps be claimed by Redlands. We are also ready to receive two thousand refugees, if that is inevitable—but they would be on reduced rations and they would be forbidden to reproduce. We too would have to limit our families, for it would be necessary to restore the population to its traditional figure *within five years*."

The Council approved this citation of the laws; then Bamar shouted to the crowd: "The Council will appoint those who will leave for Redlands. There will be no more than nine. Others will be sent when we know what our brothers need."

"I want to go," begged the watchman.

"And me!" Arva added, excitedly.

Mano's eyes sparkled. "If the Council will permit, I will also go with the envoys."

Omal looked at them favorably—for he, like them, had once known those spontaneous impulses, so rare among the Last Men.

Except for Amat, a frail adolescent, the crowd waited passively for the Council's decision. Submissive to millennia-old rules, accustomed to a monotonous existence, troubled only by the weather, the people had lost its taste for initiative. Resigned, patient and endowed with great passive courage, nothing about adventures excited them. The enormous deserts that surrounded them, devoid of all human resources, weighed upon their actions as well as their thoughts.

"There is no reason why Targ, Arva and Mano should not go," old Bamar remarked, "but it's a long journey for Amat. Let the Council decide."

While the Council was deliberating, Targ studied the sinister expanse. A bitter dolor accumulated within him. The Redlands disaster weighed on him more heavily than his brothers, for their hopes only extended to the slowness of the final decay, while he persisted in imagining fortunate metamorphoses—and the circumstances offered a bitter confirmation of Tradition.

II. Toward Redlands

The nine gliders flew toward Redlands. They did not stray far from the two roads that electric cars had followed for centuries. The ancestors had constructed huge refuges of stainless steel with planetary resonators and numerous less important relays. The two roads were well-maintained. As the electric cars used them sparsely and their wheels were fitted with highly elastic mineral fibers, and as the people of the two oases also knew how to make partial use of the enormous forces their forebears had mastered, the maintenance was more a matter of supervision than work. The ferromagnetals rarely appeared there and only inflicted insignificant damage; a pedestrian could have walked for an entire day without sensing any harmful influence, but it would not have been prudent to pause for too long, and especially to fall asleep. Many victims had, like Elma, lost all their red blood corpuscles there and died of anemia.

The Nine were not in any danger; each of them was flying a light glider that could have accommodated four people. Even if an accident overtook two thirds of the machines, the expedition would not be compromised. Endowed with a near-perfect elasticity, the gliders were built to resist the rudest impacts and to withstand storms.

Mano had taken the lead, Targ and Arva were flying almost in convoy. The young man's agitation was increasing incessantly, and stories of great catastrophes faithfully handed down through the generations haunted his memory.

For 500 centuries, humans had only occupied derisory islets on the planet's surface. The shadow of decay had long preceded the catastrophes. In a very ancient epoch, in the early centuries of the radioactive era, the decrease of the waters had already been observed; many scientists predicted that humankind would perish as a result of the desiccation—but what effect could those predictions have on people who saw glaciers covering their mountains and countless rivers irrigating their settlements?

The waters did, however, diminish, slowly but surely, absorbed by the Earth or volatilized in the firmament.[40] Then came the awful catastrophes. Extraordinary rearrangements of the crust occurred; sometimes, earthquakes destroyed ten or twenty cities and hundreds of villages in a single day; new chains of mountains were formed, twice as high as the ancient ranges of the Alps, the Andes and the Himalayas; the water was gradually exhausted with the passing centuries. Metamorphoses became visible on the surface of the Sun whose effects, according to uncomprehended laws, were echoed on our poor globe. There was a lamentable sequence of catastrophes; on the one hand, mountains were raised up to heights of 25,000 to

---

[40] Rosny's narrative voice adds a footnote here: "In the upper atmospheric regions, water vapor was perpetually being decomposed by ultra-violet radiation into oxygen and hydrogen; the hydrogen escaped into interstellar space." At this point in the text the narrative voice's frequent use of the collective personal pronoun implies that it is the voice of one of the Last Men, but the story's final passages are incompatible with that pose.

203

30,000 meters; on the other, immense quantities of water disappeared.

It is on record that, at the beginning of these sidereal upheavals, the human population had attained the figure of twenty-three billon individuals. Those masses had enormous forces at their disposal. They could split atoms—as we still do ourselves, albeit imperfectly—and did not worry overmuch about the flight of the waters, so advanced were their artificial methods of cultivation and nutrition. They even imagined that they would soon be able to live on organic produce manufactured by chemists. Several times, this ancient dream appeared to have been realized, but every time, strange maladies or rapid degenerations decimated the groups subjected to experiments. It was necessary to stick to the aliments that had nourished humans since their remotest ancestors. In truth, these aliments had undergone subtle metamorphoses, as much by virtue of techniques of animal husbandry and agriculture as by virtue of scientific manipulations; reduced rations sufficed to maintain an individual human, and the digestive organs underwent a significant diminution, in less than 100 centuries, while the respiratory apparatus increased in size as a direct consequence of the rarefaction of the atmosphere.

The last wild animals disappeared; edible animals, by comparison with their ancestors, were veritable zoophytes, hideous ovoid masses with limbs transformed into vestigial stumps and jaws atrophied by force-feeding. Only a few species of birds escaped the degradation and acquired a marvelous intellectual development. Their gentleness, beauty and charm increased through the ages. They rendered unexpected services, by virtue of their instincts, more delicate than those of their masters, and those services were particularly appreciated in laboratories.

The people of that powerful epoch lived an anxious existence. Magnificent and mysterious poetry was extinct. There was no more savage life; no more immense near-empty spaces: the woods, the heaths, the marshes, the steppes and the fallow ground of the radioactive era. Suicide ended up as the most redoubtable malady of the species.

In 15 millennia, the terrestrial population declined from 23 billion individuals to four billion; the seas, departed into abysses, no longer occupied a quarter of the surface; the great rivers and great lakes had disappeared; the immense and funereal mountains were swarming with people. Thus the primitive planet reappeared—but bare!

Humans were, however, struggling desperately. Although they could not live without water, they imagined that they could manufacture what they needed for domestic and agricultural usage—but the useful materials were becoming rare, save at depths that rendered their exploitation derisory. It was necessary to fall back on methods of conservation, on ingenious methods of managing the flow and extracting the maximum effect from the nourishing fluid.

Domestic animals perished, incapable of adapting to the new vital conditions. The people tried in vain to reconstitute more primitive species; 200,000 years of devolution had exhausted their evolutionary energy. Only the birds and the plants resisted. The former recovered a few ancestral forms, which adapted to the new environment. Many, becoming wild again, constructed their eyries at heights where humans could no longer pursue them because of the rarefaction of the air that accompanied, albeit on a lesser scale, that of the waters. They lived by depredation, and employed such refined cunning that they could not be prevented from maintaining themselves.

As for those birds that lived among our ancestors, their fate was initially dire; attempts were made to reduce them to the status of edible creatures—but their consciousness had become too lucid; they fought desperately to avoid that fate. There were scenes as hideous as those episodes of prehistoric times when humans ate humans, when entire peoples were reduced to servitude. The horror struck home; gradually, people ceased to brutalize their planetary companions and made peace with them again.

Meanwhile, the seismic phenomena contained to remold the Earth and destroy cities. After 30,000 years of conflict, our ancestors understood that the mineral realm, vanquished for millions of years by plants and animals, was taking a conclusive revenge. There was a period of despair that brought the human population down to 300 million, while the seas were reduced to a tenth of the terrestrial surface. Three or four thousand years of respite brought about a certain renaissance of optimism. Humankind embarked on prodigious labors of conservation; the war against the birds ended; people restricted themselves to putting them in conditions that did not permit them to multiply, and extracted precious services from them.

Then the catastrophes resumed. The habitable territories shrank again—and, about 30,000 years ago, the supreme rearrangements took place. Humankind found itself reduced to a few territories scattered across the Earth, which had become as vast and formidable as in the primal epochs; outside the oases, it became impossible to procure the water necessary to sustain life.

Since then, a relative calm has been produced. Although the water supplied to us by the well hollowed out in the abyss has further decreased, reducing the population by a third, and two oases have been abandoned, humankind has persisted; undoubtedly, it might survive for another 50,000 or a 100,000 years.

Industry has declined enormously; of the forces that our species used in its heyday, the humans of the oases only employ a small fraction. Communication apparatus and mechanical labor have become less complex; many millennia ago it was necessary to renounce the spiraloids that transported our ancestors through the air at a speed ten times greater than our gliders.

Human live in a state of signation, sadly and quite passively. The spirit of creation is extinct; it only reawakens, atavistically, in a few individuals. By continual selection, the race has acquired a spirit of automatic obedience, and by the same token, its laws have become immutable. Passion is rare, crime non-existent.

A sort of religion has arisen, devoid of worship or ritual: a respectful dread for the mineral. The Last Men attribute a slow and irresistible will to the planet; initially favorable to the realms to which it gave birth. The Earth let them acquire great power; the mysterious moment when it condemned them was also that when it began to favor new realms.

Presently, its obscure forces favor the ferromagnetal realm. It cannot be said that the ferromagnetals have participated in our destruction; at the most, they have assisted in the annihilation—fatal after all—of wild birds. Although their appearance dates back to a distant epoch, the new beings have scarcely evolved. Their movements are surprisingly slow; the most agile cannot travel ten meters an hour—and the bismuth-plated stainless steel enclosures of the oases are an insurmountable obstacle to them. To do us any immediate harm they would require an evolutionary leap entirely out of keeping with their anterior development.

The existence of the ferromagnetal realm was first discovered during the decline of the radioactive era. They were bizarre violet stains on "human iron"—which is to say, the kinds of iron and iron compounds that had been modified for industrial usage.[41] The phenomenon only appeared on products that had been recycled many times over; ferromagnetal patches were never discovered on "primitive iron." The new realm was, therefore, only capable of birth in the human environment. That important fact gave our ancestors much to think about. Perhaps we had been in an analogous situation with

---

[41] Rosny is presumably thinking of steel, but the chemical composition of "human iron" is probably irrelevant; what he has in mind is probably a process analogous to the one he imagined operating in "The Skeptical Legend," whereby their incorporation into living flesh causes molecules to undergo a subtle and permanent metamorphosis, which is a component of the evolution of the planet.

regard to some anterior life, whose decline had permitted the hatching of the protoplasmic egg.

Be that as it may, humanity had observed the existence of the ferromagnetals in good time. Once scientists had described their rudimentary manifestations, no one doubted that they were organized beings. Their composition is odd; it comprises only one substance: iron; if other substances are sometimes mingled with it in very small quantities, they are so many impurities, harmful to ferromagnetal development; the organism disposes of them, unless it is very weak or infected by some mysterious malady. The structure of iron in the living state is, however, very variable: fibrous or granular, soft or hard, etc. The whole is plastic and does not contain any liquid. What characterizes the new organisms most of all, however, is an extreme complication and continual instability of their magnetic state.

That instability and that complication are such that the most stubborn researchers have been obliged to renounce, not only the calculation of precise laws, but even approximate rules. It is probably in this feature that it is necessary to see the dominant manifestation of ferromagnetal life. When a superior intelligence reveals itself in the new realm, I think that it will primarily reflect that strange phenomenon—or, rather, that it will be a blossoming of it. In the meantime, if ferromagnetal consciousness exists at all, it is still elementary. They are still at a stage when the need to multiply dominates all others.

Even so, they have already been subject to a few important transformations. The writers of the radioactive age inform us that each individual consists of three groups, with a marked tendency in each group to helicoid forms. They could not, at that time travel faster than five or six centimeters in 24 hours. When their agglomerations were broken up, they took several weeks to re-form. Nowadays, as previously noted, they can attain speeds of two meters an hour; moreover, they comprise agglomerations of three, five, seven or even nine groups, the forms of the groups having acquired considerable variety.

One group, composed of a considerable number of ferromagnetal corpuscles, cannot subsist in isolation; it requires completion by two, four, six or eight other groups. A series of groups evidently involves cohesive forces, without it being possible to specify how. Apart from the sevenfold agglomerations, ferromagnetals perish if any one of their groups is killed. On the other hand, a ternary series can re-form with the aid of only one group, and a quinquenary series with the aid of three groups.

The reconstitution of a mutilated series is very similar to the reproductive mechanism of ferromagnetals; that mechanism retains a profoundly enigmatic character so far as humans are concerned. It operates *at a distance*. When a ferromagnetal is born, one invariably observes the presence of several other ferromagnetals. According to the species, the formation of an individual takes between six hours and ten days; it seems to be exclusively due to phenomena of *induction*. The reconstitution of an injured ferromagnetal is carried out by means of analogous processes.

Presently, the presence of ferromagnetals is almost harmless. Things would doubtless be different if humankind expanded.

At the same time as they were thinking of combating the ferromagnetals, our ancestors sought some method of turning their activity to the advantage of our species. Nothing seemed opposed to the possibility that ferromagnetals might, for example, serve industrial purposes. Had that been the case, it would have been sufficient to protect machinery—which once appeared to have been achieved without overmuch expense— in a manner analogous to that in which we protect our oases. That seemingly elegant solution was attempted; the ancient annals report that it failed.

Iron transformed by the new life demonstrated a resistance to any human use. Its structure and its exceedingly variable magnetism made it into a substance that was unamenable to any combination or any *directed* work. The structure seemed to become uniform and the magnetism to disappear at

209

temperatures close to melting point—and, of course, when melting actually occurred—but when the metal was cooled again, the harmful properties reappeared.

In addition, people were unable to stay for very long in ferromagnetal regions of any size. In a short time, they became anemic. After a day and a night, they found themselves in a state of extreme weakness; they were not long delayed in falling unconscious, and if they were not rescued, they would die.

The immediate cause of this fact is not unknown: the proximity of ferromagnetals tends to rob us of our red blood corpuscles. These corpuscles, almost reduced to the state of pure hemoglobin, accumulate at the surface of the epidermis and are then extracted by the ferromagnetals, which seemingly decompose and assimilate them.

Various measures can counteract or slow down this phenomenon. It is sufficient to keep walking to have nothing to fear; it is even better to travel by electric car. If one clothes a tissue in bismuth fibers, one may brave the enemy influence for at least two days. It is weaker if one lies down with one's had pointing northwards. It weakens spontaneously when the sun is close to its zenith.

As the number of ferromagnetals decreases, of course, the phenomenon is proportionately less intense; a point comes at which it is annulled, for the human organism is not without resistance. Finally, the ferromagnetal influence diminishes in proportion to the inverse square of distance, and becomes insensible beyond ten meters.

One can readily imagine that the disappearance of ferromagnetals seemed necessary to our ancestors. They entered the conflict methodically. In the era when the great catastrophes began, that conflict demanded heavy sacrifices; a selective regime became operative among the ferromagnetals; it was necessary to deploy immense forces to restrict their rapid reproduction.

The planetary modifications that ensued handed the advantage to the new realm; in compensation, their presence

210

became less disturbing, for the quantity of metal necessary to industry decreased periodically, and the seismic disorders brought forth vast masses of native iron that was intangible to the invaders. Thus, the war against them relented to the point of becoming negligible. What did the organic peril matter, by comparison with the immense sidereal peril?

Presently, the ferromagnetals scarcely bother us. With our encircling walls of red hematite, limonite or feldspar, coated with bismuth, we believe ourselves to be impregnable—but if some improbable revolution brought water close to the surface again, the new realm would oppose incalculable obstacles to human development, at least on any large scale.

Targ darted a long glance over the plain; everywhere, he could see the violet tint and peculiarly sinusoidal forms of ferromagnetal agglomerations.

"Yes," he murmured, "If humans were to spread out again, it would require the recommencement of the ancestors' work. It would be necessary to destroy the enemy or make use of it. I fear that destruction might be impossible; a new realm ought to bear within it elements of success that defy the expectations and forces of an old realm. On the other hand, why should we not find a means of permitting the two realms to coexist, and even to assist one another? Yes, why not, since the origins of the ferromagnetal world lie in our industry? Is that not an indication of a profound compatibility?"

Then, raising his eyes toward the great peaks of the Occident, he continued: "Alas, my dreams are ridiculous. And yet...and yet...do they not help me to survive? Do they not give me a little of that youthful happiness that the human soul has lost forever?"

He straightened up, as his heart skipped a beat. In the distance, in a cleft in the Mount of Shadows, three large white gliders had just appeared.

III. The Homicidal Planet

The gliders seemed to brush the Purple Tooth, which was inclined over the abyss. An orange shadow enveloped them; then they gleamed silver in the midday sun.

"Messengers from Redlands!" Mano exclaimed.

He did not learn anything from his companions on the road—their first words were, in fact, no more than a cry for help. The two squadrons increased their speed; soon, the pale masses were sinking down toward the emerald aircraft from High Springs. Greetings were exchanged, followed by a silence; their hearts were heavy; they heard nothing more but the faint hum of the engines and the whirr of the propellers. They felt the cruel strength of the deserts, over which they seemed to be flying as masters.

Finally, Targ asked, in a fearful voice: "Does anyone know how bad the disaster is?"

"No," replied a pilot with a swarthy face. "That won't be known for some time. We only know that the numbers of dead and wounded are considerable—and that's not all! We fear the loss of several springs." He bowed his head with a calm bitterness. "Not only is the crop lost, but many provisions have disappeared. Even so, if there are no further quakes, with the aid of High Springs and Devastation, we can survive for a few years. The race will temporarily suspend its reproduction, and perhaps we won't need to sacrifice anyone."

For a little while longer, the squadrons flew in convoy; then the pilot with the swarthy face changed direction; those from High Springs drew away.

They passed between the redoubtable peaks, above gulfs and along a slope that had once been covered in meadows; now, the ferromagnetals were multiplying their generations there.

Which proves, Targ thought, *that the slope is rich in human ruins!*

Again they flew over vales and hills; about two-thirds of the way through the day, they were 300 kilometers from Redlands.

"One more hour!" Mano exclaimed.

Targ searched the distance with his telescope. He perceived, still blurrily, the oasis and the scarlet region that had given it his name. The spirit of adventure, inflated after the encounter with the big gliders, reawakened in the young man's heart. He accelerated the velocity of his machine and overtook Mano.

Flocks of birds where circling over the red zone; several advanced toward the squadron. Fifty kilometers from the oasis, they arrived in considerable numbers; their calls confirmed the disaster and predicted imminent quakes. Targ, his heart contracted, listened and watched, without being able to say a word.

The desert earth seemed to have been subjected to the bite of an enormous plough; as they came closer, the oasis displayed its collapsed houses, its broken wall, its almost-buried crops, and wretched human ants swarming over the debris.

Suddenly, an immense racket split the air; the flight of the birds was strangely interrupted; a frightful quiver shook the expanse.

The homicidal planet was completing its work!

Only Targ and Arva uttered cries of pity and horror. The other aviators continued their course, with the calm sadness of the Last Men. The oasis was still there. It resounded with ominous plaints. Pitiful creatures could be seen running, crawling or shivering; others remained motionless, struck dead. Sometimes, a bloody head seemed to emerge from the ground. The spectacle became more hideous as they were better able to make out its episodes.

The Nine hovered, uncertainly—but the flight of the birds, initially enfevered by fear, calmed down. No further shock was imminent; they were able to land.

A few members of the Grand Council received the delegates from High Springs. The speeches were sparse and rapid. As the new disaster demanded all available efforts, the Nine joined in with the rescuers.

The lamentations seemed intolerable at first. Atrocious wounds had defied the fatalism of adults, and the screams of children were like the strident and savage soul of Pain.

Finally, anesthetics brought their benevolent aid. Acute suffering sank into the depths of unconsciousness. They only heard rare screams, the cries for help of those who were trapped beneath the ruins.

One of these cries attracted Targ's attention. It was fearful rather than painful; it had an enigmatic and youthful charm. For some time, the young man could not pinpoint its source. Finally, he discovered a hole from which it emerged more clearly. Blocks of stone interrupted the watchman; he had to move them aside carefully. It was continually necessary to pause in the work before muted mineral threats: holes formed abruptly, stones collapsed, or suspect vibrations were heard.

The cries had fallen silent; nervous tension and fatigue covered Targ's forehead with sweat.

Suddenly, all seemed lost; a section of wall crumbled. The digger, sensing that he was at the mercy of the mineral, bowed his head and waited. A block brushed him; he accepted destiny—but the silence and immobility were resumed. Looking up, he saw that a huge cavity, almost a cave, had opened up to his left. In the shadows, a human form was lying. The young man lifted up the living wreckage, with difficulty, and emerged from the debris, just as a new collapse rendered the tunnel impassable.

It was a young woman, or a girl, dressed in the silvery one-piece costume of Redlands. Before anything else, it was her hair that caught her savior's attention; it was the luminous sort that atavism hardly brought back to humankind once in every 100 years. As bright as precious metal, as fresh as water

214

gushing from a deep spring, it seemed the very fabric of love, a symbol of the grace that had adorned womankind through the ages.

Targ's heart swelled, and a heroic tumult filled his skull. He glimpsed magnanimous and glorious deeds, which were never accomplished any more among the Last Men. And while he was admiring the red flower of her lips, the delicate line of her cheeks and their nacreous rosiness, her eyes opened, which were the color of mornings when the Sun is vast and a gentle breeze blows over the wilderness.

IV. In the Depths of the Earth

Dusk had fallen. The constellations had lit their delicate flames. The taciturn oasis was hiding its distress and pain. Targ was walking near the encircling wall with a feverish soul.

It was a dreadful moment for the Last Men. The planetaries had announced a series of immense disasters. Devastation had been destroyed; the waters had disappeared from Two Equatorials, Great Dale and Blue Sands; they were decreasing at High Springs; Bright Oasis and Brimstone Valley announced that they had experienced ruinous quakes or rapid deletions of liquid.

Humankind entire had suffered disaster.

Targ climbed over the ruined wall and went into the mute and terrible desert.

The Moon, almost full, rendered the fainter stars invisible; it lit up the red granites and violet batteries of the ferromagnetals; a pale phosphorescence undulated periodically, a mysterious sign of the activity of the new beings.

The young man advanced into the wilderness, heedless of its funereal grandeur.

A shining image dominated the heartbreak of the catastrophe. It carried him away like a "double" of the vermilion hair; the star Vega was twinkling like a blue eye. Love became the very essence of his life, and that life was more intense, more wonderfully profound. It revealed to him, in its plenitude, the world of beauty that he had anticipated, and for which it would be better to die than to live for the dismal ideals of the Last Men. Periodically, like a name that had become sacred, the name of the woman he had pulled from the rubble came to his lips: "Erê!"

In the grim silence—the silence of the eternal desert, comparable to the silence of the great ether in which the stars sparkled—he advanced further. The air was as motionless as the granite; time seemed dead, space represented another space than that of human beings: an inexorable, glacial space full of ominous images.

There was, however, life there, abominable in being that which would succeed human life: sly, terrific and unknowable. Twice, Targ stopped to watch the phosphorescent forms in action. Darkness did not put them to sleep at all. They were moving, for mysterious ends. The fashion in which they slid over the ground was unexplained by any organ. He quickly lost interest in them, though. The image of Erê captivated him; there was a confused relationship between this walk in the wilderness and the heroism awakened in his soul. He was vaguely in search of adventure: an impossible, chimerical adventure—the discovery of Water.

Water alone could give him Erê. All human laws separated him from her. Yesterday, he would still have been able to dream of marrying her; it would have been sufficient for a daughter of High Springs to be welcomed, in exchange, in Redlands. Since the catastrophe, the exchange had become impossible. High Springs would receive exiles, but would condemn them to celibacy. The law was inexorable; Targ accepted it as a superior necessity.

The Moon was bright; it displayed its disk of nacre and silver over the western hills. Hypnotized, Targ steered toward it. He came into a rocky region. The traces of the disaster were there too: several had toppled, others had split; there were crevices everywhere in the sandy ground.

"One might think," the young man murmured, "that the quake had attained its greatest violence here. Why?" His dream retreated slightly; the environment excited his curiosity. *Why?* he asked himself, again. *Yes, why...?*

He stopped periodically to study the rocks, and also by reason of prudence; the disturbed ground was full of pitfalls. A strange exaltation gripped him. He thought that, if a route to water existed, there was a good chance that it might be revealed in such a profoundly altered place as this.

Having lit the torch that he was never without while he was traveling, he ventured into various fissures and corridors. All of them narrowed rapidly, or terminated in dead ends.

Finally, he found himself in front of a mediocre cleft at the base of a tall and very broad rock, into which the quakes had only eaten slightly. It was sufficient to look at the crack, sparkling in places like crystal, to deduce that it was recent. Targ, judging it negligible, was about to draw away when two scintillations attracted his attention. Why not explore it? If it were not very deep, he would only have a few steps to take.

It turned out to be more extensive than he had hoped. Nevertheless, after thirty paces or so it began to narrow; soon, Targ thought that he could go no further. He stopped, and scrupulously examined the details of the walls. The passage was not yet impossible, but it was necessary to crawl. The watchman scarcely hesitated; he wriggled into a hole whose diameter scarcely exceeded the breadth of a man. Sinuous and strewn with sharp stones, the passage became narrower still; Targ wondered whether it would be possible for him to go back.

It was as if he were wedged in the depths of the ground, a captive of the mineral: a small, infinitely weak thing that a single block of stone could reduce to particles—but the fever of an enterprise begun was palpitating within him; if he abandoned his task before it became utterly impossible, he would hate himself and scorn himself afterwards. He persevered.

His limbs bathed in sweat, he advanced through the entrails of the rock for a long time. In the end, he was on the point of fainting. His heartbeat, fluttering like loud wing-beats, began to weaken. He was no longer anything but a paltry palpitation; courage and hope fell away like discarded burdens. When his heart recovered some force, Targ judged it ridiculous to have embarked on such a primitive adventure.

Would I not be a madman?

He began to crawl backwards. Then, an atrocious despair overwhelmed him; the image of Erê appeared to him so vividly that she seemed to be with him in the fissure.

My madness would be worth more than the fearful wisdom of my peers...forwards!

He recommenced the adventure. He wagered his life savagely, determined only to stop when confronted by the insurmountable.

Hazard seemed to favor his audacity. The crevice broadened; he found himself in a deep basalt corridor whose vault seemed to be sustained by columns of anthracite. A sharp joy gripped him; he began to run. Anything seemed possible—but stone is as full of enigmas as the green forests used to be.

Suddenly, the corridor came to an end. Targ found himself in front of a dark wall, from which the torch scarcely drew a few reflected gleams. Nevertheless, he did not cease exploring the walls—and he discovered, at a height of three meters, the opening of another crevice.

It was a slightly sinuous crack, inclined at about forty degrees from the horizontal, large enough to admit the passage of a man. The watchman considered it with a mixture of joy and disappointment. It attracted his chimerical hope, since the way was not, after all, definitively closed; on the other hand, it seemed discouraging because it would take him in an upward direction.

"If it doesn't go down again, there's more chance that it will take me back to the surface than into the underworld," the explorer muttered.

He made a gesture of insouciance and challenge—a gesture that was foreign to him, as to all present-day men, and which echoed some ancestral gesture. Then he set about scaling the wall.

It was almost vertical, and smooth—but Targ had brought an arcum-fiber ladder, which aviators never forget. He took it out of his tool-bag. Having served for several generations, it was as flexible and solid as in its earliest days. He unrolled the light and delicate structure and, seizing it in the middle, gave it the necessary impulsion. It was a maneuver that he executed to perfection. The hooks at the end of the ladder griped the basalt without difficulty. In a few seconds, the explorer reached the cleft.

He could not retain an exclamation of annoyance—for, although the crevice was perfectly practicable, it climbed up at a rather steep slope. All his efforts would therefore have been in vain!

Even so, having rolled up the ladder again, Targ set off along the fissure. The first stages were difficult; then the floor leveled out and a corridor developed in which several men could have marched abreast. Unfortunately, the slope was still upwards. The watchman reckoned that he must be about 50 meters above the level of the exterior plain; the subterranean voyage had become an ascent!

He marched towards the denouement, whatever it might be, with a tranquil bitterness, reproaching himself for his mad adventure. How could he expect to make a discovery more important than anything humans had found for hundreds of centuries? Would it suffice for him to have a chimerical character, a soul more rebellious than others, in order for him to succeed where collective effort, employing admirable equipment, had failed? Did not an attempt like his demand resignation and absolute patience?

Distracted, he did not notice that the slope had become gentler. It had become horizontal before he awoke, with a start. A few paces in front of him, the tunnel began to descend.

It descended smoothly, over a length of more than a kilometer. It was broad, deeper in the middle than at its edge; walking there was generally comfortable, only occasionally interrupted by a block of stone or a fissure. Doubtless, in some distant epoch, a subterranean watercourse had eroded a passage here.

Debris accumulated, however, some of which was recent; and then the exit seemed to be blocked again.

"The tunnel doesn't stop here," the young man said. "It's the realignments of the Earth's crust that have interrupted it—but when? Yesterday... 1000 years ago... or 100,000 years ago?"

He did not pause to examine the rubble, among which he recognized the traces of recent convulsions. All his perspicacity was concentrated on discovering a way through. It did not take him long to spot a fissure. Narrow and high, hard, bristling and awkward, it did not betray him; he found *his* tunnel again. It continued its descent, ever more spacious; eventually, its mean breadth was in excess of a hundred meters.

Targ's last doubts vanished. A veritable subterranean river had once run here. The conviction was encouraging *a priori*, but on reflection, it worried the oasis-dweller. It did not follow from the fact that water had once been abundant that it was nearby. On the contrary! All the springs presently utilized were far from places where the liquid of life had once flowed...it was almost a law.

Three times more the tunnel appeared to end in a cul-de-sac; each time, Targ found a way through. It did end, though; an immense gulf appeared before the man's eyes.

Weary and sad, he sat down on the stone. This was a moment more terrible than when he had been crawling through the stifling tunnel higher up. Any further attempt seemed bitter folly. He had to go back! His heart rebelled against his mind, though. The soul of adventure rose up, increased by the astonishing journey he had just made. The gulf no longer frightened him.

"What if it is necessary to die?" he exclaimed. Already, he was in search of granite projections. Abandoned to rapid inspiration, he had descended, miraculously, to a depth of thirty meters when he made a false step and lost his balance.

"Finished!" he sighed.

He fell into the void.

V. The Abyssal Depths

An impact stopped him—not the rude impact of a fall on granite, but an elastic impact that was nevertheless violent enough to stun him.

When he recovered consciousness, he found himself suspended in darkness and, by groping, he discovered that a ledge had hooked his tool-bag. The bag's straps, attached to his torso, were retaining him. Like his ladder, they were made of arcum fiber; he knew that they would not give way. On the other hand the bag might become detached from the ledge.

Targ felt strangely calm. Unhurriedly, he calculated his chances of doom and salvation. The bag was looped over the projection close to the attachment of the straps, in such a way that it had a strong hold. The explorer felt the rocky wall. Apart from the ledge, his hand encountered smooth surfaces, then emptiness. His feet found a support to his left—which, after groping around somewhat, he judged to be a little platform. By gripping the upper ledge with one hand and bracing himself on the lower one, he was able to shift his weight to the other support.

When he had found what seemed to be the most comfortable position, he succeeded in detaching the bag. Freer in his movements then, he shone the beam of his radiator in every direction. The ledge was wide enough for a man to stand up on it, and even move about slightly. Above him, there was a crack in the rock that would permit the hooks of the ladder to be firmly fixed; after that, an ascent seemed practicable, back to the place from which the oasis-dweller had fallen. Below him, there was nothing but the gulf, with vertical walls.

I can climb back up, the young man concluded, *but descent is impossible...*

He was no longer thinking about anything but escaping death; nothing agitated his mind but resentment of the vain effort. With a long sigh, he let go of the upper ledge and, hanging on to the cracks, he succeeded in establishing himself securely on the lower ledge. His head was buzzing; torpor was overtaking his limbs and his brain. His discouragement was so great that he felt himself succumbing gradually to the vertiginous appeal of the abyss. When he collected himself, his hands instinctively wandered over the granite wall, and now perceived that it curved away at about waist height. He bent down then, and released a feeble exclamation. The ledge was at the entrance of a cavity, which the beam of the torch revealed to be considerable.

He laughed silently. If he was bound for defeat, at least he would not have had an adventure that was not worth the trouble of attempting!

Having assured himself that he was not missing any equipment—especially that the arcum ladder was in good order—he went into the cave. It displayed a ceiling of rock crystal and gems. At every movement of the lamp, mysterious and magical flashes were ignited. The hearts of the countless crystals awoke in the light; it was a subterranean twilight, furtive and dazzling, an infinitesimal hail of scarlet, orange, jonquil, hyacinth and emerald light. Targ saw a reflection of mineral life there—the vast and minuscule, menacing and profound life that had had the last word with men, and would one day have the last word with the ferromagnetic realm.

At that moment, he was not afraid of it. However, he studied the cave with the respect that the Last Men owed the muted existences which, having presided over the world's Origins, retained their forms and energies intact.

A vague mysticism stirred within him—not the hopeless mysticism of the fallen oasis-dwellers, but the mysticism that had once guided hazardous hearts. Although he still mistrusted the traps of the Earth, at least he had the faith that succeeds successful efforts and transports the victories of the past into the future.

After the cave came a corridor of capricious slopes. Several more times it was necessary for him to crawl in order to pass through. Then the corridor resumed; the slope became steep, to the point that Targ feared a new gulf. That slope became gentler; it was almost as comfortable as a roadway—and the watchman descended safely, until the traps took hold again. Without the corridor narrowing in height or in width, it was closed off. There was a wall of gneiss, gleaming slyly in the lamplight. The oasis-dweller sounded it in every direction; no substantial fissure was revealed.

"It's the logical conclusion of the adventure!" he groaned. "The abyss, which has toyed with the efforts, the genius and the apparatus of humanity entire, cannot be favorable to a tiny solitary animal!"

He sat down, worn out by fatigue and sadness. The road would be hard now! Beaten down by defeat, would he even have the strength to follow it to the end?

He stayed there for some time, crushed by his distress. He could not make the decision to go back. Periodically, he shone his lamp on the blank wall. Finally, he got up—but then, seized by a sort of fury, he stuck his fists into all the slender fissures, tugged desperately at all the projections...

His heat began to beat faster. Something had moved.

Something had moved. A section of the wall oscillated. With a muted grunt, and with all his strength, Targ attacked the stone. It pivoted; it almost crushed him. A triangular hole appeared. The adventure was not finished yet!

Breathless, and full of suspicion, Targ went into the rock, bent double at first, and then upright, for the fissure expanded with every step. He was going forward in a kind of somnambulistic state, expecting new obstacles, when he thought he saw another gulf.

He was not mistaken. The fissure ended in a void—but to the right, an enormous sloping mass stood out. To reach it, Targ had to lean out and pull himself along by the strength of his wrists.

The slope was practicable. When the watchman had covered 20 meters, a strange sensation gripped him. Taking out his hygroscope, he held it out over the gulf. Then, he positively felt the pallor and the chill settle in his face...

In the subterranean atmosphere, vapor was floating, as yet invisible to the light. Water was nearby!

Targ uttered a yell of triumph; he had to sit down, paralyzed by the surprise and joy of victory. Then, uncertainty took hold of him again. The living fluid was undoubtedly there, about to appear; but the disappointment would be all the more unbearable if it were only an insignificant trickle or a small pool. With slow steps, full of dread, the watchman resumed the descent. The evidence multiplied; gleams became perceptible at intervals...

And abruptly, as Targ went around a vertical projection, the water appeared.

VI. The Ferromagnetals

Two hours before dawn, Targ found himself back on the plain, on the edge of the crevice where his voyage to the land of shadows had begun. Terribly tired, he studied the scarlet moon on the rim of the horizon, like a red furnace ready to go out. It disappeared. In the immense darkness, the stars were reanimated.

The watchman wanted to get under way again then. His legs seemed to be made of stone, his shoulders sagged dolorously, and such languor spread through his entire body that he let himself collapse on a block of stone.

With his eyelids half-closed, he recalled the hours that he had just spent in the abyssal depths. The return journey had been frightful. Despite the fact that he had taken care to leave evidence of his passage, he had gone astray. Then, already exhausted by his previous efforts, he had almost fainted. The time seemed immeasurably long; Targ was like a miner who might have spent long months within the cruel Earth.

Even so, here he was, back on the surface where his kindred lived; here were the stars that had exalted the dreams of humankind throughout the ages; soon, the divine dawn would reappear in the expanse.

"Dawn!" stammered the young man. "Daylight!"

He extended his arm toward the east, in a gesture of ecstasy; then his eyes closed again, and—without being conscious of it—he lay down on the ground.

A red light woke him up again. Raising his eyelids with difficulty, he perceived the immense orb of the sun on the horizon.

Come on! Get up! he said to himself—but an invincible torpor nailed him to the ground; his thoughts drifted numbly; fatigue preached renunciation to him. He was about to go to sleep again, when he felt a slight prickling sensation over his entire epidermis—and he saw on his hand, alongside the scratches that stones had inflicted on him, characteristic red dots.

"The ferromagnetals," he murmured. "*They're drinking my life!*"

In his lassitude, he could barely recall the adventure. It was like something distant, foreign, almost symbolic. Not only did he not feel any pain, but the sensation became almost pleasant; it was a sort of dizziness, a slow and shallow drunkenness that must have resembled euthanasia...

Suddenly, the images of Erê and Arva traversed his memory, followed by a surge of energy. "I don't want to die!" he moaned. "I don't want to!"

He vaguely relived his struggle, his suffering, his victory. In the distance, in Redlands, life attracted him, fresh and charming. No, he did not want to die; he wanted to see the dawns and dusks for a long time yet; he wanted to fight the mysterious forces.

And, summoning up his dormant will, with a terrible effort, he tried to stand up.

VII. Water, Mother of Life

In the morning, Arva had no suspicion of Targ's absence. He had worked hard the day before; doubtless, worn out with fatigue, he was sleeping late. After two hours of waiting, however, she became anxious, and ended up knocking on the door of the watchman's chosen room. There was no response. Perhaps he had gone out while she was asleep? She knocked again, then pressed the door-switch; as it rolled back, the door revealed an empty room.

The young woman went in, and saw that everything was in good order: the arcum bed was lifted back against the wall; the washstand was tidy. There was no evidence of the recent presence of a man. A certain apprehension gripped the visitor's heart.

She went to find Mano; they both interrogated birds and humans alike without obtaining any useful reply. That was abnormal, and perhaps worrying—for the oasis, after the earthquake, was full of pitfalls. Targ might have fallen into a fissure or have been caught up in a collapse.

"It's more likely that he's gone out in the morning sunlight," said the optimistic Mano. "As he's an orderly fellow, he'd have tidied his room first. Let's go find him."

Arva was still anxious. Communications having become uncertain, and many radiolinks having been broken, their research made no progress.

As midday approached, Arva was wandering sadly through the rubble in the borderlands of the oasis and the desert when a flock of birds appeared, calling loudly: "Targ is found!"

226

She only had to climb up on the wall to see him, still distant, approaching with a heavy tread.

His clothes were torn; there were cuts gashing his neck, face and hands; his entire body expressed fatigue—only his eyes retained a certain vigor.

"Where have you been?" Arva cried.

"I've been deep into the Earth," he replied—but he did not want to say any more.

The rumor of his return spread rapidly, and his traveling companions came to see him. One of them having reproached him for delaying their departure, however, he replied: "Don't criticize me, for I bring great news."

This reply surprised and shocked his listeners. How could a man bring news that was not known to other men? Such words had had meaning, once, when the Earth was unknown and full of resources, when hazard dwelt among living beings and individuals or peoples opposed their destiny—but now, when the planet was exhausted, when men could no longer struggle against one another, when everything was resolved by inflexible laws and no one could anticipate perils before the birds and the instruments, they were absurd.

"Great news!" the man who had reproached him repeated, disdainfully. "Have you gone mad, watchman?"

"You'll soon see whether I've gone mad! Let's go in search of the Redlands Council."

"You've made them wait."

Targ did not reply. He turned to his sister and said to her: "Go fetch the woman I saved yesterday. Her presence is necessary."

The Grand Council of Redlands was meeting at the center of the oasis. It was not complete, several of its members having been killed in the disaster. The attitude of the survivors showed no trace of dolor, and little of resignation. Fatality had entered into them, as present as life itself.

They welcomed the Nine with an almost inert calm, and Cimor, who was presiding, said in a uniform voice: "You brought us aid from High Springs, and High Springs has been struck itself. The end of humankind seems very close. The oases no longer know which of them is able to help the others..."

"They should not try to help one another any longer," added Rem, the chief supervisor of the waters. "The law forbids it. It is equitable, when the waters drain away, that solidarity should disappear. Each oasis will determine its own fate."

Targ stepped in front of the Nine and said: "The waters might reappear."

Rem considered him with tranquil scorn. "Anything might reappear, young man—but they have disappeared."

Then having darted a glance at the back of the room and perceived the luminous hair there, the watchman continued tremulously: "The waters will reappear for Redlands."

Placid disapproval appeared on some faces; everyone remained silent.

"They will reappear," Targ cried, forcefully. "And I can say so, because I have seen them."

This time, a faint stir, born of the one image that was able to excite the Last Men—the image of gushing water—passed from neighbor to neighbor. Targ's tone, by its vehemence and sincerity, almost engendered hope—but doubt returned swiftly. Those overly bright eyes, the wounds and the torn clothing encouraged suspicion, although rare, that madmen had not yet disappeared from the planet.

Cimor gave a slight signal. A number of men slowly encircled the watchman. He saw the movement and understood its significance. Untroubled, he opened his tool-bag, took hold of his slender chromographic apparatus and, unrolling a leaf, displayed the evidence that he had collected in the bowels of the Earth.

They were images as precise as the reality itself. As soon as they struck the eyes of the people nearest to him, exclamations burst forth. A veritable thrill, almost an exaltation, took possession of the audience, for everyone recognized the redoubtable and sacred fluid.

Mano, more impressionable than the others, yelled in a resounding voice. The cry, reverberated by the radiolinks, expanded outside; a multitude swiftly surrounded the hall. The only delirium that could still lift up the Last Men intoxicated the crowd.

Targ was transfigured; he was almost godlike. Like the hearts of old, hearts went out to him with a mystic enthusiasm; faces blossomed, bleak eyes filling with fire; an immeasurable hope broke through the long atavism of resignation—and the members of the Grand Council themselves, lost in the collective being, abandoned themselves to the tumult.

Only Targ could obtain silence. He signaled to the crowd that he wanted to speak; the voices died down and the surge of heads became calmer; ardent attention dilated their faces.

The watchman, turning toward the blonde gleam that Erê mingled with all the dark heads of hair, declaimed: "People of Redlands, the water that I have discovered is on your land; it belongs to you—but human law gives me a right to it; before surrendering it to you, I claim my privilege!"

"You shall be the first to join us," said Cimor. "That is the rule."

"That's not what I ask," the watchman replied, softly. He made a sign to the crowd that they should let him through. Then he headed toward Erê. When he reached her, he bowed and said, in an ardent voice: "It is in your hands that I place the waters, mistress of my destiny. You alone can give me my reward."

She listened, surprised and tremulous, for such words were never heard any longer. At a different moment, she would scarcely have understood them—but in the midst of the exaltation of hearts, with the enchanted vision of the subterranean springs, her entire being was disturbed; the magnificent emotion that was agitating the watchman was reflected in the maiden's pearly face.

VIII. And Only Redlands Survives

In the years that followed, there were only feeble earthquakes, but the last catastrophe had sufficed to kill off many oases. Those that had seen all their water disappear could not recover any. At High Springs it had drained away for eighteen months and then vanished into unsoundable gulfs. Only Redlands had known great hope. The expanse found by Targ provided abundant water, less impure than that of the springs that had disappeared. Not only was it sufficient to maintain the survivors, but they had been able to welcome the small group that had been saved at Devastation and many inhabitants of High Springs.

There, all possible help stopped. The heredity of 50,000 years having adapted them to inexorable laws, the Last Men accepted the judgment of destiny meekly. There was, in consequence, no war; only a few individuals attempted to bend the rules and came to Redlands as beggars. They could only be refused; pity would have been a supreme injustice and a breach of trust.

As their provisions were gradually exhausted, each oasis designated the inhabitants that were to perish. The old were sacrificed first, then the children, save for a small number that were reserved in case of a possible revival of the planet, then all those whose bodies were diseased or puny.

Euthanasia was contrived with extreme gentleness. As soon as the condemned had absorbed the marvelous poisons, all fear was abolished. Their waking hours were a permanent ecstasy, their slumber as profound as death. The idea of annihilation delighted them; their joy increased until the final torpor. Many brought the appointed hour forward. Gradually, that became a contagion. In the equatorial oases, no one waited for the provisions to run out; water still remained in a few reservoirs when the last inhabitants had already disappeared.

230

It took four years to annihilate the people of High Springs; then the oasis was seized by the immense desert, and ferromagnetals took the place of humans.

Following Targ's discovery, Redlands prospered. The oasis was reconstructed further east, in a territory where the rarity of ferromagnetals rendered their destruction easy. The clearance, the construction work and the capture of the waters was completed in six months. The first harvest was good, the second marvelous.

In spite of the successive demise of other communities, the people of Redlands lived in a sort of hope. Were they not the chosen people, in favor of whom, for the first time in a hundred centuries, the implacable law had bent?

Targ maintained that state of mind. His influence was great; he had the attraction and symbolic prestige of triumphant individuals. His victory, however, did not impress anyone else as much as him. He saw it as an obscure reward for—and, even more so, as a confirmation of—his faith. His spirit of adventure blossomed; he had aspirations almost comparable to those of heroic ancestors—and the love that he felt for Erê and the two children born to her was mingled with dreams of which he dared not speak to anyone, except for his wife or his sister, for he knew that they were incomprehensible to the Last Men.

Mano knew nothing of these fevers. His life remained direct. He scarcely thought about the past, much less the future. He savored the uniform mildness of days; he lived, with his wife Arva, an existence as careless as that of the silvery birds whose flocks flew over the oasis every morning. As his first children, by virtue of their robust constitution, had been among the emigrants welcomed into Redlands, only a fugitive melancholy gripped him when he thought about the wasting away of High Springs.

By contrast, that wasting away tormented Targ; his glider took him back to his native oasis many times. He searched for water stubbornly, straying far away from the protected roads, visiting the terrible extents where the ferromagnetals enjoyed the life of young realms. With a few men from the oasis he sounded a hundred gulfs. Although the research was in vain, Targ was not at all discouraged; he taught his followers that discoveries had to be merited by dogged effort and great patience.

IX. Fugitive Water

One day, as he was coming back from the desert in his glider, Targ noticed a large crowd near the big reservoir. With the aid of his telescope, he made out the supervisors of the Waters and the members of the Grand Council; a few miners were emerging from the capture well. A flock of birds came to meet the glider; from them, Targ learned that the spring was causing anxiety. He landed, and as quickly surrounded by an anxious crowd, whose members put their trust in him. He felt a chill in his bones when he heard Mano say: "The waters are receding."

All the voices confirmed this sad news. He questioned Rem, the senior supervisor of the Waters, who told him: "The level has been checked at the edge of the expanse itself. The reduction is six meters."

Of them all, Rem had the most immovable face. Joy, sadness, dread and desire never appeared on his cold lips or his eyes, which were like two fragments of bronze, and in which the sclerotic was scarcely visible. His professional knowledge was perfect; he was master of the entire tradition of the captors of wells.

"The water-level isn't immutable," Targ remarked.

"That's true! But the normal withdrawals never exceed two meters, and they're never abrupt."

"Are you certain that they are at present?"

"Yes; the recorders have verified it; their progress is normal. They haven't registered anything this morning. It was

232

about midday that the diminution began, so it has reached more than 1.50 meters an hour." His mineral stare remained fixed; his hand had not twitched; one could scarcely see his lips move.

Targ's eyes were palpitating, as was his heart.

According to the divers," said Rem, "no new fissure has formed in the bed of the lake. The problem must therefore be with the springs. There are three main hypotheses that might account for it: either the springs are blocked, they've been diverted, or they're drying up. We still have some hope." The word *hope* fell from his mouth like a block of ice.

"Are the reservoirs full?" Targ asked.

Rem almost made a gesture. "They always are—and I've given orders to dig supplementary ones. Within an hour, all our forces will be fully active."

It was as Rem had said. Redlands' powerful machines hollowed out the granite. Until the first star appeared, a stupor reigned over the oasis.

Targ had gone underground. There was now a rapid and danger-free access route, thanks to tunnels excavated by the miners. In the beams of searchlights, the watchman considered the subterranean location that he had been the first person to reach. He studied it feverishly.

Two springs fed the lake; the first opened out at a depth of 26 meters, the second at 24. The divers had been able to get into one of them, but with difficulty; the other was too narrow. To obtain some supplementary information, work had been undertaken in the rock, but a collapse had given rise to fears. Might not the excavation generate fissures through which the waters could be lost?

Agre, the oldest member of the Grand Council, had said: "This water was given to us by the Disaster; without that, it would have remained inaccessible. Perhaps it also hollowed out its present route. Let's not carry out haphazard endeavors; it's sufficient that we have brought to a successful conclusion the ones that were indispensable."

These words seeming wise, they resigned themselves to mystery.

As dusk approached, the level was declining more gradually, and a wave of hope ran through the oasis, but Targ and the supervisors of the Waters did not share that confidence; if the losses were attenuating, it was because the level had descended below the widest outflow fissures. The water presently contained in the lake could go down to four meters and, if the springs remained inactive, that—together with the supplies in the reservoirs—would be *all the water the Last Men possessed.*

All night, the Redlands machines hollowed out new reservoirs; all night, too, the water, mother of life, never ceased to disappear into the abysms of the planet.

In the morning, the level was down to eight meters, but two reservoirs were ready, which rapidly received their provision. They absorbed 3000 cubic meters of liquid. Filling them further reduced the level; the mouth of the first spring was exposed. Targ went into it before anyone else, and perceived that the rock had been subject to recent transformations. Several crevices had formed, and masses of porphyry were blocking the passage; it was necessary to give up attempts to specify the disaster for the time being.

A second day passed, funereally. At 5 p.m., the subterranean outflow and the filling of a reservoir lowered the waters to the level of the second spring, whose orifice had completely disappeared.

From that moment on, the losses ceased; it became virtually futile to hasten the construction of further reservoirs. Rem persisted, even so, in bringing the work to a conclusion, and for six days the men and machines of the oasis labored.

At the end of the sixth day, the exhausted Targ, his heart feverish, stood outside his house meditating. Silvery darkness enveloped the oasis. Jupiter was visible, a sharp semicircle cleaving through the ether. Doubtless the great planet had also created realms, which, having known the freshness of youth and the strength of ripeness, were dying of anguish and penury.

Erê came out. In a ray of moonlight, her long hair was reminiscent of a soft warm light. Targ drew her to him, and murmured: "I have rediscovered the life of olden times with you. You are the dream of genesis; merely in sensing your presence, I believed in numberless days. Now, Erê, if we cannot recover the springs, and are unable to discover any new water, within ten years the Last Men will have disappeared from the planet."

X. The Earthquake

Six seasons passed. The supervisor of waters had immense tunnels dug in order to recover the springs. All of them failed. Illusory fissures or impenetrable gulfs frustrated the efforts. From one month to the next, hope decreased in hearts and minds. The long atavism of resignation descended upon them again; their passivity seemed even greater than before, in the same way that chronic maladies are aggravated after a respite. All faith, however slight, abandoned them. Death already had their bleak lives in its grip.

When the time arrived for the Grand Council to decree the first round of euthanasias, more of the living were willing to volunteer than the law required. Only Targ, Arva and Erê refused to accept their fate.

Mano became discouraged. It was not that he had gained in foresight—even more than before, he gave no thought to tomorrow—but the fatality had become present to him. When the euthanasias commenced, he had such a sharp sense of impending death that all energy abandoned him; darkness and the light seemed equally hostile to him. He lived in listless funereal anticipation. His love for Arva disappeared along with his self-regard; he took no interest in his children, sure that euthanasia would soon take them away. Speech became odious to him; he no longer listened; he remained taciturn and torpid for entire days.

Almost all the inhabitants of Redlands led a similar existence. No effort stimulated their pitiful energy, for work had virtually ceased. Save for a few fields of plants, maintained to produce fresh seeds, almost all cultivation had been abandoned. The water in the reservoirs demanded no care; it was shielded from evaporation and purified by fully-automatic apparatus. As for the reservoirs themselves, it was sufficient to subject them to daily inspections facilitated by automatic measuring-devices. Thus, there was nothing to disturb the lethargy of the Last Men. Those who resisted atrophy most strongly were the least emotional individuals, who had never loved anyone and scarcely loved themselves. They were perfectly adapted to millennia-old laws, displaying a monotonous perseverance, strangers to all joy as to all pain. Inertia dominated them; they maintained themselves against any excessive depression and all abrupt resolutions; they were the perfect products of a condemned species.

In contrast, Targ and Arva maintained themselves, by means of a superior emotionality. Rebelling against the evidence, they opposed to the formidable planet small ardent lives full of love and hope, palpitating with the vast desires that had kept animal life alive for millions of years.

The watchman had not abandoned any of his research; he carefully kept a fleet of gliders and electric cars operational. He did not even allow the principal planetaries to fall into ruins, and monitored the seismological apparatus.

One evening, after an excursion to Devastation, Targ was sitting up on his own in the dark. Through the transparent metal of his window, a constellation was visible that had been known in the Age of Fable as Canis Major. It included the brightest of all stars, a sun much vaster than our own. Targ extended his inextinguishable desire toward it, and thought of what he had seen in the middle of the day, while he was flying close to the ground.

It was in an exceedingly bleak plain, where only a few solitary stone blocks stood forth. The ferromagnetals displayed their violet agglomerations everywhere. He scarcely paid any heed when he perceived to the south, on a bright yellow surface, a variety with which he was unfamiliar. It produced individuals of considerable height, each formed of eighteen groups. Some attained a total length of three meters. Targ calculated that the mass of the largest could not be less than forty kilograms. They moved more easily than the previously-known ferromagnetals; in fact, their velocity reached half a kilometer per hour.

"That's frightful," murmured the watchman. "If they got into the oasis, might we be vanquished? The smallest gap in the encircling wall might put us in mortal danger."

He shivered; an anxious tenderness drew him into the neighboring rooms. By the orange light of a Radiant he contemplated Erê's astonishingly luminous hair, and the innocent faces of his children. His heart melted. Merely in seeing them alive, he could not imagine the end of humankind. What! The youth and mysterious power of generations was within them, so full of energy—and all that was to vanish? That a valetudinarian race, slowly broken by decadence, should do that was logical—but not them, not their flesh, as pretty and as new as that of the people of the pre-radioactive era.

As he returned, thoughtfully, a slight tremor shook the ground. He scarcely had time to notice it before the immense calm descended on the oasis again—but Targ was full of suspicion. He waited for some time, with his ear cocked, listening. Everything remained peaceful; the grey masses of the location, profiled by the powdery light of the stars, seemed immutable, and in the implacably pure sky, Aquila, Pegasus, Perseus and Sagittarius were inscribing the passing minutes on the clock-face of infinity.

Am I mistaken? The watchman thought. *Or will the quake prove to be genuinely insignificant?*

He shrugged his shoulders, with a slight frisson. How could he even dare to think that an earthquake might be insignificant? The most infinitesimal was full of menacing mystery!

Anxiously, he went to consult the seismographs. The first apparatus had registered a slight tremor—a delicate trace scarcely a millimeter long. The second apparatus gave no evidence of any sequel to the phenomenon.

Targ went to the bird-house; they no longer kept more than twenty. When he arrived they were all asleep; they scarcely raised their heads when the watchman switched on the light. They must, therefore, have scarcely felt the tremor, very briefly, and they were not anticipating a second.

Even so, Targ thought that he ought to alert the chief watchman. The man in question—an inert person with slow wits—had not noticed anything.

"I'll make my rounds," he said. "We're checking the levels every hour."

Targ was reassured by these words.

XI. The Fugitives

Targ was still asleep when someone touched his shoulder. When he opened his eyes, he saw his sister Arva, who was very pale, looking at him. That was a sure sign that something was wrong; he sat up abruptly.

"What's happening?"

"Fearful things," the young woman replied. "You know that there was an earthquake last night, since it was you who recorded the fact?"

"A very slight tremor."

"So slight that no one, apart from you, even noticed it—but its consequences are terrible. The water in the large reservoir has disappeared! And the southern reservoir has three large cracks!"

Targ had gone as pale as Arva. Hoarsely, he said: "No one was checking the levels, then?"

"Yes. Until this morning, the levels didn't vary. Only then did the large reservoir suddenly begin to empty. In ten minutes, the water was gone. In the southern reservoir, the cracks revealed themselves half an hour ago. At most, we'll be able to save a third of its contents."

Targ's head was bowed and his shoulders hunched. He looked like a man who was about to collapse. Full of horror, he murmured: "Is this, finally, the end of the human race?"

The catastrophe was complete. As they had exhausted, for the requirements of the oasis, all the granite reservoirs except for those that had just been struck by the accident, the only water they had left was that held in arcum basins. It was sufficient to quench the thirst of 500 or 600 human beings for a year.

The Grand Council met. It was a glacial and almost taciturn assembly. The people who composed it, apart from Targ, had reached a state of perfect resignation. There was scarcely any discussion: nothing but the reading of laws and a calculation based on invariable givens. The resolutions were, in consequence, simple, clear and pitiless.

Rem, the senior supervisor of waters, summarized them: "The population of Redlands still amounts to seven thousand inhabitants. Six thousand must submit to euthanasia this very day. Five hundred must die before the end of the month. The remainder will decrease week by week, in such a manner as to maintain 50 people until the end of the fifth year. If no new water has been discovered by then, it will be the end of humankind."

The assembly listened impassively. All reflection was vain; an incommensurable fatality enveloped their souls. And Rem continued: "Men and women over 40 cannot continue living. Except for 50, they must all accept euthanasia today. As for children, nine families out of ten cannot retain any; the others may only keep one. The choice of adults is determined in advance; we have only to consult the medical lists."

A feeble stir of emotion ran through the assembly. Then the heads nodded, as a sign of submission, and the crowd outside, to whom the radiolinks had communicated the deliberation, fell silent. Only a slight melancholy darkened the youngest faces.

But Targ was not resigned. He ran back to his home, where Arva and Erê were waiting fearfully. They clutched their children; emotion welled up in them—young and tenacious emotion, the source of ancient life and vast futures.

Beside them, Mano was dreaming. Their anxiety had only surprised him momentarily. Fatalism lay upon his shoulders like a boulder.

At the sight of Targ, Arva cried: "I don't want to! I don't want to! We shan't die this way!"

"You're right," Targ replied. "We'll meet misfortune head on."

Mano came out of his torpor to say: "What will you do? Death is closer than if we were 100 years old."

"It doesn't matter!" cried Targ. "We're leaving!"

"The Earth is empty, so far as humans are concerned," said Mano. "It will kill you painfully. Here, at least the end will be gentle."

Targ was no longer listening. He was absorbed by the urgency of action; it was necessary to flee before midday, the hour appointed for the sacrifice.

Having visited the gliders and the electric cars with Arva, he made his choice. Then he divided between the vehicles the water and foodstuffs he had in store, while Arva topped up the fuel. Their work was rapid. By 9 a.m., everything was ready.

They found Mano still plunged in his torpor, and Erê packing useful clothing.

"We're about to go, Mano," said Targ, touching his brother-in-law's shoulder. "Come with us!"

Mano slowly shrugged his shoulders. "I don't want to die in the desert!" he declared.

Arva threw herself upon him and hugged him with all her affection. A little of his former love warmed him up, but he was immediately seized again by the inevitable. "I don't want to!" he said.

They all begged him, for some time. Targ even tried to drag him away by force; Mano resisted with the invincible power of inertia.

As it was getting late, they unloaded the provisions from the fourth glider and, after one last plea, Targ gave the signal to depart. The aircraft took off in the sunlight. Arva directed a long glance at the dwelling where her husband was awaiting euthanasia, then, shaken by sobs, she flew off into the boundless wilderness.

XII. Toward the Equatorial Oases

Targ headed for the equatorial oases; the others harbored nothing but death.

In the course of his explorations, he had visited Devastation, High Springs, Great Dale, Blue Sands, Bright Oasis and Brimstone Valley; they contained some nourishment, but not a drop of water. Only the two equatorial oases retained meager reserves. The nearer of the two, the Equatorial of the Dunes, 4500 kilometers away, could be reached the following morning.

The journey was abominable. Arva never stopped thinking about Mano's death. When the Sun reached its zenith, she uttered a long funereal wail—it was the hour of euthanasia! Never again would she see the man with whom she had lived the loving adventure.

The desert extended its vast expanse. To human eyes, the ground was terribly dead. The other life was, however, increasing there, for it was the time of reproduction. They could see it swarming over the plain and the hills, redoubtable and incomprehensible. Sometimes Targ cursed it; sometimes a fearful sympathy awoke in his soul. Was there not a mysterious analogy, and even an obscure fraternity, between these creatures and humans? Certainly, the two realms were less distant from one another than either was from the inert mineral realm. Who could tell whether their consciousnesses, in the fullness of time, might have reached an understanding?

Thinking about that, Targ sighed—and the gliders continued to plough through the blue oxygen, toward an unknown so terrible that merely thinking about it caused the travelers to feel a numb chill in their flesh.

In order to guard against surprises, they made a halt before dusk. Targ selected a hill surmounted by a plateau. The ferromagnetals seemed to be scarce there, of species easy to displace. On the plateau itself there was a crag of green porphyry with propitious hollows. The gliders landed; they were secured with the aid of arcum ropes. Being made of materials chosen for their extreme resistance, they were, in any case, virtually invulnerable.

It transpired that the rock and its surroundings only sheltered a few groups of ferromagnetals of the smallest size. Within a quarter of an hour they had been expelled and it was possible to set up the camp.

Having had a meal of concentrated gluten and essential hydrocarbons, the fugitives waited for nightfall. How many other creatures similar to themselves had suffered analogous distresses in the immense ocean of the ages? When scarce and solitary family groups roamed the hostile land with wooden clubs and frail stone tools, there had been nights when humans trembled with hunger, cold and fear at the approach of lions and rainstorms. Later, shipwreck victims had wailed on desert islands or on the rocks of some murderous shore; travelers had become lost in the bosom of carnivorous forests or marshes. The dramas of distress were innumerable! But all those unfortunates had the prospect of a life without limits before them; Targ and his companions could not anticipate anything but death.

Even so, thought the watchman, looking at Erê's and Arva's children, *this tiny group contains all that is necessary to remake humankind.* He uttered a groan.

The polar stars rotated around their narrow track; for a long time, Targ and Arva meditated, wretchedly, next to the sleeping family.

The next day, they arrived at the Equatorial of the Dunes. It lay in the heart of a desert that had once been formed of sand, but which the millennia had hardened. The landing chilled the hearts of the new arrivals; the cadavers of the last people to yield to euthanasia still lay there, unburied. Many Equatorials, having preferred to die beneath the open sky, were visible amid the ruins, motionless in their terrible slumber. The dry air, infinitely pure, had mummified them. They could have stayed in that state for an interminable time, supreme witnesses of the end of humankind.

A more menacing spectacle disturbed the sadness of the fugitives: swarming ferromagnetals. Their violet colonies were visible on all sides, and many of them were considerable in size.

"Forward march!" said Targ, with enthusiasm and anxiety.

He had no need to insist. Aware of the peril, Arva and Erê hurried the children along, while Targ studied the location. The oasis had only suffered minor damage. Storms had damaged a few dwellings and knocked over planetaries and radio-links; the majority of the machines and power-generators should be intact—but the watchman was particularly worried about the arcum reservoirs. There were two of them, largely depleted, whose location he knew. When he reached them, he dared not touch them at first; his heart was beating fearfully. When he finally made the decision, though, he shouted, in a paroxysm of excitement: "Intact! We have water for two years—now let's find shelter."

After a long search, he chose a tongue of land close to the western wall. There were only small numbers of ferro-

243

magnetals there; a protective barrier could be constructed within a few days. Two spacious dwellings spared by the weather were available.

Targ and Arva explored the larger of the two. The furniture and the instruments proved to be solid, scarcely covered by fine dust; a certain subtle presence was perceptible everywhere. As they entered one of the rooms the visitors were gripped by a profound melancholy; two humans were lying side by side on the arcum bed. For some time, Targ and Arva contemplated the peaceful forms, which life had once inhabited, and which had been stirred by joy and pain.

Others would have taken a lesson in resignation from that, but they—full of bitterness and horror—stiffened themselves for the struggle to come. They got rid of the corpses and, after making sure that Erê and the children were safe, expelled a few groups of ferromagnetals. Then they had their first meal on the new land.

"Courage!" murmured Targ. "There was a time, in the depths of Eternity, when a single human couple existed; our entire species is descended from them! We are stronger than that couple, for if it had perished, humankind would have perished. Here, several might die without destroying all hope."

"Yes," sighed Erê, "but water covered the Earth!"

Targ looked at her with a boundless affection. "Have we not found water once already?" he said, in a low voice.

He remained motionless, as if his eyes were blinded by an internal dream—but he roused himself to say: "While you look after the house, I shall examine our resources."

He explored the oasis in every direction, evaluating the provisions left behind by the Equatorials, making sure that the power-generators, machines, planetaries and radiolinks were working. The industrial treasure of the Last Men was there, ready to support any renaissance. Besides, Targ had brought his technical books from Redlands, and annals rich in ideas and memories.

The presence of the ferromagnetals worried him. In some areas they were accumulated in redoubtable masses; he had only to pause for a few minutes to sense their muted labor.

If we have any descendants, he thought, *the war will be long and hard!*

He eventually arrived at the southern tip of the Equatorial. There he stopped; in a field that had once contained cereals he had just perceived ferromagnetals of the large variety that he had discovered in the desert near High Springs. He felt a tightness in his chest, and a cold breath passed over the back of his neck.

XIII. The Interim

The seasons went by in the eternal gulf. Targ and his relatives were still alive. The vast world enveloped them with its menace. Before, when they had been living in Redlands, they had already been subject to the melancholy of the deserts that announced the end of humankind, but thousands of their peers had, after all, occupied the supreme refuge along with them. Now, they fell victim to a more complete distress; they were no more than a minuscule trace of the former life. From one pole to the other, in all the plains and on all the mountains, every part of the planet was hostile, save for that other oasis in which euthanasia had devoured creatures who had abandoned all hope, without remission.

They had surrounded their chosen terrain with a protective wall, further consolidated the water reservoirs, assembled and sheltered the provisions—and Targ often left, with Erê or Arva, on missions of discovery across the desert expanse. While searching for the creative water, they collected hydrogenated matter everywhere. Such matter was rare; hydrogen, released in immense quantities in the times of human power, and also when attempts had been made to replace natural water with industrial water, had almost disappeared. According to the annals, the greater part of it had decomposed into sub-atomic particles and dissipated in interplanetary space. The rest had been drawn, by ill-defined reactions, into inaccessible depths. Targ, however, gleaned enough useful substances to increase the provision of water significantly—but it could only be a temporary expedient.

Targ was particularly preoccupied with the ferromagnet-als. They were prospering. This was because they had, beneath the oasis at a mediocre depth, considerable reserves of human iron. The ground and the surrounding plain covered a dead city. Now, the ferromagnetals extracted subterranean iron at a much greater distance as they grew in size themselves. The latest arrivals—the Tertiaries, as Targ named them—could, if they took their time about it, extract it from a depth of some eight meters. Furthermore, the displacements of metal even-tually opened breaches in the earth into which the Tertiaries could introduce themselves. The other ferromagnetals were contriving similar effects, but incomparably weaker—besides, they never descended to depths of more than two or three me-ters.

With respect to the Tertiaries, Targ soon observed that there were scarcely any limits to their penetration; they des-cended as far as the fissures would permit. It was necessary to take special measures to prevent them from mining the ground on which the two families lived. The machines hollowed out tunnels within the enclosing wall, whose walls were lined with arcum and bismuth plates. Pillars of granite cement, bedded in the rock, ensured the solidity of the vaults. This vast project lasted several, months; the power-generators, together with flexible and subtle machines, allowed the work to be carried out without fatigue. According to Targ's calculations, it ought to resist all the damaging effects of the ferromagnetals for 30 years, even on the hypothesis that the latter's multiplication was fairly prolific.

XIV. Euthanasia

After three years, thanks to the contribution made by the hydrogenated substances, the supply of water had scarcely decreased. The solid provisions remained abundant, and there were still those at the other oasis. No trace of any spring had been discovered, however, although Arva and Targ had scoured the desert indefatigably, at enormous distances.

The fate of Redlands troubled the refugees' minds. One or other of them had often sent out appeals via the Great Planetary; no one had replied. The brother and sister extended their journeys as far as the oasis several times. Because of the inexorable law, they dared not land, but they flew overhead. No inhabitant deigned to acknowledge their presence, and they saw that euthanasia was doing its work. Many more people than the regulations demanded had died. By the 30th month, scarcely 20 inhabitants remained.

One autumn morning, Arva and Targ left on a journey. They intended to follow the dual carriageway that had linked the Equatorial of the Dunes to Redlands since time immemorial. On the way, Targ would veer off toward a region that had attracted his attention on a previous trip. Lodged in one of the relay-stations, Arva would wait for him. They would be able to talk to one another easily, for Targ was carrying a mobile radiolink, which could transmit and receive voices at a range of more than a thousand kilometers. As on their previous expeditions, they would be in communication with Erê and the children, all the planetaries at the oasis and the relays having been maintained in good order.

There was no danger threatening Erê, save for those so far beyond human strength that they posed no greater risk to them than to Targ and Arva. The children had grown; their wisdom—as precocious as that of all the Last Men—was almost adult. The two eldest, one of whom was Mano's son and the other the watchman's daughter, were perfectly well able to operate the machines and power-generators; they were worth as much as anyone in combating the blind enterprise of the ferromagnetals. A sure atavism advised them. Even so, Targ had spent long hours the previous day inspecting the family enclave and its surroundings. Everything was normal.

Before the departure, the two families assembled around the glider. As with every departure, it was an emotional moment. In the horizontal light, that little group was the entire hope of humankind, all of its will to live, all the old energy of seas, forests, grasslands and cities. In the distance, in Redlands, those whose hearts still beat were no more than phantoms.

Targ enveloped his family and Arva's with a long loving gaze. The brightness of the fair-haired race had passed from Erê to her daughter; the two gold-clad heads were almost touching. What freshness emanated from them! What profound and tender legends! The others, in spite of their swarthy faces and anthracite eyes, also had a singular youthfulness: either Targ's ardent gaze or Mano's aptitude for happiness.

"Oh, how hard it is to leave you!" he exclaimed. "But it would be even more dangerous for us all to go together!"

All of them, even the children, knew that salvation was out there, in some mysterious corner of the desert. They also knew that the oasis, the center of their existence, would still be occupied. Besides, did they not communicate several times a day by means of the planetaries?

"Let's go!" said Targ, finally.

The subtle frisson of the motors was audible from the wings of the gliders. They took off, and dwindled in the pearly sapphire morning light.

Erê saw them vanish over the horizon. She sighed. When Targ and Arva were no longer there, fatality weighed more heavily. The young woman watched the oasis with fearful eyes, and every gesture the children made awoke her anxiety.

Bizarrely enough, her fear evoked dangers that were no longer of this world. She feared neither the mineral realm nor the ferromagnetals; she dreaded seeing unknown men emerge

248

from the depths of the inhabitable immensity. That strange resurgence of ancient instinct sometimes made her smile, but sometimes also caused her to shiver—especially when the evening imposed its dark vibrations on the Equatorial of the Dunes.

Targ and his companion sailed vertiginously through the aerial sea. They loved speed. The many journeys they had undertaken had not been able to extinguish the joy of challenging space. The somber planet seemed defeated. They saw its sinister plains and its sharp rocks advancing, and the mountains seemed to be rushing upon them as if to annihilate them—but with a slight gesture, they triumphed over abysses and mighty peaks. Frightful, flexible and submissive, the motors sang their low-pitched hymn.

When the mountain was past, the light gliders descended toward the desert again, where the vague, slow and ponderous ferromagnetals were moving. How pitiful and derisory they seemed! Targ and Arva knew their secret strength, though; they were the conquerors. Time was before them, and in their favor; things were coincident with their obscure will. One day, their descendants would produce admirable thoughts and command marvelous forces...

Targ and Arva decided to go straight to Redlands first. Their hearts went out to the ultimate shelter of their peers, with a passionate desire in which there was dread, distress, profound love and chagrin. While people were still alive there, there was some subtle and tender promise. When they had finally disappeared, the planet would seem even more lugubrious, the deserts vaster and more hideous.

After a brief nocturnal pause spent at one of the relay-stations, the voyagers had a conversation with Erê and the children by means of the planetary; it was less to reassure themselves as to bring the family together at a distance. Then they headed for the oasis; they succeeded in reaching it by midday.

It seemed immutable. As they had left it, so it was outlined in the lenses of their telescopes. The arcum dwellings gleamed in the sunlight; the radiolink platforms were visible, along with the garages for electric cars and gliders, the energy-transformers, colossal and delicate machines, the apparatus that had once drawn water from the bowels of the earth, and the fields where the last plants had grown. Everywhere, the image of human power and subtlety persisted. Given the signal, incalculable forces could have been unleashed and directed, enormous tasks accomplished. So many resources remaining as useless as the vibration of a ray of light in the infinite ether! The impotence of human beings was structural: born with water, they were vanishing with it.

For a few minutes, the gliders hovered over the oasis. It seemed to be deserted. No man, woman or child appeared at the threshold of any of the dwellings, on the roads or in the uncultivated fields—and that solitude chilled the hearts of the visitors.

"Are they dead, at last?" Arva murmured.

"Perhaps," Targ replied.

The gliders descended far enough to skim the roofs of the houses and the platforms of the planetaries. There was the silence and stillness of a necropolis. Even the dust in the dormant air was unmoving. Nothing was stirring but slow groups of ferromagnetals.

Targ resumed his flight. He saw two individuals on the threshold of a dwelling and hesitated for a few minutes as to whether to call out to them. Although the inhabitants of the oasis no longer comprised anything more than a pitiful group, Targ venerated his Species in them, and respected the law. That was engraved in every fiber of his being; it seemed to him as profound as life itself, redoubtable and tutelary, infinitely wise and inviolable—and since it had exiled him from Redlands forever, he bowed before it.

Thus, his voice trembled when he addressed himself to the people who had just appeared.

"How many living people are there in the oasis?"

The two men raised pale faces, which expressed a strange serenity. Then, one of them replied: "We are still five. This evening we shall be delivered!"

The watchman's heart contracted. In the gazes that met his own, he recognized the misty light of euthanasia.

"May we descend?" he said, humbly. "The law has exiled us."

"The law is finished!" the second man murmured. "It disappeared at the moment when we accepted the great cure."

At the sound of voices, three other living individuals appeared: two men and a young woman. They all looked at the gliders with ecstatic expressions.

Targ and Arva landed then.

There was a brief silence. The watchman examined the last of his peers avidly. Death was within them; no remedy could combat the delightful poisons of euthanasia.

The woman, who was very young, was much the palest of the five. Yesterday, she had still borne the future; today, she was older than a centenarian.

"Why did you want to die?" Targ exclaimed. "Has the water run out, then?"

"What does water matter to us?" whispered the young woman. "Why should we live? Why did our ancestors live? An inconceivable folly made them resist, for millennia, the decree of nature. They wanted to perpetuate themselves in a world that was no longer theirs. They accepted an abject existence, solely in order not to disappear. How is it possible that we have followed their pitiful example? It's so pleasant to die!"

She spoke in a slow, pure voice. Her words made Targ feel horribly sick. Every atom of his flesh rose up against such resignation—and the placid joy that lit up the faces of the dying was still incomprehensible to him. Even so, he kept quiet. What right had he to mingle the slightest bitterness with their end, since that end was no longer avoidable?

The young woman closed her eyes. Her feeble exaltation was extinguished; here breath was slowing down with every

251

passing second. Leaning against an arcum wall, she repeated: "It's so pleasant to die!"

One of the men murmured: "Deliverance is at hand."

Then, they all waited. The young woman was lying on the ground, scarcely breathing. An increasing pallor invaded her cheeks. Then she opened her eyes gain, momentarily, and looked at Targ and Arva with pitying tenderness.

"The folly of suffering remains within you," she stammered. Her hand was raised, and fell back slowly. One last shudder agitated her flesh. Finally, her limbs stiffened and she expired as gently as a little star on the horizon.

Her four companions studied her with happy tranquility. One of the murmured: "Life has never been desirable, even in the times when the Earth determined the power of human-kind."

Horrorstruck, Targ and Arva remained silent for some time. Then they piously wrapped up the woman who had been the final representative of the Future in Redlands. They did not have the courage to stay with the others, though. The absolute certainty of their death filled them with apprehension.

"Let's go, Arva," said Targ, softly.

When his glider was flying in convoy with Arva's, the watchman said: "Now we and our children are truly the last—the only—hope of the human species."

His companion turned a tearful face toward him. "In spite of everything," she stammered, "it was a great relief to know that there were people still living in Redlands. How many times that has consoled me! And now...now..." Her gesture indicated the implacable extent of the huge western mountains. Wildly, she cried: "It's all over, Brother!"

His own head had slumped forward—but he reacted against the pain. His eyes sparkling, he proclaimed: "Death alone will destroy my hope."

For several hours, the gliders followed the line of the highway. When the region that had attracted Targ's attention appeared, they slowed down. Arva chose the relay-station at which she would wait. Then, the planetary having brought the voices of Erê and the children, the watchman set off into the wilderness alone. He already knew the lie of the land, vaguely, over an area that extended twelve hundred kilometers to either side of the road.

The further he went, the more chaotic the terrain became. A chain of hills presented itself, and then, once again, the broken plain. Targ was now flying through unknown territory. Several times he descended to ground level, but a vertigo urged him to press on further.

An immense red wall barred the horizon. The aviator flew over it and sailed over the abyss. Gulfs were hollowed out there, gulfs of darkness, whose depths were indeterminable. There was evidence of immense convulsions everywhere; entire mountains had crumbled, others were twisting, ready to collapse into the unsoundable void.

The glider described long parabolas over the impressive landscape. The majority of the gulfs were so wide that aircraft would have been able to descend into them in dozens.

Targ lit his searchlight and began the exploration at random. First, he flew into a crevice open at the bottom of a cliff. The light seemed to dissolve in order to reach the bottom, which was revealed to be devoid of any issue.

A second gulf appeared more propitious for adventure at first. Several tunnels extended into the earth; Targ explored them without any profitable result.

The third expedition was vertiginous. The glider descended more than two thousand meters before touching down. The bottom of the immense hole formed a trapezium, whose smallest side was two hectometers long. Caves opened everywhere. It took an hour to explore them. All but two were limited by blank walls. By contrast, those two included numerous fissures—but too narrow to permit the passage of a man.

"No matter!" murmured Targ, just as he was about to abandon the second cave. "I'll come back."

Suddenly, he had the strange impression that he had felt ten years earlier, on the eve of the great disaster. Taking out his hygroscope, excitedly, he consulted the needle, and released a cry of triumph.

There was water vapor in the cave.

XV. The Vanished Enclave

For a long time, Targ walked through the darkness. His thoughts were sparse; an immeasurable joy filled his flesh. When he recovered himself, he thought:

There's nothing to be done for the present. To reach the mysterious water, it's necessary to discover a way through, elsewhere than at the bottom of the gulf, or to hollow out a passage. It's a question of time or a question of work. In the former case, Arva's presence will be infinitely useful; in the second, it will be necessary to go back to the Equatorial of the Dunes and bring back the necessary apparatus to capture energy and cut through the granite.

While reflecting thus, the young man had made preparations to get under way. Soon, the glider was describing the spiral curve that would take it back to the surface. Two minutes later he emerged from the gulf; the watchman immediately orientated his portable radiolink and sent out a call.

There was no response.

Astonished, he increased the intensity of the transmission. The receiver remained mute.

Targ was gripped by a slight anxiety; he launched a circular call, which went forth in all directions successively—and, as the silence persisted, he began to fear some unfortunate occurrence. Three hypotheses presented themselves: either there had been an accident; or Arva had left the refuge; or, finally, she had fallen asleep.

Before sending out another call, the explorer determined his present position with minute exactitude. Then he imparted the maximum intensity to the radio-waves. They would agitate the receiver microphones with such force that Arva would hear them even if she were asleep.

Yet again, the expanse yielded no response.

Had the young woman definitely left the refuge? She would certainly not have done that without a very good reason. At all costs, he had to catch up with her.

He was already under way again, flying at top speed.

In less than three hours, he had covered a thousand kilometers. The relay-station was clearly visible in the ocular lens of the aerial telescope. It was deserted! And Targ could not see anyone in the vicinity. Had Arva gone away, then? But where? Why? She could not have gone far, for her glider was still at anchor...

The final minutes were intolerably long; it seemed that the speedy vessel was no longer going forward; the young man's eyes had misted over.

Finally, the refuge was there. Targ landed in the middle, tethered the apparatus and ran forward. A cry of lament sprang from his throat. Arva was lying on the other side of the road, set against the vertical bank—which had rendered her invisible. She was as pale as the young woman who had succumbed to euthanasia in Redlands a short while before. To his horror, Targ saw a swarm of ferromagnetals—Tertiaries of the largest size—pressing around her.

With two abrupt movements, Targ attached his arcum ladder; then, descending to the young woman's side, he put her over his shoulder and climbed back up.

She had not moved; her flesh was inert; kneeling down, Targ tried to detect a heartbeat, but in vain. The mysterious energy providing the rhythm of life seemed to have faded away. Tremulously, the watchman placed the hygroscope on the young woman's lips. The delicate instrument revealed what hearing had been unable to discover: Arva was not dead—but her unconsciousness was so profound that she might die at any moment.

255

The cause of her condition seemed to be obvious; it was due, if not solely, at least in large measure, to the action of the ferromagnetals. Arva's singular pallor was evidence of an excessive loss of hemoglobin.

Fortunately, Targ never travelled without carrying instruments, stimulants and traditional remedies. He injected two doses of a powerful cordial, a few minutes apart. Her heart resumed beating, albeit very weakly.

Arva's lips murmured: "The children...the Earth..." Then she fell into a sleep that Targ neither could nor ought to combat—a fateful and salutary sleep during which he injected a few milligrams of "organic iron" every three hours. It would require at least twenty-two hours before Arva would be able to tolerate a brief awakening. It did not matter! The greatest anxiety had disappeared. The watchman, knowing that his sister was in perfect health, was not afraid of any mortal consequence.

Even so, he remained nervous. All in all, the event was unexplained. Why had Arva been lying at the bottom of the embankment? Had she—she who was so vigilant and agile—suffered a fall? It was possible, but improbable.

What should he do? Stay here until she had recovered her strength? It would take at least two weeks for her to recover completely. Better to go back to the Equatorial of the Dunes. There was nothing fundamentally urgent. The adventure on which Targ had embarked was not one of those whose outcome depends on a few days.

He went to the large planetary and transmitted a call. As before, on emerging from the gulf, he received no reply. Immediately, a terrible emotion took hold of him. He repeated the signals, giving them the maximum intensity. It became obvious that, for some enigmatic reason, Erê and the children either could not hear him or were unable to respond. The two alternatives were equally ominous. There was surely a connection between Arva's accident and the planetary's silence.

An intolerable dread was gnawing at the young man's breast. His legs were trembling, obliging him to lean against the planetary's supporting structure; he was incapable of making a decision. Finally, he tore himself away, bleakly resolute, and examined all the parts of his glider with anxious attention. He laid Arva down on the largest of its seats, and took off.

It was a lamentable journey. He only paused once, at dusk, to attempt another call. Having obtained no reply, he wrapped Arva up tightly in a silica-wool blanket and injected her with a dose of cordial larger than the earlier ones. She scarcely shivered in the depths of her torpor.

All night, the glider cleaved through the starry darkness. The cold being too intense, Targ went around the Skeleton Mountains. Two hours before dawn, the austral constellations appeared. The traveler, his heart beating faster, sometimes looked at the Southern Cross and sometimes the bright star that was the Sun's closest neighbor, whose light only takes three years to reach the Earth. How beautiful the sky must have been, when young creatures studied it through the foliage of trees, even more so when silvery clouds mingled their fecund promise with the tiny lamps of infinity. And there would never be any more clouds!

A delicate light pearled the east, and then the enormous disk of the sun rose. The Equatorial of the Dunes was not far away. Through the objective lens of the aerial telescope, Targ sometimes glimpsed, through gaps in the dunes, the wall of bismuth and the arcum dwellings, amber-tinted by the morning light.

Arva was still asleep, and a further dose of stimulant did not wake her. Even so, her pallor was not as livid; her arteries were throbbing weakly, and her skin did not have the translucent stiffness that was suggestive of death.

She's out of danger! Targ assured himself—and that certainty soothed his pain.

All his vigilance was directed toward the oasis. He strove to catch sight of the family enclave, but it was still hidden by two small hills. Finally, it appeared, and Targ wrenched the glider's tiller convulsively; it dived abruptly, like an injured bird.

The entire enclave, with its houses, its hangars and its machines, had disappeared.

XVI. In the Eternal Night

The glider was no more than 20 meters from the ground, traveling at top speed. It was about to fall vertically and smash when Targ straightened up reflexively. Then, lightly tracing an elegant parabola, he resumed his flight as far as the edge of the enclave.

Having landed, the watcher remained motionless, paralyzed by grief, in front of an enormous and chaotic ditch. There, beneath the darkness of the Earth, lay the beings that he loved more than himself.

For a long time, the thoughts crawled through the poor man's brain in total disorder. He was not thinking about the cause of the catastrophe; he was simply feeling an obscure ferocity, attaching to it all the misfortunes of that dismal week. Images followed one another at random. He continually saw his nearest and dearest, whom he had left two days before. Then, the tranquil figures were snatched away by an unnamable horror. The ground opened up. He saw them disappear. Their faces were terrified. They called out to the man in whom they had put their trust, and who—perhaps at the very moment of their death—had thought that he had vanquished Fate.

When he was finally able to think more clearly, the Last Man tried to work out what had happened. Was it another earthquake? No—no seismograph had recorded the slightest tremor. Besides, apart from a few hectares of the oasis and the desert, the enclave alone had been affected. The event was the consequence of anterior circumstances; the undersoil, having been fractured had collapsed. Thus, the misfortune that had ruined the supreme hope had not been a major convulsion of nature but an infinitesimal accident, on the scale of the feeble creatures it had engulfed.

Targ, however, believed that he could see therein the same cosmic will that had condemned all the oases...

His pain did not leave him inactive. He studied the ruins. They offered not the slightest vestige of human endeavor to his gaze. Power-generators, machines for digging, boring, crushing and cultivation, gliders, cars and houses had vanished into a formless mass of stones and rubble. Where were Erê and the children buried? Calculation only permitted a rough and perhaps deceptive approximation; he had to act on guesswork.

On the northern side, Targ assembled the apparatus necessary for clearing and digging; then, having condensed the atomic energy, he attacked the immense ditch. The machines hummed for an hour. Jacks lifted up the blocks of stone and threw them aside automatically. Cobalt paraboloids shoveled out the smaller debris, and the slow and irresistible impacts of the pile-drivers equilibrated the walls as the excavation progressed. When the trench had reached a depth of twenty meters, a glider appeared, then a large planetary with its granite pedestal and accessory structures, and then an arcum house.

Their placement made Targ's calculations more exact. Assuming that the catastrophe had surprised the family in or near the house, it was necessary to extend the excavation westwards. If Erê or the children had been able to reach the planetary responsible for communication between the Equatorial of the Dunes and Redlands—as Arva's accident led him to suppose—then he ought to continue his search in a southwestern direction.

The watchman set up apparatus in both the probable locations, and resumed work. "Humanized" by the incalculable effort of generations, the vast machines had the power of the elements and the delicacy of slender hands. They lifted out boulders, and amassed heaps of earth and small stones without any fits and starts. It only required light pressure to orientate them, accelerate them, slow them down or stop their progress. In the hands of the Last Man, they represented a greater power than had been possessed, in the primitive eras, by an entire tribe, or an entire people.

An arcum roof appeared. It was twisted and crumpled, and an occasional section had fallen in, but precise indications allowed him to recognize it. Since the landing at the Equatorial of the Dunes, it had sheltered all the affections, dreams and hopes of the last human family.

Targ stopped the machines that had begun to lift it up, and considered it, with fear and tenderness. What enigma was it hiding? What drama was it about to reveal to an unfortunate worn out by misery and fatigue?

For several minutes, the watchman hesitated over the resumption of his work. Finally, after enlarging one of the rents, he let himself slide down into the dwelling.

The room he went into was empty. A few blocks of stone were obstructing it, one of which had torn away a wall-bed and crushed it. A table had been smashed to pieces, and several soft aluminum vases flattered by impacts.

The spectacle had the indifferent character of material destruction, but it was suggestive of more disturbing scenes. Trembling from head to toe, Targ went into the next room. It was as empty and devastated as the first. He visited every corner of the house in succession—and when he found himself in the last room, a few steps from the entrance door, his anguish was mingled with amazement.

"It's quite natural, though," he whispered, "that they should have fled outside at the first sign of danger."

He tried to imagine how the first impact had occurred, and what concept of the peril Erê would have been able to form. Nothing came to him but contradictory ideas and sensations. Only one impression remained fixed: that instinct must have taken his family toward the Redlands planetary. It was, therefore, in that direction that it was logical to direct his attention. But how? Had Erê reached the Great Planetary or had she been killed on the way?

The words that Arva had stammered came back to the watchman's memory. The circumstances gave them meaning.

Erê or one of the children—perhaps all of them—had almost certainly got that far. It was, therefore, necessary to resume work as quickly as possible—which would not prevent the commencement of a communicating tunnel.

Having made his resolution, Targ raised the entrance door and attempted a rapid exploration—but blocks of stone and rubble confronted him with an insurmountable obstacle. He went out again through the roof and started the machines working again to the south-west. Then he rearranged the northern apparatus and started them on digging out the tunnel. He also attended to Arva, whose lethargy was gradually taking on the appearance of normal sleep.

Then he waited, vigilantly, his eyes fixed on the docile machines. Sometimes, he rectified their endeavor with a furtive gesture; sometimes, he stopped a pick, a blade, a screw or a turbine in order to examine the terrain. Finally, twisted and distorted, he perceived the tall stalk of the planetary and the sparkling dish. From then on, he never ceased to direct the effort, only using the subtler equipment that, when the occasion demanded, lifted up the large stones or heaped up the smaller debris.

And he released a lugubrious lament, like a cry of agony. A light had just appeared: that flexible and living gleam that he had perceived on the day of the disaster amid the ruins of Redlands. His heart froze; his teeth chattered. With his eyes full of tears, he slowed down all the machinery, only allowing the metal hands to act, gentler and more skillful than human hands.

Then he stopped everything, and lifted up against his chest, with raucous sobs, the body that he had loved so passionately...

At first, a thrill of hope cut through his convulsion. It seemed to him that Erê was still not cold. Feverishly, he put the hygroscope to the pale lips.

She had disappeared into the eternal night.

For a long time, he looked at her. She had revealed to him the poetry of former ages, dreams of an extraordinary youth transfiguring the dismal planet; Erê was love, in which there was something vast, pure and almost eternal. And while he held her in his arms, he seemed to see a new and innumerable race live again.

"Erê! Erê!" he murmured. "Erê, youth of the world! Erê, last hope of humankind!"

Then his soul hardened. He placed a grim and bitter kiss on his companion's hair, and set to work again.

He brought them all out, one by one. The mineral realm had been less ferocious toward them than the young woman; it had spared them a slow death, the slow dispersal of vital energy. Stone blocks had smashed their skulls, opened their hearts, crushed their torsos.

Then, Targ sank down on to the ground and wept endlessly. Grief had overwhelmed him, as vast as the world. And the words of the dying woman in Redlands resounded through his pain like the knell of the immensity…

A hand touched his shoulder. He sat up with a start. He saw Arva leaning over him, livid and unsteady on her feet. She was so exhausted that no tears came to the corners of her eyes—but all the despair possible to feeble creatures was dilating her pupils. In a colorless voice, she murmured: "We must die! We must die!"

Their gazes met. They had loved one another profoundly, every day of their lives, through all their dreams and all reality. They had held the same hopes in common, passionately— and in their infinite misery, their suffering was still fraternal.

"We must die!" he repeated, like an echo. Then they hugged one another—and, for the last time, two human breasts beat against one another.

Then, in silence, she raised to her lips the iridium tube that never left her. As the dose was massive, and Arva's weakness extreme, the euthanasia only took a few minutes.

"Death...death..." the dying woman stammered. "Oh, how were we able to fear you?"

Her eyes darkened, a pleasant lassitude extended her limbs, and her thoughts were completely annihilated, while her breast exhaled its final breath.

And there was only one human being on Earth.

Seated on a block of porphyry, he remained shrouded in his sadness and his dream. Once more, he made the long voyage up the stream of time, which had so ardently exalted his soul.

First, he saw yet again the primitive sea, still warm, where life was abundant, unconscious and insensible. Then came the blind and deaf creatures, extraordinary in their energy in boundless fecundity. The vision born, the divine light created its minuscule temples; the creatures born of the Sun became aware of their existence—and firm ground appeared. The populations of the water expanded on to it, vague, confused and taciturn. For three hundred thousand years they created subtle forms. The insects, the amphibians and the reptiles inhabited the forests of giant ferns, the profusion of calamites and arrowheads. When the trees put forth their magnificent torsos, immense reptiles also appeared. The dinosaurs were as tall as cedars, pterodactyls soared over the vast marshes...

In that era, the first mammals were born, paltry, clumsy and stupid. They prowled around, wretched and so small that it required a thousand of them to equal the weight of an iguanodon. For interminable millennia, their existence remained imperceptible and almost derisory. They flourished, however. The time came when it was their turn, when their species rose up in force in all the corners of the savannah and all the shadows of the forests. They were now the ones that took on colossal form. The dinotherium, the ancient elephant, the rhinoceros armored like an old oak, the hippopotamus with the insatiable belly, the urus and the aurochs, the macherodus, the giant lion and the yellow lion, the tiger, the cave-bear and the blue whale, as massive as several diplodocus, and the sperm

263

whale with the cavernous mouth, aspired the scattered energies.

Then the planet allowed humankind to prosper; its reign was the most ferocious, the most powerful—and the last. It was the prodigious destroyer of life. The forests died, and their countless guests; every animal was exterminated or debased—and there was a time in which even subtle forces and obscure minerals seemed enslaved; the conqueror went so far as to capture the mysterious force that had assembled atoms.

"That very frenzy announced the death of the Earth...the death of the Earth for *our* reign!" Targ murmured, softly.

A frisson agitated his grief. He realized that what still existed of his flesh had been transmitted, *without pause*, since the very beginning. Something that had lived in the primitive sea, in the nascent slime, in the marshes, in the forests, in the bosom of the savannahs, and among the innumerable cities of humankind, had never been interrupted, until it reached him. And here he was! He was the last human being whose heart was beating on the face of the Earth—a face that had become immense once again!

Night fell. The firmament displayed those charming fires that eyes of trillions of human beings had known. Only two eyes remained to contemplate them!

Targ listed those he had preferred to the others, and then he saw, rising yet again, the ruinous star, the pitted star, silvery and legendary—to which he raised his sorry hands...

He uttered one last sob; death entered into his heart—and, refusing euthanasia, he emerged from the ruins and went to lie down in the oasis, among the ferromagnetals.

Then, a few particles of the last human life entered humbly into the New Life.

THE NAVIGATORS OF SPACE

To Binet-Valmer,[42]
his admirer and friend,
J.-H. Rosny Aîné.

Preface

Everything is ready. The perfectly transparent sublimated argine walls of the *Stellarium* possess a resistance and an elasticity that render them practically indestructible. A pseudo-gravitic field inside the apparatus will ensure a stable equilibrium to both people and objects.

We have a space at our disposal whose total volume is three hundred cubic meters; our supplies of hydralium are sufficient to provide oxygen for three hundred days; our hermetically-sealed argine suits will permit us to move about on Mars under terrestrial pressure, our respiration being ensured by direct or pneumatic transformers. In addition, the Siverol devices will allow us to dispense with respiration for several hours by virtue of their globular action and their anesthetization of the lungs. Finally, our supplies of concentrated food, which we can return to their primitive state at will, are assured for nine months.

The laboratory is equipped for all physical, chemical and biological analyses; we are abundantly provided with destructive apparatus.

---

[42] Binet-Valmer was the signature used by Jean Gustave Binet (1875-1940), a prolific novelist and journalist nowadays most famous for his correspondence with Marcel Proust.

In sum, the propulsion, pseudo-gravitic equilibration, normal respiration and artificial combustion are adequate for three seasons. Allowing three months to reach Mars and three months to return, we shall have three full months to explore the planet, in the event—the least favorable—that we do not find any resources of nutriment and respiration there.

I.

8 April. Our vessel is sailing through eternal darkness; the Sun's rays would strike us forcefully through the argine if we had not disposed devices that attenuate, diffuse or suppress the light at our discretion.

Our life is as arid as that of captives; in the dead expanse the stars are merely monotonous points of light; our work is limited to meager matters of conversation and surveillance; all that the apparatus needs to do until the landing is rigorously determined. No obstacle has arisen that demands a change of course. Our interior life is subordinate to machinery. We have books, musical instruments and games. The spirit of adventure sustains us, an immeasurable hope, somewhat deadened by waiting.

The prodigious speed at which we are traveling is equivalent to a supreme immobility. There is a profound silence; our apparatus—generators and transformers—make no noise; their vibrations are of an etheric order. Thus, nothing reveals the bolide launched into the interstellar wilderness.

21 April. Unspeakably uniform days. Tedious conversations. Little appetite for reading or work.

27 April. My chronometer indicates 7:33. We have just eaten: extract of coffee, bread and "reconstituted" sugar. A light supplement of oxygen gave us an appetite and is making us almost cheerful. I'm observing my two companions with a certain sense of renewal; lost in the deserts of space, I feel closer to them than to my brothers.

Antoine Lougre must have been earnest since childhood. His gravity isn't sad; it accommodates flashes of gaiety, the joys of a colt shaking itself. He has long head with rounded corners, like the Scandinavians, but not their hair color; his is the color of tar. His eyes are the color of bilberries; his complexion that of lightly-seasoned meerschaum. He's tall, relaxed in his movements; his speech, as precise as a theorem, corresponds to the mathematical nature of the man.

Jean Gavial has hair as red as a fox's coat; copper-colored stars constellate his grey-green eyes; his complexion is as white as cream cheese, sown with pale red patches; his sensual and joyful mouth makes his face laugh. He's a solid creature, vaguely artistic, who hates metaphysics and transcendental mathematics, but an experimental magician and a seer of the infinitesimal. This enemy of differential and integral calculus carries out extraordinary feats of mental arithmetic; figures appear to him in phosphorescent streaks.

As for me, Jacques Laverande, a rather idle human being—a unicorn-rider—I conceal a foggy temperament beneath a tropical simulacrum: hair, eyes and beard as black as lignite that seem have been grown in some Mauritania, pale cinnamon skin, the nose of an arrogant pirate...

The elective affinities that have bound us together since college maintain a nonchalant but irreducible amity.

For the 100th time, Antoine mutters: "Who knows whether the Earth might have been alone in having produced life? In which case..."

"In which case, the Sun, the Moon and the stars really were created for its benefit," Jean laughs. "That's false. There's life out there."

"There's even some here," I say, extending my hand.

Antoine laughs vaguely. "Yes, I know—the innumerable Coexistence. But is that still life?"

"I believe in it as in my own life."

"Is it conscious, though?"

"Conscious and unconscious. All consciousnesses and all unconsciousnesses—and among them, consciousnesses compared with which yours would probably be worth no more than that of a crab."

"Thanks, on the crab's behalf!" said Jean. "I admired them in my childhood and I've always esteemed them…"

"Fifty lunar expeditions have yielded no result!" Antoine retorted.

"Perhaps they didn't look hard enough—and perhaps life there isn't comparable to ours."

"It *can't* be incomparable," Antoine complained, with a trace of humor. "The Moon is made of the same primitive elements as the Earth; its evolution was more rapid, but analogous: a mouse grows, lives and disappears more rapidly than a rhinoceros. There was a time when the Moon had seas, lakes and rivers in which it wrapped up nitrogen and oxygen. Don't we know that for certain?"

"But that was billions of years ago! In that time, a fossil record like ours would have been completely annihilated."

"Skeletons, yes…but not all traces."

"A vain dispute! Anyway, the evolution of Mars must resemble ours more closely."

"Who's contesting it?" said Antoine. "That's why I'm going there."

"You're slandering yourself!" Jean retorted. "You're going there because you're essentially a sportsman. It pleases you to be, along with us the first man to land there. That's all right—we congratulate ourselves on being guided by the spirit of adventure, as those poor fellows in their caravels once were!"

More days, even slower and more monotonous, in the black abyss, in the eternal mystery. Space! We know no more about the reality it conceals than the people who believe in the void or those who invent worlds of four, five, six or n dimensions, no more than Zeno,[43] Descartes, Leibniz or our Arenaut,[44] the conqueror of interstellar space.

One morning, Antoine, who is a little long-sighted, murmurs: "Mars has ceased to be a star!"

In the plenary monotony of our life, that almost qualifies as an Event. Now, every morning, we seek avidly to calculate the grandeur of Mars. Soon, the shape of the planet becomes precise. To the naked eye, it is a minuscule moon, a moonlet that would still be little more than a dot beside our satellite, but which is clearly circular all the same. Every three or four days, we get the impression of an increase, and now the diameter of Mars is a fifth of the diameter of Selene. It's a pretty little red-tinted moon.

"I'm reminded," says Jean, "of a little lady's watch, compared to a sturdy chronometer."

The little lady's watch becomes a twin sister of the moon, tinted pale scarlet. Growing incessantly, it does not take long to appear much larger than the sun or the moon; with the telescope, we can make out precise features on its surface: chains of mountains, vast plains, shiny expanses that that might be water or ice, white regions, probably covered in snow...

To the innocent eye, it's a colossal orb, a moon twenty times—then fifty times, then more than a hundred times—more extensive than the selenitic star. As we get closer, the star seems less luminous. Similar at first to a disk of polished copper, it pales and takes on an almost matt aspect; soon, its substance depicts a mixture of metal and terra cotta, in which

---

[43] Rosny's reference is to "*l'Éleate*" (the Eleatic); I have assumed that the reference is to Zeno (the famous paradox-monger), who was often called Zeno of Elea to distinguish him from a namesake, rather than Parmenides or Xenophanes.

[44] This term (*Arénaut* in the original) appears to be derived from Ares—the Greek equivalent of Mars—and presumably refers to a scientist who made the voyage that the three adventurers are undertaking practicable.

red is dominant, but in which multicolored patches appear. Mars's two rapidly-moving moons are vaguely discernible.

1 June. There is no more star. Mars has become a world, distant still, in which the eye can distinguish the confused shapes of mountains, plains and great valleys—which, transformed by the vertiginous rapidity of our course, is growing incessantly. The formidable moment is close at hand. We're ready; we turned the *Stellarium* around some time ago.

Jean is monitoring the decreasing power of the engine, we're controlling our fall with the aid of an anti-gravity field, and our space-time clocks are keeping track of durations and distances with minute exactitude. It's a matter of reaching Mars at zero velocity. Unless there's a breakdown, which is a remote possibility, the most we have to fear is a slight jolt when we're a short distance from the ground—but it's soon clear that there won't be any; the regulation is perfect, our speed is insignificant, and when we're very close to the ground, it becomes imperceptible.

We land softly; our apparatus ceasing to oppose any resistance to Martian gravity.

II.

Close to the equator, there is a spacious valley between high hills, almost mountains. We're not hoping to find water; our telescopes haven't revealed any rivers or lakes—not even a pool or a stream; a few shiny patches at most, toward the poles. It's certain, though, that a sharp cold—a freezing cold—must reign there, we preferred to land here, leaving easy verification until later. After all, it wouldn't take our machine more than an hour to make a circuit of the planet.

"I feel too light!" Jean complained, after a silence.

"Me too!" said Antoine.

"And me," I added. "I think I could jump over a ten-meter wall."

"Like lions and tigers—but the sensation isn't pleasant. We'll adapt in time; let's increase our gravitational field slightly."

Through our transparent walls we examine the locale with the naked eye and with telescopes. The arid ground, as hard as rock and a dirty red in color, seems sinister.

"We've seen," Antoine says, "that this valley is set between medium-sized and high mountains, and that it's disposed to receive water through a network of ravines. Moreover, the temperature here ought to be much more favourable to the existence of liquid than at higher altitudes."

"Ought to be, yes—but do we really expect to find liquid water? Vapor at the most! At any rate, if we don't find vegetation in this zone and other favourably-located regions, we can conclude that Mars is more sterile than our deserts!"

"Thus reasoned the legendary warrior who perished at the siege of Milan!"[45]

"Eh? It's the fundamental principle of scientific reasoning!" Antoine replied. "But look there!"

We followed the direction of his arm and perceived some singular structures. In terms of their color they were scarcely any different from the ground, which was red—or rather, reddish; it was their shape that rendered them discernible. After a few moments, we counted four kinds.

The first comprised zigzag strips; at each angle, there was a kind of node. The whole was flat on the ground; the breadth of the strips was twice or three times as great as their thickness, the latter seeming not to exceed two or three centimetres.

The figures of the second sort formed spirals, but spirals with irregularly undulating lines, with a thick node at the cen-

---

[45] This reference is presumably to the 14th century Charlemagnian romance "The Siege of Milan," but I cannot trace the specific quotation.

ter. They too lay flat on the ground, and were no thicker than the lightning-shaped figures.

The third sort seemed to be a more complex variety of the first; from one rather large node sprang a series of zigzag lines, but there were no secondary nodes.

"One might describe them as exceeding flat octopodes with lightning-shaped tentacles!" Jean remarked.

"And without eyes!" I added.

"But what does this mean?" Antoine muttered. "Is it a bizarre mineral? Is it vegetation? Is it a sort of sedentary animal life—after all, we don't observe any movement?"

"None!" Jean confirmed, the objective lenses of his binoculars fixed on the strange figures. "Let's get closer!"

We moved closer, and were able to assure ourselves that the surface of the structures was partly covered by a mixture of semi-transparent bubbles and a sort of polychromatic mildew, from which the carmine tint derived.

"All the same, it's still vegetation that they resemble most," Antoine concluded.

This conclusion was soon confirmed by the appearance of other lightning-shaped forms, in radial tentacles and spiraloids, some of which attained considerable lengths: five, ten or 20 meters.

"Let's make a short expedition in the chimerical search for water," Jean proposed.

We set the ship in motion, very slowly—scarcely 15 kilometers an hour—making frequent stops, but without discovering water. A more rapid excursion uphill was no more productive. There was nothing but stone, the desolation of lunar landscapes interrupted by increasingly rare pseudo-vegetation.

On landing again, we made an interesting discovery. In a location where the pseudo-vegetation was abundant, Jean pointed out moving bodies. These bodies were also flat, orange in color, with blue or violet patches; we soon discerned that they had ribbon-like prolongations—feet or pseudopods—on which they seemed to slide rather than walk.

What took the place of a body had contours so irregular that the creatures seemed formless at first glance. In fact they possessed a mossy surface with a multitude of pores, wrinkles, cavities and projections. As we moved a little deeper into the valley, it did not take us long to perceive others slightly different in form and various in hue, all remarkable by their confused flat structure and their mossy, sometimes spongy, surfaces. We could now count at least a dozen kinds. Two of these entities attained a length of a hundred feet. It was impossible to say whether they had organs or a head, but they all displayed the ribbon-like prolongations that served as feet.

"The ribbon-feet are very imperfectly differentiated," said Jean. "The head must be the part that precedes the rest when they move."

"The preceding part bears some resemblance to a grape or some other soft or spongy fruit. If that's the head, it's composed of distinct but conjoined compartments. I see nothing that evokes the idea of sense-organs—nothing distantly resembling eyes, ears, nostrils...nor is there a mouth—unless there's one among the cavities in the moss or the sponge. Those that pause in the vicinity of the pseudo-plants don't look as if they're consuming them..."

"Still no water!"

"Perhaps it's subterranean...unless these life-forms don't make any use of it."

"It's time that we took account of the composition, the pressure and the hygrometric state of the atmosphere."

Taking responsibility for this operation, I went to the narrow chamber designed for communication with the exterior world. Entrance to it was through a hatch—which, once closed, was rigorously isolated from communication with the atmosphere of other chambers. Then, at will, one put the measuring devices in contact with the environment. That operation being sufficient, for the moment, I flicked a switch and soon observed that the pressure was almost nine centimeters, the temperature five and a half degrees above zero; the humidity proved to be very low, but the hygrometer did clearly indicate the presence of water vapor.

When I communicated these results to my companions, Antoine exclaimed: "You really said five and a half degrees *above* zero?"

"278.5 degrees absolute."

"That's impossible. I didn't expect any more than *minus* five degrees. The pressure astonishes me too. As for the water vapor—that's in conformity with expectations."

"In conformity or not, possible or not, everything is as I've told you."

Then there's a mystery—two mysteries..."

"Ten mysteries!" Jean mocked. "And these mysteries probably result from the Martian atmosphere being fractionally more liable than ours to impede the loss of heat. So let's analyze the atmosphere..."

Half an hour later, the summary analysis was concluded. The proportion of oxygen was surprising—almost two-sevenths of the fluid drawn off; a third of it was nitrogen, there was a small quantity of an unknown gas, one ten-thousandth of carbon dioxide, and various substances in extremely minimal quantities, sometimes mere traces.

"We're almost at home, all the same!" said Antoine, serenely.

"And on the track of the mystery—I'll wager that it's the unknown gas that limits Martian radiation."

"We'll see. In the meantime, there's enough oxygen for us to be able to move around in the open air, with the aid of our condensers, and to renew the *Stellarium*'s supplies indefinitely."

"Shall we make an initial sortie?"

"It's rather late in the day," Antoine objected. "Obviously, it's easy enough for us to travel to a luminous zone, but I'm curious to see the Martian night."

In the rarefied air, the dusk was necessarily even briefer than in the tropical regions of Earth. The solar furnace sank into the depths of the Occident; it remained suspended between two mountains momentarily, and had no sooner disappeared than the stars were shining in an incomparably clear sky. The spectacle was broadly similar to what we had seen during the days of our voyage, but on that distant world it prompted a small crisis of poetry in Jean: a flood of epithets and, I believe, the recitation of a few verses.

We were about to put on the light when we were struck by an extraordinary phenomenon. Whichever way we turned, we perceived networks of phosphorescence—a phosphorescence so faint that it did not hide the stars, and marvelously colored.

These networks formed luminous columns—horizontal, vertical and oblique—which often intersected and whose colors did not extend beyond yellow on the spectral scale, while mounting all the way to the extreme violet. Luminous formations circulated within them, various in color, composed of oddly-intertwined filaments. These formations, slightly brighter than the columns, were no more of a hindrance to the perception of the stars, even the fainter ones.

"Almost the same intensity as the Milky Way," Antoine remarked.

Even so, the Milky Way was less perceptible through the columns than in the numerous interstices of the networks.

After a time, we became convinced that the formations were moving, with a great freedom, accelerating, slowing down, stopping or reversing direction. They seemed to be spiraling through the columns and capable of attaining great speeds; some were traveling at twelve kilometers a minute. The violet formations were the most rapid.

"Is *that* alive?" Jean muttered.

"We may doubt it," Antoine replied, "but it's probable."

On rare occasions the formations quit the columns and set off into the black expanse, where their progress slowed down or their movement became more capricious.

"Yes, it's strongly suggestive of life," said Jean. "However, I daren't believe…"

"No need for belief. Let's limit ourselves to trying to distinguish the real from the possible. This *might* be life—if so, what an enigma!"

"Etheric life? Nebular life?"

"A function of the planet, in any case, since we've seen nothing comparable in interplanetary space—and doubtless participating as much in the Ether as the Nebula."

We then observed the phenomenon with binoculars, and although the phosphorescence of the columns seemed almost invariable, that of the moving formations varied so harmoniously that it was reminiscent of a luminous symphony.

Soon a new particularity struck us. Several columns having collided with the *Stellarium*, the phosphorescence ceased at the wall it encountered, to reappear at the surface of the opposite wall; moreover, the segments were connected by thinner columns that went around our vessel. As the columns were usually straight, or so slightly curved that the curvature was hardly perceptible, we had to conclude that the junction had been formed in consequence of our arrival. To convince ourselves of it, we displaced the *Stellarium* and broke several columns. Those we left behind reformed very rapidly; those that remained in contact with our vessel took some time to establish the junction.

As for the living (?) formations, everywhere a rupture was produced, they were projected into the black expanse. A few lingered there; others rejoined a column or the segments of interrupted columns.

"Phantasmagorical!" Antoine muttered. "If they're not living organisms, no more are they entities analogous to our meteorological phenomena...much less to solid minerals or liquids!"

"I opt deliberately for life!" Jean declared. "The inhabitants of Mars, with which we were hoping to exchange elementary verities, exit on planes that will probably not permit any intellectual communication."

"Really?" I put in. "Firstly, there might be other forms; then again, what do we know about the possibilities of these?

Why shouldn't there be at least abstract analogies between them and us? Already, if they're alive…"

Antoine cut me off. "We'll think about that later. I'd like, if possible, to establish observational details…"

"The one doesn't get in the way of the other!" I said. "I'm continuing to watch—and while watching, I'm asking myself whether Mars might not be more complex than Earth— in an evolutionary sense—and whether there might be a third plane of life somewhere."

"I approve! But we've already got the outline of a classi-fication—oh, the most rudimentary possible. You've noticed that the formations include paler sections, which form some-thing like vacuoles in the mass. Now, I observe that the more rapid and precise the movements seem, and the better-executed the changes of direction, the more numerous the va-cuoles are. Compare those that have five or six vacuoles with those that only have one or two; the contrast is striking.

That was correct. The "formations" with multiple va-cuoles attained speeds of three to seven kilometers an hour; the formations with single or double vacuoles scarcely at-tained a tenth of those speeds.

In every direction, certain formations were pausing; we observed that during the pause, exceedingly thin lines linked formations that possessed the same number of vacuoles to-gether. The intensity of these lines was unstable; we saw it increase and decrease without being able to discern any rhythm. As soon as the formations started moving again, the lines were invariably broken.

"Do you know what?" Antoine exclaimed. "The varia-tions of the lines express spontaneous changes…they probably constitute a language that uses infinitesimal vibrations in a manner analogous to our sound-waves!"

"So," said Jean, "you no longer doubt that these forma-tions are alive—dissimilar as they are to anything that has been conceived by the most imaginative of our scientists and artists!"

We continued to study the strange spectacle for some time, without discovering anything that added significantly to what we had already observed; then we switched on the light, which rendered the formations invisible, and we had our evening meal.

If everything goes as it did today, we will only see the manifestations of these existences during the night...

III.

"What shall we do now?" asked Jean, when we had finished the meal.

"If you want my opinion," I said, "I'd like to return to the diurnal zones."

"In the hope of encountering organisms more like ours?"

"Yes. Besides, the ones we saw during the day were much less distant from us than the luminous formations."

"What if we were to analyze the atmosphere more minutely first?" said Antoine.

Naturally, we found the substances revealed by the summary analysis again, but the unknown fluid could not be classified; it seemed to be extremely complex.

The carbon and nitrogen comprised isotopes, so the atomic weight of the carbon reached 12.4, while the atomic weight of the nitrogen was reduced to 13.7.[46] Argon, neon,

---

[46] When Rosny wrote this story it was not yet known why "atomic weights" varied from round numbers, usually slightly (the atomic weight of carbon having been calculated at 12.01, that of nitrogen at 14.01). We now know that it is because of the presence in natural samples of minute traces of isotopes containing one or two extra neutrons—C-13 and C-14 in the case of carbon—but the existence of the neutron was not confirmed until 1932, so Rosny's assumption that there might be different forms of elements, with slightly different atomic

278

etc. were present in infinitesimal quantities. As already mentioned, the proportion of oxygen was surprising.

"The presence of nitrogen and carbon dioxide makes the existence of organisms with a similar composition to terrestrial organisms possible," Antoine remarked.

"Yes, but what about the isotopes?" Jean exclaimed. "The nitrogen may not matter, but the carbon surprises—even astonishes—me. So faithful to helium on our own world, here it seems to join with other atoms! That's inconceivable!"

"The fact speaks for itself! I suspect that a carbon thus composed might act differently from our own in an animate world. We shouldn't be astonished, therefore, to find sharp differences between our fauna and flora and Martian fauna and flora."

"Add to that the physical influences: the density of Mars, the intensity of gravity, temperature, the duration of the seasons..."

"Are you tired?" Jean asked. "If not, we can go back to the daylit regions..."

"My chrono indicates that it's bedtime," Antoine replied. "Since there's nothing urgent, let's take one more look at the aerial formations, and make another sortie after we've slept. It's best to proceed in an orderly manner."

Having no good reason to object, Jean accepted the need for sleep. For another half-hour we observed the aerial formations—which permitted us to classify them more accurately and confirm the belief that they really were vital manifestations of a more subtle nature than the most subtle terrestrial manifestations.

---

weights, remains a trifle vague; his subsequent reference to carbon's "loyalty to helium," in association with a notion of "isotopes" that had not yet been precisely refined, reflects the notion that a carbon atom (AW 12) was essentially equivalent to a "compound" of three helium atoms (AW 4).

After that, we sank into unconsciousness until the Martian dawn—which arrived after a similar number of hours as it would have *back home*, at a comparable latitude.

When I woke up, Jean was making the morning coffee, whose aroma concentrated the dreams of my pilgrimage twice a day. The re-expanded bread was already warm, as fresh as if it had just come out of the oven; combined with vitamins, condensed sugar and butter it became a perfect nutriment.

A cook by vocation, Jean offered us irreproachable coffee and toothsome slices of bread and butter.

"The body of Christ!" said Antoine, who was the most epicurean among us. "Let us be thankful for this breakfast..."

"To think that we are still mortal, who are drinking our coffee on another planet!"

"I consider it more astonishing still that we have drunk it in interplanetary space," I said. "Here, at least, we find ourselves in a world homologous to our own."

"We're invading the house next door. Thus far, it doesn't seem very comfortable. Let's get ready to go out."

"But first, let's consult the birds."

We had brought six—two sparrows, a chaffinch and three canaries—which, like us, had remained healthy during the journey.

Picking up the chaffinch's cage, Antoine took it into the compartment that communicated with the exterior on demand. A little suction pump was able to condense the Martian air. When he had finished breakfast and our toilette, we observed that the finch had not suffered in the least.

"As was to be expected!" said Jean.

"Almost—but the effect of the unknown gas might have been harmful. It seems that it's not. Nevertheless, we'll take a few precautions."

Ten minutes later, equipped with ordinary respirators, condensers, weapons and tools, we set foot on the surface of the planet, where we walked as lightly as if our strength had been tripled. Thanks to the condensers, we were breathing without difficulty.

"Forgive a small fit of enthusiasm!" Jean exclaimed, brandishing his ice-axe.

His explanation made a singularly pleasant impression on us; in that rarefied milieu we had expected to be able to talk and hear only with extreme difficulty—but for some enigmatic reason, the atmosphere conducted sound quite well.

The air was perfectly clear. The Organisms were abundant, some immobile, like our plants, others mobile, like our animals, the fastest moving at the speed of pythons, the slower ones scarcely at the speed of slugs. None seemed to be bilaterally symmetrical, and yet they bore no resemblance to our radially symmetrical organisms.

"First of all, how many feet do they actually have, if these ceaselessly deforming ribbons are feet?"

"They seem, at any rate, to be taking the place of feet."

These...*zoomorphs* make use of them for movement, but their slithering is also reminiscent of crawling."

"One, two...three, four...eight! They have eight feet?"

"Yes, but...ah! Here's a ninth—which only appears at intervals..."

The movements of the appendages were bizarre: sometimes folded back, sometimes zigzagging, sometimes approximately helical, these pseudo-limbs were obviously very transformable.

"We need to turn some of them over, if possible," I said.

"Come on, then!" Jean replied, approaching an organism almost as long as a rat, which was moving sluggishly.

With a deft movement of his ice-axe, he succeeded in turning the creature over, whereupon it was enveloped by a fluorescent halo, which faded away after a few seconds. It waved its appendages desperately, trying to recover its natural position.

"That fluorescence is interesting!" Antoine muttered.

"Nine feet!" Jean announced.

"Correct!"

"Let's see, then! The appendages are fixed in threes; each triad forms a shallow curve..."

"That's true…and perhaps quite characteristic."

"Extremely characteristic, because…" Antoine stopped, hesitantly. Before he had resumed speaking, we had made the same observation as him: the three series were separated by two delicate furrows, which delimited three zones.

"I'd hazard a guess," said Antoine, "that instead of being radially or bilaterally organized, these creatures are ternary!"

"Let's make sure…"

Jean successively turned over two other organisms different in size and form. Like the first, they were enveloped by the fluorescent halo and they revealed two furrows and nine appendages arranged in threes.

"All ternary—as if the duality manifest in the majority of terrestrial species were represented here by a trinity."

"But what if these are inferior creatures?"

We looked for agile organisms. Visibly conscious of our presence, when we tried to approach them, they made off.

Eventually, we succeeded in cornering a zoomorph of fairly considerable size in a crevice, and Jean set about using the same method to turn it over. A broad violet halo shone forth.

Uttering a cry of surprise, Jean dropped his ice-axe. "Damn it!" he said, feeling his arm—and as we looked at him anxiously, he added: "Not broken—but the strangest sensation! An intense cold—a sort of prickling that extended all the way to the bone. It didn't resemble anything I've felt before! At any rate, these animals—if one can call them animals—can defend themselves. I felt something before, with the slow ones…but very slight."

"I don't think that fluorescence is negligible!" muttered Antoine.

As we moved toward our friend, we had opened an exit, through which the Martian animal escaped.

"It could have been worse," I said. "The haloes of the largest ones must be fatal."

"Very dangerous, at least. In sum, this planet doesn't lack character…"

"We haven't seen anything yet! How are these entities put together? What are they made of? If it's oxygen, hydrogen, carbon and nitrogen their life could be homologous to terrestrial life, but if they're made of other elements the gap increases."

"The chemical analysis will be relatively simple, but the composition of the organs might be terribly complicated."

"Let's begin at the beginning," Jean concluded, capturing a small-sized creature.

We went back to the *Stellarium*, which was barely five hundred meters away.

Antoine was still pensive. "Do living creatures exist here that are capable of attacking this?" he murmured, when we arrived at the vessel.

"None that we've seen," Jean affirmed.

"Imagine colossi comparable in size to the diplodocus of old and our present day whales. Wouldn't their immense haloes have an effect on our hull—or couldn't they simply radiate a homicidal energy through it?"

"We have what we need to respond—by radiation or by explosives."

"Yes, but...what about surprises?"

As he was speaking, Jean started, and he extended his arm toward the Martian orient.

Antoine's hypothesis was revealed in a formidable reality. Three hundred meters away, a colossal and frightful creature had just appeared, comparable in size to an iguanodon, the Biblical Leviathan, and sperm whales. Flattened, like all the structures of its realm, it was nevertheless elevated, by reason of its size, three feet above the ground.

"About forty meters long...fifteen broad," I murmured.

"Let's go back in," said Antoine, evidently worried.

Sheltered within the *Stellarium*, we examined the monster with our binoculars.

"It might perhaps be prudent to go up a little way," I suggested.

"Let's wait and see," Antoine replied.

As the colossus remained motionless, we were able to analyze the details of its form—its "formless form," as Jean put it—at leisure. It seemed to us to be similar to those of other organisms, save for a few details, but the enormity of the zoomorph made it seem more hideous.

"That's because we don't yet know how to differentiate these structures."

The animal (?) began to move, quite slowly. It stopped close to the *Stellarium*. We had the impression, perhaps illusory, of a hesitation. Whatever it was, it soon drew away, and its speed became extraordinary.

"A hundred kilometers an hour!" said Jean.

"In spite of the trepidations of its appendages, it doesn't seem to be running or crawling...if it weren't touching the ground, I'd say that it's flying."

"Who knows whether it might not be using a movement between flight and sliding," said Antoine. "We'll see. In the meantime, let's get to work!"

We divided up the task. I was to carry out the dissection; Antoine and Jean removed a little of the substance—with some difficulty—for chemical, spectrographic and radiographic analysis.

The organism was dry, devoid of liquids. Its gases and solids were of an incomparably elastic nature: submitted to powerful pressure and traction, the solids flattened out or stretched considerably, but as soon as the experiment ceased they resumed their original form.

We had a great deal of difficulty tearing or cutting them. Their porosity proved to be remarkable. The interior of the body, very close to the surface, where the creature flattened out, included numerous vacuoles but nothing that resembled organs.

I continued to palpate it, rather vainly, but my companions had already made some impressive discoveries. The analysis revealed very small quantities of nitrogen, carbon and hydrogen; the essential substance was formed of oxygen compounds, nitrocarbon and boron oxide, with small proportions of magnesium, arsenic, silica, calcium and phosphorus, plus as-yet-undefined traces of various substances known and unknown.

"These things compose a realm completely different from ours," Jean declared.

Antoine acquiesced with a nod of the head, and I said in my turn: "The difference, in my opinion, is rendered more striking by the absence of liquid. I suspect that circulation is essentially gaseous."

"One could also imagine solid circulation—after the fashion of particles moving in inter-atomic spaces."

"In any case, the primary anatomical analysis remains fruitless."

"Given that you're a prince of histology," said Antoine, amiably, "I conclude that the enigma is profound."

"What are we going to do now?"

"First, it's particularly important to extend our exploration of the surface. Let's take a look at other regions…"

"Another one!" cried Jean.

"Another what?"

"Another giant—even vaster than the first."

We turned round, and discerned a monster that must have been at least fifty meters long. It was heading straight for the *Stellarium*.

"Let's lift off!" I said.

Gripped by an ardent curiosity, Antoine put a hand on my shoulder, while Jean, petrified, seemed not to have heard. The enormous creature approached our transparent vessel rapidly—undoubtedly aware of its presence, for it stopped as soon as it reached it.

An immense halo was manifest, and I felt chilled to the bone. Antoine, who was livid, shivered. Jean leaned on the wall, his eyes haggard.

A second, weaker, halo froze us further; at the same time as I felt an indescribable sensation, extremely disturbing, which was not reminiscent of any known sensation. It caused a constriction in my chest and seemed to stop my heart beating.

How long our torture—for it was a torture—lasted, I don't know; perhaps 30 seconds, perhaps several minutes.

When we recovered our senses completely, the enormous organism had disappeared.

Antoine, as usual, was the first to recover his strength and self-possession. "We've just escaped death!" he remarked, in a voice that hardly betrayed his emotion. "If it weren't for the *Stellarium*, we'd have sunk into the eternal night."

I couldn't help saying, with a hint of reproach: "Because nobody listened to me!"

"We were wrong—quite wrong...especially me, who yielded to an unhealthy curiosity. *Mea culpa!* All the same, it's as well to know. Tomorrow night, we won't run the immense danger that we ran unconsciously last night. It would only have required two or three of those monsters to gather around us to annihilate us in our sleep, in spite of the walls!"

"Provided that they're active at night," Jean remarked.

"The second halo was far less powerful than the first," Antoine went on. "Proof, it seems, that these emissions require a great expense of energy."

"Was that brute conscious of what it was doing?" Jean muttered. "Or was it acting under the influence of a physical excitation provoked by the proximity of unusual substances?"

"Or unusual creatures," I added.

"Through the wall...that completely impermeable wall?"

"Since our eyes can see through it as clearly as an atmosphere, why shouldn't a sense analogous to our vision be involved?"

"That's true," said Antoine. "There's no reason to refuse *them* senses sensitive to our infinitesimal vibrations."

While speaking, we had raised the *Stellarium*, whose gravitational compensator maintained us fifty meters from the Martian surface.

"I assume that the halo can't do us any great harm here," said Jean, in an aggrieved tone. "Its radiation must obey the inverse square law of distance."

Antoine's face was somber. "I assume so—although these brutes might, after all, perhaps be capable of channeling their emissions...in which case, goodbye inverse square law. It's scarcely probable, though; that one, like the smaller ones, is *enveloped* by a luminous carapace. All the same, we might be handicapped in our excursions."

"In spite of our radiation-shields and mini-torpedoes? Besides, a simple beam of radiation, suitably selected, will doubtless be sufficient to keep the aggressors at a distance."

"Doubtful!" said Antoine. "But it costs nothing to try."

We chose for an experimental subject a zoomorph of medium size, at which we directed obliquely radiations of various frequencies, progressively increasing the dosage. The zoomorph proved utterly indifferent to long waves, waves in the visible spectrum and the shorter ultra-violet waves, but beyond the Ramières rays, it gave signs of agitation, and when we reached the Bussault rays, it drew away at an accelerated speed in the opposite direction.[47] We prolonged the exposure momentarily, then attacked a second, third and fourth zoomorph, with the same success.

"In principle, we've succeeded," I said, "but I won't be reassured until a giant confirms our results. If I'm not mistaken, here comes one now..."

A colossus had just appeared around the corner of a rock. As it was some distance away, we moved closer before subjecting it to a shower of Bussault rays. It seemed to manifest a certain hesitation, but it continued to advance almost directly toward the source of the radiation.

"Let's increase the intensity!"

The effect was not long delayed. The zoomorph stopped, and then retreated. With a suitable discharge, and orientating

---

[47] The electromagnetic spectrum had not been completely "mapped" when Rosny wrote this story, and X-rays were still sometimes called "Röntgen rays" after their discoverer; the idea that new varieties of radiation might be discovered, and named after their discoverers, thus seemed very plausible.

the *Stellarium* with respect to various azimuths, we could insure ourselves against any chance of error.

"Well," said Antoine, lightly, "we're masters of the situation, at little expense—for the energy deployed is, after all, feeble. I confess that I was quite worried—consternated even. Not that I doubted our means, but I feared an excessive expenditure of energy...but there we are!"

"There'll be other dangers."

"Silence, Jeremiah! We'll overcome them. Now, let's get under way for other zones."

It suited us to travel rather slowly, in order not to miss any interesting regions, and to zigzag somewhat, to enlarge the field of observation.

After an hour and a half, we had scarcely traveled more than 100 kilometers parallel to the equator, while tracing oblique lines four or five leagues long. The desert regions were succeeded by regions frequented by zoomorphs. Jean, impatient for new discoveries, proposed a high-speed flight.

"We can resume our snail's pace afterwards."

"A straight course?"

"Oh no! Many turns to the right and left of the track."

The *Stellarium* flew on at 1000 kilometers an hour, with pauses during which we scrutinized the locales. The hour went by without any notable results, and we were already wondering whether to resume the slow excursion when Jean exclaimed: "Something singularly reminiscent of water!"

"Yes, singularly," I added.

A large bright brown sheet was shining very weakly in the sunlight, as if it were covered with slightly polished gauze; moving ripples left no doubt as to its fluidity. The sheet was about as large as Lake Annecy.[48]

"Water? Is that water?" Antoine muttered. "It has an odd color."

"I've known muddy water of the same hue!"

---

[48] The surface area of Lake Annecy is about 27.6 sq. km.

"Almost, yes—but rarely. At any rate, it's still a liquid…and on this disconcerting planet, it's the first hint of it. Let's take a look at close range."

"Prudently."

"This time, we won't all leave home at the same time."

As soon as we were close to the lake, we became certain that the brown color was the normal color of the liquid. A profound and delightful emotion gripped us. This world was no longer incompatible—and how sadly!—with our own. The flexible forms that were undulating on the shore and in the surrounding plain seemed incontestably analogous to our vegetation. For a few minutes, we were in a kind of ecstasy, to the extent that Jean's eyes were full of tears.

Although no plant clearly replicated a terrestrial form, they all bore some resemblance either to our grasses, our ferns, our shrubs, our trees, our mushrooms, our mosses, and even our lichens and algae. However, the pseudo-mosses were as large was willow-trees, the pseudo-mushrooms grew to heights of seven to ten meters and the pseudo-lichens developed tresses as long as our algae, while the tallest trees were no larger than a hazelnut tree and were much stouter than ours—with the result that, in spite of their low stature, they sometimes attained the circumference of baobabs; one might have thought them the remnants of enormous trunks sawn off a few feet from the ground, on which a multitude of thin branches was growing.

The vegetation was various in color, the ensemble being somewhat reminiscent of the shades of forests at the height of autumn, when the crows resemble immense bunches of flowers.

While we were savoring the delight of being in a near-terrestrial locale, other discoveries excited us; animals appeared in their turn. From the outset, there was no doubt: here, incontestably, were creatures analogous to our animals, even though there was an assortment of structures that were astonishing to our sublunar eyes.

Of quadrupeds there were none; these animals, large or small, had five feet, the fifth being different from the others and seemingly playing a more complex role. As on Earth, some animals were moving on land, others swimming in the water or flying in the air. No feathers, but hair, scales and bare skins. No tails at all. Multiple eyes, the number of which varied according to species, without there ever being less than six—eyes that were generally smaller than the eyes of our quadrupeds, but of the same sort, endowed with a superior brightness. No ears or visible nostrils; mouths in which the dentition formed a solid block...

Various sizes, although we saw no animal as large as a zebra. In broad terms, the bodies resembled terrestrial bodies; as well as skulls that were roughly comparable to the skulls of wolves, cats, bears, tortoises and birds, others were perfectly triangular or formed as exact pyramids.

Many of the kinds of feet found on our planet have equivalents among the Martian animals apparent on the shore or the plain, but the aerial varieties all have five wings capable, as we soon saw, of performing the functions of feet, and the aquatic animals five fins, four lateral and one ventral.

I am accumulating our observations as if they were simultaneous—in reality, it took us hours to make them.

At first, we flew very slowly over the locale—which frightened the aerial organisms but appeared to leave the inhabitants of the water and land indifferent. Then, having perceived none of the zoomorphs of the previous region, we decided to study the successive zones at the edge of the lake and on the plain.

From the outset, we had observed that the majority of Martian animals were herbivores; they were roaming around tearing apart and chewing vegetation. Soon, we witnessed carnivorous scenes especially among small-sized organisms.

We had to wait two hours to discern a struggle between two aerial creatures; the victor transported its victim into a crack in a rock. Then we saw an animal the size of a wolf bring down and tear apart an animal not much smaller than itself.

"The terrestrial inferno!" Jean groaned.

These scenes were rare, the number of herbivores far surpassing the number of carnivores.

"Shall we make a sortie?" I asked.

"I was about to propose one," Jean replied.

The lot selected Antoine to stay aboard the *Stellarium*, which would follow us at a distance; if it were too close, it would hinder our observations by causing the animals to flee.

Furnished with autonomous respirators, ray-guns and mini-torpedoes, and enveloped in our pressure-suits, Jean and I went out on to the lake-shore. First of all, we took a little water from the lake; it was noticeably heavier than terrestrial water and gave off an indefinable, vaguely aromatic odor that was not unpleasant.

"Its density is equivalent to one and a half times that of our old oceanic liquid," Jean remarked, "and its evaporation must be feeble. Is it just water? I'm almost sure that it isn't. We can find out."

Each of us was equipped with a little analysis kit, which permitted a few summary experiments. Warmed in a minuscule test-tube, the Martian liquid required a significantly higher temperature than water to cause it to boil. Its specific density was approximately 1.3.

Having put away our minuscule apparatus, we began our excursion along the shore of the lake.

The animals avoided us, except for the smallest, which were probably unaware of our presence. There was no apparent panic or curiosity, however.

"We must simply be unknown to them," said Jean. "Hence the spontaneous mistrust...but it's purely instinctive."

Sometimes, an animal less prudent than the rest stopped some distance away to observe us with its multiple eyes, but if we walked toward it, it did not take long to run away.

"Those are perhaps the most intelligent. They're trying vaguely to figure us out. What luck, Jean, if we were to encounter quasi-human beings!"

"Or what bad luck! What if they were as intelligent and as ferocious as humans?"

"The *Stellarium* is close at hand."

"The trap might be even closer! One well-hidden ambush, and we'd be fried!"

"Look out!"

An animal similar to a carnivore, one of which we had seen at work before setting out, had just appeared. Very thickset, it attained the stature of a large Newfoundland dog, and displayed a muzzle similar to a five-sided prism; its six eyes gleamed like glow-worms. Its hide was violet-tinted, reminiscent of hairy lichen.

"Perhaps it has a keen desire to taste the unfamiliar flesh!" my companion muttered.

An animal of another kind suddenly appeared, vaguely reminiscent of our weasels, but a weasel with a helical mouth and a stature equal to that of a wild boar; it was being perceived by an animal of the same kind as the one that had first come into view. Caught between two fires, it tried to move away obliquely, but a third enemy materialized and it found itself caught in a triangle.

"That resembles a terrestrial scene, point for point," said Jean. "A red deer or a roe deer surrounded by wolves."

The hunted beast tried to pass between two aggressors. It failed. One of the carnivores seized it by the nape of the neck, and in a flash, the other two fell upon its flanks. Jean made as if to intervene, but it was already too late; the aggressors had opened the victim's throat, from which ran a sulfur-yellow liquid—doubtless Martian blood—and its belly was ripped open.

"I was about to fire a ray!" Jean said. "Although the planet seems to me to permit the renewal of our energy-supplies many times over, however, it's better to economize our resources."

"All the more so as we're not here to alter the course of events that have been going on for thousands of years!"

Pensively, we continued on our way. Because humans are perhaps the most adaptable of animals, we already felt familiar with the locale, with its plants and animals—and even with the weight deficiency that had made us feel ill before. On the other hand, we were glad to be able to move swiftly and effortlessly; as for respiration, thanks to the condensers that supplied us with concentrated Martian air, it was perfect.

"If there are edible plants and animals—edible for humans—there's nothing to prevent us from living on Mars for an unlimited time," Jean remarked. "There seems to be a possibility of finding everything necessary for quotidian existence here, and renewing the energy reserves for the return journey. Eh? What's this coming toward us?"

What was coming toward us was not very reassuring: an apocalyptic creature twelve meters long, simultaneously reminiscent of an alligator, a python and a rhinoceros. Low-slung, with a rounded torso, a thick pyramidal muzzle and head of which projected a sort of long horn, a hide that was bare on the flank, scaly on the back and hairy on the muzzle, the beast advanced with a wriggling motion that gave it the appearance of crawling. Stout feet were agitating beneath it.

"Is it crawling or walking?" I exclaimed.

"Both!" my companion replied. "The movement of the feet is, if I dare say so, in synchrony with the twisting of the body. We've nothing as ugly as that on Earth."

On seeing us, the beast had stopped, and its eyes—it had a dozen of them—directed a gaze at us that sometimes went out and lit up again, as if commanded by circuit-breakers.

We got our ray-guns and mini-torpedoes ready, just in case.

"That thing must weigh as much as several elephants," said Jean.

"Five or six."

We noticed that all the visible animals had fled at panic speed—proof that the monster was redoubtable.

After a brief pause, it started moving again, and it was obviously heading straight for us.

"All right, old chap!" said Jean—as he sent forth a beam of Bussault rays.

The beast's writhing became convulsive, but it did not stop; in fact, it accelerated its progress. I launched a beam in my turn, and this time the effect seemed decisive; the enormous mass stopped dead, and the eyes went out. Soon, it turned round and moved away, heavily and painfully.

"It's hurt!" I said. "Should we finish it off?"

"No need—and it might take too much energy. I reckon it's out of action for some time. But here's Antoine!"

The *Stellarium* was, in fact, there. We exchanged a few signals with our friend—who, completely reassured, retired to a distance.

"Still no equivalent of the creature that lit the first fire at the end of the Tertiary!" Jean muttered. "It seems, however, that if there's any chance of meeting one, there's no place more favorable than the shores of this lake?"

"Eh?" I said. "Perhaps it's already aware of our presence. It might be hiding, its quasi-human eyes fixed upon us, setting some ambush for us. Who can tell?"

Jean shrugged his shoulders and burst out laughing.

When we had climbed a hill, a forest was revealed—a forest of pseudo-mushrooms, simultaneously impressive and baroque.

"One might really take them for gigantic cloves and colossal columellas," I said, "apart from a few unexpected festoons and a few helical appendages. A unique texture...a thallus...nothing resembling leaves..."

Animals appeared and disappeared slyly; airborne individuals took off on their five wings; some of them were tiny, no larger than cockchafers, others much the same size as tits, pigeons, crows or even falcons. They had no feathers, no beaks and no tails; their muzzles were most commonly shaped like flattened arches.

"They're still the ones least reminiscent of terrestrial life," Jean murmured. "Their five wings, especially, seem unusual. Note that during flight, they're disposed in a fashion somewhat akin to helicopters. In the same way that the apocalyptic beast seemed to be running and crawling at the same time, they seem to be flying and swimming at the same time."

"They have to be clever, in an atmosphere as thin as this! Their wings also seem to be extraordinarily vigorous."

We had reached a clearing, in which nothing grew but some sort of paltry lianas and pseudo-lichens. It was strewn with rocks, similar to standing stones, and while I stopped to examine some of them, Jean drew ahead by a hundred meters or so. Something must have caught his attention, which caused him to move into a narrow gully between two blue rocks, larger than the others. I lost sight of him.

A few minutes went by; then, not seeing my companion reappear, I searched for him with my gaze. There was no sign of him. I headed for the blue rocks in my turn.

Two creatures emerged, which differed from all those that we had already seen. Standing on three feet, their torsos vertical, there was something positively human about them. Even their faces, whose skin was bare, in spite of their six eyes and the absence of a nose suggested some kind of homology with our species.

How can I describe those faces, though? How can I convey an impression of their harmonious form, comparable to that of the most beautiful Greek vases, or the ravishing nuances of their skin, simultaneously evocative of flowers, crepuscular clouds and Egyptian enamels? None of those gross fleshy appendages that are our noses, ears and lips, but six marvelous eyes, compared with which our most beautiful terrestrial eyes are no more than the wing-cases of cockchafers or scarabs—eyes through which pass all the gleams of auroras, morning meadows, rivers at sunset, oriental lakes, oceans, storms, clouds...

The creatures walked strangely, on three feet that were raised in turn. When they stopped, the feet formed an acute-angled triangle, the middle foot slightly to the left of the front and rear feet. As for their height, it was visibly equal to that of Spaniards or southern Italians.

While I was studying them, in a fit of surprise and admiration, they drew away and disappeared behind the trees—but others appeared some distance away. One of them was carrying something that resembled a coiled piece of liana; I felt my legs go numb.

Aiming my ray-gun, with difficulty, I fired a beam of radiation. Two creatures tottered; they all shivered and disappeared behind a block of stone. The numbness only lasted another half-minute, but a profound anxiety had gripped me.

As loudly as I could, I shouted: "Jean! Jean!"

A dozen upright creatures emerged, but much further away than their predecessors. They only stayed momentarily; the *Stellarium* was descending into the clearing. By the time it was a few dekameters from the ground, the clearing was deserted.

Antoine was already emerging from the exit hatch. "Have you seen Jean?" I cried.

"Jean? No, I haven't seen him," Antoine replied, in the tranquil voice that he maintained through the worst anxieties. "I arrived over the clearing just as you headed for the blue rocks. I saw the upright creatures appear; I understood that there was danger—and here I am!"

"Jean has disappeared—and those creatures are evidently redoubtable. Like us, they can strike at a distance, and the energy they use paralyzes the muscles. I suspect that only the distance saved me!"

While I was speaking, we never ceased scanning the expanse with our binoculars. Occasionally, a luminous face appeared in the distance, and then vanished.

"We can't abandon Jean," said Antoine, "but what are we to do? To risk ourselves out there would probably be fatal. Creatures that know how to project energy at a distance are intelligent enough to set a trap for us—easy enough to do, since there are so many of them."

296

We looked at one another in immeasurable distress.

"Something bad will happen to us if we remain here," Antoine continued. "It's surprising that we're still safe. Let's get back into the *Stellarium*. In any case, that offers us the best chance of discovering something. Come on!"

He drew me to him and dragged me away. It seemed highly likely that Jean was already dead.

We hovered above the forest, if it could be called a forest. There was nothing but Aerials and wild pentapods—no trace of the Verticals.

"The *Stellarium* has probably frightened them," said Antoine. "Let's go up higher!"

We climbed above the clearing without discovering anything, but once we had moved a few kilometers away we had no difficulty seeing the Verticals. They were wandering placidly or occupied in strange tasks. Occasionally, we saw one of them point the bizarre machine that had nearly stunned me at some pentapod; the animal was not long delayed in staggering and falling.

"They're definitely the equivalent of human beings on this planet," Antoine said.

I thought the same; furthermore, the movements of the beings gave rise to an activity completely different from those of other creatures, if only by virtue of their diversity.

"So long as they've spared Jean!" I sighed.

We came back to the clearing repeatedly, executing maneuvers in every direction. Nothing! As the hours passed, our faint hopes dwindled. Oh, how vain and ridiculous the expedition now seemed!

"How did we dare to come here in such a small number?" I said, five or six hours after our friend's disappearance. "We weren't crazy, though."

"It's only necessary to regret stupid actions," Antoine retorted, severely. "All explorers risk their lives. That's the rule. How many of those perished who set out in Columbus's or Magellan's caravels, or Cook's ships, or ventures into forests, scrublands or deserts. How many others died who set course

for the moon or landed on it? Their task was inferior to ours."
Firmly, he added: "Perhaps I'll die here, but I don't believe I'll
regret coming."

"We should have set out in greater numbers!"

"It would have been necessary to build several *Stella-*
riums, and thus to wait—for a long time—for money and men
to be found, at the risk of being anticipated. There's no proof,
in any case, that a larger party would have succeeded. If Mars
contains many Tripeds armed like those who have abducted
Jean, it might have been more dangerous for twenty, thirty or
forty to come than two, three or four. Haven't we made the
sacrifice of our lives?"

The day passed; fate condemned us to spend the night
over the forest. We saw the Imponderable Living Beings reappear, but our hearts were too heavy for us to devote ourselves
to observations or scrupulous experiments. Even so, we took
better account of the individuality, the spontaneity and also the
"speciation" of the Ethereals.

Their movements were as discontinuous as the movements of a crowd in our city streets—more discontinuous,
even, more varied and more variable—although associations
of movements were formed for inconceivable ends.

Often, exchanges of phosphorescence, changing
rhythms, with repetitions and pauses, suggested the notion of a
language. There might or might not have been authoritative
control within the groups; the number of those composing
them varied from two to several hundred—once, in fact, we
saw thousands of complex filaments whose length (stature?)
attained seven or eight meters, moving through a near-vertical
column of networks. That multitude rose up through the column at great speed, as if it were trying to reach the stars.

In spite of our anguish, we rose up along with that singular multitude. It climbed to a height of several hundred kilometers. The column had faded out some time before; the Ethereals were creating a less obvious pathway, which was erased
behind them. In the end, they stopped, but their agitation in

place created a collective palpitation from which fluorescences escaped.

After approximately half an hour, the crowd descended toward the planet again.

"We've witnessed a great etherosocial event, if I might call it that," Antoine murmured, when we had resumed our maneuvers above the forest. "I think those life-forms are far superior to ours!"

"They seem to be unaware of us, though, while we can see them! Isn't that a superiority on our side of the account?"

"Haven't we been unaware, throughout almost all of our ancestral evolution, of the microbes that nevertheless decimate humankind? Would you say that the microbial killers of negroes, redskins, Egyptians and Greeks were superior to the people they destroyed, who did not know of their existence?"

"Who knows?"

There was a pause. We directed beams of light at the cryptogamic forest, hoping against hope that we might see our poor companion. We sent out radiant signals in vain.

Antoine took the first watch and I slept for a few hours—the feverish sleep of the condemned, with its nightmares and bewildered awakenings.

It was still dark when my turn to be on watch arrived. Until dawn, I never ceased describing circles above the bleak forest. My soul really was mortally depressed; in this strange world, even if Jean had not been a dear friend, I would have felt his loss as an intolerable diminution of my own person. The journey across the interstellar abyss, the isolation in a star lost in the depths of space, had made the three of us into a single being.

Dawn finally came, immediately mutated into broad daylight. I looked down hopelessly at the huge thalluses and the creeping plants. Suddenly, my heart leapt: emotion swept through me like a cyclone, traversed by lightning-flashes.

Jean was there!

He was there, in the same clearing from which he had disappeared, next to the blue rocks.

I sent forth a "hailing" beam, to which he replied by repetitive signals—signals in our radiostenographic vocabulary.

He said: "Safe and sound. I'm among the homologues of our human race. We understand one another, very vaguely. They're gentle—gentler, I think, than humans. They captured me by stunning me; I haven't been subject to the slightest violence. Their astonishment and curiosity are intense. They ardently desired to know where we come from; I finally succeeded in making them understand…"

"But how could you eat…and breathe?"

"As for respiration, nothing to fear—they left me two respirators—but I'm hungry…thirsty, especially. Their water isn't drinkable for humans. I dared not eat their food…they've guessed that…"

"You're not free?"

"No, and I doubt that they'll let me go, until I can explain. Send me water—water above all."

"Soon, my dear Jean. I'll wake Antoine."

Antoine, who was sleeping as badly as I had slept, got up at the first appeal, and was stupefied by the sight of our companion, alone in the clearing.

I explained the situation rapidly, while Jean stenotelegraphed: "I've been able to assure myself that their 'fluidic bombardment' only passes through objects of no great thickness—five or six centimeters at the most; it becomes harmless in passing through more than that. It doesn't threaten life; it produces unconsciousness. At 100 meters its effectiveness is already much reduced. Take your precautions in consequence."

"Good!" said Antoine. "We'll send down the provisions."

Rapidly, we made up a parcel and dropped it from some two hundred meters above the ground, its fall being slowed by a small gravitic field opposed to the Martian field.

During that fall we saw some twenty Tripeds emerge from underground, who watched the operation with evident curiosity.

"Thank you," Jean telegraphed, when he had taken possession of the provisions. "I hope to give you precise information next time."

We saw him eat and drink, without anyone interfering, but when he wrapped up the parcel again four Tripeds emerged from underground to take him away.

"What does that signify?" Antoine muttered. "Are they sparing him permanently, or is it only a respite?"

"I have an idea that they won't do him any harm—unless they think that they're under threat themselves. They want to know what we are and where we come from. Think what our state of mind would be in analogous circumstances!"

"A civilized state of mind—but what if they're savages?"

"I imagine that they're more likely to be 'retrogrades'—underground habitation implies the impoverishment of the planet."

"Possibly! At any rate, their weapons—the fluidic bombardment that Jean mentioned—appear to indicate a present or past civilization."

"And how captivating it is!"

"Anthropocentrist!" cried Antoine. The Ethereals, not to mention the Zoomorphs, ought to appear much more exciting! These are only a sort of equivalent of Terrans..."

"That's true—but which of them, deep down, interests you the most?"

"I have the same weakness as you, damn it! Then again, there's Jean—safe and sound, but captive. Until he's set free, that's where the poignant episode, the tragic turn of events, will take place..."

"He must be set free!"

Antoine shrugged his shoulders sadly. "How? Even if the Tripeds are powerless against the *Stellarium*, and even if our rays are sufficient to vanquish them, they're holding Jean—his life is at their disposal. We can only count on chance or the good will of his kidnappers."

"I shan't despair of that good will."

"Nor I—but it's a baseless impression."

"Their gentle treatment of Jean…"

"Might be a trick! I'm thinking about Cook's massacre."

We spent long hours—even bleaker than the hours of darkness—hovering over the forest. In the middle of the day Jean reappeared in the clearing and immediately stenographed: "I firmly believe that their mores are very gentle, gentler than ours, and that they don't wish me any harm. A sign language is slowly being established between us. I've been able to make them understand that we come from another world. There's no doubt about their intelligence; it must be the equivalent of human intelligence, with particularities that are related to their structure. Since yesterday we've received many visitors, who come from other regions…"

"Do you think that their society is increasing or decreasing?"

"Deceasing—there's no doubt about that. Like humans, they belong to an animality whose life depends on liquid. Now, their liquid—their water—has become rare, and is perhaps not the same water as in the past."

"Can we hope for your liberation?"

"I'd dare to bet on it…"

One by one, Tripeds had emerged from underground. They were attentively observing the exchange of signals between their prisoner and the navigators of the *Stellarium*.

"They really are very beautiful!" said Antoine.

"Much more beautiful than us!" I sighed.

We were able to observe their gait and gestures at our leisure. As I have already said, they only moved one leg at a time, in such a way that their steps were taken in three stages; their gestures were in some respects very similar to and in some ways greatly different from ours. The extremity of each of their upper limbs was "digitized" but did not exactly form a hand; the extremities that replaced our fingers emerged from a sort of shell; there were nine of them to each hand and we soon noticed that they could curve over in every direction, without the movement of any one of them influencing the movement of others. They thus obtained, at will, the most various dispositions, and could grip several objects at the same time, in different directions. Their garments were made of a sort of mossy vegetation that was exactly fitted to the body.

One of them, who as standing close to Jean, was observing our friend's gestures, and ours, with a particularly intense attention.

"This is an important person," Jean told us. "He has a certain influence over the others—he's the one with whom I'm designing a system of signals—but it will require a few days more to exchange elementary ideas."

"Do you still have food and water?"

"Until tomorrow morning."

At that moment, the influential individual traced various signs.

"I think I understand that he's trying to reassure us about the future," Jean said. "Fundamentally, I sense more melancholy than anxiety."

IV.

A week vanished into the imponderable. We communicated with Jean every day. More than once we thought about disembarking in the clearing, but the captive asked us to wait a little longer. Because our continuous presence was unnecessary, we made long excursions. They revealed three zones inhabited by Tripeds: three zones of lakes and canals that, in combination, scarcely attained the extent of the Mediterranean.

The lakes scarcely extended beyond the tropical regions, although we found several of them in latitudes that would have enjoyed a temperate climate on Earth. Elsewhere, there was nothing but more or less diluted vapors that sometimes resembled light mists, or—in the polar regions—fields of snow.

303

There could scarcely have been more than seven or eight million Tripeds on the entire planet. The majority lived underground; the others, much smaller in number, lived in stone dwellings whose style was vaguely reminiscent of the Roman style.

These dwellings—evident vestiges of the past—were always part of an important agglomeration. One might have thought these cities entirely composed of large and small Roman churches, the majority of which had fallen into ruins—which left little doubt as to the decadence of the Tripeds. Many centuries, perhaps millennia, before there had been seven or eight cities as populous as Paris under Louis XIV or London under Cromwell; they now contained a few hundred individuals in total.

It was easy to tell that the Tripeds' industry was in complete decadence. They constructed tools, some of which were reminiscent of terrestrial tools, agricultural machinery and mechanical means of transport. The last-named, which were rare, did not move on wheels—they seemed to crawl rather swiftly over the ground. Once, no doubt, the Tripeds had had flying machines; they communicated at a distance by means of apparatus whose mechanism escaped us, but which evidently used waves.

It did not take long for our presence to become known; we were observed with the aid of instruments similar to our own binoculars and presumably constructed on the same principles. As we passed by, crowds assembled in the cities; elsewhere, groups emerged from underground; the agitation and curiosity seemed lively.

In sum, the Tripeds displayed the vestiges of a civilization once comparable to the terrestrial civilization of the nineteenth century; we conjectured that, following the successive abandonment of many industries, their science had diminished over the centuries.

As for their animals, very few attained the size of our elephants, giraffes or large buffaloes.

The domain of the Tripeds and their Realm only comprised a rather restricted fraction of the planet—a tenth at the most; it stopped part way between the equator and the poles. The surface occupied by the zoomorphs was more extensive and extended much further to the north and the south; the future belonged to them.

Was the retreat of the Tripeds due to a conflict between the Realms, to the impossibility of living in certain regions or to a spontaneous decadence? We made little attempt to answer these questions; nevertheless, *the presence of Zoomorphs excluded that of the Tripeds.* What seemed evident to us was that the realm of the Zoomorphs was much less ancient than the other.

"The future is theirs!" said Antoine, one day when we had traveled through several zones. "They'll possess the whole planet eventually!"

"They already possess three-quarters of it. What about the Ethereals?"

"They, my friend, are so far in advance of us that I have renounced any thought of forming an idea of their future."

"Are they really in advance of us? More subtle, undoubtedly, less exposed to brutal contingencies—but perhaps after all, less intelligent…"

"Possibly. The very essence of their organization nevertheless appears to me to be of a higher order."

"Do you think so? One may doubt it. Free electrons have movements more ample and rapid than those of a living cell, but I deem them inferior to a cell nevertheless."

"A poor comparison. We're dealing here with a complex organization of radiations…radiant cells, if I might put it like that. In sum, it's a vain discussion. We can only resort to our intuitions—woefully inadequate, alas!"

On the eleventh day, we saw Jean appear in the middle of the clearing, alone. Not a single Triped was visible.

Our friend raised a smiling face toward the *Stellarium*. "I'm free!" he affirmed.

My heart was beating furiously. Jean went on: "As you see, they're keeping their distance. In any case, I've been able to convince them that, if they had evil designs, they would be impossible against our vessel. Their weapons are inadequate, their instruments are incapable of penetrating the argine walls and they don't possess any powerful explosives. Besides, they don't wish us any harm! They've told me that repeatedly. I can't have misunderstood it."

While he was radiotelegraphing, the *Stellarium* descended into the clearing. We finally landed, and Jean found himself back with us.

The immense sadness ceased to weigh upon us. Hope sounded its fanfares. For several minutes we exchanged incoherent words of joy.

Then Antoine asked: "You really think they're harmless, then?"

"They're already naturally inclined to a gentleness greater than human beings...a gentleness that includes a great deal of resignation."

"Why resignation?"

"They know that they and their entire Realm are in a state of decay. They know it in a sort of innate manner, as well as by tradition. Our presence naturally inspires a great curiosity in them, and gives them—if I've understood rightly—a vague hope."

The *Stellarium* remained stationary on the edge of the clearing. Gradually, Tripeds had arrived, who were maintaining their distance. One of them came closer and waved its right arm in a rhythmic manner.

"It wants to welcome you," said Jean, who replied to the Triped's gestures.

"What shall we do?" asked Antoine.

"Give me a cup of coffee!" said our friend, laughing. "The absence of coffee was a poignant privation."

I immediately put the water on to boil, while Jean continued: "If you'll permit it, I'll return to them for two or three hours every day, in order to perfect my sign language. During

306

that time, you can continue your explorations... You must have made some exciting discoveries."

"We've discovered Triped cities—but why do some of them live on the surface and others underground?"

"There are, I think, two different patterns of evolution. Without fighting one another, or hating one another, the Subterraneans scarcely socialize with the others. They too have veritable cities, or townships."

"The cities on the surface are mostly made up of ruins. In cities that could accommodate 300,000 or 400,000 Tripeds, there are 10,000 at the most—sometimes fewer."

"Then the subterranean cities, fully inhabited, are more recent. That of my friends doesn't contain more than 2000 inhabitants. I can go across it in any direction...ah! The coffee!" Jean sniffed the odorant vapor avidly.

"We've surpassed many ancestral things...but we've added nothing to them!" he exclaimed, as he finished his coffee. "Of everything we've brought with us, nothing else reminds me more tenderly of the Earth."

"Do you think that we can definitely prolong our sojourn?" I asked.

"From the energetic point of view, we can find everything we need...in the same way, as you know, it will be easy for us to renew our oxygen supplies. There remains the matter of nourishment. The Tripeds' doesn't suit us..."

"It's only a matter of nitrogenous substances. As for hydrocarbons..."

"We'll take charge of that..."

"There are nitrogenous aliments," Jean went on, "but they contain substances whose elimination might give us an acceptable substitute. In their present state, they're not poisonous...but they don't provide nourishment."

"An adaptation that might take years!"

Jean's return brought the joys of spring. The dreams of previous times rose up once again from the abyss, from the depths of the immeasurable spaces in which our native planet floated.

"All the same," Jean muttered, "I'll be glad to see her again!"

Every evening, we turned toward *her*, as she became a resplendent star. We beheld her again, we poor atoms, conquerors of the ether, humble navigators of the imponderable ocean...

Nonetheless, we had no regrets; nostalgia did not extinguish the passion for knowledge.

"A time will come when fleets of *Stellariums* will go from planet to planet! Humans are only tiny creatures—but what tiny creatures they are!"

V.

Every day, Jean spent three or four hours among the Tripeds, and then participated in our explorations. Antoine and I were impatient to do as he did, but it was necessary to wait until the sign language was less embryonic.

We took lessons with Jean, who brought back a new "word" every day. In this work of cerebral adjustment, the Tripeds showed themselves to be superior to humans, being endowed with a greater abstract agility—is it not the case that among us, old peoples in decline are always more abstract than peoples who are still young?

On returning from one of his absences, Jean remarked: "We already possess two hundred terms of exchange. With 600 or 700 terms, many things can be expressed quite well—after all, some subtle classical authors made use of no more than 1200 or 1500 words!"

As Jean and his Triped friends perfected their "dictionary" we obtained more precise information regarding the present and past of Mars. It confirmed our conclusions. The memory of a superior power and knowledge persisted among the Subterraneans; once the Tripeds had practiced an ingenious and diverse industry, which involved productive factories, innumerable means of terrestrial and aerial transport; they had been able to use subtle energies, since, even now, they communicated over long distances and made use of radiation weapons for attack and defense.

We also learned that no war had broken out between Tripeds for millennia. The incompatibility of races had not translated itself into any brutal act, much less homicidal encounters.

"They destroy certain animals, however," said Jean. "I think I understand that they have often gone to war with *the other Realm*. Thus far, the explanation remains a trifle confused."

"I doubt that they mean the Ethereals."

"Surely not! It might be a question of the Zoomorphs—which, if I understand correctly, gain territory incessantly."

"The two Realms can't co-exist, then?"

"I suppose not."

That question fascinated us. Jean promised to do everything possible to obtain details. He brought them three days later.

"I understood this time. The Realms can't live on the same ground, at least after some time. In addition to conflicts with the superior Zoomorphs—murderous conflicts for the two Realms—the soil gradually becomes incapable of producing vegetation. It's poisoned; the animals perish and life becomes untenable for the Tripeds. It is, in consequence, essential to repel the slightest incursions. Having taken refuge in their subterranean tunnels, our friends are sheltered from their adversaries. Even if there are fissures, the Zoomorphs' emanations are neutralized and absorbed. The Tripeds can plan attacks, which don't kill but merely render the Zoomorphs' sojourns difficult. Unfortunately, the numerical weakness of the Tripeds, which gets continually worse, restricts their field of action; some territories are inevitably abandoned or ill-defended.

"At this moment, the battle is fierce in one southern region—I don't know exactly how far away it is from here. The

Zoomorphs, being very numerous, are gradually gaining ground. I sense that the Tripeds are hoping that we might intervene…"

"There's almost nothing we can do," said Antoine.

"What if Mars furnishes us with the necessary raw energy? I think it will do so without any great difficulty."

"We could see—and, in any case, study possible means."

VI.

The first meeting was gripping.

It took place a short distance from the *Stellarium*, under the umbrella of an enormous plant. There were five Tripeds, whose multiple eyes looked at Antoine and me strangely.

Everything about them was unusual; no terrestrial image was exactly adaptable to their structure, and yet a thousand subtle analogies arose at the sight of them, giving rise to an indescribable sympathy from the very beginning.

Gazes dominated all other expressions of their harmonious faces by a considerable margin. None of the six eyes had the same shade as another, and every shade varied indefinably. That diversity and those variations suggested an agile life whose charms far surpassed all human charms. Oh, how dull the most beautiful eyes of terrestrial women and children would have seemed by comparison! The impression, so sharp at first, increased further by the second; soon, even Jean's keen gaze seemed grievously insignificant.

In our indescribable solitude, the signs that Jean had taught us were forcefully engraved in our cerebral, nervous and muscular memory. We made use of them almost familiarly. Besides, our interlocutors' comprehension was rapid and precise; their intuition easily filled in lacunae.

"I know already," said the one who appeared to be the dominant individual, "that you come from the neighboring world. You are superior to us…and superior to our ancestors."

I thought I discerned a melancholy in the multicolored gleams of his eyes.

"Why superior?" said Antoine. "We're merely different."

"No, no...superior. Our world is smaller...we have not lasted long enough. It is a long time now since our strength departed. We are also vanquished. We know already that you are conquerors. You must be the masters of your world."

"Yes, we dominate the other living things..."

"We are always retreating! We occupy no more than a tenth of the planet. The creatures that are displacing us are not our equals...but they can live without liquids."

I hesitated before saying: "Do you love life?" It was necessary for me to repeat the question in three ways.

"We do not love it greatly. We would not be unhappy without the *Others*. For a long time, our forefathers knew that our race was bound to disappear. That no longer saddens us; we only wish to disappear without violence." After several attempts, he succeeded in making himself understood. "All living things have their end of the world. It does not come more quickly for each of us than for those who preceded us; we may even live longer—and since our number diminishes from century to century, all that we can wish for is that the *Others* will give us time. Perhaps you will help us?"

The bizarrerie of adaptation! I got used to those flat faces, which lacked the fragment of flesh, fundamentally so ugly, by means of which we breathe and smell; I got used to that skin, which had so little in common with ours, and to those strange branches that replaced our hands. Already I felt that, by degrees, everything would seem normal.

More than their physical structure, I was fascinated by the idea of their eternal silence. Not only was their language visual, but they averred that they were incapable of emitting any sound comparable to articulated sound, or even to the cry of the most obscure terrestrial animal.

"Is it because they can't hear anything?" Antoine asked.

"I've asked the question without any result," Jean replied.

311

Antoine tried to pose it in his turn; he could not make himself understood. The notion of articulate speech—and, undoubtedly, any notion of audition—was absolutely foreign to them.

"On the other hand," said Jean, "they perceive by touch vibrations of the ground that we don't perceive at all—with the result that the approach of a creature is signaled in darkness with a precision that humans cannot attain."

"Could their sense of touch detect aerial waves, up to a point?"

"Yes and no. If the waves are very powerful they perceive them by the vibration of the ground or objects."

While we were exchanging these items of speech other Tripeds had arrived.

"This time there are two 'women,' " Jean remarked. "I can't quite bring myself to call them simply 'females.' "

He had no need to point them out: slightly taller than the males, they were more different from them than our counterparts are from us. There is no point in attempting to depict their grace and seductiveness; when I had exhausted all the metaphors of the poets—having summoned up flowers, stars, forests, summer evenings, spring mornings and the metamorphoses of water—I would still have said nothing! There was no relationship to human beauty or animal beauty. My imagination searched in vain for benchmarks of evocation and illusions of memory. How certain their charm was, though! Every passing minute confirmed it. Was it necessary to admit that beauty is more than a simple adaptation of a fraction of the universal reality to our human reality?

I had always considered that the human face, with the soft protuberance of the mucus-producing nose, the ridiculous appendages of ears and that mouth in the shape of an oven—repugnant, in sum, by virtue of its brutal function—was not in itself superior to the snout of a wild boar, the head of a boa constrictor or the maw of a pike, and that it acquired all its seductiveness from an instinct similar to that which guides a hippopotamus, a vulture or a toad. The contribution of esthetic reality thus seemed to me to be subordinate to our physical structure, and would be entirely different if we were constituted differently. The young female Martians gave the lie to this theory; the most gracious of them, especially, demonstrated to me, with forceful evidence, the possibility of *beauties perceptible to us and yet completely foreign to our environment and our evolution.*

The conversation continued, and took a positive turn. The Tripeds asked whether we might be able to help them combat the invasion of a part of their territory. They did not find it easy to fight against the small or large Zoomorphs. For the colossi, it was necessary for them to combine the emanations of a great many ray-guns; they also had to maintain themselves at a distance, lest they sacrifice a considerable number of combatants. In sum, the energies that the Tripeds had at their disposal were too weak.

"Were your ancestors better armed?" I asked.

"Our distant ancestors, yes. But in those days, the enemies of our Realm were small in size and only occupied sterile regions. No one guessed the future role that the creatures would play. When the peril became evident, it was too late. We no longer possessed means powerful enough to destroy the large enemies. All our efforts have been limited to opposing their advance."

I am summarizing the Tripeds' replies, which were only obtained after numerous questions, and elucidated with difficulty.

"Are your enemies organized?" asked Antoine.

"Not exactly. There is no direct understanding—nothing that resembles a language—and we do not know whether it is appropriate to speak of intelligence. They act according to an instinct incomprehensible to us. When the invasion of a territory has begun, the enemies accumulate, and then the inferior organisms begin to increase...and when they have been in the area for a while, the ground is poisoned. Our plants can no longer live there."

"Are the invasions rapid?"

"Quite rapid once they have begun...and more frequent as time goes by. Once, hundreds of centuries ago, the invasion was so slow that it was almost imperceptible; it was limited to desert regions. Our own decrease had already begun. Now, we often lose fertile regions. The invasion that has begun in the south is very threatening, and will cost us dear if it succeeds."

"We shall discuss the matter!"

For some time, my friends and I stood there looking at one another.

"We already know that we can intervene," said Antoine, "but at the price of a considerable expenditure of energy. Our means, as they are at present, do not permit it. It's necessary to know whether Mars is able to furnish us with new resources. Solar radiation is too weak here for our transformers to derive a radioactive surge directly. A supplementary derivation is required from Martian materials."

"I think the planet can provide it," Jean affirmed.

"Let's get to work!"

The Tripeds watched our mysterious conversation avidly. They knew already that signals emanated from our mouths; they were trying to take account of lip-movements.

Jean turned toward them and signed: "We will attack your enemies if we find the necessary energies." After several repetitions he succeeded in making them understand. Because the Tripeds employed a form of energy hitherto unknown to us for loading their weapons, they ended up catching on to what he meant.

"We will help you!" said the influential Triped. "But how do you know that our intervention will be useful?"

"Because we have already encountered your enemies, and have discovered how to put them to flight."

At these words, there was a lively agitation among the Tripeds; their multiple eyes literally lit up their faces.

More impatient than the males, one of the "women"—the more graceful—asked: "Have you seen the largest among them?"

314

"Yes—several as long as the distance between me and that rock."

How we were able to decipher the joy of the Tripeds, so different in its manifestations from our human joys, remains inexplicable. The eyes, above all, revealed it to us, with their continual variations—and the emotion of the curious young female was singularly seductive.

VII.

Habituation—the preliminary form of adaptation among humans and animals—tightened our relationship with the Tripeds. We became so used to their presence, their forms, their movements and their customs that it soon seemed as if we had been among them for a very long time.

As I have said, their dwellings were underground, although they spent a substantial part of the day in the open air. I now knew the reason for that, which was simply the need to escape the excessive nocturnal cooling—a reason all the more peremptory because a mild temperature reigned at a certain depth, accompanied by light emanated by the planetary subsoil.

It had not even been necessary to excavate refuges; the planet had a great number of caverns linked by tunnels; they could often be accessed by slopes of varying steepness, all the way down to two or three thousand meters underground. Triped industry had made these natural habitats more comfortable in places.

Sometimes, a sequence of caves extended for considerable distances, including expanses of water, some of which were little lakes. The lighting grew brighter the further down one went. We became convinced that it was due to radioactive phenomena, although we found no substance similar to our Violium, the ancient Radium, or even Planium.

315

"Undoubtedly," Antoine remarked, one morning, "the radioactive release has been exhausted in the superficial layers, while it is probably even more active lower down."

"If it is radioactivity," Jean put in.

"Either way," I said, "it's a pity that we can't use these energies to replenish ours."

In the absence of radioactive elements, we had discovered elements whose combination developed extremely high temperatures and produced high-frequency radiation; no more was necessary to achieve the atomic dislocations necessary to our work. We had succeeded in providing ourselves with considerable energies that were easy to renew.

Furthermore, fortunate experiments had permitted us, by means of successive eliminations, to transform Martian water into terrestrial water and render edible three of the aliments consumed by the Tripeds. We were thus able to prolong our stay indefinitely.

In the meantime, we had increased our intimacy with some of our hosts. Conversations had become increasingly easy, virtually automatic when they concerned familiar matters.

The Tripeds' industry retains the vestiges of an industry analogous to the human industry of the nineteenth century. They make ingenious use of solar radiation and use it to produce high temperatures; they practice a metallurgy little different from ours, but they do not weave any fabrics. Their clothing and blankets are made with the aid of a sort of mineral moss obtained by sublimation, which they are able to endow with a surprising resilience and flexibility. Their beds are made of large elastic strips, which they suspend from panels or beams by means of four, six or eight hooks. Their furniture includes too many variations for me to pause to describe it; in any case, it offers analogies with human furniture of various epochs and cultures.

As for their agriculture, it is, in a way, "radiant;" they do not disturb the soil much, but submit it to the influence of waves and currents before sowing; the roots of plants easily dissolve the humus thus prepared. Since time immemorial, the Tripeds' meals have been composed exclusively of liquefied nutrients, which they absorb with the aid of tubes comparable to reeds.

Their personal and social life is very free. One might say that the era of crime is over for them, and the era of virtue too. As they have no need of any effort to respect the liberty of others, they no longer know poverty or wealth; everyone does his share of the work as naturally as an ant, while retaining his individuality.

Tripeds capable of violence have become extraordinarily rare; they are considered to be insane. Does that mean that they have no passions? Yes, they do, and powerful ones—which do not, however, harm their neighbors. The worst could well have been love. They are subject to it as imperiously as we are, but over time, jealousy has disappeared. The male or female who does not find favor or no longer finds favor suffers violently; he or she cannot even conceive any longer that anyone might wish to infringe upon their freedom of choice. Multiple love is frequent and causes no more drama than the love of a mother or a father for several children.

This tolerance might be explained by the futility sensed and recognized for selection. For long series of millennia the Tripeds have been under no illusion regarding their decadence; they accept it without bitterness and savor it as fully as we savor the joy of living. One day when I was conversing with the friend who understands us most fully, he said to me: "Why should the death of the species sadden the individual? Does not everything pass, for every living being, as if the entire world disappeared with him?"

Obviously! But it might have been the case that the decline cast a melancholy shadow over their souls. On the contrary, the expectation seemed to bestow a sort of collective serenity on the Tripeds.

How do they love? It took me long months to acquire a notion of that, which is certainly imperfect, but as extensive as human organization permits. Some nuances doubtless remain foreign to me, as the perception of sound is to the Tripeds. Their physical love remains an enigma more mysterious than the love of flowers. Their embrace—for their nuptial act is an embrace—seems extraordinarily pure. It is the entire body that loves, in a fashion that is somewhat immaterial. At least, if matter is involved, it must be in the form of dispersed atoms and imponderable fluids.

The birth of a child is a poem. First, the mother is entirely enveloped by a halo, which, as it condenses on her bosom, becomes a luminous vapor. She then suspends a delightful shell from her shoulders—a sort of large pale flower—in which the infant condenses, takes on the form of its species, and then begins to grow. Its nourishment is invisible at first, emanated from the mother.

To my imagination, the birth and primary growth of these beings has something divine about it; all the terrestrial infirmity and ugliness is banished therefrom, as they are banished from the nuptial caress.

While we made our preparations—which required more than three months—we were able to study the structure of our friends more closely.

Their vision is much more complex than ours; it extends into the infra-red and the ultra-violet; their three pairs of eyes register different ranges. One, situated at the top, only has a distinct perception of the part of the spectrum that extends from orange to extreme indigo. The middle set of eyes discerns the red and infra-red. Finally, the third pair is adapted to the particular exploration of the violet and ultra-violet rays, up to the highest frequencies.

Their sense of touch is extremely varied. They perceive weak vibrations in the ground; the approach of another Triped or a Pentapod is signaled to them by magnetic induction, as are variations in atmospheric conditions—thus, the absence of hearing is largely compensated.

All their arts are visual, but the arts in question are not static, like our painting, drawing and sculpture; they are dynamic arts in which light—*their* light, much more extensive and varied than ours—replaces sound. I have sometimes had a presentiment of the exquisite and infinitely nuanced nature of such arts but—alas!—only a presentiment. My efforts to understand—I won't say a symphony, but a simple luminous melody—remain fruitless.

I had an adventure, the strange and most captivating of my life. Chance, which leads destinies on Mars as it does on Earth, returned me several times in the company of the graceful creature that I mentioned above. Because she was avid to understand the mystery of our world, and doubtless because a confused sympathy attracted us to one another, we helped chance along and saw one another repeatedly.

She had rapidly learned to make use of our optical alphabet, she manifested an ardent curiosity regarding the world from which we had come, and made intense efforts to penetrate its mystery.

I made every effort to describe our humankind, which she judged much superior to the Tripeds, since we had crossed the frightful interstellar abyss. She never let up asking questions or learning; a perpetual enchantment shone in her eyes—the most marvelous among the marvelous eyes of her kind.

The sentiments that attracted me to her were decidedly indefinable. They included a wholehearted admiration, the pleasure of discovering some subtler beauty every day, a magical delight that exalted me as the goddesses had once exalted mystical Hellenes, and a tenderness with no analogy to any known tenderness—neither love, which seemed impossible by destination, nor the kind of friendship that involves a greater familiarity of souls, nor the gentleness that arises at the sight of a baby. No, it was in truth an incomparable sentiment, which I did not seek to compare to any other.

I remember walks in the forest, on the lakeshore or on the ruddy plain. I lived in a fairyland, uplifted by a fervor that abolished duration and dispensed the "bright" innocence of children and young animals.

One day, we stayed out late by the lake. Night fell—the pure night of Mars, with stars more sparkling than those seen

319

on our highest mountains. "Grace" manifested an admiration for terrestrial prodigies that was becoming a cult—but in that indescribably pure air the splendor of the Ethereals appeared.

Gripped, I contemplated that divine spectacle for some time, and then—for we were still visible to one another—I sighed: "Because of them, Grace, Mars is superior to the Earth."

Her reply, which surprised me profoundly, was: "I don't believe that."

"And why don't you believe it?"

"I'm not sure that these brilliant life-forms are superior to yours, or even to mine. There's no proof of it—none! And I also think that something similar must exist on Earth, which you have not yet perceived, just as our distant ancestors had *not yet* perceived those…"

"Perhaps they didn't exist!"

"In that case, their evolution must have been very rapid—too rapid for them to be superior…"

We looked at one another in the darkness; Grace's eyes shone like the constellation Orion; her life seemed to expand subtly over my face.

"If even Earth has not yet produced them, it will produce them—in greater abundance and with more brilliance than Mars. Your planet must outshine ours in every respect!"

We returned through the forest, pensively—and that night, I loved her even more.

I loved her more, with further nuances. An unprecedented intimacy began to develop: an exaltation of the soul, a heartfelt sensuality foreign to the brutal sensuality of terrestrial animality.

She too seemed increasingly avid for my presence. One day, I said to her: "Don't human beings seem very ugly to you, Grace?"

"I thought so at first," she replied, "although that ugliness has never seemed unpleasant to me. Now, I think that your bodies and faces can have their beauty. I don't know about you any longer. I await your arrival with impatience…I find an unfamiliar charm in our encounters that astonishes me."

"It's very kind of you to say that, dear Grace—I was dazzled right away!"

In the limbo of the unconscious, it seemed that a world was in the process of construction; supernatural entities were rising out of the depths; a mysterious light illuminated legends; possibilities were springing forth from creative eternity—and I sensed Grace's world combining with the obscure world of my ancestors.

How can I describe that emotion, which mingled the stars with the beating of a paltry human heart, which invaded me as the equinoctial waves invade an estuary?

VIII. The War with the Zoomorphs

Our preparations lasted longer than we had expected, but they were finally concluded. Assured of our provisions of energy and food, we declared ourselves ready to fight the Zoomorphs.

About two-thirds of the way through the summer,[49] the *Stellarium* touched down three kilometers from the invaded region. It comprised a plain bordered by low hills; two lakes and a few canals rendered its possession particularly precious to the Tripeds.

We had constructed a dozen powerful ray-guns for our friends' usage. The *Stellarium* was carrying five more. We had flown over the territory more than once, which was not yet permanently occupied, although several hundred giant Zoomorphs had killed or chased away the animals.

---

[49] Rosny inserts a footnote: "It is well-known that the Martian year—and, in consequence, its seasons—is twice as long as ours."

The invasion stopped abruptly at a broad gap in the terrain, which had once been the bed of a river. The invaded territory comprised approximately 300,000 hectares. Zoomorphs of any size never stayed there for more than a few days; the ones that left were replaced by approximately equal numbers of newcomers.

No regularity determined the arrivals and departures, any more than the movements of Zoomorphs within the area. We searched in vain for any trace of organization, unable to discern anything but chaotic trajectories.

"I hoped to discover some sort of collaboration," said Antoine, "if not akin to that of a beehive or an ant-hill, at least like that of migratory birds, but I can't detect anything similar. Even so, the invasion seems quite clearly-defined, limited by the dry river-bed. That bed isn't an obstacle—we've seen them cross more difficult terrain."

We knew, moreover—by courtesy of the Tripeds—that it was always the same. Every irruption of Zoomorphs had its limits, and no further push ever occurred until the invaded terrain had been entirely adapted to the life of its conquerors. There was a mystery of "incoherent unanimity" therein, as is sometimes produced in the development of the species, genera and families of terrestrial fauna.

"Let's renounce the attempt to understand," said Jean.

"And let's get ready to act! It won't be easy. When we've expelled a hundred colossi, we'll hardly have begun. They'll probably be replaced."

"Who knows? The instinct that guides their invasion might also notify them of an unavoidable peril. Let's proceed methodically. Let's begin by clearing an initial zone, as economically as possible."

We alerted our allies and distributed the apparatus, which they had learned to use. Then Jean said to the one who had been appointed, by the tacit consent of the Tripeds, the leader of the expedition, and whom we called the Implicit Chief: "Don't do anything until you've been given the signal. We're going to clear the loop of the river."

The *Stellarium* rose up to a low altitude. We saw the colossi roaming around the invaded territory in every direction, amid a legion of small and medium-sized Zoomorphs—which was reminiscent, from a distance, of a swarm of large bugs.

The loop, situated to the north-east, extended for a length of 1000 meters and a breadth of between 1100 and 1200 meters. A dozen of the colossi were moving about there.

Knowing from experience what radiations were efficacious, we projected a beam that immobilized and then put to flight an enormous Zoomorph. A few rays sufficed to keep it going in the right direction; as soon as it was out of the loop, we attacked a second, and then a third.

Five were successively expelled, but while we were taking aim at a sixth, we saw two new ones arriving at great speed.

"Exactly as we feared!" said Antoine. "How many more will come, over such a vast extent? How can we maintain a radiation barrier? What an expenditure of energy!"

"Although it requires a fairly intense energy to make them flee, perhaps a weaker emission will be sufficient to hold them at a distance," Jean suggested.

"Perhaps—but it's an entire plan of campaign that you're sketching there. Let's first take the advice of experiment."

At that moment a powerful Zoomorph approached the entrance to the loop. We directed a slender thread of radiation at it. At first, it seemed unaware of the attack and continued to advance—but its speed soon slowed down.

"It's stopping!"

It did, indeed, stop, and remained stationary for some time. Finally, it began to retreat.

"We'll be able to make important economies!" Antoine exclaimed, joyfully.

Nevertheless, to encourage our allies, we agreed to an expenditure of energy considerable enough to complete the clearance of the loop. Every time a monster from outside attempted to go through the pass, we stopped it at little expense.

After three-quarters of an hour, our task was ended; the loop now only contained negligible Zoomorphs. The Tripeds could get rid of them by their own means. Our success enthused our allies—who, until then, had followed our advice like sacred orders.

"The experiment is decisive," Jean said, then. "It's an important item of information. By taking our time, we can save energy. But I glimpse something more important than that economy, which is that accumulators with a feeble yield will be sufficient to maintain the Zoomorphs at a distance everywhere. The Tripeds will easily learn to construct such apparatus—which, once deployed, will draw their present energy requirements and reserves from solar radiation. Thus, the present frontiers will become impregnable."

While Antoine guarded the loop Jean and I went back to the Tripeds; they welcomed us with a frenzy of enthusiasm. Thousands of scintillating eyes gave their faces a fantastic gleam and coloration. The "women" especially were carried away: moving flowers, palpitating blooms in which the pupils shone like prodigious glow-worms.

In a rush of gratitude, Grace said to me: "What are we compared to you? Poor powerless creatures! How beautiful life must be on Earth, and how happy your humble little friend..."

"Grace, dear Grace, there are no creatures as seductive as you on our planet, and no spectacle comparable to your face! Oh, doubtless you're unaware of the charm of our rivers, the sweetness of our meadows and our forest-clad hills, the exciting fervor of our oceans, the sunsets that fade gently in the depths of the sky, and the enchanted world of flowers—but that sparse beauty cannot equal your luminous perfection..."

"Rivers...waters that run...waves that rise and break, as you have described them, must be divine. I sense that memories are being reborn within me that are not my own, which come from the depths of our ages, from the times when Mars too had Living waters!" Her entire body quivered with enthusiasm as she repeated: "Living waters..."

324

We succeeded in reaching an understanding with the Tripeds regarding the general attack. It would gradually expand, departing from a corner of the invaded territory—the corner by which the reconquered loop was surrounded.

This disposition seemed to us to be preferable to an action that was overstretched at the start; it would permit us to familiarize the Tripeds with the economical deployment of the apparatus, and would not leave any gap through which the giant Zoomorphs might insinuate themselves unexpectedly, which might expose our allies—and perhaps us—to great risks.

The attack began about two-thirds of the way through the day, with a moderate expenditure of energy. After a few hours we had driven the invaders back to a distance of three kilometers, from a surface of about 500 hectares. There remained a considerable number of small Zoomorphs, whose expulsion would have required such an expenditure of time that it was necessary to renounce it temporarily.

Night fell. We established a fan-shaped barrage of rays, admittedly weak but sufficient to keep the invaders at a distance.

"It will be impossible," Jean remarked, "to maintain a barrage when we've cleared a territory five or six times as extensive—we won't have enough machines."

"Then let's think about fabricating smaller accumulators."

That was relatively easy, now that we had developed our machine-tools, all the more so because the barrage devices, in addition to their smaller dimensions, did not require the same precision as the others.

We communicated our project to the Implicit Chief, who understood its importance.

A luminous multitude crowded around the large fires dispersed on the plain; the Triped camp reminded us of the entries when combatants bivouacked on the eve of battles, before the epoch of radiation warfare, from the era of hand-to-hand combat of primitive humans armed with pikes, clubs and spears to the battles of giant canon and airplanes. A mystical hope returned to the crowd a little of the racial ardor that had disappeared such a long time before.

"It seems that our world has been rejuvenated!" Grace told me. "The dream of the Future is reborn! Many of our people hope that Earth will reanimate Mars..."

"What about you, Grace?"

"I don't know. I'm happy...I feel that I've grown."

A poet of olden times wrote: "You looked at me in my night/With your beautiful starry gaze/Which dazzles me!"[50] A hyperbolic image of Earth, but far inferior to reality here! Grace's eyes, more varied and also more variable than our dull terrestrial eyes, were truly comparable to a constellation of great multicolored stars.

We had gone out of the camp, and in the cold darkness the Ethereals were multiplying their mysterious movements. With a mystical exaltation, rendered more mystical still by Grace's presence, my imagination went out to them.

"We'll never understand them!" I said, in a melancholy tone.

"It's better thus," she replied. "It's better not to understand too many things."

What tenderness emanated from her! I quivered in the utmost depths of my being. "Oh, Grace, it's you that I'd like to understand!"

"I'm simple—how much simpler than you! My inclinations guide me, and I don't seek to know what they hide..."

"Why come to me?"

"Because I'm happy beside you!"

She stroked me; I felt a mysterious fluid passing through me, more ineffable than a perfume, more evocative than a melody. I was born into a singular and charming life, which prolonged the image of Grace in the past and the future.

---

[50] The quoted lines are from Victor Hugo's *Les Contemplations* (1856).

The chill increased. I brought her back to the fires. We stopped near the Implicit Chief, whose daughter she was. He looked at us with a serene curiosity, astonished, I think, by the intimacy that had grown up between his daughter and me—and which, all things considered, pleased him. It would have seemed absurd to suspect a sexual attraction; the incompatibility of Tripeds and humans was too great! Even if such an attraction had revealed itself to be possible, the father would not have conceived any anxiety.

As I have said, the extraordinary fluidity of Martian love, stripped of all gross apparatus and any brutal or baroque gesture, excludes all repugnance, hatred and jealousy. No father or mother intervenes in the predilections of their children. Two lovers can be faithful by virtue of an exclusive affection without being linked by social rites or individual promises. As for children, for many millennia they have been the responsibility of the community, which finds it politic to take an interest in their fate.

In sum, the family does not exist in the terrestrial sense, although children are as beloved as ours. There are none of the painful doubts that still trouble so many humans regarding the authenticity of filiation; the Tripeds have been granted the privilege of an infallible instinct, which allows them to know immediately whether a new-born is theirs or not.

If my preference for Grace pleased the Implicit Chief, it was because he felt a keen inclination for Terrans himself. His imagination, more than that of other Tripeds, was comparable to that of the Ancestors. Our coming—he told me subsequently—had awakened atavistic dreams in him and rendered to the Future and its Possibilities a seduction previously extinct. That evening, he asked me: "Is our sky as beautiful as yours?"

"It is incomparably more beautiful by night," I replied. "We have nothing similar to these luminous life-forms that agitate beneath stars brighter than ours. Your nights would be superior in everything if they were warmer, as ours are in summer, even in the lands where winters are harsh."

"Those warm nights must be very pleasant!"

"They have a great deal of charm."

"And what of your days?"

"I find them preferable to yours, but you might not like them at all. Our plants are more colorful and more numerous; they produce flowers from which other plants are born, and which are almost as striking as your womenfolk. Three quarters of the Earth's surface are covered by waters that run or palpitate; the hour that precedes daylight and the one that follows it are much brighter than on Mars."

"We are nothing," he said—and a melancholy expression passed over his magical eyes. "How much shorter life on our planet will be than on yours! Already the radiant age is past—and it never permitted our Ancestors to cross the abysms of space. Too small and too far away from the sun, our world could not accommodate an evolution comparable to that of your world!"

"I find that quite astonishing. We only have one sort of life—you have three!"

"There was only one in the time of the Great Power! As, in spite of everything, life has begun on your world in much the same manner as it did here, I think that it will multiply in its turn, when the decline of humans has begun. It's logical to suppose that the multiplication in question will be much more surprising than it is here!"

Two fires were enveloping us with their benevolent radiance, and I observed once again that the Tripeds' abstract faculties surpassed ours.

"I don't understand," I said, "why, given your subtle intelligence, you have renounced creativity."

"We didn't renounce it spontaneously. It required an immense lapse of time, and countless ordeals, to abolish the creative faculties."

"But since you understand so easily things that are foreign to your civilization…"

"Yes, we understand…I even think that we might learn everything that is done on Earth—but we no longer know how to draw new notions from our ancient notions…we don't

328

know how, and we've lost the taste for it. It seems so futile to us! Perhaps it would only be a cause of unhappiness—for the return of that sharp anticipation, inestimable for young races, would be despairing for old ones. A thousand times better not to think about the future, to narcotize ourselves in the present in which we only suffer while inferior life-forms threaten us. And yet, since your arrival, something stirs within me—a strange desire for renewal...the aspiration for a vaster and more intense life!"

He threw a few blocks of fuel on the fire, and remained there, meditatively.

IX. The Catastrophe

In the four days that followed, we slowly extended the cleared zone and occupied, by joining it up with the terrain we had initially conquered, about 1800 hectares. Then it was necessary to rest, not because our energy supplies had been significantly deleted—we were renewing them without any great difficulty—but because it had become difficult to maintain an effective barrage.

We then put all our efforts into the fabrication of defensive accumulators. Four of these little devices, put in working order, were emitting radiations in a fan along a line a kilometer long, but five kilometers remained to be covered, which was a considerable hindrance to us in the attack.

It was therefore decided that we would work to complete our means of making war, and for ten days the entire camp set to work constructing them. On Earth, it would have been difficult to recruit novices capable of understanding a complicated task as rapidly as the Tripeds, and carrying it out efficiently. On the other hand, one would have found much more initiative among the terrestrials. Our friends, even those of the elite, scarcely passed the level of assimilation; they did the work marvelously, but they were strangely short of initiative. Every gesture, rapidly learned, became automatic, but whenever something unexpected occurred, we had to intervene.

Even so, the fabrication progressed much more rapidly than it would have advanced on Earth in similar circumstances, and the Tripeds delivered machines to us in quantity, all exactly similar to the models.

Nearly two weeks passed, and almost all of the line to be covered was already defended; thanks to their feeble output, the accumulators recharged themselves easily by means of solar radiation.

Once the work was organized, the very automatism of the Tripeds gave us the leisure to examine the Zoomorph Realm more closely. In the invaded zone as in the zones occupied for a long time by these organisms, it did not take us long to remark that there was nothing comparable to the vegetable/animal division characteristic of terrestrial life, and also of Martian life in the Realm to which the Tripeds belonged. All the Zoomorphs took aliments from the ground, but the superior Zoomorphs were "carnivores" *as well*.

The absorption of aliments took place over the surface of the body; the Zoomorphs did not possess any orifice adapted for swallowing substances. It was all done by a sort of osmosis.[51] Whether the nourishment was taken from the ground or from living beings, it entered into the organisms as infinitesimal corpuscles. Victims only perished exceptionally; after a period of torpor in which all vital action was suspended, they usually ended up by being reanimated.

It was easy for us to capture Zoomorphs of small or medium size and to study their anatomy; thus far it has been impossible to understand exactly how their organs function, or even to determine their presence.

---

[51] Rosny inserts a footnote: "Editor's Note: A detailed study of Zoomorphs and a complete account of hypotheses regarding their organization will be published subsequently, by our hands."

As I have already noted, the constitution of higher Zoomorphs is trilateral; the inferior species have a structure as confused as the thallus of a mushroom or an alga. Inferior or superior, they all exhibit numerous vacuoles, often disposed in chains or triangles. We suppose that these vacuoles serve particularly for circulation and nutrition.

For want of liquids, circulation is doubtless achieved by projections of microscopic particles; in several "vivisected" Zoomorphs we have been able, with the aid of a high-powered magnifying-glass, to follow currents and whirlpools of elements that seem homogenous to the circulation of blood and sap.

At the outset we believed that certain Zoomorphs remained attached to the ground; we were not mistaken; all Zoomorphs can move, but the individuals of rudimentary species can only do so after long intervals of immobility, probably when they have impoverished the location to which they are fixed.

The flattened form of Zoomorphs indicates, I think, that they require a large surface successfully to attack the inert or living solids from which they obtain their subsistence. This is all the more probable because they seem to absorb few substances from the atmosphere; the rigid ground must, given this principle, play the greater role in their formation—and because they do not put down roots, it is not surprising that they embrace and extend themselves superficially.

It is also noticeable that the flattening of the structure is slightly less marked among the predatory Zoomorphs—but as they continue to demand the principal fraction of their nutrition from the planet, that development is of scant importance.

There is no indication of an instinct of association among the Zoomorphs—and I am not talking about a refined instinct, like that of ants, termites and bees, or even wasps or beavers, but an instinct as like that which assembles flocks of migratory birds, bison herds or wolf packs. The actions of Zoomorphs are strictly individual. There is not even any trace of family ties.

331

Fecundation is external; the new-borns seem to spring from the ground, so tiny is the seed, and while still almost invisible they seem already to possess the integral features of their species.

Can one speak of the intelligence of Zoomorphs? We would rather say that they are entirely at the mercy of "tropisms," which become more various as the individual is more highly evolved. We have searched for races of directive organs or organs of transmission; we assume that these functions emerge from the disposition of vacuoles. Where one would expect to find a head, as in a terrestrial or Martian animal, one finds no particular material structure, but several systems of vacuoles inside which multitudes of corpuscles move with a remarkable regularity.

As for the vacuoles disposed in chains or linked by fine canaliculae, everything leads to the supposition that they replace our nervous and muscular systems.

Nothing is more bizarre than the trajectories of these flat and formless individuals, which seem to move at hazard, tracing innumerable zigzags until they are solicited by some lure or some danger.

When a prey-Zoomorph discerns the approach of a Zoomorph predator, it flees instantly; it has a good chance of saving itself for, at a distance varying according to species—but never very great—it ceases to be perceptible. Besides which, hunting is not continual, as in our forests and savannahs; even the predatory Zoomorphs live primarily on the soil and the atmosphere, it is only occasionally that they go in search of prey.

By comparison with the life of Zoomorphs, the life of Martian animals and vegetables almost ceases to seem strange to us. The plants are reminiscent—more or less confusedly but still reminiscent—of our plants. The superior animals are homologues of our vertebrates; the running of some and the flight of others—the five feet or five wings—have ended up seeming natural to us. As for aquatic species, their five fins make them more comparable to our batrachians than our fish.

Among all of them, circulation is liquid; it is a kind of blood that nourishes their bodies, even though the blood may be violet, blue or green. The vessels that contain it recall our veins and arteries, although a single heart is replaced by two, three, four or five convulsive pockets, according to the species.

They have mouths; their multiple eyes are true eyes; the digestive organs do not differ overmuch from those of many terrestrial animals. If we had never seen birds, or fish, or insects, they would doubtless appear as singular to us as Martian animals—but we would recognize, eventually, a kinship between mammals and the birds, the fish or the insects. Thus we find homologies between Martian organisms and ours, although it is necessary to recognize a fundamental difference from the Zoomorphs, and even more so from the Ethereals.

As for the Tripeds, we ended up considering them actually as people, although their evolution has separated them more obviously, in a few respects, from our superior animals than from the majority of the higher Martian creatures. Every day, however, their vertical stance, and their mentality especially—astonishingly close to ours—their emotionality, their charm, and the charm of their womenfolk above all, increased a familiarity and intimacy that made them our otherworldly family.

During the night, we maintained the habit of taking refuge in the *Stellarium*, established behind the camp. In the early days, one of us would stand watch; then a profound sense of security caused us to abandon that precaution; all three of us slept as tranquilly as if we had been living in an earthly house.

Generally, the Tripeds woke up before us. A few hundred of them, tempted by the caverns, had established themselves beneath the reconquered ground; others came and went as they pleased.

One morning, we were woken up by a knocking on the hull of the *Stellarium*, and perceived numerous Tripeds, who were evidently upset—which, for want of being able to express their emotion by means of voices, they were making manifest in violent gestures.

As soon as they saw that we were up, they multiplied signals; we knew immediately that the Zoomorphs had breached the barriers.

"All the barriers?" asked Antoine, extremely surprised.

"No!" replied several Tripeds at the same time—the signs were not confused as words would have been. "Only on the right...a host of enemies. A large number of our people have perished."

"We're on our way!"

The *Stellarium* was already lifting off, and we were soon hovering above the multitude. Seven enormous Zoomorphs—the largest was almost a hundred meters long—were moving among the bodies of Tripeds that had been struck down. Other Tripeds were lying in the dry bed of the ancestral river, and beyond that, a large number of our friends were gesticulating desperately.

On the extreme right of the formerly-reconquered territory, there was no longer a single Triped alive—which permitted us to take the offensive immediately. Since it was impossible to attack all the monsters head-on, we adapted a divisive tactic. Each Zoomorph was maneuvered in turn, and as we proceeded more intensively than usual, we obtained rapid retreats. At a rate of five seconds of irradiation per individual, we were able to return to each Zoomorph twice a minute—and as the rays always fell in the same direction, the flight was orientated as we desired. In any case, out of inertia, the Zoomorphs did not attempt to turn back; even in the intervals of respite they followed the line that we wanted them to follow.

It only took us a quarter of an hour to clear the area, after which Jean went out to examine the radiator on the far right.

"The axis of the apparatus was tilted upwards a few degrees," he declared on his return. "In consequence, the rays were no longer level with the ground. The Zoomorphs simply passed under the beams."

"Is it repaired?"

"Naturally."

"That will teach us to stabilize the inclination more firmly!" said Antoine. "Such a small thing! Now let's make inquiries of our friends."

While we were exchanging these brief words, the Implicit Chief had hurried forward. He seemed profoundly emotional. His body was trembling like a birch tree in the wind, and he thanked us vehemently. "We didn't dare turn another apparatus against the invaders," he said, "for that would have opened up a new access to those outside."

"Irrefutable, for them!" I muttered, thinking about their deficit of initiative.

Antoine pointed at a group of prostrate Tripeds. "Do you think they're dead?" I asked the Implicit Chief.

A bleak sadness lit up in our ally's gaze. "I think so—but among those who were able to flee into the fissure, many will be saved."

"Do you have remedies?"

"Against this kind of injury, none. When victims don't die, they emerge from unconsciousness sooner or later, and the recovery is complete after a few hours or days." He lowered his head and added, shivering: "My daughter!"

Devastated, I demanded to get out of the *Stellarium*.

"I'll go with you," said Antoine. "We must help these poor devils."

I dared not interrogate the chief; I examined the bodies in terror.

"She isn't among these," he said. "She was able to cross the limit."

My emotion—oh, how profound it was!—was mingled with the fear of that very emotion. That small existence, previously lost in the depths of the heavens, in the droplet of red fire that trembles by night among the minuscule solar nightlights, that creature so dissimilar to human beings and all the living creatures that surround human beings, how much anguish and distress she caused me! Crushing impatience and

335

violent hope combined with terror—all the drama of love and death!

Meanwhile, I followed the Implicit Chief, and we arrived at the edge of the long ravine that had been a river when there were still rivers in that condemned world.

Bodies were lying pell-mell: a hectic crowd, like a population of ants forced to flee by a flood; a few Tripeds were trying to care for the injured.

Already I was next to Grace, motionless and seemingly breathless, her body rigid. I remembered the morning when my sister Clotilde died, when the abysms of nothingness had swallowed up the universe.

The Implicit Chief guessed what I was thinking. "She isn't dead!" he said.

Leaning over, he studied his daughter attentively. His eyes, darkened by sadness at first, radiated more lively gleams. Reassured, and because he was the Animator, he began examining other bodies.

How long did I remain alone next to Grace? Less than a quarter of an hour, I think—but the duration, full of a tumultuous flux of sensations, was indefinitely dilated. Then Tripeds came, who transported her into a shelter warmed by a radiator not unlike our allies' weapons.

Time resumed its normal rhythm; the emotions ceased their tumult; I believed in Grace's resurrection, and the Implicit Chief increased my hope every time he visited.

Nevertheless, when she opened her eyes, I was so affected that I remained paralyzed. The beautiful eyes were initially reminiscent of a constellation veiled by the vapors that rise from ponds in autumn; then the light sprang forth like a nascent dawn. She looked at me with an astonished affection that became increasingly tender.

Eventually, she said: "The monsters are vanquished, since you're beside me."

"Yes, they've been driven back."

Joy radiated like the perfumes emanating from the odorifier, and Grace's sentiments became focused, metamorphosing, expressed by gestures so slight that we were communicating almost directly from mind to mind.

There was a pause, which would have been a silence between beings using speech. Things that could not be said were in the air, mysterious migratory birds of the soul.

Then she said: "I'm very glad to see you beside me *now*. It's as if your presence has caused me to be reborn. I'm so happy that you can understand me."

At these words, an unknown exaltation lifted me up. "I too am singularly happy," I said. "With a happiness as new as the morning of my life!"

I had leaned forward; our shoulders touched; Grace put her arm delicately around my neck. I then had the prescience of a sensation that surpassed all human sensations...

But the Implicit Chief came in, accompanied by Antoine.

"There's no longer any danger," the Implicit Chief said. "She will have recovered all her strength by nightfall." As Antoine and I looked at one another interrogatively, he added: "It's always the way. The recovery is never incomplete."

He was not mistaken. From the next day onwards, Grace no longer felt any malaise. I saw her again every day, while the hostilities resumed. They were soon brought to a conclusion.

In the interim, more barrage devices had been constructed. To obviate any lack of initiative on the part of the Tripeds, we carefully anticipated all the circumstances that might arise, and enumerated the measures that it was necessary to take in each case.

They were thoroughly familiar now with the manufacture of radiators, and—as I have said—their skill, promptitude and exactitude far surpassed ours; they were planning to construct enough machines to defend all their frontiers.

"We shall learn from our neighbors all that you can teach us," said the Implicit Chief, on the day when he began sending back the bulk of his army to their native caverns. "They will teach others. Your science will provide our species with increasingly better protection against invasions. The Envoys of the Earth will have saved their humble Martian brothers!"

Epilogue

And the days went by. We met other groups of Tripeds. On a vast plain we established a luminous generator so large and so intense that it had to be perceptible on Earth. On a clear night, we sent the first call-signals, according to the dot-and-dash system that the men of the previous century used for transmission—a system so perfect and so simple that it could translate human language in as many different ways as there are senses and forms of energy.[52]

We were immediately understood, for we were repeating signals already employed by explorers of Earth. Ten radiogenic stations replied to us; we had, in brief, news of the Earth as precise as that exchanged by means of radio-waves from city to city and continent to continent. Antoine and Jean received "stellar radiograms" from their families and I—who had lost mine—received a few friendly messages.

Our voyage excited a frenetic enthusiasm over the entire planet. The newspapers declared it the greatest event of the century, some the greatest event in human history...

My predilection for Grace increased further. I saw her for longer periods every day, and my sentiments became so strange that I was afraid to analyze them. How could I define those beautiful frissons, those prodigious waves? There was nothing resembling them in my humble pilgrimage. The idea that it could be love, in the human sense, seemed absurd to me, and even repulsive. The poor sensation of *our* sensuality

---

[52] Rosny inserts a footnote: "The Morse system, which can be addressed to sight, hearing, touch, and even to smell and taste, and can utilize all our movements and employ almost all perceptible energies."

was completely numbed; its wakening with respect to Grace would, I think, only have filled me with disgust and shame.

However, it was certainly desire that I felt in her presence; every time our bodies made contact I felt that marvelously pure tenderness that I had felt on the day of her resurrection. Might it be love, all the same? If so, it is as foreign to our pitiful love as Grace is to human femininity.

Because no words could express it, and because Grace undoubtedly would not have understood it, I contented myself with experiencing it, and we wandered like happy shadows through the forest, along the shores of silent lakes and in the subterranean depths.

One day, we came into a spacious cave in which an aquamarine light rose from the ground and ran along the walls. The legend of Mars had been inscribed in the stone, at the time when the young planet had created the first thinking beings.

We were sitting on an ancient stone, whose substance, one dispersed in innumerable tiny creatures, no longer formed anything but a heavy and melancholy block, in which obscure energies vacillated and whirled interminably.

It was there that I felt, with a dazzling certainty, that Grace had become dearer to me than any other living creature, and could not help telling her so.

She shivered from head to toe, like foliage; her beautiful eyes filled with enchanted gleams, and she placed her head gently on my shoulder. Then—oh, how can I describe it? It was an embrace, nothing but an embrace, as chaste as the embrace of a mother picking up her child—and all the joys of yesteryear appeared as poor crooked things: the sudden joys blowing on the wind, the perfumes on a hill, the resurrection of the morning, the divine lies of sunsets, and the entire fable of Woman, so patiently constructed over the millennia, and Woman herself, at the time when I thought her the greatest intoxication in the universe...

Nothing remained of it. It all disappeared in that miracle, which seemed the very miracle of Creation.

Editors' Note

As this text goes to press, we hear that the second voyage of the *Stellarium* has been completed and that the fabulous explorers have visited their friends in the Other World again. The volume relating the observations and experiment of a scientific order will appear soon. It will be followed by the narrative of the second voyage, this time transmitted from Mars itself.[53]

---

[53] This note was probably optimistically deceptive in its claim that the sequel had been completed. It is worth noting that it cannot be referring to a completed version of "Les Astronautes," since the latter text makes no pretence to being "transmitted from Mars itself."

THE ASTRONAUTS

I.

Memories float in an atmosphere of fable. A nostalgia as charming as the September evening carries me "into the eternal night, through the dead expanse" toward the red star on which I once lived for several seasons.

Level with the occident, a timid glimmer of light increases and rises toward the stars. Earth's minuscule companion, the Moon emerges, the color of copper, immense, ten times higher than the Eglise Saint-Michel, seeming to hold the entire village of Mièvres in its lap. As it does so, it blots out colossi lost in the depths of the stellar expanse, although the paltry Mars, a microbe of space, is brighter, seen from here, than the triple Sirius.

My old garden, with its twisted trees, its coarse grass and its wild flowers, becomes a witches' heath.

The atmosphere has shivered; the *Albatros*, Antoine's blue rocket, descends in a spiral and lands as lightly as a dragonfly on the terrace of the orchard.

Antoine, Jean and Violaine, with whom I shall soon resume travel through interstellar space, get down.

Politely but imperiously, Jean has imposed Violaine upon us. It is not his will that spoke, but rather that of the beautiful daughter of men. She does not resemble her brother. You would think her the offspring of a hot country, with her serpentine black hair, her eyes of black fire and her harmonious body, while Jean manifests the appearance that we confer on the blood and red-haired warriors of Celtic Gaul. For the sake of principle, Antoine and have I resisted for a month, but Violaine's determination will triumph tonight. Deep down that doesn't displease us. During the interastral journey and life on Mars, we lacked feminine input—the small attentions that that add grace to everyday life.

"Your garden looks good in the moonlight," Jean says. "It's alive; nature has bestowed the royal gift of joy upon it."

Antoine raises his eyebrows, verifies Jean's affirmation with a circular glance, and says, indifferently: "That's true. The moonlights suits it."

"It's delightfully old," Violaine puts in, turning her charming face toward the stars. She points at Mars. "I shall see it at close range, then."

"Good," says Antoine. "You've made *our* final decision." He does not laugh, but his smile grows broader, to the point of seeming hilarious, and he mutters: "You'd be wrong to think that you're going to amuse yourself. First, there's the voyage shut up in the *Stellarium*."

"In the world of stars."

"Around the Sun! For monotony, one can't do better. As for Mars itself, it's not a very enjoyable spectacle."

"No, but an exciting one!" she retorts, vehemently. "Go on—you're all in a hurry to see it again, each in your own way: Jean with exaltation, Antoine with insatiable curiosity, and you, Jacques, with love."

"True," I say.

"And for me, I know that it will be a voyage to enchantment."

This time, Antoine bursts out laughing, in his hollow and dry manner. "You're Jean's sister all right, in spite of appearances, you young African!"

II.

The time has come. The *Stellarium* is about to carry us into the unsoundable depths. It's not the furtive departure of the last time. Our workmen have talked, and a multitude has arrived by land and by air. It is surrounding and flying over the enclosed field, and occupying all the neighboring roads, emitting a rumor like a herd of livestock.

At intervals, a shout goes up, which is echoed, frantic, enthusiastic and also vaguely threatening.

The *Stellarium* is ready. The last checks have been carried out. We say our farewells to the Earth. A few tears, embraces, words…and the astral vessel is sealed upon us.

Antoine has taken out his watch. Jean and I are at the controls.

"Ten o'clock!"

That is the signal.

Through the indestructible but elastic walls we can hear the howls and roars of the crowd, and see its frantic eddies—but not for long. Soon, there is no more than a confused agitation of airborne and terrestrial insects…then countryside and cities; then a blurred surface and a few last aviators.

"That's it!" Antoine murmurs. "Space has us in its grip."

"And we have it in ours!" retorts Jean the Bold.

Violaine, who is slightly pale, adds: "Slaves and masters."

Days, and more days. It's strange, after all, that we have so little fear. Alone in the wilderness—and what a wilderness! There are no resources in this vast environment, which is, for our material lives, absolute emptiness.

That there is instead, I suspect—or rather, as I believe—a swarm of existences incompatible with ours, only a few indications are beginning to reveal to our most subtle instruments, prolongations of ourselves. There is only an infimal, indirect perception of *something*.

The terrestrial atmosphere reveals itself to us perpetually by its resistance and its breaths, from the lightest morning breeze to the cyclones that rise up and sink large ships, uproot trees and knock down monuments. Here, there is nothing—*nothing*. No resistance, no movement, save for the material movement of planets, no revelation.

343

Even so, the four of us retain an impression of perfect security. Violaine, who has not been hardened, as the rest of us have, by an earlier journey, quickly becomes accustomed to it. Perhaps she has even less sensation of risk than her three companions. Familiar, spontaneous, with slight caprices, she is all the youthful and feminine grace of Earth aboard this interstellar vessel.

III.

Within three days, we land.

First we set down in a region occupied by the zoomorph realm. It is a sinister place, like all those from which life homologous to terrestrial life has disappeared: red soil, which was once fertile, but which many thousands of years of dryness have petrified: on the horizon, a chain of mountains, bare and menacing, bristling with peaks: a funereal conclave that renders us thoughtful.

"It's admirably melancholy," Violaine murmurs. "The reign of rock, the realm of sterility."

"Oh, no!" Jean ripostes. "On the contrary, a marvelously fecund place. Here the second kind of Martian life abounds. You've been alerted, Violaine—open your eyes!"

We are still inside the *Stellarium*, but the transparent hull allows all the details of the location to penetrate.

Violaine looks more attentively. She begins to discern the strange structures that made such an impact on us during our first voyage. By virtue of their color and scant thickness, they are scarcely distinguishable from the ground, but as soon as one pays attention to their forms one no longer sees anything else; a strip of ground close to the *Stellarium* is literally covered with them.

The majority are immobile.

"Oh!" Violaine exclaims, her eyes sparkling. "Over there, though! See how they're moving!"

"Pay attention to the principal forms," Antoine tells her. "The zigzag ribbons with nodes at the angles, the spirals with the bluish centers and the opaque masses from which the linear threads emerge."

Hypnotized by amazement, Violaine contemplates these fantastic organisms. "Are they really alive?" she murmurs.

"There's no doubt about it."

"It's true that some are reminiscent of flattened cephalopods."

"A false analogy! They have no relationship to any terrestrial animal or plant."

"Oh, I want to go out."

Jean starts laughing. "Calm down little sister. First get used to the weight deficit."

"That's true—I no longer weigh as much. It's rather disturbing when one moves..."

"You get used to it," Antoine remarks. "Taking the mass of Mars into account, and the distance to the center, your weight is reduced by about three fifths."

"It's as if, on Earth, I weighed no more than twenty-five kilos?"

"Right!"

Here and there, a Zoomorph moved, without it being possible to discern the mechanism of its progress. The cilia were moving in a strange fashion, but did not give the impression of serving directly for propulsion.

"Notice, Violaine, that the majority, especially on the terrain where they're most abundant, are less than a decimeter in length, and that the largest ones are no more than a meter. Their effluvia can't reach us inside the *Stellarium*. They have to act together. In any case, within a certain distance, they only project radiation if they're touched. If they perceive our presence, they must be quite confused."

"While the giants seem to perceive it!" said the young woman, laughing. "I haven't forgotten your stories or your reports, gentlemen. And I'm by no means unaware, even though I was not part of your expedition, that the Zoomorphs are absolutely solid—and that, in consequence, their circulation and their nutrition must be assured either by gases or microscopic particles. We also know that the majority of the Zoomorphs live at the expense of the ground, from which they extract matter and energy, but that others are, in addition, carnivores of a sort, although they neither kill nor injure their prey; they content themselves with removing—by osmosis, I think—an essential complement of nourishment."

"Good—we have nothing more to teach you," Jean concluded.

"Nothing to learn! I only know the theory; now I need to see and understand. That's more complicated." She interrupted herself, her eyes staring, and extended her arm. "That's one of their monsters, isn't it?" She was pointing at an immense ochreous shape with orange strips, which was moving rapidly about 300 meters away. "The largest reptiles of the Secondary Era weren't as long as that!"

"But a great deal thicker! That monster's an immense pancake! Look out—it might attack us!"

The *Stellarium* rose up to an altitude of fifty meters. We examined the colossus with our binoculars. It stopped, its appendices and cilia contracting. We could see its three lateral zones, separated by furrows, quite clearly.

"A triple octopus, a vast mushroom and a leviathan bug—made up of three bugs each the size of a brontosaurus—all at the same time," Violaine murmured, thoughtfully. "But all those images are false. The comparisons fail as soon as they're imagined. Ah! It's getting under way again."

It headed for the area where the little and medium-sized Zoomorphs were swarming. It reached it. We saw it extend itself over some fifty of its paltry kin. Bluish phosphorescence enveloped the group.

"A carnivore!" said Jean. "It's devouring its victims' energy."

"They won't die of it!"

Violaine, excited to the point of exaltation, remarked: "This world is less cruel than our own, then?"

"Who can tell? Everything is so different. Our experiments haven't yielded any conclusive revelation of a sensitivity, unless it's very obtuse, let alone an intelligence analogous or homologous to ours. We've never observed any alliance or solidarity, or the slightest sign of affective instinct."

"Which doesn't prove anything," said Antoine.

"No, nothing," Jean agreed. "Even if they don't act in concert, they nevertheless have their methods of invasion and conquest."

"So do our lichens, grasses and trees—and how energetically. Who believes, though, that they make concerted plans and have elective affinities?"

We remained there, observing, for some time. Other Zoomorphs of medium size passed by. Their cilia quivered as they moved, but did not provide any support, and their progress was most often disordered, never clearly directional.

"In fact," said Violaine, "they don't have limbs, do they?"

"No," Jean replied. "We haven't been able to discover the function of the cilia. I'm inclined to believe that they help to summon motive energies."

"I'd like to walk on the planet's surface," Violaine said. "It seems to me that I'll only get a precise sense of the reality outside. In here, I'm still bound to the Earth."

Zoomorphs were now appearing from every direction. At any moment, a colossus might approach our refuge.

"Let's find a less populous spot!" Antoine proposed.

The *Stellarium*, which had landed in the course of the discussion, took off just in time to avoid danger; two monsters were arriving at great speed.

"We wouldn't have been able to get away, Violaine, if we'd let them come any closer. One alone nearly caused our death before. Two would probably be sufficient to rid the planet of our curiosity."

One of the monsters passed over the very ground on which we had landed. The other was very close to it.

"Fortunately, they can be kept at a distance," Violaine murmured.

"Yes, we're better armed than before. Our portable ray-guns are more powerful too."

The *Stellarium* was already a long way from the landing-ground. Antoine brought it to a halt above a long valley through which one of the great rivers of Mars had flowed, incalculable ages ago.

"I assume that a magnificent tropical life once flourished here," said Jean. "And we know that the planet's flora was beautiful—it still is."

"The primitive flora must have been even more so. Our Triped friends are more distant from it than we Terrestrials are from our primary flora."

By evoking ancient fecundity, the structure of the location rendered the present petrifaction more striking.

"Shall I have the joy of setting foot on this wild terrain?" asked Violaine. She was standing next to me. I was glad. I was gently and tenderly intoxicated by her proximity. I was free of the confused dread that accompanies the most reassuring Earthly love...but nevertheless, I had a passionate desire to see Grace again.

"We can," Jean agreed, having scanned the valley with his binoculars. "There are no large Zoomorphs on the horizon, and few medium-sized ones."

The *Stellarium* settled on a plateau. No gravitational field was added to the feeble Martian weight.

"Let's arm and armor ourselves!"

A quarter of an hour later, we bore a considerable resemblance to those deep-sea divers one sees in old engravings—so different from our own aquatic explorers. Thus equipped, we emerged from the *Stellarium*.

We could not help being inconvenienced by our lightness, even though we had become accustomed to it during our first voyage. Every step carried us further than we expected. Gradually, though, equilibrium was restored, although it was a slower process for Violaine, who nearly fell over several times. She laughed, however, delighted with the lightness in spite of the inconvenience.

"It's like a dream!" she said—and then added: "It's so dead that one ends up feeling sympathy for the Zoomorphs." Gaily, she started to run—and this time, after several gigantic bounds, lost her balance.

She got up immediately, hardly having felt the fall. "No terrestrial animal would be able to match me," she said—not even the swiftest hare...or an eagle or a falcon."

She set off again, moderating her pace. I followed her, trying not to go quickly but moving nevertheless at a vertiginous speed.

Suddenly, I lost sight of her. She had just disappeared behind a large red rock. No longer having her in sight, in that formidable desert, made me anxious. I accelerated my pace and rounded the rock.

She was lying on the ground, motionless. Several meters away was a huge Zoomorph enveloped by a bluish light, which went out before I got close. In spite of my anguish, I did not lose a sense of necessity—a jet of radiation stopped the monster in its tracks. Although large in size it was not a colossus. Soon, it began to retreat, slowly at first, and then swiftly.

Livid, her limbs inert, Violaine had the indecisive appearance of a corpse. I was bending down to pick her up when Jean and Antoine appeared. We looked at one another, not daring to say anything. The impassive Antoine seemed as disturbed as us. Finally, trembling in every limb, Jean said: "I'm a fool!"

He had no need to say any more; I felt that I was sharing his remorse. I thought that I was as responsible as he was. Antoine, however, had already recovered his composure. He applied his ear to Violaine's breast. His eyelids quivered—a sign, in him, of sharp emotion.

"Well?" cried Jean, exasperated by anguish.

Antoine made no reply. We knew him too well not to deduce what his silence signified.

Jean tried to listen in his turn, but he was obliged to abandon that attempt. The noise of his own arteries would not have permitted him to perceive a normal heartbeat. Deafened by the tumult of my own blood, I failed too.

"There's nothing for it but to go back to the *Stellarium*," said Antoine, whose face had almost resumed its normal appearance.

Jean picked Violaine up, and we went back to the vessel. Antoine and I took bounds of several meters. Again we were forced to restrain ourselves; at top speed, we could not maintain our equilibrium. Because he was carrying Violaine, Jean had more stability even though he was moving more rapidly than he would have been able to do on our native planet and making maximum effort.

Near the *Stellarium*, a terrible spectacle stopped us; three colossal Zoomorphs were barring our path. One of them was at least 50 meters long, the others nearly 40.

"Idiots!" Antoine muttered. "We've been idiots!"

Our apparatus was certainly safe from any attack. Ten or twenty Zoomorphs acting together would have been incapable of doing it any harm, even if these monsters had been equipped with muscles like terrestrial monsters, and had launched their mass at a vertiginous speed—but their mass was greatly diminished by their slender thickness. Besides, Zoomorphs never employed brute force; their levels of radiation, terrible for us, posed no danger to the *Stellarium*.

Would our ray-guns be adequate to drive all three of them away? Wouldn't the energetic expenditure be too great for a prolonged battle? All the more so because it would have been highly dangerous to act at short range; they would perceive our presence, rush toward us—and their velocity would be too great for us to have any possibility of escape!

"It would doubtless be best," I said, "to attack the largest one together?"

"Let's be careful!" Antoine replied. "I think it's best to attack them all at once, with a moderate expense of radiation.

That will doubtless suffice to hold them in respect, initially...perhaps even to drive them away, after a few minutes..."

"But if they take too long to go away," Jean remarked, "we'll exhaust our energy before having obtained a conclusive effect."

I was of the same opinion. We had no time to lose; the chances of saving Violaine were decreasing by the second.

"Well," said Antoine, "let's try both methods. I'll attack the largest one."

Jean and I having each made our choice, the attack began. For two minutes, it seemed ineffective, the Zoomorphs neither advancing nor retreating, although they gave signs of agitation.

Jean's energy reserves, and mine, employed without restraint, were beginning to run low.

"You see!" Antoine said, softly.

Jean did not reply. He had just taken possession of Violaine's ray-gun, and was already making use of it to double the intensity of the attack.

The Zoomorph retreated almost instantaneously, and drew away at increasing speed. Then, attacked by three ray-guns simultaneously, the one that I had chosen as a target—which was already giving signs of distress—drew away in its turn.

Before we had joined our ray-guns to Antoine's, the third Zoomorph began to withdraw; a blast of radiation accelerated its retreat. The way to the *Stellarium* was free.

We had no lack of means to reanimate Violaine, if she had not ceased living. By degrees, we started up the artificial respiration apparatus. Antoine prepared the cardiac stimulator and oxygen insufflator.

Violaine's heart remained inert. No mist tarnished the glass of the dew-detector. Then Antoine intervened with the cardiac stimulator, while I forced three small doses of oxygen into her lungs. Several minutes went by, in mortal suspense— and then Jean uttered a loud exclamation: "Ah! Finally!"

The heart had begun to beat again; a slight mist appeared on the detector's glass. There was one more minute of anxiety, and then the young woman's eyes opened.

Jean and I were weeping like infants.

IV.

"It's understandable that our friends the Tripeds haven't been able to resist these formidable creatures," said Antoine, when order was restored again. "The instinct that leads them to attack us is rather surprising. Strictly speaking, we don't belong to the same realm as the Tripeds and pseudo-animals of Mars."

"We're from a homologous realm."

"But so different! Not much more than the composition of our flesh and internal liquids. It's evident nevertheless that if we were to found a Martian colony, that colony would find deadly enemies in the Zoomorphs."

Violaine was listening, pensively. Her face retained no trace of the near-fatal accident. Personally, I was subject to the retrospective fear that is so violent in imaginative people. The idea that her apparent death would have become eternal within another minute or two set my heart hammering.

"I don't believe," she remarked, "that it's a matter of instinct. It's something like a reflex. Our presence is doubtless sufficient to provoke a radiant reaction."

"That's entirely possible," said Antoine.

"The most primitive terrestrial creatures might have been subject to similar impulses of aggression or defense. Our purely organic appetites and repulsions still are. The odor or sight of a foodstuff is sufficient to excite a physical or chemical desire."

"Our viscera are great laboratories of physics and chemistry!" Jean exclaimed. "Life would be impossible otherwise."

The image of Grace suddenly appeared to me with an extraordinary intensity. I was gripped by an overwhelming desire to see her again—a singular thing, at a moment when Violaine had awakened such powerful emotions.

"Isn't it time that we went to find our friends the Tripeds," I murmured.

"I was just thinking the same thing," said Violaine.

Our gazes met. Might a rivalry arise between that beautiful human woman and the marvelous Martian female? Could Violaine have the merest inkling of the nature of an affection so different from any terrestrial affection? It was certainly love, and of incomparable force, but as pure as love must be for a flower.

"All right—let's go see our friends."

We scarcely had any need to get our bearings; during our first sojourn, we had explored Mars in every direction several times over. Scarcely 3000 kilometers separated us from Triped lands.

"It must still be night there," Jean observed.

"Yes, but dawn is not far off. Then again, Violaine hasn't seen the Ethereals yet. We'll make a stop on the far side of the equator while waiting for daylight."

"Just as long as our friends have been able to keep the Zoomorphs at bay."

"They will have been able to in the region that we fortified, but it's only too certain that the Zoomorphs are advancing elsewhere—fortunately, with extreme slowness. They'll require several hundred centuries to invade all the lands that the Tripeds still occupy. I estimate that their first invasions must date back millions of years. Their progress must have been imperceptible at first. It has accelerated over the millennia.

"What proportion of the surface area still belongs to the Tripeds?"

"To the Tripeds and their pseudo-animal and pseudo-plant realm, perhaps an eighth—still a considerable extent, the surface area of Mars being not much different from that of our continents, as there are no oceans here. There's very little surface water in the majority of the territories invaded by the Zoomorphs. When I say water…"

"Yes, I know," said Violaine, "you mean a *kind* of water."

"Exactly—but from which we've learned to extract distilled water."

"In sum, it's not only the Zoomorphs that are driving the Tripeds back, but also the desiccation?" said the young woman.

"Yes. Even so, there must be many reservoirs of subterranean water here."

While they were talking, the astroship, moving at low speed, crossed the equator and entered the dark region. The starry sky appeared abruptly, and the conversation ceased. The *Stellarium*, having slowed down further, finally came to a standstill on a plateau, at the top of a hill. Then, all four of them contemplated the sky in silence.

Violaine immediately was astounded by the innumerable legions of the Ethereals. They formed a palpitating Milky Way, radiant and profound, in which luminous dots were moving in every direction with vertiginous rapidity.

They could still see the starry sky, however, with periodic eclipses, and the large topaz-emerald star that was the Earth.

"Oh, that's beautiful!" Violaine sighed.

"Beyond beauty and ugliness," Jean remarked.

The young woman quickly discerned the moving constellations and groups of constellations formed by the Ethereals. "You're right!" she murmured. "It's beyond beauty."

"It's better," Antoine muttered. "What we call beauty is merely a human fable. Even on Earth, it bears no relationship to reality."

"That's why one can apply the term as easily here as on Earth," I said. "It's sufficient for us to have a corresponding sensation. So far as I'm concerned, I'm sensitive to the moving beauty of these creatures."

"I congratulate you," said Antoine, ironically.

We fell silent, exalted by the prodigious spectacle. I was astonished that we had ever doubted that the Ethereals were living beings. Their movements did not exhibit any uniformity, or any energetic servitude. Not only were they circulating in all directions, but every one of them, and every group, seemed to be moving haphazardly. It is true that molecules also move in all directions and that their trajectories vary continually, but they do not partake of the alternation of order and disorder, repose and activity, which immediately characterizes the Ethereals.

It took more than an hour to cool our enthusiasm; then the *Stellarium* got under way again, very slowly, at 1000 kilometers an hour. Even so, the Triped region did not take long to appear, in the pale light of dawn. We landed on a low plateau that overlooked the plain. As soon as the Sun appeared, visibility spread out over a vast extent. In the rarefied atmosphere, the details of the location appeared with extreme clarity.

"A land of dreams," said Violaine, after a silence. "Almost terrestrial dreams. That wood over there is reminiscent of a wood of gigantic and fantastic mushrooms, and it's a sort of red grass that's growing on the plain. As for the lake, without the strange plants that surround it, it reminds me of Lake Zurich."

The flying creatures rising up slowly from the plateau astonished Violaine. "Five wings—and what wings! Perhaps pterodactyls looked like that."

"Not at all," said Antoine. "No reptile, bat or bird, nothing feathered or hairy: a sort of velvety fly."

One of the flying creatures, as large as an eagle, alighted on a rocky ridge a hundred meters from the aeronauts.

"It has at least six eyes!" the young woman exclaimed.

"Seven to be exact, Violaine," said Jean, "and three feet—but here come the quintupeds."

There were three of them, at the foot of the slope. One seemed to be a caricature of a leopard, in spite of its rectangular maw, its multiple eyes and its five feet. The other two, brick-red in color, were more reminiscent of bears, although they had some kind of felt instead of hair. All three animals were about the size of Nordic wolves.

"Carnivores or herbivores?" Antoine muttered.

Each of the animals had six eyes of different shades—sapphire, ruby, emerald, amethyst—gleaming even more brightly than the eyes of our felines in semi-darkness.

"Our insects also have multiple eyes," Violaine remarked.

"Yes, but their sight is so limited that they're hardly aware of it."

"Except in their own way, which permits them, in all innocence—lice, fleas, bugs, mosquitoes—to exploit us as prey. That's their good luck."

"No more than it is ours! I think that if insects could see us clearly, as we see them, they would have exterminated humans a long time ago, along with many other mammals, birds, reptiles and amphibians."

At that moment, Violaine exclaimed: "Oh—they're herbivores!"

The three animals had, indeed, begun to browse, strangely, with the horny arcs that served them as teeth.

"Hey!"

The herbivores were running away. An apocalyptic animal had just appeared, the size of a rhinoceros, with a head like a truncated pyramid and the eyes of an octopus scattered over a giant face. Its pelt was blue and silky, similar in texture to the tall silk hats of yesteryear.

"It's frightful and magnificent!" Violaine exclaimed.

Its immense eyes had just perceived the humans—who, having emerged from the *Stellarium*, had advanced to the edge of the plateau. It uttered a roar—you might have mistaken it for a blast from a trombone—and then bounded up the slope.

"I believe it intends to devour us," said Antoine, placidly. "Let's see about that, comrades." He pointed his ray-gun at the wild beast and fired a beam of radiation. The brute stopped in alarm, took two or three steps forward, then retreated and fled with meteoric speed.

"It bounds as well as a tiger!" remarked Jean, admiringly.

"Six meter leaps."

The carnivore had already covered the best part of a mile when other beasts came into view, one about the size of a wolf, the color of sulfur, with a muzzle like a huge seashell and a helical mouth, the other as black as night, with a long parabolic body and five spatulate feet, which seemed to be crawling and walking at the same time. The latter was chasing the former. Both stopped at the sight of the blue colossus, which reached the sulfur-colored beast in three bounds.

"It puts me in mind of a prehistoric scene," said Jean. "In fact, these monsters are no more surprising than the fabulous monsters of the Secondary Era, or even the fauna of the virgin forests that, until recently, humans permitted to grow over vast territories."

"If Mars didn't have other kinds of life than that of animals and plants of which this location offers us specimens," said Antoine, "as well as the Tripeds, who represent a pseudo-humankind, the originality of the planet would be meager—but with its Zoomorphs and Ethereals, I reckon it to be a creation superior to our sublunar bubble."

"Temporarily, if Earth follows a slower and more ample progress, as it almost certainly will."

"We shall have equivalents of the Zoomorphs and Ethereals in time."

"Us!" exclaimed Violaine, laughing. "I believe it!"

After a hesitation, the black beast had retreated in the face of superior force, and the leviathan had just opened up its victim, from which a golden liquid was spurting.

"All things considered, and in spite of my grudge against the Zoomorphs," said Jean, "their manner of nourishing themselves at the expense of the weak is less gross than that ferocious devouring."

357

"And among the Ethereals, there's probably no contest for elements or energy."

"In that case, old tapir, progress has a direction in this small world?"

Raising his arms in a gesture of uncertainty, Antoine replied: "Let's try to make contact with our friends the Tripeds."

"Let's hope that we haven't mistaken their habitat. They might cook us."

"Do you think so?" said Jean. "Our legend has surely spread throughout Tripedy; I think we'll be made welcome everywhere. The real reason for preferring our friends to others is that we've created a language that they alone understand. Anyway, they're nearby."

"Over there, behind the agamic forest."

A few moments later, we were flying over the forest whose enormous vegetable structures sometimes resembled mushrooms as big as oak trees, sometimes trees like mosses or fabulously magnified lichens.

"The clearing," Jean announced.

It was, indeed, the clearing in which I had stayed while Jean, having gone into the forest, had been captured by Tripeds.

"We thought you were lost here," I murmured, putting my hand on our friend's shoulder. "We didn't suspect that it was the threshold of the promised land."

"Let's go down," said Antoine.

The *Stellarium* landed in the middle of the clearing, between four enormous blocks of red and green stone, one of which was vaguely reminiscent of a sea-lion.

Jean, Violaine and I disembarked, while Antoine remained on watch in the *Stellarium*.

"It was over there, Jean, that you disappeared, between those two rocks."

Jean started laughing. "I shall disappear there again," he cried.

"Not without us," Violaine begged.

"I want to!" said Jean. "There's no danger."

"Let's be careful just the same," I said. "It's possible that our friends have moved away."

"I don't think so."

We advanced as slowly as possible, for as soon as we adopted the rhythm of terrestrial walking we began to take huge bounds.

"Tortoise pace, eh?"

All three of us stopped, almost simultaneously.

"There they are!" cried Jean. "Our friends—or some of them, at least."

"Are they really the same ones?" asked Violaine.

"I recognize one of them," I said.

"And I recognize three," Jean added.

There were six, who had taken a step back when they first saw us—but they were immediately reassured, and one of them was already "talking" to us—by which I mean that he was expressing himself by means of signs created by the Tripeds and ourselves.

Violaine examined the fantastic creatures avidly. She recognized them easily; we had brought a great many photographs back to Earth. Her astonishment was no less keen for that, and increased as the Tripeds came to meet us.

"What beautiful eyes!" she exclaimed. "They're ornamented with them all over! Their complexion is admirable; our most beautiful petals hardly manifest shades as delicate."

We continued going forward to meet the Tripeds and soon reached them. Jean had entered into conversation with one of them. We learned that nothing had changed since our departure, but that the invasion of the Zoomorphs was continuing, albeit slowly, in various parts of the territory occupied by the Tripeds, animals and plants.

"But have they crossed our barriers?"

"No, and we've succeeded in constructing others for our brothers in the most endangered regions." But he added, in a melancholy fashion: "We're going to disappear!"

Shivering, Violaine watched the Triped's gestures, and her brother's, with a passionate delight. She confessed to me

359

that she was disorientated by the strange limbs and the absence of those fragments of flesh, the nose and ears, that are graceless in themselves and often ugly, comic or baroque, not to say repulsive, in our fellow humans.

"I shall get used to it very quickly, though," she added. "The form of the cheeks is as exquisite as their hue, and the entire head seems as harmonious as a beautiful amphora from Athens or Corinth. Lit by the magical fire of their eyes, I think I'll end up finding them beautiful."

"You'll find their females more beautiful still," I said.

"I know that they're quite different."

"As you've been able to see in our photographs: taller, with thinner faces. You'll recognize them immediately, although they don't have signs as visible as breasts."

The conversation between Jean and the Triped was continuing. As it was mute, I could follow it fairly well while listening to Violaine.

"You already know that our friends' dwellings are underground. It's a domain of warm and well-lit caves and tunnels. They're able to live there secure from Zoomorph invasion, but they need a rather extensive surface area because of their plant nourishment. They find water in the caverns."

"It's *their* water, isn't it? Which we can only drink after purification?"

"Transformation, Violaine, for chemical intervention is necessary."

There was a pause in the conversation between the Triped and Jean, who had quickly asked to see the Implicit Chief. The Tripeds invited us to follow them.

We soon arrived at a kind of natural porch. A gently-sloping corridor descended toward the caves. After walking for five minutes there was a bend in the corridor. The Tripeds lit the way for us with the aid of little blocks of stone that emitted a yellow phosphorescence, bright enough to allow us to see. It was a soft light that did not penetrate very far but was quite sufficient for short-distance viewing. Little by little, the wall of the tunnel became phosphorescent in their turn; that

360

light, almost imperceptible at first, became increasingly distinct thereafter.

In this fashion we reached a cave in which the accumulated light permitted us to see for a long way.

"Splendid!" Violaine murmured. "A cathedral that could contain St. Peter's in Rome twenty times over."

Regularly-shaped excavations were hollowed out in the walls, from which dozens of Tripeds emerged. Among them was the Implicit Chief—and close behind him was the female who had helped me to discover "a magical delight that exalted me as the goddesses had once exalted mystical Hellenes, and a tenderness with no analogy to any known tenderness."[54]

Would there be the fatal deception of recommencements? Already, an infinitely delicate atmosphere was emanating from her. Violaine lost her prestige; her beauty was dulled and blurred by mist; she was too similar to myself.

Besides, Grace was hypnotic; she was contemplating me in a dazed manner. "It's inconceivable," she whispered.

As the young Martian female came forward, her atmosphere resumed its "nascent state"—that strange and subtle voluptuousness with no resemblance to any Earthly voluptuousness, which seemed to endow me with a new sense.

I would search in vain for a comparison; any metaphor would be vain and deceptive. Neither the vegetal perfumes of flowers, leaves or herbs, nor the intoxication of mornings on which it seems that the universe had just been born, nor the purest love has any resemblance to that sensation, much less love in its brutal state.

Only Grace had made me feel that on the surface of Mars, although she had very beautiful sisters. It is probable that particular affinities and mysterious mutual influences were involved, since nothing similar had been produced in Antoine, or even in Jean, who was more sensitive and emotional than me.

---

[54] The quotation is from "The Navigators of Space."

"I dared not believe that you would come back!" she said. "It's too great a happiness for us to see one another again!"

Absence had not caused her to forget any of the sign language created by the Tripeds and us. Her joy radiated around her, and rendered her more fascinating.

"Only the impossible could have stopped me!" I replied.

Pure as our affection was, we did not want to say any more, not out of modesty—that word has no meaning here—but because our intimacy was shy. At least, it was for me—but I sensed that it was for her too, either by intuition or illusion.

A crowd had gathered, wondering and joyful. Its silence—the eternal silence of the Tripeds, for whom sound does not exist—was, however, bizarrely tumultuous. I can find no other term to express the luminous delight that brightened their faces: so many sparkling eyes comprised a kind of astral illumination, reminiscent of a living crowd of constellations.

The conversation with the Implicit Chief lasted for some time; it was agreed that we would discuss with him and the most learned Tripeds the means of combating the Zoomorph invasion everywhere. This time, it would be necessary to take account of the threatened peoples—in fact, all the peoples of the periphery in contact with the enemy and not yet provided with defensive apparatus.

We already knew that the domain occupied by the Tripeds and their realm must be equal to twice the area of Europe. The rest of the surface, as vast as Asia and America combined, had escaped them.[55]

"Many peoples have already been initiated into the system of defense that you created for us," said the Implicit

---

[55] The author inserts a footnote: "It is necessary not to lose sight of the fact that the present surface of Mars no longer has any seas, but only lakes; because of that, the area potentially available to the Tripeds could be compared, in extent, to our continental lands—but the Zoomorphs already held about four-fifths of it."

Chief, "but they have not yet tried it out. It seems, too, that the dwarf Zoomorphs are becoming more resistant to the radiations. If they adapt themselves completely, the danger they pose will be as serious as the large ones, for they reproduce more rapidly."

"Yes," said Jean, "that's the rule on Earth, and probably a universal rule."

The Implicit Chief spontaneously raised the question of our supplies. Anticipating our return, he had prepared drinkable water—*terrestrial water*—according to the prescriptions left by Jean, and had sowed some cereals and spores of an edible lichen that we had brought on our first voyage. The cereals had only yielded negligible results, but the lichens had multiplied profusely. That was good news, for, although scarcely substantial, the lichens would at least provide a purified nutriment with which to avoid scurvy. Not that we had omitted to vitalize our condensed nutriments, but, if our sojourn were to be prolonged further than that of our first voyage, our cultures might be "anemiated." Then again, we would take pleasure in eating fresher vegetable matter; this time, we had brought seeds originating from arctic and mountain regions.

The conference with the Implicit Chief needed to be prolonged even further. Grace and I agreed to see one another the following day.

"Who knows whether we might not succeed in growing a few nutritious vegetables?" said Jean, when we were back on the *Stellarium*.

"It would be the beginning of the colonization of Mars!" Violaine exclaimed, enthusiastically.

"Perhaps, one day, Mars will belong to humans," said Antoine.

"Oh!" I cried. "I don't want that at all! The native ferocity of our peers still persists in the 20th century. There are brutes on Earth who would pitilessly exterminate our Triped friends."

"Perhaps not."

"They'd reduce them to slavery, then," said Violaine, indignantly.

"A moderate slavery might suit our friends," Antoine remarked.

"No, no!" I said, with disgust. "It would be abominable. The Tripeds aren't unhappy. Their decadence has ceased to make them suffer. Down with the terrestrial colonizers!"

"What will be, will be," Antoine retorted, phlegmatically. "In any case, the hour has not come, nor even the century. If humans are to become true conquerors of Mars, it won't happen for 200 or 300 years."

"Well," said Jean, "I believe that it won't happen. There's too little air, and I can't imagine an entire population rigged out in respiratory apparatus, which would be unbearable on a permanent basis."

"Unbearable? Go on! I got used to it before."

"Because you spent the better part of the time aboard the *Stellarium*. But why shouldn't the colonists build dwellings equipped with air-condensers? The cultivation of the soil, over large areas, would only take up a small part of the laborers' time."

"The colonists would be essentially sedentary, then?" I asked. "A scarcely tempting ideal."

"Would it be very different from what happens on Earth, for the majority of people?"

"Not for children, or for a respectable fraction of adolescents."

We paused to watch a herd of animals grazing in a large clearing. You might have thought them strange serpents clad in a sort of orange cotton wool—serpents with feet, five of them, according to the norm—with heads like large beetroots. They did not seem unduly troubled by our presence, although they manifested a keen agitation on perceiving that they were being watched by two enormous Aerians that were hovering over the clearing.

"The eagles of Mars!" Violaine exclaimed.

"More like condors."

Their five emerald-colored wings were vibrating gently; we could see their multiple eyes sparkling. Instead of beaks they had enormous funnel-like muzzles. The orange animals stopped grazing; they huddled together, tremulously.

"An old terrestrial scene, in sum, in spite of the differences between the organisms," said Jean. "Mars has engendered ferocious life, exactly like our world. If the Tripeds had ended up going to war, their ancestors would have massacred one another just like ours."

"In that sense, Zoomorphic life will be a progress toward less cruelty, since their prey is merely *exploited*."

"What about the Ethereals?" asked Violaine.

"We don't really know anything about them yet, but we assume that they don't destroy one another," Jean replied. "How I'd like to find a means of communicating with them!"

Having described several circles, the Aerians fell like stones. One of them seized a serpentine creature; the other paused at an altitude of a few meters.

"Let's play the role of providence."

"We only need to move forward," Violaine affirmed, taking the lead at a run.

She was not mistaken. On seeing this upright creature arrive, quickly followed by two others, the Aerians resumed their flight, while the herbivores, huddled together, remained motionless, all a-tremble.

"They seem exceptionally stupid to me," said Jean.

At any rate, they were very fearful, for they were literally swaying on their five feet.

"It's astonishing that their species has been able to survive!" muttered Antoine.

We were close to them now; we would probably have been able to knock them down without their trying to defend themselves.

Finally, abruptly, as if the animals were waking from a dream or a trance, they fled at great speeds into the depths of the forest.

"Good!" said Jean. "I can explain their existence a little better. Alternations of passivity and alertness...that's found, less obviously, in many terrestrial animals."

We did not take long to get back to the *Stellarium*.

V.

The next day, we received a visit from the Implicit Chief. He came to talk about the Zoomorphs, and he added precise details to the previous day's revelations.

"I propose a general tour of inspection," said Antoine.

"Beginning with the limits of the Triped domain?"

"With a few incursions into the interior?" asked Violaine.

"Naturally! After a first tour of inspection."

"The Implicit Chief can accompany us if he wishes."

When consulted, the Chief accepted enthusiastically. "Can we take a second passenger?" he asked. "My daughter, whom you know, has a surer and more rapid vision than mine. No one understands you better; she has been a great help in preparing the defensive apparatus."

My heart had begun to beat faster, and I turned away to hide my disturbance from Violaine. It was absurd, of course, since my love for Grace had no relationship to terrestrial love, being further removed therefrom than my friendship for Jean and Antoine. Pure as it was, though—purer than the purest of human sentiments ever is—sexuality was mingled within it, in a sublimated and quasi-supernatural form, and Violaine would have been jealous if she had understood. Was it possible that she did understand? Not directly, undoubtedly, not really, but by transposition, by false analogy. In any case, she should not suspect anything immediately.

Meanwhile, Jean had replied to the Implicit Chief: "There would even be space for several extra passengers."

When the Chief had gone, Violaine murmured: "His daughter...the most brilliant of the Tripeds, whom we saw in the caves?"

"The most brilliant, yes."

"I found her very charming!"

That exclamation seemed soothing, which was also absurd. What revelation might rise up in Violaine's soul, what kind of jealousy? Could a woman be jealous of a rose?

An impression persists, however, which no amount of reasoning can destroy. The example of the rose is specious, anyway. Does not an excessively intimate friend, an excessively pampered pet, dog or cat, without there being anything equivocal about it, often arouse jealousy in an impassioned woman? After all, even a predilection for roses may create umbrage, when it absorbs the soul of the beloved too extensively.

I am getting lost in the void. Violaine will never divine what there is between Grace and me, and the rest is fiction.

Since yesterday, the *Stellarium* has sheltered Grace and the Implicit Chief. Grace is delighted to see us constantly as we are, free of our respiratory apparatus. Outside the *Stellarium*, she has only seen me like that at intervals, during our first sojourn.

Naively, she says:[56] "Humans are much more beautiful than we are. What poor creatures we are in comparison to you, especially to *her*. The Earth that produced her is divine!"

I repeat these words to Violaine, who is coquette enough to be delighted by them. She replies: "Tell her that I find her very beautiful."

Grace's eyes become dazzling; there is a symphony of multicoloured fire, which puts one in mind of a sextet in light.

---

[56] The author inserts a footnote here to remind readers not to forget that conversations with Martians are carried out by means of signs.

"By comparison with those eyes," Violaine murmurs, "ours are mere guttering candles."

It is understood aboard that we shall make a voyage of exploration in all directions, not only above territories occupied by animals, plants and Tripeds, but above the much more numerous regions where the Zoomorphs reign. These regions save for their edges, are completely unknown to the Tripeds; they have only been able to go into them at continual risk to their lives.

The progress of the *Stellarium* is extremely slow, and pauses are frequent. Sometimes it hovers motionless in order to give our guests a better view of the landscape.

"It's true, alas, that we have been exiled from the greater part of our planet," said the Implicit Chief, sadly. "For vast numbers of years, no Triped has been able to travel through immense territories. The entire Earth belongs to humans, doesn't it?"

"Apart from the reactions of nature, which are sometimes terrible—but our aircraft can carry us everywhere, and settlements have been founded in the most hostile regions. The last conquest, in the twentieth century, was that of the continent and islands surrounding the South Pole."

"What grandeur is yours!"

"It will come to an end, alas. And I don't believe that it will be very distant. Perhaps a million years."

The *Stellarium* floated slowly over locations where desert regions and magnificent vanished civilizations were displayed. All of it was now completely occupied by Zoomorphs. Immense monuments sometimes made us think of an amalgam of the ruins of Angkor and Luxor, without the resemblance surpassing a certain analogy, and sometimes comprised strange heaps in which artificial rocks alternated with giant termitaries, parabolic dwellings arranged in spirals, contorted pyramids and serpentine towers without definable forms. Sometimes, we might have believed that we were looking at a colony of giant corals.

"Mysterious!" muttered Jean. "How did they live in those?"

The Zoomorphs were swarming in the cities, especially the smaller Zoomorphs.

The massive vestiges of ancient civilizations were succeeded by deserts in which the ruins had ended up being confused with the soil of deserts that were utterly bare or deserts of sinister-seeming red rocks and vertiginous mountains.

The Implicit Chief and Grace contemplated the ruins and primitive surfaces with equal avidity, but the mountains excited them most of all. They were much higher and more varied than those visible in the Triped regions.

"It's frightful and splendid," said Grace. "Are you also the masters of your mountains?"

"We have observatories and dwellings on the highest."

"Higher than these?"

"Perhaps the summits of the Himalayas and the Cordilleras are a little higher—and all white, covered in eternal snows."

She read our explanations, marveling like a child at a fabulous fairy tale. "How happy I am!" she said, her eyes shining.

The Implicit Chief also seemed happy. His movements and his gaze were livelier.

"It's the pressure," said Antoine. "It's causing them to experience a kind of euphoria. There's a danger of eventual fatigue. For them, the *Stellarium* is a tank of compressed air."

It cannot be said that the Implicit Chief and Grace were listening to us, since they could not hear anything, but they deduced that we were talking about them—and when the Chief spoke, in slightly exaggerated gestures, his speech fitted in strangely with Antoine's.

"Do you always have as much air, on your world?" Grace asked.

"Yes," Antoine replied. "This is our average pressure."

"That explains your superiority," said the Chief, "and that of our distant ancestors."

"When the pressure becomes too tiring, don't hesitate to tell us—we'll go outside."

"I don't think that it will tire us overmuch; we have a considerable adaptive ability; we can regulate the rhythm of our breathing and ration our intake of air. At this moment, we're no longer breathing as rapidly; if we begin to feel ill, we'll breathe even more slowly."

"Without having to think about it?"

"Mechanically."

Having passed over the high peaks, we flew over a bleak plain where the dry bed of a great river was still visible; then came a deeper depression where the waves of a sea had once danced. Thanks to the *Stellarium*'s slow speed and occasional pauses, the Implicit Chief and his daughter were able to contemplate their ancestral patrimony, now forever lost to the Tripeds, at their leisure.

They gazed at the scenery with a passionate interest, especially the Zoomorphs in incalculable numbers, grazing the energy of the ground or sliding at various speeds, sometimes as slow as the slowest tortoises, sometimes more rapid than eagles in full flight.

"They will take everything that remains to us," said the Implicit Chief. There was an unaccustomed rebelliousness and anger in his attitude and his expression.

"He's less resigned," Jean observed.

"An effect of the pressure."

The *Stellarium* moved more rapidly. We saw a city—what else can I call it?—appear: a mass of helical towers, spiral houses, sinuous pyramids, spires that might have been Gothic in their contortion and quasi-cyclopean ruins that was both chaotic and ordered. The whole had a decorative harmony that reminded me of drawings made by mediums, which are sometimes fantastically seductive.[57] We did not have to

---

[57] Spiritualist mediums sometimes engaged in "automatic drawing" as well as "automatic writing," sometimes producing

wonder whether it had any inhabitants; they emerged from everywhere, pointing at the *Stellarium* and making signals to us that we knew to be welcoming gestures—for the *Stellarium*, which had already gone everywhere during our first sojourn, was familiar to the entire Triped population. It had become legendary, as we soon learned; although not much inclined to mysticism, the Tripeds had devoted a cult to it. They all knew that we had been victorious in fighting the Zoomorph invasion of our friends' territory and the frontier cities; our arrival awoke vast hopes.

"Let's stop here," Jean proposed. "These citizens are showing signs of agitation; I'd like to see them at closer range."

"Oh, me too!" exclaimed Violaine.

The *Stellarium* landed on a hill overlooking the city.

It was agreed that I should stand guard. The Implicit Chief went out, and I was left alone with Grace.

The agitation of the crowd that gathered at the foot of the hill contrasted with its absolute silence. In addition, the Tripeds moved around with a lightness that, in combination with the rarefaction of the air, muffled the sound of their progress. They surrounded Jean, Antoine, Violaine and the Implicit Chief, gesticulating frantically. I would have been anxious had I not been familiar with the gentleness of the Martians. There was a moment when our people were so tightly surrounded that I could hardly see them. Then, in response to a signal from the Implicit Chief, the crowd moved off toward the city and vanished between the houses and monuments.

---

images of other worlds. The supposed images of Mars by "Helen Smith" reproduced in the best-selling *From India to Mars* (1899) by Theodore Flournoy are anodyne, but the actor Victorien Sardou (1831-1908) produced some highly imaginative depictions of life on Jupiter while he was a member of Camille Flammarion's circle; it is presumably these that the narrator has in mind.

When there was no longer anyone at the foot of the hill I was gripped by a great emotional disturbance; born of reality, the dream became real again, but remained fantastic. Grace's magical eyes enveloped me with a "tender" light, a marvelously variable light of love. It was a song of light, as soft and penetrating as a female choir heard on a crystalline night beneath a cloudy sky beside the strangest of Oriental lakes.

"I love you, charming daughter of Mars," I said, "so different from my human sisters."

"I'm so happy to be with you," she replied. "How I've longed for this moment!"

Chimerical, impossible love exalted my every fiber. Grace had drawn closer. Her atmosphere enveloped me, magnetically, and for the first time since our arrival I hugged her to my bosom: a prodigy; an inconceivable magic; an indescribable creative youth; an intimate revelation of another universe than the human. And the miracle was complete. From bodies trembling like grass in the wind emanated a sensuality devoid of gesture, a superhuman sensuality that rendered the grimacing sensuality of human love derisory. It required nothing but an embrace, the chastest and most innocent imaginable, to create that happiness, beyond all the dreams and beautiful mirages created over time by perishable creatures desperately attempting to surpass their destiny.

What did the duration that limited the miracle matter? It left no lassitude—nothing but an exceedingly gentle and tender languor. I was "bathed" in mystery and I did not try to mingle it with conjectures regarding my privilege; what is certain is that something within me was in accord with Martian nature, and something in Grace a reflection of terrestrial life.

When Violaine came back with her companions, she remarked, after having scanned me with a rapid glance; "That's strange. I've never seen you with that dreamy expression."

"Dreamy expression?" I became slightly—very slightly —anxious under that frank gaze.

"Yes," she said. "Hallucinated, in some way. It's not unappealing, though."

"An otherworldly expression!" said Jean.

"But we are on another world," Antoine put in. "Here, faces have six eyes and heads have no ears."

Violaine stood very close to me and asked, in a low voice: "Do you love me?" She was more than usually attracted.

"Ardently," I said. It was not entirely true. I loved her calmly—but I did love her. The ardor would come back later.

In the days that followed, we visited several cities, as many on the Martian surface as in the underground caverns. The life of the caverns was predominant, though; the caves were ingeniously fitted out, linked together in hundreds by corridors and provided with ventilation systems created by distant ancestors.

"Perhaps humans will also end up in caves," Antoine suggested.

"If, as on Mars, the caves are warmed by radiations whose origin we don't yet know," Jean remarked. "A rather sad life, on the whole."

"They don't see to find it so."

The Implicit Chief could only give us sketchy information. For a long time, the Tripeds had kept no records, being submissive to regulations that were thousands of years old, resigned to a decadence that was unaccompanied by any individual suffering. Spared all warfare, ignorant of hatred, incapable of murder, their material life is hardly burdensome. There is no overpopulation. The exceedingly slow invasion of the Zoomorphs is compensated by the automatic decrease of the birth-rate. The two phenomena are complementary, for the Tripeds have absolute control over their fecundity. They can interrupt the formation of embryonic lives without any suffering for their women.

Their entire being participates in their magically pure sexual intercourse; as I have said, there is nothing brutal about it, nothing but an intoxicating embrace. If any substance is

373

involved, it must be in an imponderable state: a radiation of atoms more subtle than the perfume of flowers. We have seen that a mother, after several weeks, is enveloped by an almost invisible light, which slowly condenses, like a miniature cloud. Then, sheltered in a delightful "shell," a sort of large pale flower, the child gradually takes shape, nourished by an invisible substance. One can imagine how easy it is to interrupt the chain of metamorphoses well before the new individual has emerged from the limbo of sensation.[58]

Love among the Tripeds is, therefore, a voluptuous dream, and their sensuality is incomparably superior to ours. Have they always had that privilege? I suspect that it developed in the epoch when their species was in full bloom. Perhaps their ancestors had knowledge that permitted them to perfect their organic functioning, and to transform the organs themselves.

In spite of their resignation—or, rather, their adaptation to a progressive and conclusive disappearance, the end of life for all—the Tripeds desired to retain the as-yet-considerable part of the surface that the Zoomorphs had left them. Thus, our intervention, during our first voyage, had excited universal enthusiasm. In imitation of our fluidic barriers, other barriers had been created, although with less skill. Some of them, although imperfect, hindered the enemy infiltration.

To bar the route to the invaders everywhere would take many years, perhaps a century. The perimeter of the domain, almost twice that of our European domain, required vast numbers of machines and colossal supplies of radiation, and, subtle as it was, the Tripeds' industry was far from being adequate to the task—as was their activity. They were not lazy, but their labor had been drastically moderated for thousands of years.

They all worked, it is true, without distinction of sex, from their youth until an advanced age. None of them avoided

---

[58] The author inserts a footnote: "Triped females can conceive without intercourse with the male. It is sufficient that both of them desire it for some time, *intensely*."

their tasks, although their individual liberty was complete. It was a triumph of mutual aid, spontaneously organized, regulated by custom without laws or penal obligations. For the many centuries and millennia that they had been ignorant of murder, and almost of violence, they had not needed a judiciary apparatus, or any kind of social servitude. In sum, there was no intensive labor, their machines being as moderate as themselves. That was not adequate to bring the task that our defensive apparatus demanded to a successful conclusion. It was not sufficient to continue, it was necessary constantly to produce the necessary energy.

Our dream, therefore, was to create a frontier zone that would stop the invaders *by itself.*

Before anything else, it was necessary to create establishments to capture large quantities of energy in various districts, and equipment sufficiently complex for direct combat against the Zoomorphs.

"It's a veritable revolution for the Tripeds," Antoine remarked. "It's difficult to calculate the global effort that they'll have to supply. In any case, a continual effort sufficiently considerable to demand an increase in activity."

"Which won't please them," I said. "Their extinction appears to be proportional to the increase of the Zoomorphs, or very nearly. Those presently alive are scarcely under threat."

"In sum," Jean concluded, "the profit will be for future generations—a profit that might be illusory, since the race might make its exit meekly, by its own means."

VI.

One evening, when we were contemplating the sky, the stars and—most of all—the Ethereals, Jean said: "Who knows whether it might be possible to communicate with them?"

"Possible, doubtless," Antoine retorted, "but so improbable that, for us, it might as well be impossible."

"If, by chance, they were much more intelligent than us," I remarked, "there would be a chance of success. You've already admitted that they're essentially superior."

"Essentially, yes. But suppose they're still in the earliest phase of their reign—by analogy, something like the first terrestrial creatures of the Primary Era."

"For what it would cost us," said Jean, his eyes fixed on a column in which the Ethereals were manifesting a vertiginous activity, "it would be absurd not to make the attempt."

We did not go any further that evening. On the far horizon the Earth rose, a coppery jade star that we contemplated affectionately; it would take so little to prevent us from ever returning to it. Jean's words, however, rendered more concrete an idea to which we often returned. Another incident gave him a singular impulsion. It was during a visit that we made with the Implicit Chief to the ruins of a temple that had been abandoned while the Tripeds still retained their creative genius. The ruins in question, which were not very ancient—perhaps 5000 or 6000 years old—were composed for the most part of carved blocks, sometimes bearing a number of symbols, which we judged to be inscriptions.

"They are, indeed, inscriptions," the Implicit Chief affirmed, "but we can no longer decipher them. One of them, however, according to my great-great grandfather, reports an attempt at communication between our ancestors and the luminous life-forms."

"Eureka!" Jean exclaimed, enthusiastically.

Antoine nodded his head, excited in his abstract fashion, his eyes suddenly vague, devoid of gaze, and his eyebrows furrowed. I was no less excited than they were.

"But you haven't retained any trace of that communication?" I asked the Implicit Chief.

"No, none—nor had my great-great grandfather. If the attempt succeeded, all communication between the luminous life-forms and us ceased hundreds of thousands of years ago." In a melancholy fashion, he added: "It's lost, like so many admirable things. I don't even know the purpose of most of the tools you see there. As I've often told you, we're poor decadent creatures, who don't even know a thousandth of what *they* knew, and our power has diminished more than we know."

Thus spoke the Implicit Chief, and—I don't know why—his speech, although similar to so many others in which he testified to the Tripeds' decline, struck us more keenly than all the rest. With a placid sadness, he added: "I am alone in regretting it, and only on certain days. Decadence is not a disease; often I reckon it is a good thing." After a pause, he went on: "If only we were conclusively protected from the arid creatures, life would be happy for me and the others."

My distracted companions paid hardly any attention to these words. Jean's expression was revealing an increasing agitation; Antoine's, contracted, testified to an intense preoccupation.

When we went back to the *Stellarium*, Jean said: "Why shouldn't we try to do what the ancient Tripeds might perhaps have done?"

"It's a matter of knowing whether we're as intelligent as they were," said Antoine. "I doubt it."

"Eh? We may doubt it, if we please, provided that it's a provisional doubt that doesn't prevent action."

"My doubts are stimulants!" Antoine retorted, phlegmatically.

That evening, we began experiments—or, as Jean put it, opened hostilities. As had been agreed during the day, we traced luminous signs on a board. Naturally, we adopted the method that was, in a sense, classical—one that our ancestors had tried in the nineteenth century and our contemporaries had improved. We had encountered only failure; neither Mars nor Venus, nor any other planet, had ever replied. With the aid of a phosphorescent substance we traced simple geometrical figures on the board: triangles, squares, circles and ellipses. The figures thus assembled seemed to us to have more chance of attracting attention than a single figure, even if it were repeated.

A few hours passed. Nothing, naturally.

"It would have been prodigious to obtain an immediate reaction from the Ethereals," Antoine remarked.

"Is it certain that no reaction was produced?" I said.

Jean, who was observing the columns and luminous groups attentively, said in his turn: "I haven't observed anything irregular, at any rate."

"Of course not!" muttered Antoine, who had started laughing softly. "It will take time for us to be able to distinguish the normal and the abnormal in these creatures."

"Do you think I don't know that?" Jean retorted, with a hint of bitterness. "I agree that I'd have done better to say that I didn't notice anything at all."

"Conclusion?"

"No conclusion. We remain in the dark, not knowing whether our appeal has failed, or even knowing whether it has been noticed. We don't know anything. Nevertheless, we have to repeat the experiment for several days, in order to attract the Ethereals' attention."

"That's what we shall do."

"Amen," said Jean. "I have a feeling, Antoine, that it will be necessary to have recourse to something other than the visual. Everything inclines us to suppose that a mode of perception analogous to our sight is foreign to them. In the meantime, let's repeat the first experiment carefully."

We repeated it carefully for six days running, for the sake of conscientiousness.

"Nothing prevents us from repeating it endlessly," said Jean, on the sixth day, "but we ought to undertake other simultaneous exercises."

He had no need to say so. His intention corresponded to ours. We thought it quite improbable, in fact, that the Ethereals had means of perception corresponding to our senses. Given the lack of those senses, we had a better chance of achieving our goal with the aid of rhythmic signals, commencing with the most rudimentary.

"To what extent, and in what form—if one can speak of form in this context—are they conscious of our presence?" Antoine asked. "They presumably confuse us with the objects that they go around."

"That's plausible," Jean agreed. "They're probably unaware of the *living* existence of Zoomorphs, Tripeds and everything else living on Mars alongside them."

"Which wouldn't bode well for our enterprise," I added. "I refuse to believe it, for it would be necessary to write off an intelligence having a least some analogy with our own."

"Why?"

"Don't animate obstacles, by virtue of their perpetual displacement, and various actions and reactions, have a general and particular rhythm quite different from inanimate objects? If they're intelligent, the Ethereals can't have failed to perceive that."

"But without necessarily concluding that the obstacles are alive," Antoine contended.

"Agreed—but the difference must give beings whose thoughts have any relationship with ours, however distant, cause to reflect."

"Let's pass on to the Deluge. What signals should we adopt?"

"I can't think of anything simpler than Morse code in a radiant form," Jean suggested.

"That's very rudimentary," said Antoine, pulling a face.

We tried radiant Morse code for several days, within the limits of visual radiation, and in the infra-red and ultra-violet, all the way to X-rays. It had no more success than the geometric designs.

On the seventh day, Antoine complained: "It definitely is a wild goose chase."

"A noble pursuit," said Violaine.

It should be noted that these attempts did not waste much time; once the apparatus was set up, it functioned automatically. Afterwards, it was sufficient for one or other of us to keep an eye on events during the two or three nocturnal hours devoted to the experiments.

"A noble pursuit if you wish," I said, "but another failure. I've got an idea!"

"I'll stand aside to let it pass!" Antoine joked.

"Well, it's that our radiant Morse signals are too slow in frequency to be perceived by the Ethereals. Let's accelerate them."

"Not a bad idea. Let's accelerate them."

Quite rapidly, we set up an acceleration device, of which we had all the necessary components, complemented by an apparatus for successive deceleration. The frequency of the signals was multiplied by a thousand.

Still nothing.

After two days, we multiplied them by a hundred thousand, then a million, and a billion.

For two hours, we repeated the word *homo* endlessly.[59]

The operation required little attention, so we engaged in rambling conversations or trivial tasks.

One evening, Jean's voice awoke me from a meditation. "The miracle is accomplished!" His bright eyes were shining with enthusiasm, his cheeks quivering.

"What?" said Antoine, straightening up with a start.

"They've replied!"

"No? No?" I said, simultaneously credulous and incredulous.

He had no need to insist; the decelerators were connected to an evidential plaque imbued with a fluorescent material, and the plaque was repeating, at regular intervals:

. . . __ __ __   __ __   __ __ __

We looked at it, astounding. Then Violaine murmured, gratefully: "A new era is beginning."

---

[59] It is not obvious why the astronauts think it appropriate to open communication with a Latin word rather than a French one, especially as they switch to French thereafter.

We were saturated with enthusiasm. If we had had any doubt, it would have been dissipated when Jean sent a new signal: "I am," which was immediately repeated.

"Ah!" said Jean, putting his hands together. "If I had any faith, I would pray."

"But we are praying!" Violaine retorted. "Our attempt has been one long prayer. I was sure that they're alive, but I never really hoped that a link could be established between material creatures and creatures of radiation."

"Personally," said Jean, softly, "I already entertained a timid hope during our first voyage."

"Mystics are often right!" Antoine concluded. "Besides, the radio-wave technology permitted us to hope."

VII.

Prodigious as our first success was, it did not give us any certainty with respect to the future of our relations with the Ethereals. After all, communication had only been achieved in its most embryonic form; they knew that we existed, that we were living beings like them and that we were attempting to know them and make ourselves known to them. It was a clean slate, with a simple mutual notion of existence. It was now necessary to cross abysses of discrimination to go beyond that.

Our first victory dissuaded us from despair. Jean, following the norms of his nature, was full of faith and hope. We first set out to suggest the notion of identity and the verb "to be," which implies existence. To succeed in that we made use of the terms "you" and "me," applied alternatively to one or other of us, and then simply the verb "to be."

It required much probing to arrive at that result, and intuition played such a considerable role, especially on the part of the Ethereals, that I feel incapable of explaining it—all the more so because my memory only registered the major phases, without any perceptible relationship between them. It was, in a sense, the cerebral development of a little child. Every day brought a new element of discrimination; soon, it was evident that the Ethereals could distinguish us individually and understood the verb that commanded all the others.

For our part, we now had a fairly clear perception of the group with which we were corresponding. It was composed of nine quite distinct individuals. They had not precise forms, but each of them comprised a dozen small luminous centers of various shades and intensities, linked by multicolored lines and helices. The distance between the centers, like the movement of the lines and helices, varied continually. *A priori*, these movements made any precise distinction between individuals, but we eventually finished up by recognizing them, at first with difficulty then quite easily, thanks to repetitions, the creators of habit and automatism; besides, variable as the forms of our correspondents were, they gravitated around a median form.

As it accelerated, the progress became so rapid that no one, I think, was able to define its phases. The fact is that the Ethereals had taken command, and we were soon no longer able to doubt that their intelligence was far in advance of ours. They not only knew how to create methods, but also to make us understand them with an extraordinary clarity.

To begin with, they learned our language; after some time, the slightest indication was sufficient for them. The slightest analogy suggested fecund generalizations to them. Thanks to them, our procedures were subject to prodigious improvements; the acceleration and deceleration devices required fewer and fewer intermediate materials. That was only a preliminary phase, however; it did not take the Ethereals long to want to understand us better and to reply to us in our own fashion. Everything became relatively easy when, following their instructions, we had installed a radio-transmitter of sufficient frequency. The radiations derived from our voices were communicated to them directly.

The day eventually arrived when we heard them—a moment as fabulous as the one when we received their initial response. To hear voices that did not exist, emitted by beings which cannot emit or perceive sound, and to reply to them with our voices transformed into universal radiations, infinitely surpassed anything we had hoped for in our wildest dreams. When we heard the first words emanated by the Ethereals, Jean, always more inclined than the rest of us to exteriorize his enthusiasm, exclaimed: "You're right, Violaine! It's a new era of life, not only for this world but perhaps for all the sister planets of Earth and Mars."

A bad line of 19th century verse came back to memory: "Men will become as gods!"[60]

"They *are* the gods!" muttered Antoine, pointing at the Ethereals.

"Who knows?"

"Do you doubt that their intelligence infinitely surpasses ours?"

"No! I don't doubt that, but perhaps we have potential for development that they do not. We've succeeded in leaving our planet. Will they ever succeed in leaving the environment of Mars? We guessed that they were alive, but it seems that they ignored us totally at first."

"That's because we were negligible to them."

"Just as they were to us. Nevertheless, I admit their superiority, with the reservation that it does not extend to all our faculties or all our possibilities."

---

[60] The exact form of the line cited by the author does not correspond to any source that I can identify, but the promise itself—attributed to the serpent in Eden—is widely quoted. The most notorious 19th century French citation is in René de Chateaubriand's *Génie du Christianisme*, but that hardly qualifies as a line of verse let alone a bad one. (It is possible that the author's "*mauvais*" [bad] refers to the morality of the sentiment rather than the quality of the writing, although the grammar of the line, as rendered in French, is certainly incorrect.)

"For myself," said Jean, "I believe they're capable of overtaking us in *every* respect."

"I don't deny it—but I doubt it."

"We'll try to find out," said Antoine. "First, it will be very interesting to know whether they have organizations superior to human organizations."

"Surely they do," affirmed Violaine, with a violence shot through with indignation. "It's obvious that their communication between individuals is much more perfect than ours, and it must be the same for their collectives and multitudes—as proven by the movement of their columns, which often comprise vast numbers of individuals and collective agitations that we sometimes witness."

"On those points," Antoine agreed, "I'm entirely inclined to share your views, but not with respect to stable institutions and our 'social memory.' Have they anything analogous to our libraries, which conserve the past and summarize all our knowledge *externally to ourselves?* Have they in their activity a manner of existence intermediate between mineral and colloidal life, as between humans and the terrestrial surface? It's hardly probable."

"They must have something better."

"We shall see."

Our intercourse with the Ethereals became veritable conversations, which would have been almost intimate but for a serious physiological obstacle; what we took a minute to say unfolded, after successive accelerations, in a tiny fraction of that time, on the order of one trillionth. They replied at the same speed, but their words, after being slowed down, arrived at the speed of our own voices. They had, in consequence, to await our responses for an immense interval, relative to the rhythm of their existence. By contrast, their responses reached us instantaneously, but were reeled off with an unaccustomed rapidity. For example, in a trillionth of a second they could make such progress that it took us a trillion times as long—ten minutes, for example—eventually to follow it.

Instantaneity on one side, almost infinite slowness on the other; one can easily imagine the great awkwardness in our communications.

Let us summarize this schematically. Antoine addresses an Ethereal. He speaks for five minutes. The response is instantaneous. An Ethereal speaks for a trillionth of a second. The reply, after successive decelerations, takes ten minutes to unfold. It is therefore necessary for it to await Antoine's reply for those ten minutes—an extremely long time so far as it is concerned. Obviously, during the interval, it is going to occupy itself with something else.

Fortunately their lifetimes are not proportional to their vibratory speed—as they made known to us—or conversation would have been practically impossible. Organisms make adjustments—otherwise, would we be able to perceive frequencies as practically distinct as those of light and sound?

VIII.

The group that conversed with us—since, as I said above, our communications were becoming veritable conversations—was not absolutely stable. To begin with it had comprised nine individuals; now it was larger, sometimes a dozen, fifteen or even twenty. However, five of the original Ethereals were always present. We had given them the names of stars: Antares, Aldebaran, Arcturus, Vega and Sirius.

Although the colors of the centers, lines and helices were variable, red and orange appeared more distinctly in Antares, Aldebaran and Arcturus than in Vega or Sirius—which, for that reason, seemed to us to be predominantly blue or violet. Slight as the difference was, it was perceptible, and we learned that it was not without significance; the polarity of the first three was opposed to the polarity of the other two, although that opposition did not have the same significance as the one between positive and negative electrical elements.

All five were keenly interested in our existence, especially Aldebaran and Vega. Something that astonished us profoundly was that their voices—those voices that *did not exist*—exhibited some difference. It did not take us long to understand that this resulted from the rhythmic elements of each of the five Ethereals, the states that determined the "harmonic individuals."

It was Aldebaran who replied to us first on the day when we posed the question of Space and Time. Antoine began by defining persistence and change. It was necessary to add a few terms to our common vocabulary.

The Ethereals listened, asked questions and made suggestions, and then Aldebaran concluded: "The changes that you perceive directly are extremely slow by comparison to those we perceive directly ourselves. You can, however, conceive—without perceiving them—of much more rapid changes. Your slow changes are an illusion; the obstacles that we encounter, and which seem motionless to you, appear to us from the outset to be assemblies of radiation all of whose components are destroyed and reconstructed incessantly. They are aggregations without individuality. Know too that everything is alive.

"As for you, you are aggregations more active still, but organized. We do not understand what you call time and space, but we conceive of coexistence, change and number—thus, at present we are eight who are listening to you, who coexist without being confused. We communicate with one another much more directly than you."

From subsequent conversations, it transpired that they did not have a *species memory* as persistent as that of humans—no archives of a long past, no technology, no weapons, nothing analogous to books conserving thought and science, or disks conserving sounds and images—but *in themselves*, they had numerous and various elements permitted them to create means of communication with us—to understand, for example, in their fashion, a radio-transmitter—and, as they had so often proved, to understand us so intimately that they had contrived to emit radiations that were eventually transformed into sound.

They understood, albeit abstractly, that we die periodically and reproduce ourselves. Strictly speaking, they do not die. At the end of a time that they are unable to determine since they cannot conceive of abstract time,[61] the intensity of their life diminishes; then the members of a group of Ethereals renew themselves, and the renewal often involves considerable changes of structure. Renewed, the individual only retains a confused and soon-annihilated memory of its anterior life.

"It's as if they die without dying and are reborn without rebirth," Violaine observed.

We did not succeed in determining clearly how they understand one another—what they have that corresponds to our language. It must involve extremely complex combinations of radiation, which demand, as our communication does, a constant intervention of intuition.

Let us imagine, to get a grip on the idea—for it does not correspond to any certain reality—that everything we express in speech has to be completed by the listener. One would rightly say that something is happening similar to the transmission of our thoughts and sentiments, with many errors of interpretation—an ever-imperfect and often false comprehension of both sentiments and ideas. Our lacunae or false interpretations are, however, more a symptom of insufficient discrimination than of the insufficiency of language. Among the

---

[61] It is not entirely clear what the author means in saying that the Ethereals cannot conceive of abstract time, since they can understand change and velocity, and their subsequent speech is full of temporal references. The author might have in mind Henri Bergson's contention that time had been misrepresented in Cartesian and Newtonian philosophy, which likened it to a "fourth dimension," and ought rather to be considered as a process of "becoming." Rosny sympathized with that view, but it is hard to believe that he could have been satisfied with the vagueness of the account given here.

Ethereals, language evokes in the speaker something that really passes to the other, not by integral reception but by a development of which I only understand a tiny fraction. To put it another way, the language, while having a relatively broad significance in itself, serves to establish mental states, to bring organisms into concordance, to create a sort of mental identity between two or more individuals.

If we imagine a conversation between Aldebaran and Antares, it would consist of a series of phrases, operating as linguistic triggers, which would end up reproducing in one of the interlocutors, almost identically, that which is occurring in the other. One Ethereal can address several of its fellows, but cannot perceive several simultaneous replies distinctly. It is important to note that each individual remains master of its thoughts. It only creates, as much by questions as answers, a state of pseudo-identity in the other, within the limits that it sets.

Let us try to translate this by supposing that humans were endowed with some faculty analogous to the one I have attempted to define. In a conversation with another person, every time I started to speak I would determine a mental state approximately similar to the one that is causing me to speak— an abstraction made, instinctively or voluntarily, by something I cannot specify. My interlocutor will understand me with no errors or lacunae. His emotional state will also be analogous to mine. It is necessarily the case that our nervous systems are vibrating in an almost-identical fashion *at the moment when we are in communication.*[62]

The Ethereals have no experimental sciences, or even mathematics, in the sense that we understand them. Mathematics would not be any use to them. They solve the most subtle theorems of problems concretely, to perfection—and their

---

[62] The author inserts a footnote: "Among the Ethereals, this concordance is more extensive. Between individuals of the same species, it seems to involve the totality of the organisms."

science, which is personal rather than social, is an immediate function of their life. It involves series of realizations in all the domains of their activity, which far surpass ours.

Even their structures embody knowledge that is innate or acquired in a flash, which are only revealed to us by dazzling but untranslatable suggestions. One essential fact is that their science involves nothing but radiations. It is in the form of radiation that they perceive what we call gases, liquids and solids—in a word, matter. Our physics and chemistry thus have no meaning for them. They only perceive the so-called material world in its radiant state—which, in verity, is capital in universal existence as in ours. The corpuscles that form matter, being nothing more than bound radiance, flow and renew themselves in the fashion of a river. All constancy is, in sum, nothing but dispersion and reformation in the same order, with the same density, within the radiant aggregations that constitute substance.

It does not follow from the fact that the Ethereals only perceive bodies in the form of radiation that their knowledge is less extensive than ours, but it is a different knowledge. It gives them direct access to the secrets of physical influences and the combinations called chemical. It allows them to perceive the internal transformations of the radiant clouds that are bodies to them—but that knowledge of the infinitesimal hides a considerable fraction of the effects of mass from them; thus, they had no clear idea of the organic life of Mars, nor any organized life except their own. In that regard, we were an essential revelation for them.

It is necessary to remark here that, if the Ethereals go around bodies when they encounter them, it is not because they cannot go through them—but in passing through them they are subject to painful sensations, which they naturally avoid. These influences would be more intense, and thus more painful, if they decided to penetrate into the interior of the planet.

IX.

Is the life of the Ethereals narrowly attached to the existence of Mars? It seems so. They cannot imagine that they might exist outside that influence. Mars is their center of energy; when they draw away from its surface, beyond a certain distance, soon becoming numb, they no longer have the same motive force and their thought is gradually extinguished. They are then drawn back toward the planet, and as they approach it their vitality is renewed—from which one may conclude that they are a function of an essentially Martian radiation, which decreases with distance.

Would the Earth furnish them with a tolerable environment? I cannot see how one could verify that, the Ethereals being incapable of crossing interplanetary spaces.

How did the Ethereal realm originate? To what modifications has it been subjected through the ages? These questions are insoluble, since the Ethereals have no records and their memories do not extend beyond a period so brief that they cannot obtain an abstract notion of time therefrom. For them, all that exists is a kind of present, ceaselessly in the process of transformation, devoid of distant benchmarks in the past; hence they have no tradition, and nothing that resembles our general or individual history—and yet they have an innate science that far surpasses the sum of our concrete and abstract science, a more lucid consciousness, a more rapid, more numerous and much surer intelligence than our consciousness and intelligence. Among them, the past, in its essentials, is incorporated into their structures—if one can speak of structure—and that is the basis that gives me a conjectural sense of the transformations of their realm, which could never be likened by analogy to the strata that furnish us with traces of ancient organisms conserved within the entrails of the Earth.

Are the Ethereals as individualized as humans? It seems so, but we have seen that they can communicate more intimately between themselves, to the point of blending their minds, provided that there is mutual consent.

They have no knowledge of sex; few Ethereals are born, those which are alive are approximately immortal (see above). Generation seems to be the result of an emanation, followed by a radiant condensation, due to more or less numerous groups. The rare births are compensated by the fusion, also very rare, of two Ethereals.

There is no hatred, and no conflict—individual or plural—among them. The causes that give rise to rivalries are non-existent. There is no occasion to dispute their nourishment; energy is furnished superabundantly, and I do not think it is possible for them to harm one another; one Ethereal is powerless to cause another to suffer by virtue of any forcible breach of its integrity. Theirs is a situation analogous to the one we would be in if we could neither kill nor injure one another.

If they have no enemies, do they have friends? Incontestably. Thus, Aldebaran is particularly attached to Vega, and Arcturus to Antares. The entire group comprising Antares, Aldebaran, Arcturus, Vega and Sirius is particularly close, and, as it is with this group that we have communicated since the beginning—although many other individuals often involve themselves in our conversations—it is they who have informed us most intimately about Ethereal life.

We have tried in vain to understand that which corresponds in them to our pleasures and pains. To begin with, nothing comparable to our scale of physical suffering and pleasures. The world of torture has no meaning for them. Their radiant joys, like their sadnesses, give rise to phenomena that we can glimpse, but cannot understand and never will understand, except symbolically.

X.

With the aid of a crew of Tripeds, we have constructed a kind of blockhouse on the top of a hill a short distance from a region occupied by Zoomorphs. Equipment has been set up there, designed for communication at any distance, for astronomical observation and physico-chemical experiments, and for the production of a breathable atmosphere, along with powerful energy condensers. We are completely safe there from the most redoubtable Martian animals, and we would also be able to withstand legions of giant Zoomorphs.

There is a striking contrast between the regions where the Zoomorphs reign and the regions where the Martian flora and fauna still persist. Only the mineral is manifest in one part, save for the Zoomorphs, which themselves seem to be minerals endowed with life.

An infinitely desolate plain extends to a chain of mountains. There is no movable soil there, nothing but hard bleak rock, a bare and—apparently—utterly sterile desert. In reality, there is an extraordinary fecundity, since an innumerable Zoomorph population finds the elements necessary to its subsistence there.

We know that all Zoomorphs, even those that draw energy from others, can subsist without any other alimentation than that supplied by the ground. The species that remain immobile are not, like our plants, attached to the ground. Moreover, the immobility is never complete; if their displacements escaped us at first, it is because they are only perceptible over a very long period; Zoomorphs of that sort advance at half a millimeter an hour, little more than a centimeter a day, while others, especially the giants, attain fantastic speeds of more than 100 kilometers an hour. It is understandable that a first approximation, like that of the beginning of our preceding voyage, had made us think that the great majority of the Zoomorphs were fixed to the soil. We had never stayed long to watch the same individuals, even for an hour.

As for zoomorph generation, we are still far from understanding its mechanism. On the one hand, it is very slow. On the other, it involves groups. There is no trace of sex, nor of individual reproduction. The groups seem to give rise to scattered corpuscles—a sort of dust in the bosom of which almost imperceptible nebulae form, confused sketches whose evolution is too slow for it to be followed conveniently. It will take a long time for us to arrive at any precise notion of it.

One day, I was dreaming at the junction of two locations, one rich, comparable to terrestrial life, the other despairingly desolate. Zoomorphs were circulating in every direction, but not crossing the boundary that separated their bleak zone from the vegetated zone.

A giant Zoomorph, 50 meters long, found itself in confrontation with the most monstrous of the Martian animals, as massive as an Earthly rhinoceros but with longer legs. There was a striking contrast between the organism flattened against the ground, which was reminiscent of a bug as vast as the shadow of a sperm whale or a blue whale, and the enormous carnivore, three meters tall, clad in red silk, its pyramidal head illuminated by six enormous eyes, like searchlight beams. The distance separating them was no more than twenty meters.

"One would think that the carnivore perceived the presence of the Zoomorph," said Violaine, who was sitting beside me.

"It's possible, Violaine, but scarcely probable. I don't think any emanation reveals the Zoomorph's presence, and its appearance is as mineral as the ground on which it rests. If the carnivore were conscious of the other's life, it would know that Zoomorphs have means at their disposal against which it is powerless."

"What if it were very stupid?"

"The level of its intelligence is only a secondary issue; instinct is sufficient. It's probable that our carnivore is unaware of the presence of the enemy, and vice versa, unless it's simply indifferent. Remember your adventure, Violaine."

"I remember. My presence was recognized at a distance."

"And you were attacked—like us, in fact. I'm therefore inclined to believe that it's necessary to be in their domain for the Zoomorphs to attack, and the idea gives rise to more than one conjecture. Outside of their zone, they don't perceive anything, or everything in the other zone leaves them indifferent—or, finally, their fluidity is much less effective there. Notice that that the frontier is not crossed from either side, under normal circumstances. The ground presumably informs the two reigns, but it's perfectly normal that, being strangers to all Martian evolution, nothing warns us except for the different appearance of the zones."

I fell silent, charmed by Violaine's presence. Her somber beauty was sumptuous that day: the beauty of daughters of Iberia, which envelops them with a voluptuous aura. Terrestrial dreams rose up: the odor of young leaves, lawns and wild roses. I remembered a summer evening when Regulus was about to set in the west. Young women dressed in white appeared in the starry gloom. Their luminous dresses accelerated the rhythm of my arteries. Like them, Violaine was a symbol of all human joys, the innumerable legend that has mingled with universal love.

A slight anguish was mingled with the charm: the fear of never seeing the Earth again. It would take so little to banish us to a world lost in the depths of space.

"Violaine," I murmured, agitatedly, "when shall we find ourselves once again on the bank of a river among tall Gothic poplars, while a landscape of Old France extends to the distant hills?"

I had gripped her small hand. I drew her toward me gently, and her long hair spilled over my shoulder. I plunged my face into it as if into a wave.

"I'm not unhappy here," she said. "I like the violent contrast between the two locations. We'll dream about that coppery lake, that forest, those red meadows and those fantastic beasts in future, and we'll feel nostalgic."

394

"That's true—all the more so because this is the world of our betrothal."

I hugged her to my bosom, instinct mounting tumultuously, but Violaine pulled away gently. I had never loved her as much.

"Here's the *Stellarium*," she said.

Our ship was already settling in the vicinity of the blockhouse. Antoine, Jean, the Implicit Chief and Grace emerged.

"We've identified two regions strongly threatened by Zoomorphs," said Antoine. "The invasions never take place everywhere, which is difficult to explain but of little importance; it's necessary to engage in a serious battle at the threatened points."

"I wonder..." Jean began. He did not finish. He shook his head with a feeble smile.

"What do you wonder?"

"Chimeras," Jean said. "I often think about it. An intervention by the Ethereals?"

"A lovely idea!" Violaine exclaimed.

The Implicit Chief watched us talking, but the movement of our lips told him nothing. Grace had drawn near to me, and her atmosphere poured delight into my entire being. As usual, whenever she was present, the anxiety mingled with the brightest of our hours disappeared. I translated Jean's words for her.

"What a magnificent hope!" she replied. Then, with slight melancholy: "But there's no link between them and other living things."

"We can talk to them, Grace."

"You can talk to them!"

I told her about the fabulous adventure; she followed my gestures, stunned by astonishment. "It's obvious," she said, "that we're nothing compared to the inhabitants of the Earth."

Jean, Antoine and Violaine, with the Implicit Chief, had just gone into the back room of the blockhouse.

"For me, you are the supreme beauty of life," I said.

Her charming head inclined toward my shoulder. "Why are you so much closer to my life than the others?" she won-

395

dered. "Even with my eyes closed, I'm aware of your presence; it penetrates me, while theirs is as imperceptible as if it were invisible!"

While she was speaking, I had closed my eyes, and I knew then that I too had no need to see her. There was, therefore, a fantastic affinity between us, more penetrating than the strongest affinity between two terrestrial beings.

"What have I done to deserve this?"

"When you close your eyes, Grace, can you perceive the presence of your own kind?"

"No," she replied.

"Not even when you're in love?"

A sort of gilded pallor spread over her face; I learned subsequently that it was a sign of confusion like blushing in humans.

"When I'm in love, yes."

An irresistible force impelled me to ask: "Do you love me as you love them?"

"Like them, and differently."

I could have said the same thing. I loved her with both a lover's love and a love that bore no resemblance to any other sentiment, just as the sensuality born merely of the contact of our breasts did not resemble any of our coarse human sensualities.

We rejoined my companions and the Implicit Chief, who were all very animated, but the discussion had ended.

"Why not begin immediately?" said Violaine, who was more impatient than the rest of us.

"Yes, why not?" Antoine replied.

Our friend Jean contented himself with saying: "Let's go!"

A few minutes later, having crossed the equator, we were far away from the agamic forest again, on the hill where we usually conversed with the Ethereals; they would have responded to signals sent from elsewhere, but it was here that we had assembled the apparatus necessary for our communications.

It was the middle of the night. The two satellites of Mars were visible, but their light was very faint by comparison with the light of *our* Moon. Aldebaran, Sirius and Antares—soon joined by Vega, Arcturus and some less familiar Ethereals—did not take long to appear.

The Implicit Chief watched the conversation in a state of excitement that he had never shown before. Grace was amazed and delighted—all the more so when I told her that she could speak to them in her turn, as soon as we had agreed signals necessarily as dissimilar as the Triped language was from ours, since our communications with the Ethereals, begun with the aid of a radiant transformation of Morse signals, now took the form of a triply indirect translation of our spoken language.

On that day and the following ones, we made every effort to acquaint the Ethereals with the existence of the Tripeds and with the Martian flora and fauna in general. That existence was known to them in the form I mentioned; for them, a Triped was nothing but a little radiant cloud, of which they had not conceived the collectivity, and hence the individuality. It was the same for every other plant and animal, and also for the Zoomorphs.

The knowledge that they had of our terrestrial organisms had to facilitate their knowledge of Martians—which inevitably seemed to be a curious inversion of normality. Up to a certain point, the groundwork for that knowledge had been laid by our conversations, but it remained embryonic. It required, as it had for us, the collaboration of the two life-systems. We prepared the way with repeated conversations. Soon, our imponderable friends had notions of the organized existences of the planet that rapidly became coordinated.

During his time, we had prepared signals for the Implicit Chief and Grace that would permit an initial exchange of words, very restricted as yet, with the Ethereals. In consequence, we understood everything they said to one another, but it was possible to talk to either party while only being understood by that one.

397

The Ethereals had been informed of the conflict with the Zoomorphs, but they had reservations.

"We don't know whether we can help you," said Aldebaran, while Antares added: "We must not give false hope to our friends."

XI.

The Tripeds had constructed a second blockhouse for us, half a league from the zone where the Zoomorph invasion was taking on redoubtable proportions. That zone was among the most fertile of the regions occupied by the Martians. In truth, the latter lived mainly in a series of caverns rich in beneficent energies, but they cultivated the surface.

We had found plants there which, once submitted to transformative apparatus, gave us a healthy and sometimes flavorsome nourishment.

The equipment from the first blockhouse was transported to the second, while the caverns furnished us with a limitless supply of the materials needed to produce oxygen and nitrogen—with the result that the blockhouse was provided with an atmosphere similar to the terrestrial atmosphere, save for the rare gases.

"Isn't this the happiness of Crusoes?" said Violaine one morning, as she served us coffee with slices of bread and pancakes made from a product furnished by the Martian flora, which were not dissimilar to buckwheat pancakes.

"No doubt," I replied. "All the elements of a modest Eden are assembled here."

"Speak for yourself," muttered Antoine. "For us, it still lacks something!"

I did not believe that he was suffering from that dearth, but Jean sometimes became thoughtful. Violaine and I exchanged a furtive glance. Antoine laughed sardonically, but in an amicable fashion, and a slight redness showed on the young woman's face.

Our love had remained pure, though; we were respectful of the ancient laws of terrestrial society, which are increasingly less respected. Had not almost all of humankind accepted union free of social sanction? Why should a few peoples, especially ours, retain a decrepit morality? And even while respecting them, did we not have new rights, at the distance we were from our planet?

In fact, I waited without impatience; terrestrial sensuality seemed so gross, compared to the radiant sensuality of my Martian love. I preferred to love Violaine without recourse to the singular gestures of procreation; I savored the quintessences of our adventure by bringing them closer to my adventure with Grace.

Eight days before, we had entered into conflict with the Zoomorphs—a conflict still localized, restricted to the most endangered point. The local Tripeds were working ardently to construct the necessary radiant devices. There was no lack of energy, drawn from the caverns. They revealed themselves to be skillful, and quick to understand, but lacking in initiative. Delighted by the initial results of our campaign, they showed us a keen, submissive and mystical affection.

"Let's go see where we are!" said Jean.

It required no more than five minutes of walking to reach the vicinity of the frontier. It was not that we had hastened our steps—on the contrary, we had slowed them down.

"Now I've got into the habit," Jean remarked, "the lightness of our bodies has become quite pleasant."

"It's almost as if we had wings," added Violaine.

"Wings on our feet, like Hermes."

On our arrival, Tripeds had gathered, among whom was a giant, one of the local chiefs, who already possessed the rudiments of the language created with the Implicit Chief.

"A few days ago, this territory was still entirely ours," the colossus remarked

"It will be once again, this evening," Jean replied, "And they've not yet had time to denature the soil."

"In any case," said Antoine, "the damage can be quickly repaired by transporting soil here."

We went to the invaded area, followed by a small crowd, agitated but silent by nature. The Zoomorphs were swarming among the grasses and trees. The flood of small ones had been joined by two of large size. Jean amused himself by bombarding them with Dussault rays. They gave signs of agitation and made as if to return to the bare ground from which they had come.

The little scene excited the Tripeds, who pressed around us, full of enthusiasm.

We gave a few instructions to the giant, for organizing the recovery of the ground where it was still possible. He understood us all the better for having been the first to plant defensive radiators.

"Are you not threatened as we are on your own world?" he asked.

"We're still in the victorious period that your ancestors once knew. We have dominion over the large animals but the smaller ones still resist, especially the smallest of all—and we fear the invisible ones."

"The invisible ones?" said the Triped. "We're unaware of those. If they exist, they don't do us any harm."

"Perhaps the Ethereals have destroyed them," Violaine suggested, in sonorous language.

"That's an idea!" cried Antoine. "If that's true, it gives me more confidence in the cooperation of our immaterial friends."

The defensive operations made rapid progress. A crew of Tripeds, led by the Implicit Chief, was not participating in the work and completing the instruction of the others.

Soon, a barrage a hundred kilometers long was mounted against the Zoomorphs. The system that fuelled the radiators had been improved; the machines were solid and would last a long time. Furthermore, the Tripeds had learned how to maintain and repair them.

After a few days of observation, which had permitted them to investigate the structure of the Zoomorphs, the Ethereals attempted discharges of radiation. We watched the first attacks along with Grace, the Implicit Chief, the local chief and a crowd that had gathered from all directions.

I shall always remember that night. The Earth was at its brightest; we contemplated that beautiful green-gold star delightedly, while Jupiter, brighter here than on our own planet, rose above the horizon and the moons of Mars moved vertiginously.

A legion of Ethereals had answered the appeal. Above our heads, Aldebaran, Sirius, Antares, Arcturus and Vega formed a fascinating mobile constellation, while three of the stars whose names we had attributed to them were sparkling in the sky. A hundred Ethereals assembled over the segment chosen for the initial experiment, then descended to less than 50 meters from the ground. A flood of visible and invisible radiations sprayed the Zoomorphs, causing a violent disorder among the smallest—which, after moving in every direction, fled precipitately toward the desert zone. The medium-sized Zoomorphs only gave slight signs of agitation, and the giants remained motionless. We were a little disappointed, especially Jean and Violaine. The Tripeds remained impassive.

"It's semi-successful," Jean murmured.

"It's too soon to draw any conclusion," Antoine riposted, placidly.

At the same moment, Vega told us: "Our attack was not sufficiently intense. Wait for the second attempt."

Signals were exchanged among the Ethereals; soon, more than a thousand more joined the initial aggressors.

From then on, the clearance was rapid. Fifteen or 20 Ethereals attacked each giant Zoomorph simultaneously, and the latter were not long delayed in retreating at speed. As for the small and medium-sized Zoomorphs, they were swept away in a trice.

New Ethereals having joined the "scouts," the recently-invaded zone was soon liberated.

A frenetic joy gripped the Tripeds. The Implicit Chief lost his calmness, and Grace was tremulous with enthusiasm. We Terrans looked on, marveling.

"But there's nothing to prevent the Zoomorphs from coming back," Antoine remarked, "later, if not right away. The Ethereals can't dedicate themselves perpetually to their expulsion."

Aldebaran's voice was heard at that moment—remember that our friends the Ethereals, although using radiations to speak to us, all had their own voices—explaining to us that a small minority of the Ethereals were interested in the fate of the Tripeds. The others showed little inclination to expend energy on their behalf. A large number did not think that they ought to discriminate between Tripeds and Zoomorphs. "It's because of you—because you made the effort to communicate with us—that a group is attempting to aid your friends."

"You're abandoning the conflict, then?" said, Jean, anxiously.

The voice of Sirius was heard in its turn. "No! We hope to be able to render the Triped frontiers inaccessible to the Zoomorphs by penetrating them with a weak, but effective and stable, energy."

The Ethereals did not attempt to make us understand their project. In the meantime, the apparatus that we had created for the Tripeds, once put into operation, would suffice to maintain the positions acquired.

XII.

Jean had conceived a plan to grow Martian plants on Earth, and even to transport a few small animals there.

"It won't be easy to feed them on the way," said Antoine.

"That's what I'm proposing to study," Jean retorted.

"Really?" said Antoine.

The idea seduced Violaine. There were two quintupeds, in particular, that she dreamed of transplanting, one with a helicoids muzzle, brightened by magnificent eyes and clad in scarlet, the other the color of old gold. These animals, about the size of a domestic cat, were meek and herbivorous, for it seemed impossible to nourish the carnivores of Mars on terrestrial flesh.

We sometimes spent two or three days in the same location. The *Stellarium*, constantly guarded by one of us, was moved according to our whim. All our power and security came from the ship, and we treated it reverently. The resistance of its hull was almost limitless. It was usable for at least two or three generations; the impulsion and gravitational apparatus were invulnerable. We had a mystical confidence in it, which did not dissuade us from looking after it with rigorous prudence. The slightest flaw in its integrity might make us exiles condemned to an early death. Could we survive for more than a few seasons on Mars? Confident as I was, I experienced a terrible anguish on thinking about it.

We had established a third blockhouse in an area neighboring Zoomorph zones. Like the first, it was equipped with oxygen generators, condensers and gravity-field compensators. The Tripeds had helped us with all the accessory installations, which demanded hard labor but which, thanks to them, were promptly concluded—with the result that, including the *Stellarium*, we possessed four sound shelters.

We had also constructed three helicopters, which permitted swift journeys without recourse to the *Stellarium*. Grace and the Implicit Chief often accompanied us in our explorations; their collaboration was precious to us—especially that of the young Triped female, who was endowed with more intuition than her fellows. Her mere presence continued to dispense all the noblest and purest enchantments to me.

One afternoon, Jean, Violaine and I were out walking not far from the second blockhouse; we were collecting seeds that Jean thought particularly apt at maintaining themselves for a long time without alteration—about which he was not mistaken.

Antoine was guarding the *Stellarium*.

We were wandering among giant trees, as tall as Australian Eucalyptus trees, which they did not resemble at all. They were widely separated from one another, with the result that we could see the locale clearly for a long way.

I was leaning over a violet plant when I heard Violaine say: "The *Stellarium*'s taking off."

That did not astonish me unduly; nevertheless, I raised my head. Not only had the *Stellarium* taken off, but it was climbing rapidly, reaching a considerable altitude within a minute.

"What's Antoine doing?" I exclaimed.

"Antoine is the wisest of us," Jean replied. "He must have his reasons."

The *Stellarium* continued to climb; it was shrinking with every passing second, and also drawing away laterally. Soon, it was almost invisible. Finally, it disappeared.

We experienced dread, then fear, and then terror. We looked at one another, pale and livid.

"Antoine's lost in space," Jean moaned. "He's lost control of the apparatus—something's gone awry."

Despair grew in our hearts. Antoine would perish in the boundless expanse and we, exiled, could do nothing but await death, after an agony whose slowness would render it more lamentable.

How beautiful that Earth appeared to me! The memories were rising up, innumerably: infancy; youth; those that I loved and had loved; the fine mornings when life begins again; the greenery of spring; the waters, source of all life, which always delighted me; dream-like dusks; winters when refuge is so sweet; adventures great and small...

Oh, never to see that again, to expire miserably on an ingrate planet, devoured by desert! There was Grace, though, who would have rendered life acceptable, even marvelous, if life on Mars were not impossible...

An hour has passed, as long as several days. We have taken refuge in the blockhouse. At least we have installed all the apparatus necessary to condense Martian air here, and also oxygen generators. With our helicopters, we can rejoin Grace and the Implicit Chief, and take refuge in the first blockhouse, whose equipment is more complete than that of the second...

Two hours have passed. All appearance of hope has passed. We don't have the strength to talk to one another. Jean, so prompt to react, seems more downhearted than me, and Violaine is devastated.

Evening has come. The worlds and the Ethereals are shining in the sky, and we can see the Earth, a gilded emerald, the sight of which fills us with mortal anguish.

Jean's voice emerges from the shadows: "Should we inform *them*?" He means our terrestrial friends, to whom we send news periodically.

"Not yet, Jean. What good would it do to worry them prematurely? There'll be plenty of time to inform them of our distress."

"How long can we live here?" Violaine asks.

"About three months—longer, if we succeed in further improving the nutriments we obtain from Mars."

These nutriments are as yet only a supplement; they provide some energy, but only a few of the substances necessary to repair tissues.

"We'll succeed in improving them," Jean affirms. "I have a few experiments in mind. In any case, I hope that they'll permit us to eke out our terrestrial nutriments considerably."

"Is it impossible that anyone might come to our rescue?"

"There are other *Stellariums*."

"None of which are as good as ours."

"New ones were being constructed when we left. Perhaps, then…"

A wave of despair ebbs and flows again; then distress takes hold again, more profoundly.

"Try to sleep for a few hours," Jean advises us. "I'll take the first watch."

Sleep! Is that possible?

Thoughts and sensations, born of one another, unfurl in tumult. One idea covers me with cold sweat, another awakens multitudes of images and hopes. Will it be necessary to wait for the moment when, the last vestiges of hope having been extinguished, we will sink fatally? I don't know—and what does it matter?

But what if Earth comes to our rescue after all?

Violaine, Grace…they float in the mist. A love as sad as death envelops me. Oh, poor Violaine! I can still see her out there, a little human made for a long life, so adept at happiness, whom our weakness has led to death.

I've been asleep. Youth. In the fog of semi-wakefulness I am able to think that I am on Earth: a virgin forest, a river, my old half-wild garden, the odor of morning…

A start, a surge of the heart; reality has gripped me again. I find myself on a dying world. The Earth is lost!

It's still the middle of the night. Through the little window I see the sky swarming with Ethereals, Vaguely, I search—for the thousandth time—to imagine their sentiments, their thoughts, their dreams…nascent chimeras. Who know whether they might be able to help us? Impossible. They have no idea of weight, of our movements, of our efforts, of our mechanisms. All of that is an excessively slow rhythm—and besides, they're not technologists.

A voice emerges from the shadows—Jean's. "Ought we to warn Earth? Its position is favorable tonight."

"It will be just as favorable tomorrow," I reply.

"I understand! You still hope to see Antoine again. Not me. We would have seen him some time ago, if it had been possible for him to return."

"I'm no more hopeful than you—all the same, it's better to wait another day."

"Let's wait, then!"

Dark insomnia. All my nerves are taut; periodically, my heart leaps like a wild beast. I could be happy here, though, if it were possible to survive. Violaine, terrestrial love; Grace, the miracle. I no longer have any relatives over there but a brother who doesn't much like me, and whom I rarely see. Oh, if it were not for the Earth, the astral fatherland, Grace could console me.

Dreams as vain as those of a man afflicted by a mortal illness.

An internal fog. My being floats between sleep and wakefulness; reality is lost in a fantastic unreality.

A voice wakes me up—neither Jean's voice nor Violaine's. I leap to my feet. Impossible! But yes, it really is Antoine's voice, only slightly altered by the loudspeaker. Jean is already standing up in the darkness. Violaine comes running.

"It's really Antoine's voice!" cries Jean.

"Here we are, Antoine."

"I'll be on Mars within a minute," Antoine replies. "Light up the blockhouse."

In the obscurity that envelops the planet—for the Martians live without light at night—the blockhouse shines forth. The minute passes, so short and so long, and then there is a great light in the firmament.

Scarcely a few seconds more, and the *Stellarium* settles down lightly, a short distance away from the blockhouse.

Antoine appears, as calm as usual. We cluster around him, in the delight of salvation—mingled, in me, with retrospective fear.

"What happened?" asked Jean. "The *Stellarium*…"

"The *Stellarium* is safe and sound. Until now it has not suffered the slightest damage, and that was what saved me. It followed a straight line, inflexibly."

"The accident happened to you, then?"

"Yes, me. A stupid accident. I had a sore throat; instead of a remedy, I mistakenly took a soporific. I'm very sensitive to such drugs. All in all, one of those errors that is unpardonable. When I woke up again, it took me some time to understand what had happened. In sum, I very nearly condemned us all to death! I humbly ask your forgiveness."

"You don't deserve it," said Jean, who had recovered his natural good humor.

It was one of the great moments of our lives. We remained silent for some time, overwhelmed by happiness. Never before had I perceived so profoundly our individual weakness compared with the enormous power of humankind. We were the same paltry creatures as in the times when our ancestors struggled unrelentingly for their subsistence, in the bosom of a world in which living beings devoured one another, in which the plain and the forest resounded incessantly with cries of agony. Although all that has gone, although our species has triumphed insolently over its ancient rivals, although the most powerful only live by the good will of the victors, every member of that prodigious assembly is merely a puff of smoke—and that assembly, in its turn, is merely a fugitive cloud.

XIII.

Only six or seven weeks of our sojourn here remain. We could prolong our stay but that would be dangerous; Antoine is formally opposed to it. That is the wisdom and also the honesty of each companion. The deliberation has been lengthy. Jean, always inclined to risk, ended up submitting to necessity, and Violaine too. It has been necessary to resign myself to it—with what sadness!

408

The idea of no longer seeing Grace is unbearable, even more so than on the first voyage. She has become so dear to me! Such accord, so complete an intimacy, would be impossible with a human creature. On contact with her, I acquire new vital properties; her atmosphere penetrates me intimately; she too has been subjected to a subtle metamorphosis which has drawn her nearer to my humanity. In the infinite universe, we surely form a couple that is unique, by virtue of the fusion of such dissimilar mentalities, and a certain vague resemblance.

Must I really leave her? Now that she has transformed the energies of my being, that seems to me to be a form of suicide; for a long time, the life I lived on Earth will seem a restricted form of life. The new powers of my being will be lost there; I must abandon the admirable creature who caused their birth.

Could she live on Earth? She supports the air-pressure aboard the *Stellarium* without difficulty, but she has only stayed here for short periods of time. If she died, I would believe that I had committed the most abominable crime.

It would certainly not be impossible to create a dwelling for her usage over there, and—for going out—an apparatus similar to the one we employ here, but opposite in effect, rarefying instead of concentrating.

I shall always remember this summer morning. It will appear softer, gentler, more charming, on the edge of the lake, amid a strange vegetation that is, from an Earthly viewpoint, the vegetation of the Secondary Era. Except that here, it is not a vegetation of primitive times, but of the final ages.

A troop of green and red herbivores grazes the bank; Aerians pass overhead, and an abyssal faun appears in the heavy water.

We walk slowly, in total security; I am armed with powerful ray-guns.

How happy we could have been! And even now, the future ceases to be redoubtable in my companion's atmosphere.

I have pronounced the word of great melancholy: departure. It has sounded the knell. "How I would like to see the Earth with you!" says Grace, imploringly.

For a long time, that has seemed impossible; then, intoxicated by her moving presence, I wonder if it really is impossible. Why should we not make a third voyage to Mars, in order to bring her back?

Violaine, Jean and even Antoine have mentioned the possibility. With apparatus constructed on the basis of our experiments, we could easily prolong the sojourn. As well as Grace, the Implicit Chief ardently desires to see the Earth, all the more so because he has no fear of death being entirely resigned to it.

I say to Grace: "I dread that, if anything happened to you, I would be unable to survive you."

She remains pensive momentarily; then her desire and her youth carry her away. "Nothing will happen to me!"

The embrace; the imponderable sensuality.

Finally, the voice of Aldebaran was heard. It was there with Vega and Antares, at a low altitude. It said: "We've found it!"

Those three notes invaded me with an almost painful resonances—followed by a purely joyous reaction. Violaine's small hand squeezed mine, while Aldebaran continued.

"We can create a zone along the edges of the Triped regions that the Zoomorphs will be unable to cross. Our trials are conclusive. In a few days, you'll have the proof of it—and very little energy will be required to perpetuate our work."

"Is it radiation?" Jean asked, avidly.

"It is radiation—a composite radiation that it will be easy to make known to you, which you can reproduce without overmuch difficulty. The Tripeds can also learn to produce it, and from then on will be in control of their destiny."

"Will they be able to reconquer territory?"

"Only the most recently invaded."

410

I approved of that. It did not seem to me to be desirable that a relatively young realm, perhaps in progress toward great achievements, should be annihilated by a realm whose environmental conditions were bound to disappear eventually. It was sufficient for me that the Tripeds would continue to survive without fear of premature annihilation. They asked for no more themselves.

One morning—it was, at least, morning in the sector where the *Stellarium* was at rest—the great news spread throughout the planet. The Zoomorphs were in retreat everywhere, leaving a neutral zone of varying width.

A multitude of Tripeds gathered around the *Stellarium*, making expansive gesture, exhibiting an enthusiasm rare among those resigned creatures. They had no difficulty making themselves understood; our knowledge of their language had increased greatly. Besides, the Implicit Chief had just arrived in his glider, with Grace, and was showing us his joyous gratitude.

It was a surprise on the part of the Ethereals; they had chosen to act before alerting us.

"Our species is saved!" signed the Implicit Chief, with an ardor extraordinary in that calm being.

Grace's multiple eyes gave off dazzling gleams. "The messengers from Earth have brought new life," she said.

"We mustn't rejoice too soon."

Meanwhile, Antoine was speaking to the Ethereals, invisible in the daylight. Successively, we heard the unreal voices of Sirius, Vega and Aldebaran. "We must wait," said the last-named. "It's only an experiment as yet."

"It's probable, though, that it's conclusive," Antares interjected.

"Well," I said, "let's go to the night side."

Thousands of Tripeds were crowding around the *Stellarium*. We did not have the courage to pass on the Ethereals' warnings. Then we told the latter of our desire to see them in the nocturnal sky. They consented to follow the *Stellarium*, which carried us to the other hemisphere, along with Grace and the Implicit Chief.

Soon the nocturnal sky appeared—the beautiful Martian sky of giant stars, as Violaine proclaimed, hyperbolically.

Our radiant friends were already waiting for us; to the anxious questions of the Implicit Chief—which we translated—Aldebaran replied: "If you succeed in understanding the radiation that has chased away the Zoomorphs, you can utilize it, and the Martians who come after you."

"Why not?" Jean exclaimed. "We've done more difficult things in order to enter into communication with them, ever more subtly. We shall succeed."

Antoine limited himself to nodding his head, but Violaine cried: "They'll know how to make us understand!"

I had taken up my astronomical telescope; I contemplated our native planet tenderly—and I always came back to the same thought: "If I could only take Grace there!"

Violaine pressed lightly upon my shoulder. Terrestrial love had awoken within her; I savored it gladly—but could it suffice to make Grace' absence bearable?

The rhythm of Ethereal life, so much more rapid than ours, accomplished progressions of thought in two or three days that would have taken us years.

We were delighted, but scarcely astonished, when Sirius announced to us that the experiment had definitely succeeded and that the Ethereals had already charged the ground with energies that would prevent the advance of the Zoomorphs at all points for a long time. They invited us to study the useful radiation, and especially its means of employment. I must confess that we could never form a clear idea of the radiation itself, but we were able to determine the manner of its usage and construct the first apparatus capable of producing and utilizing it.

For the Tripeds, it was now only a matter of imitating us with subtlety and precision, in which they were even more adept than humans. It was then evident that the part of Mars occupied by the Tripeds would be forbidden to Zoomorphs for many centuries—which awoke as much enthusiasm and hope in them as their passive nature permitted.

The date of the departure drew nearer; we had informed the people of Earth, who were now waiting for us with an ardent impatience.

It was finally necessary to make the great resolution.

Should the Implicit Chief and Grace go with us? They both seemed determined, all the more so when they heard that we would return to Mars the following year.

We deliberated for a long time. It was their lives that they and we would be risking. Antoine analyzed the situation with his habitual phlegm.

"The risk of the crossing is their affair. Have we not run it twice already?"

"It was especially great on the first voyage," Jean remarked.

"Obviously. All the same, it remains no less great—more's the pity. It's up to them to decide. But the sojourn on Earth makes greater demands on our responsibility. We've only stayed here four months."

"And eleven days."

"They'll have to remain on Earth for a year. Will they stand up to it? Could we do that here? Finally, there's the grave question of nutrition."

"I contend that it's resolved," said Jean.

We had certainly completed experiments—undertaken over a long period—with a view to nourishing the Tripeds with terrestrial aliments. There were some that they digested quite naturally, which could not help but astonish us. Others became assimilable for them after a few modifications. Moreover, as the Tripeds eat very little, we could carry Martian provisions, which, after desiccation, would replace the fraction of our provisions used up during our sojourn. The indefinite resources of terrestrial laboratories would surely permit effective transformations. Had we not succeeded in rendering a few Martian plants assimilable for ourselves?

"Won't the sojourn itself be deadly to them?" Antoine asked.

"That's the question. Note that they don't experience any malaise when they accompany us in the *Stellarium* at a pressure of 750 millimeters."

"Let them decide!" Antoine concluded. "They can, in any case, return here with us or others. Our voyages have provoked emulations. Who knows whether the *Stellariums* that are being constructed back there might not be better than ours? Normally, they would be."

"Yes, since we're already envisaging improvements ourselves. Earth-Mars voyages will become regular events."

"And soon banal."

We spent some time initiating the Tripeds into the new means of defense against the Zoomorphs; they understood us very well, and a kind of rejuvenation was manifest among the resigned creatures.

One morning, the Implicit Chief declared: "Grace and I are determined to make the crossing, if you'll allow it."

"You've considered everything?"

"Yes—the journey is worth the risks."

Antoine insisted on explaining the dangers of a sojourn on Earth once again. He did not want to listen, and Grace proved to be even more determined than he was. We finally gave in. The success of our two expeditions had made us optimistic.

"Oh, how happy I am!" Grace said to me.

I was happy too, intensely—with pangs of anxiety.

When everything was ready for the journey, we said our farewells to the Ethereals. We had conceived a kind of sublimated affection for the ones most familiar to us, especially Aldebaran, Vega, Sirius and Antares. Perhaps it was mutual. It seemed that they vaguely regretted our departure, though not ardently. They promised to watch over the Triped lands.

The morning of the departure arrived. It had not been announced in advance. The Implicit Chief and Grace took leave of their close kin, without any pathos. Because of the resignation that underlies their sentimentality, they have no ardent affection. Mild, patient and inoffensive by nature, passion scarcely excites them, and has not for thousands of years. The relatives of the Implicit Chief and Grace seemed barely unaffected—but the scene would, I think, have been more disturbing if Grace's mother had not vanished into the eternal night a long time before.

The departure of the *Stellarium* and its pilots appeared to make a deeper impression than that of my young friends. We had become the protectors of the species, and when the Implicit Chief announced our probable return there was a veritable explosion of joy.

"You have no regrets, Grace?" I asked, a few minutes before take-off.

"I regret leaving far less than I rejoice in it."

"In any case, if the sojourn on Earth, or even in the *Stellarium*, inconveniences you, we can bring you back."

Her eyes were shining like beacons.

Antoine gave the signal to lift-off.

XIV.

All the peoples of Earth were awaiting the arrival of the *Stellarium* with quivering enthusiasm. From one pole to the other, on mountain-sides, plains, the depths of forests and islands in remote regions of the oceans, the great news was known: people were going to see the strange beings that did not resemble our species, but played a role on Mars comparable to that of humans on Earth.

Interplanetary communication, ensured by more powerful and subtler apparatus than during our first journey, had been terse, precise and frequent. Logophones and periodicals recounted the vicissitudes of the incredible sojourn. Everyone knew, in fact, but they wanted to see. Innumerable sky-screens were to show the Implicit Chief and Grace to the entire Earth as clearly as if they were present before the spectators' eyes.

Grace and the Implicit Chief had watched the Earth increase in size. They could see better than we could, with or without telescopes; their vision far surpassed ours in acuity, delicacy and means of accommodation.

Grace awaited the moment of touchdown with a delight mingled with dread. She had withstood the journey well; the Tripeds' respiratory organs, I repeat, have an incomparable power of adaptation; they automatically regulate the quantity of air aspired, and support considerable changes of pressure without sustaining any damage. In consequence, our hosts would not suffer from the change of atmosphere—but would they withstand the climate as easily? It was probable. On Mars, whenever they leave their well-warmed tunnels, they resist very low temperatures. In general, Martians are more durable than Terrans, doubtless due to the particular evolution of their planet.

XV.

When we were no more than 200 kilometers from Earth, we reduced the *Stellarium*'s velocity—which was already much diminished—considerably.

As we had planned, we were flying over France. Its fields, forests, mountains and the great liquid plain of the Atlantic moved us to tears, while a marvelous ecstasy was manifest in Grace's shining face and multiple gazes.

"How young the world is!" the grave and pensive Implicit Chief said, eventually. "One would think that it had just been born…"

The Tripeds were even more charmed than astonished by the waters—seas, lakes and rivers—and the flow and movement of their waves.

"Here, everything can always begin again," said Grace. "Always!"

Meanwhile, Violaine, who was leaning on my shoulder, murmured: "It's true that everything here is young—even an old city like Paris, thanks to its young river, its canals and its gardens."

We were no longer alone; clouds of vortices and gliders came from every direction. My father,[63] Jean and Violaine's mother and Antoine's parents and brother escorted us, along with known and unknown friends. Grace lowered her head, intimidated, but the Implicit Chief admired the human power of the flying multitude. Behind our transparent walls, we were as visible as in the open air, and airborne reporters were taking photographs of our guests with an indiscreet ardor.

"I understand that they're wonderstruck," said Jean, "but they're annoying me."

"The other side of the coin!" Antoine added.

The multitude increased with time, troubling the joy of the return, which we had wanted to be gentle and welcoming.

"They might leave us to our families!" exclaimed Violaine. Our families did, however, form a kind of barrier.

With the aid of magnetic dishes, we exchanged a few hasty and tender words, but as several people were speaking at the same time, the conversation could not be other than confused.

Finally, the crowd became intolerable; we arranged to meet our families and close friends in my old house at Yvette and flew over the spectators.

For ten days, however, we were obliged to suffer the indiscretion of the curious and reporters.

---

[63] The reader will probably remember, although the author obviously does not, that the narrator has previously informed us—as recently as chapter XII—that his father is dead.

After the initial alarm, Grace and the Implicit Chief tolerated the importunity of the Terrestrials without too much irritation. Seeing only benevolence in the visitors and curiosity-seekers, they even found a certain pleasure in it. Soon, however, the curiosity was appeased, and we had entire days without visitors. I made excursions with Jean, Grace, Violaine and the Implicit Chief, sometimes by land and sometimes by air. Sometimes, the aquaplane set down on a river or a lake, and that was perhaps what Grace and Violaine preferred.

"It seems to me," said Grace, "that I have returned to a very ancient existence, the memory of which is like a dream."

"Even for us," Violaine replied, "the skies evoke times that have disappeared into the prehistoric night."

"And God separated the inferior waters from the superior waters!" Jean intoned.

We observed a singular evolution of sensitivity in our guests. The resigned inertia characteristic of Martians, the apathy of beings who accept their degeneration, decreased from day to day. The Implicit Chief, formerly so placid, manifested more inclination to strong emotion every way. He was conscious of it. "Even in my childhood," he said, "I was never as young as I am now."

For Grace, it was a magical world. Even more than her father, she led a new life, the charm of which increased continually. She sought out the company of Violaine, who enchanted her, and Violaine submitted to Grace's attraction. The three of us often went out together; my two loves mingled strangely, so dissimilar and yet confused in the same universal origin. I tried to analyze my sentiments, but ran into a wall of darkness. It seemed that Grace's enchanted atmosphere augmented my love for Violaine, and it is certain that I never loved my fiancée more than when the three of us were together.

The day of the wedding drew closer. Grace awaited it impatiently. It seemed that it was her own marriage that was about to be celebrated. A strange mental transposition made her want to see a son of my descendancy, as if she would be giving birth to him herself—and when I told her that, she replied: "I'm sure that he will be attached to me by a filial link. He will bear something of my race. Oh, you have nothing to fear—it will be purely internal...and yet, if ever he makes a voyage to Mars, he will feel almost an exile here!"

She spoke with an infectious exaltation. Her beautiful eyes shot forth enchanted gleams. I had no alternative but to share her singular illusion...

Our marriage was a world-wide event, the explorers of Mars being famous throughout the world, and travelers arrived from all parts of the globe. Myriads of machines filled the sky. Around our house their number, arranged in several layers, was so great that the sky could only be seen through a few narrow gaps. By night, their beacons spread a blinding light.

I found myself alone with Grace as the hour approached when I would meet Violaine. She was radiant. She pressed herself against me, embracing me for a long time, and a strange energy was added to the happiness that overwhelmed me.

"You will love her all the more for it," said the Martian female, "and I shall..."

I only found out the following day what she had decided to do, and I rejoined Violaine, simultaneously intoxicated by Martian and terrestrial love.

The next day, I got up before my wife, and found Grace waiting for me. Her enchanting eyes were full of tenderness.

"You're happy," she said. "I love your happiness. Did you think of me a little?"

"I'm always thinking about you, Grace."

She seemed to hesitate momentarily, while I looked at her admiringly, then said: "Would you like a child of mine—a child that will have retained a part of your radiance?" When I did not reply, in surprise, she went on: "Remember that Martian women can become mothers *by themselves* when they desire it for a long time and with a great intensity. I have desired it for months, and yesterday, I desired a child with such force that *one will be born*."

What a fantastic delight overwhelmed me, augmented by contact with the young Martian female!

The health of Grace and the Implicit Chief was quite unaffected. They digested a few terrestrial nutriments, which permitted the eking out of the provisions that we had brought from Mars. Meat did not suit them, although they liked fruits and vegetables. All in all, their adaptive abilities far surpassed those we had shown on Mars.

"It's probably a sort of return to the conditions of an ancestral environment," Antoine remarked. "After all, there have been epochs on Mars when the pressure, the temperature and the creatures themselves had more analogy than present circumstances with conditions on Earth. Their physiology is, in a sense, remembering..."

"While we live on Mars," said Grace, "in an environment that might perhaps be analogous to one *yet to come* on Earth."

In order to acclimate our guests more effectively, we acquired—or, rather, the Grand Council of States granted us—a high mountain valley, to which the *Stellarium* could take us in minutes, although our vortices sufficed to travel the 500 kilometers that separated us from the refuge. We spent an initial sojourn there in one of those mobile chalets that can be set up in a few hours.

A thousand meters above the domain the eternal snows began; the valley, sheltered from the wind and easily accessible to the sunlight, remained frost-free until mid-October.

We're going to try out a few seeds here," Jean said. He had brought back a large collection of seeds of the plants he had cultivated on Mars, along with small animals, only two of which had died. The others, cared for by the Implicit Chief, proved as resistant as our Triped guests.

The latter were enjoying the new period of rest, though not as much as the long voyages across the continents, especially the ocean crossings in Antoine's Argonaut, which was sometimes a ship and sometimes a gyroplane. Sailing over those vast liquid expanses reanimated a young and magnificent life in them that had been forgotten on Mars for millennia. The long watery waves plunged them into a cosmic reverie that went as far as ecstasy.

XVI.

Thus the days, the months and two seasons went by—and then began the miracle that would create a stir over the entire planet.

Inevitably, I was the first to perceive that Grace was surrounded by an almost invisible glow. Violaine did not take long to discern it too. She said to me as the light was fading one day: "We are alone in seeing the aura that is enveloping Grace..."

"Ah!" I said. "You can see it?"

Grace was walking in the garden. As the light declined, the aura became faintly visible.

"You're thinking the same thing as me," Violaine said, smiling. "Besides, *that's not all...*"

I nodded my head.

"It will be lovely!"

That exclamation left me somewhat surprised.

"It's so beautiful, their way of being pregnant, while ours..." She lowered her head in confusion. I took her in my arms, gently. "And yet, I'm happy to be a terrestrial mother!" She remained silent for a moment, pensively. "I believe she loves us very much," she went on, in a low voice. "Especially you..."

"She only ever mentions you with enthusiasm..."

"I know that, and I have a singular affection for her—an *otherworldly* affection. Perhaps that helps me to understand the affection that she has for us. I don't know how the idea came to me that she desired a child because we are expecting one...she has a sort of love for you..."

That was so unexpected that it took my breath away. A muffled anxiety was mingled with the surprise; it would have been so painful for me if Violaine were jealous...

"You look flabbergasted!" she said. "That's only natural. What harm is there in it? It's so very different from what the love of a woman would be...and so delightfully pure! If I were a man, I believe that I would feel something like that for her..."

"Oh, Violaine...!"

"Yes, and I don't think that would prevent me in the least from loving a woman. It would be as if I loved a flower...a prodigious flower...a conscious flower. I don't know whether you can understand..."

"Yes...yes I can..." I said, with a haste that I regretted immediately.

She burst out laughing, and then became serious again. "It's certain that you're very attached to Grace. You understand it better than I do. It's you, in fact, who discovered it, so to speak. I'd already guessed it before leaving Mars."

"I didn't know that!" I stammered.

Dusk was advancing slowly. Soon, a colossal scarlet sun was poised in the gap between two hills. The neighboring village church occupied a tiny corner of the firelit surface. Little by little, the shadow of the rotating Earth devoured the star, and the festival of the clouds began...

Grace's aura was now so visible that Jean and Antoine, who had just dined with us, paused.

"I suspected as much!" Jean exclaimed. "Now I'm sure."

"Bah!" said Antoine. "I've known for a week."

"And you didn't say anything!"

"Like them," Antoine replied, phlegmatically, pointing at Violaine and me. "Anyway, I could have been mistaken—better to await confirmation. And even now, although I know that it's sufficient for Martians to desire it intensely, I'm not entirely sure of the denouement. I'm wondering why she wanted it."

"She has more than one reason!" Jean exclaimed. "The most alive of Martian women, she must desire not to be the last link in a vertiginous chain of ancestry. Notice that she's more vivacious than she was on Mars. Then again, it will be a sort of commemoration of her terrestrial sojourn—for I'm assuming that she's thinking about returning to her astral homeland. And finally, because Violaine..." He stopped, and burst out laughing.

"By way of emulation?" said Antoine.

"That, old fellow, is almost slander. I'd say out of sympathy."

"Good!" said Violaine.

We contemplated the sumptuous clouds for a while; in the distance, rivers, mountains and gulfs were slowly emerging and vanishing—and Grace, in her silvery aura, shot through with fine networks of emerald, and her huge eyes, shining more brightly than the stars, mingled a living charm with the sovereign beauty of the occidental sky.

"A marvelous mode of reproduction!" Jean murmured. "Is it not proof of the superiority of Martians, at least in terms of nature?"

"Let's steer clear of that genre of hypotheses," said Antoine. "It's more like a final manifestation, before the end of Martian life."

"Disappearance," said Violaine. "But the Martians are not ready to disappear, I hope."

"In a million years, approximately. I say a million to focus our ideas—I could as easily have said fewer, or more."

"I can breathe again!" said Violaine, laughing. "Perhaps humankind won't last any longer."

"As we are surely not. Between now and a million years hence, we might have undergone a considerable transformation."

"Progress or decadence?"

"I don't know. My own opinion favors a decrease in mental activity, as in the Martians, but certainly not in the same form."

"Personally, I believe in a superior activity for a few more million years!" Jean exclaimed.

"You're very greedy."

Darkness fell. Grace and the Implicit Chief rejoined us. The young Martian female's aura reminded me of ancient fables of luminous clouds guiding individuals or populations through the desert.

Via the servants, and then the neighbors, the news spread, first around our place of residence and then, gradually, by means of phone calls and news reports, to the distant reaches of the planet. Visitors flocked; regional reporters, then provincial ones, and finally national ones from every country, invading the locale like locusts.

We obtained a relative peace by fixing two hours a day when Grace would be visible at a distance. Clouds of aircraft flew over our dwelling incessantly. We asked for privacy in vain; we could not persuade people who had come from the antipodes or the poles to leave without taking away films of the miracle...

Thus, day by day, the planet followed the metamorphosis of the mist, the concentration that rendered it more and more luminous, and finally, the marvelous shell, the huge white flower. When the child began to take form, the excitement became delirious...

Epilogue

I shall always remember that morning.

We were staying in the mountain chalet. I got up while the household as still asleep, and immediately went into the garden, with which I had been impassioned for some time. The Martian plants were growing abundantly, mingled here and there with Alpine plants. They already provided a part of the alimentation of Grace and the Implicit Chief, who ate them

424

with pleasure, although they did not prefer them to the terrestrial foodstuffs to which they had adapted perfectly.

Some ten Martian animals were living in the vicinity of the house. Jean had domesticated them completely; not only did they show no inclination to run away but, being rather fearful, waited for their hosts to wake up before going to graze at a distance. Two of them followed me in my morning stroll; the first, the size of a cat, was blue and gold, and had a corkscrew muzzle and helical legs. It performed strange somersaults as it walked, as if its feet were mounted on springs. The other, as sinuous as a weasel, was amaranthine on its back, pink underneath with emerald stripes; its legs extended almost horizontally, terminating in spatulate feet, which caused it to progress half-crawling and half-hopping.

Each of them had six large eyes, whose beauty far surpassed those of all terrestrial animals, from gazelles to tigers: six focal points through which passed all the colors and shades of the solar spectrum.

As I was daydreaming in the depths of the garden, I saw Grace running toward me; she was holding her child in her arms—a sign that its embryonic growth was concluded. The little child's eyes were already magnificent.

"I'm happy," she said. "I dedicate him to the Earth, his fatherland...and to you, who gave me the desire to give birth to him!"

I looked at him tenderly, and it genuinely seemed to me that, although it was so different, his face had a slightly human form.

"He's a Martian...I wanted him thus."

Violaine appeared on the threshold with Jean.

"The first terrestrial Martian!" Jean exclaimed. "We'll look to him for...a complement!"

He had conceived the idea of founding a little Martian colony, inoffensive by definition.

Violaine looked at the new-born intently. "He will bring happiness to ours!" she said. She was also about to give birth.

"We shall return to Mars!"

A thrumming sound made us turn our heads, and Antoine's vortex settled on the terrace.

He looked at the Martian child welcomingly, then murmured: "If he has a wife one day, that might be the beginning of a Martian colony."

"When we take him back to Mars," Jean said, "we'll find a wife for him…"

"Perhaps it wouldn't do any harm," said Antoine, "but it might, after all, be perilous. The Earth has reanimated Grace and the Implicit Chief singularly."

These words could do nothing to combat our complacency. An atmosphere of gentleness enveloped us. The landscapes of Mars mingled with the locations of the summery mountain—the conclave of silvered summits, and the pine-forests rising up from the depths, creeping up the slopes, having exterminated the oaks and the beech trees…

Afterword

"The Xipehuz" must have seemed a deeply enigmatic text to its original readers, many of whom would surely have asked at least some of the questions that the text stubbornly refused to answer. What were the Xipehuz? Where had they come from? What was their purpose? Why did they kill humans and animals, since they did not use them as nutrition?

The probability is that Rosny did not provide answers to these questions because he had no idea what the answers were. Indeed, he seems to have changed his mind about the questions in the course of the story, in which the Xipehuz initially reported as resembling "planes" disappear, leaving only their conical kin. Rosny always appears to have been impulsively spontaneous in his creativity, recording images and ideas that occurred to him without bothering to think them through in advance—and then, whenever his attempts to think them through as he continued his work ran into inevitable difficulties, simply abandoning them to mystery and often refraining from removing inconsistencies and manifest contradictions. Over the course of his entire career, however, he did continue to niggle away at the implications of his ideas. Although it would be stretching the argument too far to suggest that he built an entirely new model of the universe merely to find a means of accommodating the Xipehuz and to provide a possibility that the questions posed above might somehow be answerable, there can be no doubt that the evolution of his metaphysical notions did not precede the imagery of his literary works so much as evolve in concert with it.

In retrospect, the notion of "the fourth" universe—the "innumerable Coexistence," as one of the characters in "The Navigators of Space" puts it—allows us to construct certain plausible hypotheses about where the Xipehuz might have originated, and why (if not how) they came to Earth. They probably came from a different component of the fourth universe—one of the many independent worlds contained in the seemingly empty space within the atoms and between the stars of our own. They probably came as would-be colonists, intent on occupying the Earth as other creatures of their kind had presumably occupied some other habitable world, perhaps having cleansed it—after a long evolutionary process—of some native homologue of our organic life. They probably killed Earthly animal life simply in order to clear it out of the way.

Being impatient, like the Zoomorphs of "The Navigators of Space," rather than patient, like the ferromagnetals of "The Death of the Earth," the Xipehuz were probably intent on expanding the scope of their "realm" beyond its original habitat. Perhaps they might have done so by "space travel" within their own native cosmos, but perhaps not, either because of the same impracticability that makes interstellar travel difficult in our cosmos, or because the physical distribution of material substance in their native cosmos was very different from our own. They could not, of course, have arrived in our world by any simple process of transportation, as science fiction writers have sometimes imagined humans and aliens traveling between essentially-similar "parallel worlds," but must have done so by some mysterious process of transmutation, which allowed them to forsake their original material envelopes—essentially imperceptible to, and incapable of interaction with, the matter making up our component of the fourth universe—in favor of new envelopes, presumably homologous with their own in some exotic fashion, that were capable of such interaction.

As to what the Xipehuz are, that is eventually made clear by the story: they are living beings that have evolved from the "mineral realm" by a physical and chemical process quite distinct from that which produced the protoplasmic life of plants, animals and protozoa—probably a "dry" process unreliant on water. They are fundamentally similar in kind to Zoomorphs and ferromagnetals—and also to the Moedigen and Vuren of

"Another World," although the unperceived existence on Earth of the latter species raises further problems of hypothetical identification and explanation.

"Another World" is one of the most frustrating of Rosny's scientific romances because it demonstrates more clearly than any other the acute problems that he had in developing his ideas once he had set down the substance of their initial inspiration. Having introduced the Xipehuz—probably without the slightest idea of what he was going to do with them—he was at least able to fall back on a ready-made narrative stand-by (the most convenient form of plot leverage is violence), and, for the rest of his career, he was usually careful to keep that stand-by ready to hand. In "Another World," however, the possibility of a war between humans and Moedigen is virtually out of the question, at least within the restricted scope of the first-person narrative that introduces the story, and the author therefore had to cast around for another stand-by in order to have any prospect of an ending (narrative closure and sexual consummation have a lot in common). That one too, he was careful to keep well in hand throughout his career, although its continual use in scientific romances eventually led him to some rather peculiar extremes, as "The Navigators of Space" readily illustrates. In "Another World," however, that recourse obliged him virtually to abandon the Moedigen and Vuren, at least as a central concern of the story.

Perhaps, in retrospect, that abandonment was necessary to the completion of any kind of story at all, because the notion of another aspect of the "innumerable Coexistence" being visible to an exceptional individual is not logically coherent, at least in the form of representation given to it in "Another World."[64] Although the Moedigen and Vuren exist quite independently of animal and vegetable life, intangible as well as invisible thereto, they must interact with the mineral environ-

---

[64] Rosny subsequently made another attempt, as readers will discover in volume 2 of the series, which includes "In the World of the Variants."

ment in some way, else they could not exist at all, and the results of that interaction must be detectable. The story's narrator does point this out, but cannot carry the argument forward to any significant extent, leaving the nature of the interaction unspecified as well as unmeasured.

Presumably, the effects that the Moedigen and Vuren have on the mineral environment are perceived by human beings, but regarded as "weather phenomena" rather than the actions of purposive beings, by virtue of a curious reversal of the "pathetic fallacy" that once prompted superstitious humans mistakenly to perceive intelligence and emotion in the weather. The same train of thought is tacitly present in "The Navigators of Space," in the suggestion that there must already be an Earthly equivalent of "Ethereal" life that humans have not yet been able to perceive.

The Ethereals of Mars are particularly interesting because they complete a tripartite division of possible modes of coherent organization, in which animal/vegetable life may be contrasted with both material mineral "life" and a nonmaterial "life" whose organization and transactions are purely energetic. Although the notion that the last-named kind of organization is essentially superior to the alternatives is deliberately challenged in the text of "The Navigators of Space," it has a certain natural attractiveness because the elimination of material middlemen seems inherently more efficient—or, at any rate, less clumsy.

Rosny was not the first French writer to imagine "mineral life" or "energetic life;" both had been suggested as possibilities by Camille Flammarion—whose own scientific romances and speculative essays gave voice to the same kind of disgust for material processes of life-support that Rosny develops in "The Navigators of Space"—but Rosny developed those ideas much more elaborately than Flammarion ever had, let alone any of the other writers who had briefly touched on such notions. (Restif de la Bretonne and Didier de Chousy are notable examples.) This is, as Rosny pointed out himself, a key respect in which his work differs markedly from that of

H.G. Wells, or that of Jules Verne; it was a step beyond the range to which his most important successors, as well as his most important predecessors, were intent on confining themselves.

It did not take American pulp science fiction writers long to come up with a similar notion of evolutionary hierarchy, in which beings of frail flesh were likely to be superseded by inorganic intelligences, and ultimately by beings of "pure force," and "The Navigators of Space" was virtually contemporary with George Bernard Shaw's *Back to Methuselah* (1921), which similarly represented the "highest" form of evolution in terms of a transcendence of the material, so there was a broad consensus of sorts with respect to this issue at the time. Rosny was, however, unusual not only in the detailed attention he paid to his own constructions, but also in juxtaposing examples of his three fundamental forms of organization, crediting each with an independent evolutionary origin rather than imagining some kind of transformative process by which human minds might eventually become "etherealized."

Some of the ideas sketched out in "The Skeptical Legend" were similarly echoed in British scientific romance and American science fiction, most notably Rosny's discussion of the possibility of the evolution of new senses, including some form of "cerebral penetration." Indeed, the relative poverty of the human sensorium had been the key theme of the original text of French scientific romance, Voltaire's "Micromégas" (1745)—but Rosny attempted to bring the insights of then-modern science to bear on the discussion with an intensity that put other contemporary writers, and most of his successors, into the shade. His investigations of chemical asymmetry and the possibilities of a supersession of "bipolar life" in "The Skeptical Legend" are more unusual, but both stop some way short of any genuinely interesting speculations. By far the most unusual idea raised in the essay was, however, that of what he called "planetary physiology"—although it is actually a kind of "cosmic physiology"—and the metaphysical basis with which he supported that idea.[65]

With the aid of hindsight, we can now see how the idea of the "fourth universe" came into being as "spinoff" from the notion of planetary physiology. In order to imagine some way of linking together the distantly scattered worlds of space, to which mid-19th century astronomy had finally added an appropriate scale, Rosny had to imagine a mode of connection more immediate than the ones supplied by electromagnetic radiation and gravity. The notion that seemingly empty space was actually full of "alternative" forms of matter and energy imperceptible to our senses did not arise directly from the principle of plenitude, but rather from his antipathetic reaction to the revelation that the remainder of creation was so far removed from the Earth as to be irrevocably separated from it.

Like Camille Flammarion—and, for that matter, almost everyone else who confronted the issue imaginatively—Rosny was reluctant to accept the degree of isolation to which cosmic distances condemned humankind, but he was not prepared, like Flammarion or the writers of American science fiction, to suppose that the remedy might lie in the simple supposition that the velocity of light was not an absolute or a maximum. If light could not provide a better connection between worlds, Rosny thought, then it was necessary to invent something that would: something that would recreate the Macrocosmic being that neo-Platonist philosophers had once imagined as a Great Man. Always endeavoring to get away from anthropocentrism—perhaps not entirely successfully, but more successfully than any other writer of his or any other generation—Rosny

---

[65] It seems probable, in retrospect, that Rosny did not mean "*planétaire*" in the sense that most readers of "La Légende sceptique" would have understood it (i.e. pertaining to the planet) but in a sense more closely akin to the use he subsequently made of the same word in "La Mort de la Terre," where it refers specifically to a kind of hypothetical communication device closely akin to a radio-telescope dish.

was deliberately tentative in his sketch of a hypothetical cosmic physiology, but that tentativeness was vital to the avoidance of a misleading overspecification of the kind of extrasensory link he was trying to imagine. It is worth noting here that the same exaggerated tentativeness is painfully obvious in "Companions of the Universe," which was probably the final work of fiction in which he attempted to convey a fleeting sense of the fourth universe to his readers, although "In the World of the Variants" was not published until a later date.

Although Rosny devoted a great deal of thought to the corollary idea of the fourth universe in his subsequent fiction and non-fiction, he never returned specifically to the notion of a "planetary physiology" binding the observable cosmos into the single entity, probably because it was an idea that did not lend itself to any sort of literary development, and could not be significantly extrapolated beyond mere suggestion. It is, however, very noticeable in all of his fiction that he did retain some notion of the overall community of intelligence; it is significant that "The Xipehuz" does not end with humankind's extermination of the alien invaders but with Bakhoun's regret for the unfortunate necessity of that genocide. Similar regrets are attached in his work not merely to similar incidents, but also to virtually every description he issues of the transactions of earthly life: the necessity that obliges living organisms to consume other organisms, which one of the characters in "The Navigators of Space" describes, bluntly, as "the terrestrial inferno." As the subsequent volumes of the series will display, over and over again, Rosny's explorations of alternative patterns of Earthly evolution consistently voice his regretful disgust for "nature red in tooth and claw," and sometimes search, with a desperate but admittedly hopeless yearning, for patterns of life that might enshrine a far higher level of tolerance and co-operation.

In "The Xipehuz," barbarian humans do fight a war of extermination against the alien invaders, which only one of them has sufficient sensitivity to regret, but the war that their civilized counterparts wage against the Zoomorphs of Mars on

433

behalf of the Tripeds in "The Navigators of Space" is a much more modest affair, effectively a mere holding action. This reflects the close thematic connection between "The Navigators of Space" and "The Death of the Earth," in which the Last Men make no attempt at all to fight the ferromagnetals, even though the ferromagnetals are as eager to extract iron from human blood as from any other source. The Last Men and the Tripeds both recognize that their own existence is entirely dependent on water, that when there is no more water to sustain them, other forms of organization that are not so dependent will replace them, and that the polite thing to do is to wish those replacement species well.

In all these stories, there is a tacit recognition of the fact that, however different they are—and the differences are extreme, by any standards—there is an essential kinship between humans, animals, plants and Tripeds on the one hand, and Xipehuz, Moedigen, ferromagnetals, Zoomorphs and Ethereals on the other: a larger-than-life kinship whose essence is the "planetary physiology" that bids the entire universe—the fourth universe as well as the perceptible universe—into a single great common enterprise (an enterprise, it might be worth noting, that has no need for any kind of God, let alone the kindly kind who would have laid on the kind of serial interstellar reincarnation in which Camille Flammarion felt obliged to believe). The stories in this volume, therefore, demonstrate the continuity and connection of Rosny's speculative work as his problematic career progressed. It must also be noted, however, that within that overall continuity, they also demonstrate the extent to which Rosny's notion of the dimensions of the terrestrial inferno changed as he grew older.

In "The Xipehuz" and "Another World," the torments of life are confined to physical violence and emotional isolation, and sexual love is seen as a crucial amelioration of its hellishness. In "The Death of the Earth," too, the few Last Men who do not give way to despair and euthanasia are maintained in their resistance by the power of fraternal and sexual love. In "The Navigators of Space," however, a pattern appears that was to be further emphasized in Rosny's subsequent works, in which the vulgar aspects of sex are shifted to the other side of the moral account-book, becoming an aspect of the inferno rather than a potential source of amelioration of its ravages. Rarely content with half-measures, Rosny defines the narrator's love for a Martian Triped not merely as conceivable but as something intrinsically superior to any kind of love available to him on Earth, precisely because of its asexuality. In order to do that, he has to invent an "objective" beauty superior to any mere reflection of physiologically-ordained desire—a "poetic passion" of a higher kind than any merely human reaction.

A cynic might put this change of heart down to the inevitable effects of aging on human sexual desire and capacity—Rosny was in his 60s when he wrote "The Navigators of Space"—and thus condemn it to triviality. "The Skeptical Legend" and "Another World," however, both offer eloquent testimony to the extent to which Rosny had always felt alienated from other people, and had always, in consequence sought beauty and solace in perceptions and passions of a different kind: in the "planetary physiology" that modern science might lend to an inquisitive mind, if only one cared enough to make the attempt to grasp its fugitive substance. In the final analysis, the continuity was more important than the changes that took place within it.

SF & FANTASY

Guy d'Armen. *Doc Ardan: The City of Gold and Lepers*
G.-J. Arnaud. *The Ice Company*
Aloysius Bertrand. *Gaspard de la Nuit*
Félix Bodin. *The Novel of the Future*
Didier de Chousy. *Ignis*
C. I. Defontenay. *Star (Psi Cassiopeia)*
Charles Derennes. *The People of the Pole*
Harry Dickson. *The Heir of Dracula*
Sâr Dubnotal. *Vs. Jack the Ripper*
Alexandre Dumas. *The Return of Lord Ruthven*
J.-C. Dunyach. *The Night Orchid. The Thieves of Silence*
Paul Féval. *Anne of the Isles. Knightshade. Revenants. Vampire City. The Vampire Countess. The Wandering Jew's Daughter*
Paul Féval, *fils. Felifax, the Tiger-Man*
Arnould Galopin. *Doctor Omega*
V. Hugo, Foucher & Meurice. *The Hunchback of Notre-Dame*
O. Joncquel & Theo Varlet. *The Martian Epic*
Jean de La Hire. *Enter the Nyctalope. The Nyctalope on Mars. The Nyctalope vs. Lucifer*
G. Le Faure & H. de Graffigny. *The Extraordinary Adventures of a Russian Scientist Across the Solar System* (2 vols.)
Gustave Le Rouge. *The Vampires of Mars*
Jules Lermina. *Panic in Paris. To-Ho and the Gold Destroyers. Mysteryville*
Jean-Marc & Randy Lofficier. *Edgar Allan Poe on Mars. The Katrina Protocol. Pacifica. Robonocchio.* (anthologists) *Tales of the Shadowmen* (6 vols.) (non-fiction) *Shadowmen* (2 vols.)
Xavier Mauméjean. *The League of Heroes*
Marie Nizet. *Captain Vampire*
C. Nodier, Beraud & Toussaint-Merle. *Frankenstein*
Henri de Parville. *An Inhabitant of the Planet Mars*
Polidori, C. Nodier, E. Scribe. *Lord Ruthven the Vampire*
P.-A. Ponson du Terrail. *The Vampire and the Devil's Son*
Maurice Renard. *Doctor Lerne. A Man Among the Microbes*

Albert Robida. *The Clock of the Centuries. The Adventures of Saturnin Farandoul*
J.-H. Rosny Aîné. *The Navigators of Space*
Brian Stableford. *The Shadow of Frankenstein. Frankenstein and the Vampire Countess. The New Faust at the Tragicomique. Sherlock Holmes & The Vampires of Eternity. The Stones of Camelot. The Wayward Muse.* (anthologist) *The Germans on Venus. News from the Moon*
Kurt Steiner. *Ortog*
Villiers de l'Isle-Adam. *The Scaffold. The Vampire Soul*
Philippe Ward. *Artahe*

MYSTERIES & THRILLERS

M. Allain & P. Souvestre. *The Daughter of Fantômas*
Anicet-Bourgeois, Lucien Dabril. *Rocambole*
A. Bisson & G. Livet. *Nick Carter vs. Fantômas*
V. Darlay & H. de Gorsse. *Lupin vs. Holmes: The Stage Play*
Paul Féval. *The Black Coats: The Companions of the Treasure. Gentlemen of the Night. Heart of Steel. The Invisible Weapon. John Devil. The Parisian Jungle. 'Salem Street*
Emile Gaboriau. *Monsieur Lecoq*
Steve Leadley. *Sherlock Holmes: The Circle of Blood*
Maurice Leblanc. *Arsène Lupin: The Hollow Needle. The Blonde Phantom*
Gaston Leroux. *Chéri-Bibi. The Phantom of the Opera. Rouletabille & the Mystery of the Yellow Room*
G. Marot & L. Pericaud. *Nick Carter vs. Jack the Ripper*
William Patrick Maynard. *The Terror of Fu Manchu*
Frank J. Morlock. *Sherlock Holmes: The Grand Horizontals*
P. de Wattyne & Y. Walter. *Sherlock Holmes vs. Fantômas*
David White. *Fantômas in America*